HOW

(not)

TO FALL

in Love

Lisa Brown Roberts

HOW (not) TO FALL in Love

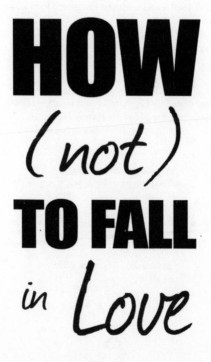

Entangled Publishing, LLC
2614 South Timberline Road
Suite 109
Fort Collins, CO 80525

Entangled Teen is an imprint of Entangled Publishing, LLC.

Visit our website at www.entangledpublishing.com.

Edited by Liz Pelletier
Cover design by Liz Pelletier and Heather Howland
Interior design by Jeremy Howland
Cover photo © iStockphoto/Solovyova

Print ISBN 978-1-62266-520-4
Ebook ISBN 978-1-62266-525-9

Manufactured in the United States of America

First Edition February 2015

10 9 8 7 6 5 4 3 2 1

For Erik, who always believed

CHAPTER ONE
September 1

"Hey Darcy! You'd better get outside. There's a tow truck hooking up your car."

I stared at Ryan, with whom I'd been in lust since seventh grade, trying to make sense of his words. It took a moment to realize he was not, in fact, admitting he'd been madly in love with me for the past five years, but was instead jabbering about my car.

"Tow truck? My car?" It was like he spoke Klingon and I didn't have a universal translator.

"Yeah." His blue eyes flashed with excitement. "You should hurry. They can really screw up your transmission." He tossed his messily perfect bangs out of his eyes. "I guess they're serious about us not parking in the handicapped spots. But dude, that's harsh."

Handicapped spots? I never parked in those. My brain finally kicked into gear and I slammed my locker shut.

"Thanks." I took off down the hall, out the main doors, then cut across the manicured soccer field toward the parking lot. As I ran, my stomach roller-coastered. Did I really park illegally? Dad would kill me if he had to pay to get my car out of an impound lot.

My Audi was already loaded onto the tow truck by the time I got there. A swelling crowd of my classmates milled around, pointing and exclaiming. The one using great dramatic expression and lots of gesturing was Sal, my best friend and queen of the theater club, AKA "DQ" for Drama Queen. Sal was always on the verge of being in full costume, like today in her weird grandma prairie dress and suede-fringed boots with fake spurs. She looked like a demented cowgirl, especially with her short, spiky black hair and goth makeup.

"I demand to see a warrant! You can't just come onto private property and take someone's car. My father is a lawyer and—"

"Can it, kid," said the tow truck driver. He hopped off the back of the truck where he'd been adjusting the cobweb of chains trapping my car. He paused before climbing into the truck, then his voice boomed loud enough to reach the whole crowd. "When the bills ain't paid, the car goes away."

I froze. Bills not paid? That was impossible. My dad was Tyler Covington, the face of Tri!Umphant! Harvest Motivational Industries. He had his own TV show. Just on PBS, but still. Money couldn't possibly be an issue.

No one had noticed me yet. Maybe I could duck behind

the other cars and hide until the tow truck left. Unlike my dad and Sal, who both thrived on an audience, I was queen of the mice, always skittering around corners and on the watch for potential traps.

Sal spotted me. "Darcy!" Everyone turned to stare. So much for avoiding the spotlight. "Darcy, come tell this man this is your car. Show him your driver's license or something!" Sal was freaking out like it was her car being towed.

The tow truck man leaned out of his window. "Like I said, if you don't pay your bills, you don't keep your car." The truck roared to life, slowing as it passed me. The driver tossed an envelope out the window. As it fluttered to the ground, Sal ran to grab it.

"When you come get your car out of the impound lot," the driver called, "bring cash. We don't take bad checks." He laughed and cranked the steering wheel hard, making my Audi wobble like a toy as he exited the parking lot.

The hive of students buzzed with excitement as Sal rushed over to hug me. Her thick black eyeliner magnified the panic in her worried brown eyes. "Oh my God, Darcy. I can't believe this. What an ass. This can't be right. He can't just take the car from—"

I held out a hand for the envelope. "Let me see it."

She handed it over and I tore it open.

NOTICE OF INTENT TO SELL

This notice informs owner TYLER COVINGTON that vehicle 2013 Audi VIN 214081094809148 has been repossessed due to nonpayment after notice to cure was sent via certified mail. This vehicle will be sold in thirty days at auction. All proceeds will be used to pay off the loan. To redeem this vehicle, bring full payment in form of cashier's check to High Plains Deals impound lot, 1301 Mountain Avenue, Denver, Colorado.

A few kids wandered closer to us, oozing curiosity. Sal glared at them. "Back off. Give her some privacy, dorks!"

Something was wrong. Horribly wrong. This couldn't be happening. But it had, in front of the entire school. The parking lot was full, with everyone leaving for the day. I imagined Ryan's face when he heard my car had been towed because it wasn't paid for, and I felt sick.

Ugh.

Things like this didn't happen at Woodbridge Academy. WA was the most elite private school in Denver. Ninety percent of the kids came from wealthy families. The other ten percent were scholarship students.

"I can't go back in there," I whispered, tilting my head toward school where my books waited in my locker. My hands shook as I crumpled the repossession notice and tried to unzip my messenger bag. Sal took the paper and refolded it neatly. She unzipped my bag and tucked the letter inside, then put her arm around me.

"We're getting out of here. Now." We hurried to her car, a yellow Beetle with daisy hubcaps and DRAMAQN on the license place.

She tore out of the parking lot, slowing only to flip off a couple of football players who yelled at her to slow down. The Beetle squealed around corners, hopping the curb more than once.

"God, Sal, chill out. This isn't a NASCAR race." I was going to hurl if she kept driving like a spaz.

She glared at me and then refocused her stare over the dashboard. "We have to get you home. Your parents need to call the tow truck company and get your car back before that asshole ruins it towing it around like a load of trash."

My stomach clenched. Did mistakes like this really happen? Did banks screw up that badly?

Sal shifted gears angrily. The way she drove her car it'd be lucky to last another year.

"Sal." I hesitated. "What if it's true? What if we do owe a bunch of money on my car? And somehow didn't pay the bills?"

She glanced away from the road to gape at me. "Are you nuts? Your family is freaking loaded, Darcy. This has to be a mistake." She chewed her bottom lip. "You can probably sue, you know. For damages to your car, pain and suffering, all that jazz. I'll ask my dad about it."

I rolled my eyes. Sometimes her never-ending drama wore me out.

"Forget it," I said. "I'm sure my dad will fix this."

"Exactly," she agreed, blowing through the stop sign at the end of my block. Her car lurched to a stop in our driveway.

"Thanks for the ride," I said, "but maybe I'll sue *you* for whiplash."

She didn't laugh. "Just get inside and get this handled. I've got to get back to school for auditions."

"Sorry." I felt a twinge of guilt. She didn't need to drive me home; I could've called my mom.

"Don't apologize. That's what best friends are for, right?" She grinned at me then peeled out of the driveway. I wondered how many speeding tickets her lawyer dad made go away.

I opened the wrought iron gate on the side of the house, looking for my dog, Toby, but he wasn't waiting for me like usual. I hurried past the swimming pool, already covered in anticipation of winter, and through the French doors into the kitchen. I had to find my dad to get him to call and get my car back.

Something was off. I didn't smell dinner cooking, which was weird since Mom, who could have her own Food Network show, always had exotic ingredients simmering on the stove.

Toby came running from the dining room, wriggling with happiness, and I dropped to my knees for a dog hug.

"Hey, boy. What's going on?" I looked into his devoted Labrador eyes as I rubbed his chocolate brown fur. "We'll run in a little bit. I need to find Dad first." I opened the pantry to grab him a Scooby snack. He caught it easily when I tossed it in the air.

"Mom?" I called, as I left the kitchen. I was starting to get worried. "Dad?"

No answer.

I wandered into the dining room. We only used it for dinners with Dad's premier clients and family holiday extravaganzas. The rest of the time it lurked empty yet imposing. The sleek, spiky silver chandelier made me think of knife blades poised above us while we ate, but Mom bought it during a European shopping spree, so we were stuck with it.

"Mom?" I yelled louder this time. Toby barked for emphasis.

I heard muffled voices from the library. It sounded like Mom and Dad talking, not Mom and one of her perky tennis buddies having their post-game Perriers. That was a relief. I couldn't deal with perky after the drama in the parking lot.

I flung open the door. "You guys won't believe this. Some jerk took my…" I trailed off when I saw it wasn't Dad with Mom, but J.J., Dad's business partner.

"Darcy." J.J. turned toward me, flashing his movie star smile. It was almost as blinding as my dad's trademark grin.

"Sorry to interrupt," I said, backing toward the door. "I thought Dad was in here." I glanced at Mom, who sat in a leather wing chair, her fingers twisting her gold serpentine necklace. Why did she look like she was fighting back tears? I glanced at J.J., whose smile had vanished.

Something inside my stomach twisted and I reached down to pet Toby, wanting to keep him close. "Everything okay?"

J.J. and Mom exchanged one of those condescending we-have-to-tell-her-something-but-let's-not-tell-her-too-much looks.

"What is it?" My stomach knot twisted tighter. "Is Dad okay?" Visions of fiery plane crashes played on the TV screen of my mind.

"Sure, sure. He's fine," J.J. blustered, not looking at Mom. "But he's, ah, had a change of plans. He won't be home tonight."

"But he's got the game tonight. He can't miss that." Dad

was the official team motivator for the Denver Broncos and never missed a game. I stared at Mom, who was staring at J.J. She still hadn't looked at me. I heard echoes of the cackling tow truck driver's laugh and a nibble of fear tickled the base of my neck.

"Mom? What's going on?" Now they both stared at the ground. Toby leaned against my leg and let out a soft whine.

"I need to talk to Dad," I said. "Because this crazy thing happened at school today with my car."

J.J.'s head jerked up. "What happened?" His voice was sharp, surprising me.

"Were you in an accident?" Worry creased Mom's face.

"No." I rubbed Toby's head. He leaned into my hand, making me feel safe like he always did. "Worse. This jerk tow truck driver took my car from the school parking lot, in front of everyone." I cringed, reliving the humiliation.

J.J. and Mom stared at each other, their expressions making goose bumps rise on my arms.

"But I thought her car was paid for," Mom whispered, her eyes fixated on J.J.

J.J. glanced at me. "Darcy, your mom and I need to talk. Alone."

I swallowed. Normally I'd leave without question, but something was seriously wrong. "No."

Mom raised her eyebrows. "Darcy. Please."

The knot in my stomach had morphed into a balloon now, swelling with anxiety and worry. "No," I repeated. I never argued with adults, but I was freaking out and needed to know what was going on. "Dad's not home for a Broncos game, which he never misses. Some jackass stole my car right in front of me. What's going on?"

"Don't say jackass," Mom said softly, but her heart wasn't in it.

J.J. loosened his tie and walked to the window, staring out at the trees bending in the breeze. I waited. I'd win this battle, no contest. I spent most of my life waiting and watching other people. Most of the time I was like a shadow no one noticed.

"Your father," Mom started, then stopped to swallow and compose herself. Her cloudy gray eyes met mine. "Your dad is taking a little vacation." She fiddled with her watch. "He's been working too hard. He needs a break."

My heart sped up. A break? Was that code for something else? A break from us? From Mom? I looked at her red-rimmed eyes. God, I hoped this didn't mean divorce. I glanced at J.J., who still stared out the window.

"So is he going up to the cabin for a few days?" I asked. "Or staying in L.A.?"

"Honestly, I'm not sure what he's doing." Mom turned to look at me. "He called J.J. from the airport to say he'd be back next week sometime."

"He called from L.A.?" I looked at J.J., willing him to turn around and tell me what he knew.

Mom spoke again when J.J. remained silent. "No, he called from our airport. As soon as he got off his plane, he got in his car and hit the road."

"He what?" That didn't make any sense. What was Dad doing? My heart raced even faster. He was a freak about keeping his word, never being late, never missing appointments. Missing tonight's game was completely unlike him.

"You have to tell her," J.J. said, his voice low. "It's already started, with her car."

The fear I'd been tamping down tore through me now as he turned toward us, his expression hard and unreadable.

"What's started?" I hated how weak and tinny my voice sounded. Why couldn't I sound strong and passionate like Sal or my dad?

"We… There might be…" My mom tried to speak but couldn't finish, tears choking her voice.

"Harvest is going broke, Darcy," J.J. bit out the words. "Which means your family is, too. So don't plan on getting your car back anytime soon."

I stumbled backward as if he'd slapped me. His words echoed in the room as Mom collapsed into sobs.

"I…but I…" I struggled for words, fear and confusion shutting down coherent thought. "But," I tried again, my voice rising in panic. "My dad… Where's my dad?"

J.J.'s mouth thinned into a bitter smile. "That's the million dollar question, isn't it?"

No one spoke, all of us staring at each other in frozen silence. I couldn't believe what J.J. said. My dad wouldn't just go AWOL. Every minute of his life was scheduled and planned. And broke? What did that even mean?

"I need to go," J.J. said. "Since Ty's not here for the football game, somebody needs to greet his clients in the stadium box." He wiped a sheen of perspiration from his forehead.

"You'll let me know?" Mom whispered. "If you hear from him again? And tell him to call me. Please."

J.J. frowned at Mom. "He hasn't called you?"

Tears spilled down her cheeks as she shook her head.

He heaved a deep sigh then lumbered across the room. He closed the door behind him without saying good-bye.

For some reason, I thought of this old movie with a badass guy who does slow-mo acrobatics to avoid flying bullets. He has to choose whether to take a red pill and wake up to reality, or take a blue pill and stay in a fake world. That was me right now. Did I want to take the blue pill and live in denial of whatever was happening with my dad? Or did I want to take the red pill and have the truth crash down on me?

I was such a wuss. I'd pick the blue pill every time.

Chapter Two

"Sweetie, can you please get me a glass of ice?" Mom's eyes blinked like windshield wipers on warp speed. "We need to talk."

So much for taking the blue pill.

"Sure." I left the room, Toby trailing behind me. I knew Mom sent me for ice so she could try to compose herself.

What J.J. said about us being broke didn't make any sense. Maybe he was exaggerating; he did that a lot. I knew because I babysat his twin sons all the time and he freaked out about stupid stuff, like the time his kids used his designer shoes as boats during bath time.

The water glass trembled in my hands under the fridge dispenser and ice cubes clattered to the floor. Toby crunched the dropped ice noisily, saving me the trouble of cleaning up.

I stared at the glass. The Tri!Umphant! Harvest logo

swirled around it from top to bottom in gold lettering.

T-houghtful

R-esponsible

I-nitiative!

U-nleashes

M-agnificent

P-ositive

H-arvest!

I sighed. Those words were more important than any prayers or political beliefs in our house. As an AP English student, I despised the phrase with its incorrect punctuation, crazy capitalization, and fuzzy meaning. As my father's daughter, I pretended to believe every word. There had to be something to it, right? Why else would so many people pay to listen to my dad talk about it?

I brought the glass to Mom and sat across from her. She stared into it before speaking. "I don't really know what's going on," she said. "I'm hoping your dad will be home soon, and everything will be okay."

"But what J.J. said about us going broke. Did he mean it? How is that even possible?"

Mom stood up and walked to the liquor cabinet, which surprised me. She wasn't much of a drinker; she always said the extra calories weren't worth the buzz. I watched anxiously as she poured amber-colored liquid over the ice cubes. She took a swig and turned to face me.

"Maybe you should go to the football game with J.J. tonight. You always have fun."

Now I wondered if Mom was the one taking the blue pill. How could she expect me to go to a game and act like nothing was going on? And hang out with J.J., who was acting so weird? No way. I leaned over to rub Toby's belly. His tail thumped softly against the rug Mom had imported from Turkey.

"No thanks. I'll skip it." I pulled out my cell and texted Dad. *"Where r u? Call asap. 911."* He always called when I used our I-need-to-talk-right-now code, which wasn't often.

"So do you think I'll be able to get my car back?" J.J. had to be wrong about that.

"I don't know, Darcy." Mom sat across from me and took another swig of her drink. My stomach fluttered. Not only was she drinking in the middle of the day, she wasn't exactly sipping, either. "We need to talk to your dad."

I waved my phone at her. "I just texted him. 911. He'll call any minute."

But he didn't call.

*M*om and I sort of watched the first half of the football game on TV while we ate a gross frozen pizza. We spent more time checking our phones and texting Dad than we did watching the game. At halftime, I went upstairs to my room, wanting to get away from Mom, who'd switched from the amber liquor to wine.

I turned on my laptop, hoping to escape my worries for a while. I logged onto Instagram and scanned everyone's latest pics, but when I saw what Ryan had posted, my heart stopped.

He'd hashtagged the photo "Repo Girl," and had the

nerve to tag me in it. The photo was of me, my mouth partly open in shock. Sal stood next to me, her arms flung up in exasperation. My car on the back of the tow truck looked fuzzy and out of focus.

My breath came in short bursts. How could he do this? We weren't close friends, or anything more, much as I'd dreamed about that. But we were hardly enemies. We'd known each other for years. I wasn't in his uber popular orbit, but he spoke to me in class, at the eco-club meetings, at parties. He *knew* me.

I scanned the comments, most of which mocked me and the repo, but not all of them.

"Dude. Why r u being a prick? Delete this or I'll pound you." That was from Mark, Sal's latest boy toy. Mark was cool; even cooler than I'd realized, apparently. A few people had echoed his comment so maybe not everyone thought I was a loser. But judging from most of the photo likes and snarky comments, Ryan had managed to turn me into the laughingstock of the whole school.

I closed my laptop and flopped back on my bed. Toby jumped up and curled next to me. I rubbed his head while staring at the ceiling. I couldn't believe Dad had just disappeared. Was he leaving Mom for good? My heart sped up to hyperdrive. I couldn't imagine them divorcing. They drove me nuts but I loved them, and they seemed to love each other. I never heard screaming arguments. They spent long weekends together all the time, flying to resort towns and leaving me home with Toby.

I had no complaints about that. I loved my time alone. I wasn't the kid who threw wild parties when her parents were gone. I was the weirdo watching old movies by myself or making jewelry while I listened to music. I invited Sal over, no one else, though I sometimes wished I had a boyfriend to hang out with when my parents were gone.

Desperate to escape the fear and anxiety bearing down on me, I put on an old romantic comedy, hoping to cheer myself up. The movie lulled me to sleep and I woke hours later to the theme music playing over and over. I turned off my TV and stumbled downstairs to say good night to Mom.

But when I walked into the family room, lured by the sounds of late night television, I found Mom passed out on the couch, an empty wine bottle tipped over on the floor.

September 17

Dear Darcy,

I'm sorry honey. So sorry. I need to get away from Colorado for a while to clear my head and focus on the next step. I miss you and your mom and love you both. Remember we will be Tri!Umphant! no matter what happens.

XO,

Dad

Chapter Three
September 23

<u>The Top Ten Reasons Darcy Covington Should
Leave Woodbridge Academy</u>

10. Her dad can't afford the tuition anymore since he's a QUITTER.

9. Repo Girl can barely afford the bus pass.

8. Woodbridge isn't a school for spawn of criminals.

7. She's

6. a

5. L

4. O

3. S

2. E

1. R

Chloe Hendricks had outdone herself. The photoshopped

pic of my dad's face had devil horns and blacked-out teeth. And dollar signs for eyes. Chloe had never liked me, maybe because it was easy for her to pick on a mouse like me.

"You need to report her," Sal growled, tearing the sign off my locker.

"For what? Not being as funny as Letterman?" I tried to sound sarcastic, but failed miserably.

I'd hoped no one had watched Letterman last night. He'd used my dad as the butt of his Top Ten list. He must've been inspired by the CNN story stating my dad was on a leave of absence, combined with all the crazy rumors swirling on the internet.

Sal tore the sign into strips, making a big production of it for the crowd watching us.

Mark joined us at my locker. "Is it still a rule, that guys can't hit girls? 'Cause I want to."

I almost smiled at him. He was as big as a truck but he had a soft, squishy center, at least for Sal and me, if not for Chloe. "No, you don't. And yes, it's still a rule."

He shook his head, huffing out a sigh. "I could key her car. Slit her tires."

"No." I punched him in the shoulder. "Go pick on someone your own size."

He grinned at me. "There is no one my own size. At least not here."

"You're too nice, Darcy," Sal said, glowering at me as she crumpled the remains of the sign and tossed it in the trash.

"Not really," I said. "Mostly I'm a big chicken. Have you seen her claws? Plus she probably has rabies."

The warning bell for class rang. Mark and Sal engaged

in major PDA, then he took off for PE.

Sal hugged me before we went our separate ways. "Someday karma will bite that bitch in the ass."

I shrugged. I wasn't sure I believed in karma anymore. Mom and I sure didn't deserve what was happening to us.

In the three weeks since Dad had disappeared, we'd been swimming upstream against a raging river of chaos, but at least we'd kept things a secret. No one knew that Tri!Umphant! Harvest had frozen our bank accounts, after Mom had spent days meeting with the board. Or that Dad had gone Kerouac, hitting the road with no destination, sending us random postcards. Or that J.J. had suddenly developed a Jekyll and Hyde personality, and was only showing scary Mr. Hyde to us.

Now everyone knew about my dad, including my long lost Uncle Charlie, who'd called last night after he saw Letterman. I'd answered the phone since Mom was passed out on the couch.

That was another new secret: Mom drinking herself to sleep almost every night.

I'd almost reached the library when my phone vibrated in my pocket. I didn't recognize the number. My heart leaped, hoping it was finally Dad.

"Hello?" I slid into a tiny hallway alcove where no teachers could yell at me for being on my cell.

"Darcy? Is that you?" His voice sounded different, not quite himself.

"Dad! Where are you?" My heart ricocheted in my chest.

"Darcy, it's Charlie. Your uncle."

My heart had slowed way down. "Oh." My voice was

barely a whisper.

"I'm sorry, sweetheart, if you thought I was him." He sounded sad and worried.

"It's okay." That had happened last night, too. Who knew brothers could sound so alike? I tried to remember the last time I'd seen Dad's younger brother or even talked to him. I'd been a little girl. I barely remembered his ponytail and scruffy beard. But he always sent a special gift for my birthday. And he laughed a lot; I remembered that much.

"I called your mom again today, but she hasn't returned my calls." I'd given him both our cell numbers last night.

She's probably still in a wine coma, said my inside voice. But my outside voice said, "I'll remind her to call you." Right. Like Mom would call.

He sighed into the phone. "Please do. And you can, too, Darcy. Anytime." He hesitated. "You should come see me. At my shop."

"Yeah." My dad hated that Charlie worked in a crummy pawn shop in the 'hood, as Dad called it. "But I don't have a car anymore."

"You don't? What happened?"

I sighed into the phone. "It's a long story."

It was his turn to sigh. "Let me think about this, and get back to you."

"Okay." I shrugged, like he could see me. What was he going to do? See if his pawn shop had any spare cars lying around?

We said our good-byes, and I snuck into a quiet corner of the library and shoved in my earbuds. I should've listened to music, something to calm the stress balloon expanding in my stomach. But instead I pulled up Letterman on YouTube.

On my tiny phone screen, Dave smirked. Up popped his Top Ten list from last night, which he read aloud while his studio audience laughed and applauded.

The Top Ten Reasons Tri!Umphant! Tyler Covington is in Hiding:

10. He didn't get the memo that self-help gurus are a relic of the 20th century.

9. Those old videos of him singing with a Christian punk band back in the 1980s resurfaced on YouTube.

8. Grecian Formula stopped making his shade of blond hair color.

7. Clients started asking for refunds when their "harvest" ended up being a stack of unpaid credit card bills.

6. He was turned down as the replacement shill for Oxi-Clean.

5. Even the family dog won't listen to his spiel anymore.

4. He tried out for *Dancing with the Stars* but even Florence Henderson AKA Carol Brady wouldn't dance with him.

3. The Denver Broncos have been on a winning streak without his pre-game pep talks.

2. PBS called. They want their tote bags back.

1. He really did abandon his family and his business to run off to a hidden island with all the money.

The video already had over 300,000 views. I wondered how many were from my classmates, thanks to Chloe.

I might as well shave my head and move to Tibet. My life was over.

O-V-E-R.

CHAPTER FOUR

After the Top Ten locker humiliation, I was hoping Mom would be home, but she'd left a note that she was at a job interview. I couldn't imagine where she'd apply, but she'd told me since all our accounts were frozen, we'd been living on credit cards, which was a bad idea.

I started some homework, but it was hard to find the motivation to finish it. I fixed myself toast and dug a wilted bag of salad out of the fridge. I missed gourmet chef Mom.

My cell rang just as I swallowed a bite of lettuce that was way past its prime.

"Darcy, it's Charlie. Again." He laughed softly, making me smile a tiny bit. It had been days since I'd heard someone laugh in a nice way rather than behind my back. "I want you to come see me tonight, so we can talk. I'd come to you, but I've got a ton of donations to sort through. We can talk while I do that here at my shop." He told me the address.

"Um." I hesitated. "I'll have to check the bus schedule, and figure out the transfers." Unlike most of my classmates who called the bus the "ghetto ride," I'd discovered I liked it, since it gave me time to read and listen to music.

"No need for that. I'm sending a driver."

"What?" Since when could my supposedly poor uncle afford a car and driver?

"Probably not the type of limo service you're used to," I heard the grin in his voice, "but I think he'll get you here in one piece."

What the heck? I chewed my lip nervously. "I'll need to check with my mom." *Before I get into a car with a stranger to whisk me away to the wrong side of the tracks.*

"Already did. I texted her and she said it's fine, as long as you're home by ten or so."

She'd actually replied to him? Shocker.

I let out the breath I'd been holding. I didn't have anything else to do, except stay home and feel sorry for myself, ignore the rest of my homework, worry about Dad, and eat too much ice cream.

Toby whimpered at my feet. He'd been spending too much time alone, just like me. "Um, can I bring my dog? Is that okay with your driver?"

I heard muffled voices, then, "Does he get carsick?"

I snorted. "Of course not."

"Good," Charlie said. "Lucas will be there in about half an hour. Probably less, the way he drives." He paused. "Lucas is my repairman, in my shop. He's a great guy, so you don't have to worry about riding with him."

I pictured a balding, overweight old guy in grungy jeans wearing a sagging tool belt. With my luck he'd have a plumber's crack, too. I sighed. "Okay."

"You haven't moved lately, have you? Still on Humboldt Street?"

"Yep." Charlie was right; I had ridden in fancy town cars with drivers, usually going to and from airports. This definitely wouldn't be the same.

After we hung up, I trudged up to my bedroom, Toby at my heels. What would my uncle and I talk about? Should I pretend it hadn't been years since I'd seen him? Tell him the gory details of my family's tale of woe? Ask him for a loan to get my car back?

I froze, my hand on the banister. Wasn't that what pawn shops did? Buy stuff from people? I ran up the rest of the stairs. In my room, I yanked open a dresser drawer and removed an old-fashioned hatbox, also a long-ago gift from Charlie. It held all my expensive jewelry from Tiffany's and Needless Markup, jewelry I never wore because I preferred to make my own with beads and wire. Selling my jewelry might be a way to get my car back. I had one week before the repo was a done deal, and Mom said there was no way we could come up with the cash the bank wanted. What would Charlie think if I asked him to buy jewelry Dad had given me?

My memories of my uncle were mostly impressions, of hugs that smelled like coffee and cinnamon, and lots of laughter. Every year when I opened my birthday package from him, I was excited to see what pepper shaker he'd sent, since that was what he always sent. My favorites were the yellow Labrador, a Fred Flintstone, and a cherubic red devil kissing the air. Once my dad had suggested I throw them away, but I'd refused.

"What good is a pepper shaker without its mate?" Dad had asked.

"Not everything has to be useful," I'd argued.

I sat at my vanity and opened the drawer where I'd hidden all of my uncle's birthday cards. On each of them, he'd sketched an image of the matching salt shaker. My fifth birthday card showed a whimsical drawing of a tiny blond angel with puckered lips, to match the red devil on my dresser. "One day these two will meet and sparks will fly!" The words swirled across the card in beautiful calligraphy.

My eighth birthday card showed a yellow Labrador puppy lying on its back, with tiny holes for salt in its stomach. "Toby needs a friend, don't you think?" said the note.

When I was young, the shakers had been my favorite toys. I'd set up elaborate adventures with all of the characters, including a pink Siamese cat and a surprised-looking chef. As I held the Labrador shaker, rubbing my fingers over the smooth ceramic, I wondered what my uncle thought of his disappearing brother.

Seventeen pepper shakers lined my vanity table. As I stared at them, I remembered when I'd last seen Charlie. It was my seventh birthday party. Dad had argued with Mom after Charlie left our house.

"He's a loser, Marilyn. I don't want him coming to her birthdays anymore."

"But Ty, he's your brother."

"He's a hippie working in some crummy pawn store.

That's not the type of role model I want around for Darcy. He doesn't even own a car, for Christ's sake."

I opened another drawer and pulled out Dad's latest postcard. It had arrived yesterday, postmarked Tennessee, with a picture of Graceland. I hoped that Elvis wasn't *his* new role model. Even though I was mad at him, I didn't want him dying of a heart attack on a toilet.

"Darcy—I know things must be hard for you and Mom right now. I'm sorry about that. Do what you need to do."

The words had infuriated me. *Gee, I'm sorry life is falling apart honey, but, ya know, figure it out. Meanwhile, I'll be driving around the country visiting random tourist traps.*

I pushed away the twinges of guilt about selling my jewelry. If I had the right buyer, it wasn't entirely disloyal. It was just transitioning the items from one family member to another. *Do what you need to do.*

The sound of the doorbell and Toby's excited barking jolted me out of my reverie. I jumped up, glancing at myself in the mirror. I could stand some lip gloss and mascara, but who cared? This wasn't exactly a hot date. I grabbed the hatbox full of jewelry and my string wallet and hurried down the stairs.

Toby was already at the door, barking his head off. Our front doors were too fancy for peepholes, so I just flung it open.

Holy shizballs.

One of the hottest guys I'd ever seen stood on the porch. Thick dark hair almost brushed his shoulders. He wore a black T-shirt and jeans, and from what I dared to look at, underneath he was all sinewy strength and lean muscle. Not a beer belly or plumber's crack in sight. And he was way closer to my age than the old guy I'd conjured in my imagination.

Toby launched himself out the door, and the guy knelt to pet him, instantly turning my guard dog into a heap of wriggling pet-me fur. The guy glanced up at me, and I caught my breath at the swirling kaleidoscope colors of his eyes: green, blue, and silver, all mixed together.

"Er. Um." I stammered. "Hi."

He grinned at me, one side of his mouth quirking higher than the other, and flashing a dimple.

Why hadn't I at least put on lip gloss?

"Hi." He stood up, looming over me as Toby bounced around his legs. "You must be Darcy. I'm Lucas Martinez, your chauffeur." He grinned and glanced down at my insane dog, then back at me. "And your scary protector is…?"

Damn. Even his voice was sexy. *Words, Darcy. Find them. Use them.* "Toby," I squeaked. I cleared my throat. "You sure it's okay if he rides in your car?" The shiny black muscle car in the driveway wasn't the falling apart vehicle I'd imagined, either.

"Sure." He shrugged. "I like dogs."

Toby rolled on his back, flaunting his stomach for a belly rub. I sort of felt like doing the same thing, but I had more impulse control than my dog.

"I'll just grab his leash. Please come in." I stepped back into the foyer, embarrassed that I'd completely forgotten all the manners Mom had drilled into me.

He smiled down at me and entered the Covington Castle. I saw his eyes widen as he took it all in: the marble floor, the enormous chandelier, the family portraits interspersed with artwork lining the walls.

"Be right back." I escaped into the kitchen and grabbed Toby's leash off a hook on the wall.

Inhale calm. Exhale stress. So he was cute, so what? Okay, way beyond cute. But still. He worked for my uncle, just doing him a favor by picking me up. I snuck into the powder room off the kitchen and brushed my hair. And found some lip gloss in a drawer. *Score.*

Back in the foyer, Lucas was kneeling again, rubbing Toby's stomach. He stood up when I entered the room. I wondered if I could sneak a Snapchat shot of him for Sal.

"Ready?" He held out a hand for Toby's leash and I gave it to him, since Toby had forgotten I existed.

"You could totally rob us if you wanted," I muttered, closing the front door and locking it. "My dog just fell into insta-love with you." As soon as the words left my mouth, I felt my cheeks flame with heat. *Nice to meet you, gorgeous driver. How do you feel about freaky girls with no social skills?*

Lucas laughed as I hurried around him and down the steps.

"Your carriage awaits," he said, stopping next to me and sweeping out his arm in a grand gesture. Still blushing, I looked away from his assessing gaze.

Once he'd closed the door behind me, I let out a long breath. I needed to get a grip. Woodbridge was full of hot guys. This was not a big deal. It must be all the stress, making my hormones overactive or something.

He slid into the driver's seat and started the car. I felt the deep rumble of the engine underneath my butt. I glanced at the dashboard, which gleamed. The car wasn't new but it was spotless. He must be one of those guys obsessed with their cars. I wondered if he washed it shirtless. If he did, he could probably charge for admission.

Stop it, I told myself. *He's your driver, not your date.* I tried to think of something non-freaky to say. "You're probably going to end up with a lot of dog hair in the backseat. Sorry."

He shot me a crooked grin as the car pulled out of the driveway. "Don't worry about it. I've got a Shop-Vac."

I suddenly wondered if my uncle had told him to be extra nice to me because my life was falling apart. The idea was almost as appalling as the Top Ten list on my locker.

He increased the speed as we turned down Sixth Avenue. "So Charlie says he hasn't seen you in a long time. He's glad you're coming to his store."

"Me too. I've never been there."

He turned toward me, surprised. "Really? Why not?"

Weren't limo drivers supposed to remain silent unless spoken to? Guilt about not seeing my uncle made me irritable. "Long story."

He shrugged. "It's kind of a long drive, if you feel like telling the story."

"You don't want to hear it. Be glad you're just the chauffeur."

He shot me a look of surprise, then a darker emotion flickered in his eyes before he turned back to the road. "So the hired help shouldn't ask questions. Got it."

Oh no. Now he thought I was a rich bitch too good to talk to him?

"I didn't mean... It's just..." Crap. Why couldn't I be

charming like my dad and Sal? It was situations like this
that made me stay in my mousy shell. He didn't say anything
for several blocks, making me feel bad that I'd snapped at
him. I reminded myself he'd driven across town to pick me
up, and was just trying to make conversation.

"My dad," I said haltingly, "Charlie's brother, he, uh,
didn't see Charlie often. I think I was seven the last time I
saw him."

I glanced at Lucas's arms resting on the steering wheel
as we waited at a red light. His skin glimmered in the sun
like Aspen leaves at their peak, golden and warm.

"Wow," he said. "That's…different."

"That's one way to put it," I said, then shifted in my
seat so I could pet Toby in the backseat. I snuck a glance at
Lucas's profile. Yep. Still hot.

We drove in silence again, until he reached for his iPod.
One of my favorite songs by a local band blasted through
the speakers. He adjusted the volume and glanced at me. "Is
this okay?"

I was glad he had to refocus on driving because those
eyes of his killed me. "Yeah," I said. "I love Ice Krystal.
They're great in concert."

He glanced at me. "Did you see them at the Gothic?
That was an awesome show."

"It was," I agreed. I'd gone to the concert with Sal and
we'd danced the entire time. It was weird to think Lucas had
been there, too. Possibly even witnessing my lame dance
moves.

"Charlie's store isn't far from the Gothic."

Wow. So all the concerts I'd seen there, my uncle had

been close by and I hadn't even known?

Lucas turned the car down an alley behind a row of old brick buildings. "We'll park in the back, but walk around to the front. You need to get the full effect, seeing it for the first time."

"Whatever you say, driver." I forced a feeble smile, and his answering grin chased away some of my anxiety.

We walked down the alley and around to the storefronts facing Broadway. I held Toby's leash in one hand and my hatbox in the other. My spazzy dog kept angling into Lucas's space.

"Want me to hold the leash?" Lucas asked.

"No thanks." It would've been easier, but I was feeling stubborn, and anxious. Handing over the leash again felt like giving up control.

"Have you done training with your dog?" Lucas asked, after he almost fell over Toby darting in front of him.

"Yes," I grumbled. "But he has a mind of his own." Especially when he's in insta-love, I wanted to say, but didn't.

I was so distracted trying to wrangle Toby that I almost walked past the shop, until Lucas put a hand on my arm to stop me. I jumped at the feel of his skin on mine, and he yanked his hand away.

He inclined his head toward the faded brick storefront. "Here it is."

I took a deep breath, feeling like I was about to meet a magic wizard who held all the answers to my questions about my dad. But then I remembered Dorothy in *The Wizard of Oz*, and reminded myself there was no such thing as real wizards.

CHAPTER FIVE

The Second Hand Story was flanked by a vacuum and sewing machine repair shop and a tattoo parlor called Inkheart. This part of town was cool in a shabby, retro kind of way.

The store's large window faced the sidewalk. Someone had put up a crazy display of toy animals frolicking under a fake tree. A stuffed squirrel had a Frisbee glued to its paw while a fuzzy rabbit flew a kite suspended from the ceiling.

I glanced at Lucas and pointed to the display. "Is this what you meant by 'the full effect'?"

He nodded, watching me warily. Did he think I'd make fun of the display?

"It's great," I said, meaning it. "Did Charlie do this?"

"I did."

"Really? I thought you were the repair guy." I forced

myself to maintain eye contact with him, drawing on the very small amount of "Tri Ty" DNA I'd inherited.

His lips quirked. "Among other things." He reached for the door and opened it, and I jumped again, this time because of the goofy Halloween "bwahahah" laugh that sounded, the kind that people rigged up on their front porches to scare little kids.

Lucas laughed as he propped open the door with his body. "No ghosts, I promise. It's just Charlie's way of announcing customers. You can go inside."

Toby dragged me into the store, excited to meet new people to fall in love with.

You can do this, I told myself. *Just breathe.*

I looked around, but didn't see anyone. Then curtains sectioning off a far corner of the store parted and my uncle walked out. He paused before grinning and exclaiming, "Darcy! I'm so glad you came."

He still had the long ponytail and scruffy beard. In his old Beatles T-shirt and jeans he looked exactly as I'd imagined him.

"Hi. So wow, you recognize me?" Duh. Who else would Lucas have brought here? I winced at my awkwardness.

Charlie chuckled, then stepped close to hug me. I held the hatbox in one arm while hugging him with the other, Toby forcing himself into the middle of our family reunion. My uncle still smelled like coffee and cinnamon.

"Of course I recognize you," Charlie said, after we hugged. "You're my favorite niece."

"And your only one," I muttered.

He grinned and looked down at Toby. "Toby. How

delightful to make your acquaintance again." He smiled at me. "Last time I saw him he was a puppy."

A little late I asked, "Is it okay if he comes in your store?"

Charlie nodded. "My store, my rules. So yes."

He glanced at the hatbox. "You still have it. Amazing. How about the pepper shakers?"

I nodded. "I have all of them."

His brown eyes, so much like my dad's, widened in delight. "You do? I'm thrilled. I was afraid your dad..." He stopped, watching me with questioning concern.

"It's okay," I mumbled.

Charlie motioned me toward a long Formica counter lined with turquoise vinyl barstools that made me think of a 1950s diner. As I perched on a stool, I glanced at the large mirror behind the counter. It reflected shelves overflowing with old appliances, glasses and dishes, ancient radios and TV sets, and wicker baskets overflowing with toys. Two of the walls were covered in murals. The images were from all around Colorado: the zoo, Red Rocks Amphitheatre, and the boathouse at City Park. The far wall was lined from floor to ceiling with more shelves.

"Oh," I gasped. I slid off the stool and hurried to one display.

I'd never seen so many salt and pepper shakers in my life. A sign on the bottom shelf caught my eye: *"Not for sale."* I bent down for a closer look and my breath caught.

There were the mates to all of my pepper shakers at home. I recognized them from my birthday cards: the yellow Labrador lying on his back, the angel kissing air, Wilma

Flintstone, a blue Siamese cat looking down his snooty nose, a laughing lady chef and the rest of the mates to all seventeen of my pepper shakers.

"I always knew you'd show up some day," Charlie said softly. He'd sidled up to me so quietly I hadn't heard him. I rose to face him, speechless.

Who was this amazing guy? And why had Dad banished him from our lives?

Charlie grinned. "Coffee? Donut?" He put an arm around my shoulder and steered me back to the counter where I was grateful to sit because my shaking legs might not hold me up. Toby had finally stopped stalking Lucas and curled up on a rug like he lived here.

Charlie lifted the lid off a round glass pastry dish piled high with donuts. A hand-lettered sign said, *"Donuts: 50¢ each or free if you tell me a good story."*

His eyes were kind. "Have as many as you want."

"I'm going to Liz's," Lucas said, shoving off from the counter where he'd been leaning, watching us. "You want anything?"

Charlie shook his head then glanced at me. "I have plain old coffee but Liz makes the good stuff. Do you want a mocha? Tea?" He flashed an apologetic smile. "I don't even know if you're a coffee or a tea person."

It was a small thing, but seeing the flash of regret in my uncle's eyes threatened to break my heart. I swallowed over the lump in my throat. "Nothing right now," I said.

Charlie glanced at Lucas. "Take your time. Darcy and I have a lot of catching up to do."

Lucas nodded, shooting me another curious glance

before he left, setting off the Halloween laugh when he opened the door.

"Now, have a donut. I insist."

I hesitated, then pointed to one with pink icing and sprinkles, my favorite. "I'll take that one." I looked at him shyly. "Do I really have to tell you a story?"

He slid the donut toward me on a paper napkin. "I have a feeling you'll be telling me plenty of them now that we're getting reacquainted. I'll put this one on your story tab."

"So you give people free food if they tell you a story? For real?"

He nodded, leaning against the counter. "It's a tradition. The first owner of this place did the same thing. Thus the name."

The Second Hand Story.

I took a huge bite of donut to give me an excuse not to talk. What could I say? *Wow, you are not what I expected at all. You are oddly cool in a hippie-ish sort of way. How can you and my OCD father possibly be related?*

"You sure you don't want coffee?" He refilled his NPR mug.

"Just water," I slurred around my mouthful of donut.

He opened a small fridge and handed me a bottle, then gestured to the hatbox. "So what's in there? Or was this your way of making sure I recognized you?" His eyes practically twinkled. How could my dad be so freaked out by this guy?

I swigged more water, stalling for time. I didn't want money to be our first topic of conversation. It seemed rude, not to mention embarrassing. He wiped the counter with a rag, oozing patience.

"It's just some…stuff. I thought maybe you might…" This was pathetic. I was pathetic.

His eyes held mine for a moment, and then he lifted the lid off the box.

"Ah," he said, looking at the jewelry. He glanced up. Concerned? Judging? I couldn't read his expression. "So you need some cash." It was a statement, not a question.

I nodded, too mortified to speak.

He rubbed his scruffy beard. It looked good on him, no matter what Dad said. "Darcy, I wish I could help, but this isn't exactly the kind of store you need right now."

"It's not why I'm here," I said, relieved to find my voice. "I wanted to see you. But while I was waiting for my *driver*," I forced a smile, "I remembered you work in a pawn shop, so I thought maybe…" I couldn't finish.

My face flooded with heat. What was I doing? I had to get out of here. I grabbed the box from the counter and slid off the stool. Toby ran to the door, and then I remembered I didn't have a car to whisk me away. Crap.

"Sit down, Darcy. Please." Charlie's voice was gentle but commanding. "I'm not letting you run away, not after waiting all these years to see you again."

I took a breath, then resumed my seat on the spinning stool, embarrassed. Looking into his kind eyes, so much like my dad's, I thought that maybe I didn't want to leave.

"Sorry," I said. "This is all just…a lot to take in."

He nodded. "I can only imagine what you and your mom are going through."

I bit my lip, unsure how much I should tell him.

"My car was repossessed." I could tell him that much.

Toby gave a long-suffering dog sigh and curled up on the rug again.

"Repo'd?" He looked stunned.

"Yeah. It was...pretty bad." I took a deep breath and plowed on. "My mom talked to the bank, and if we come up with about six grand in a week I can get the car back." I left out the part about catching up on old payments and making new ones. Mom said there was no way we could do it.

Charlie let out a low whistle. "That's a lot of cash." He looked genuinely sympathetic.

"Yeah."

"What about your mom? Can't she help?"

I shook my head. "She wants to but our accounts are frozen." I shot him a quick look. He definitely knew what that meant and so did I, now. Frozen = no access to money = Mom getting a job.

Charlie sipped his coffee. "Maybe you should try a pawn store. Not a thrift store, which is what my store is." The corners of his eyes crinkled just like Dad's when he smiled at me.

"Oh. I didn't realize..."

His grin spread like marshmallows melting in hot chocolate. "Do you know the difference?"

I should know the difference. I was a freaking honor student after all. But this wasn't exactly my usual scene. "Not really," I admitted.

"Thrift stores sell used things that are donated, usually, or stuff we buy really cheap. Pawn shops take your valuable items and loan you cash based on a percentage of the value." He snorted. "A very small percentage, but still, it's something."

I frowned. "What do you mean 'loan'? I just want to sell the stuff."

"They buy things, too, so you could walk into a pawn shop right now and come out with cash. But if you do a loan, you could buy your jewelry back. Eventually."

"I doubt I'd ever be able to come up with the money to buy my stuff back," I muttered.

He sighed. "I wish I could help with your car."

"It's all right," I said. "I'm getting used to the bus." I hesitated. "And that's not why I came here, to ask you for money. I really wanted to see you." I glanced back toward the shelf of shakers. "And those are awesome. They look just like the ones you drew on my birthday cards." I bit my lip. "I kept those, too."

Some of the sadness left Charlie's eyes, making my own heart lift. We sat in silence, taking each other in, until I heard a door slam somewhere in the back, and Lucas emerged from behind the curtains, like an actor ready for an encore. He had a to-go cup in each hand, and sat down right freaking next to me.

"Here." He slid a cup toward me. "Liz insisted, when I told her Charlie's niece was here." He glanced at Charlie, grinning. "You're lucky she's busy over there or she'd have crashed your private party way before I did."

Charlie laughed. "This is one day I'm glad she's short-staffed." He smiled at me. "I'll introduce you to her, Darcy, but I'm not done talking to you yet."

I held the cup to my nose and sniffed. "Hazelnut coffee?" I glanced at Lucas.

"Her call, not mine," he said. "I would've guessed something more complicated for you. Lots of half-caf, low-fat, double sprinkles, stuff like that."

His eyes sparked with laughter, but I wasn't amused. "You think I'm high-maintenance?"

He lifted a shoulder. I narrowed my eyes. Just because he'd picked me up in my stupid country club house didn't mean he could make assumptions.

"I would've ordered black coffee," I lied. He didn't need to know about my strawberries and creme Frappucino obsession. With double sprinkles.

Charlie pointed to his ancient coffee pot. "I have plenty of that."

"Um." I bit my lip and turned away from Lucas's smirk. "I'm okay with water. And hazelnut."

Lucas laughed next to me as Toby pinned him with his dog version of a Jedi mind-control stare, willing Lucas to pet him. Lucas caved instantly, leaning over to rub his ears, and then raised his eyes to mine.

"What are *you* drinking?" I asked accusingly.

"Cappuccino. Double shot. Extra dry."

"And you called me high-maintenance?" I never sparred like this with guys, but Lucas pushed my buttons. And I had a feeling he enjoyed doing it.

He grinned and shrugged.

Charlie chuckled from the other side of the counter. "All right, you two, settle down." He glanced at Lucas. "Darcy needs our help, Lucas." His words surprised me, and Lucas, too, judging by the expression on his face.

Lucas spun his stool so he faced me. "Do you need

something fixed?" He tucked a strand of hair behind his ear. "I'm guessing you're not here to shop for clothes."

"Lucas." Charlie's "stern warning" voice sounded like every teacher I've ever known.

Lucas shrugged, a smile playing at his distracting lips. "I'm just sayin'…"

Just saying what? What did he know about me or my falling-apart life?

"Look," I said, sighing in frustration, "whatever you think about me, I need some money and I need it fast. This is all I've got." I lifted the lid off the hatbox and slid it toward him. "Can you help me?"

His eyes locked on mine briefly, no longer mocking, then he broke the connection to peer into the box. He whistled and glanced at me. "Nice bling. You sure you want to get rid of it?"

I stared at him, trying not to be distracted by his hypnotic eyes and smoky voice. "I don't have much choice," I said.

"Her car was repossessed," Charlie said. "She needs to come up with a lot of money. Fast. What do you think, Lucas? eBay?"

Lucas stared at me, obviously shocked. "Repo'd?" He turned to Charlie and they exchanged a meaningful look. I wondered how much Charlie had told him about my AWOL dad.

"Yeah," I said. "My dad is the loser on Letterman and my family is going broke and falling apart and I just want to get my car back."

"Letterman?" Lucas frowned. So I'd found the one person in town who hadn't seen it.

"Never mind," I said, fiddling with my napkin.

Lucas spun his stool so he faced Charlie. "eBay will take too long," he said, "and you have to be eighteen to pawn it." He glanced at me. "Are you?"

I shook my head. My eighteenth birthday was six months away. My earlier frustration washed away as I sat there watching him. Of course he thought I was a high-maintenance rich girl. What else would he think after being sent to rescue me from my castle like I was a special princess?

And he was right about me not shopping here. Yeah I wore jeans, but they weren't from Wal-Mart. And I'd just showed him a box full of expensive jewelry.

While Lucas pondered my problem, I rested my chin in my hands, staring at my reflection in the mirror behind Charlie's counter. Even though middle-aged cougars thought my dad was hot and my mom had been the queen of every school dance, I'd just ended up average. Highlights from Mom's salon didn't help my boring brown hair, and I was stuck with my too small nose and too wide mouth. I could be a Picasso model.

Lucas finally spoke. "My cousin had his car repo'd once. He was able to negotiate with the bank. Have you talked to anyone at your bank?"

I felt like he'd ripped off a huge scab, exposing a gaping wound. What was I doing here, asking two people I hardly knew for help? I suddenly felt raw and drained. I needed to leave.

Charlie must've sensed this, because he moved quickly around the counter. "Let's go say hi to Liz, then I'll take you home."

"But I thought you had boxes to unpack," I said, confused.

"I can drive her home," Lucas said.

Charlie shot Lucas a cryptic look and shook his head. "You stay here. I'll take Liz's car."

"Whatever you say, boss." Lucas crossed his arms over his chest, watching me with an unreadable expression. He was probably relieved his chauffeur duty was over.

Toby jumped up, sensing something was happening. Lucas leaned over to pet him again and I caught a glimpse of a tattoo peeking out from under his shirt sleeve. I couldn't tell what it was, so I turned away before he caught me ogling him.

"Thanks," I whispered to Charlie, horrified to feel tears threatening to breach the dam. No way could I break down here. I walked quickly to the door and shoved it open, juggling my hatbox and Toby's leash. "Thanks for the ride, Lucas," I said in a voice thick with unshed tears, but I didn't think he heard me over the loud Halloween laugh.

Charlie caught up to me as I walked quickly down the sidewalk, headed for the coffee shop I'd noticed when Lucas and I had first arrived. I didn't want to meet someone else tonight, but since Charlie was my ride I didn't have much choice.

"I'm sorry, Darcy, if we upset you somehow." Charlie's voice was soft with concern.

"You didn't." I swiped tears off my cheeks with the back of my leash-holding hand. Damn it. I was not going to cry.

Charlie wrapped an arm around my shoulder, and I was stunned at how much he felt like my dad. I let out a long breath.

"Would you like to just go home?" Charlie asked. "You can meet Liz next time."

Next time? I doubted there'd be one, but I nodded, grateful for the opportunity to leave sooner rather than later.

I followed Charlie around the corner to the alley to an older hybrid car.

"I don't have a car," Charlie said, pulling a key ring from his pocket, "but Liz lends me hers whenever I need one." So that hadn't changed since Dad's anti-hippie rant ten years ago when he'd excommunicated my uncle from our lives.

Maybe I could follow my uncle's example and go car-free. The thought of doing so was agony, but it didn't look like I was going to be able to spring the Audi from repo jail.

We drove in companionable silence, except for the jazz playing from the car radio. It was like he knew I needed to recharge my batteries and not talk. By the time we got to my house I felt a little better.

"Thank you for sending Lucas to get me," I said, as the car idled in the driveway. I tugged at my hair. "Sorry you didn't get any of your boxes unpacked like you planned."

His smile was mischievous. "That was mostly an excuse to get you out of your house and down to my neck of the woods."

"Really?"

He nodded. "I'm worried about you." He glanced at our house, completely dark because I'd forgotten to leave lights on, and Mom wasn't home yet. Or else she was passed out on the couch. "Looks pretty lonely for a girl by herself."

I shrugged. "It's okay."

"I want you to come back to see me, Darcy. Regularly. Think about it, okay?"

I laughed. "You going to make Lucas my permanent chauffeur?"

"If I have to, yes."

No way was that happening. "I can figure out the bus route. It's not rocket science." I grinned, then impulsively leaned over to hug him. I closed my eyes, inhaling his cinnamon and coffee smell. His answering hug was tight, once again reminding me of my dad.

He pulled away, his expression serious. "I can't offer you money, Darcy, but I can offer you time. I'm always available to talk, or just listen. I meant what I said about coming to see me. If I'm not around, Lucas is, and he can always track me down."

Right. Like I'd just waltz into Charlie's store and hang out with that package of uber-hotness like it was no big deal.

"Want me to come inside with you?"

I shook my head, imagining Mom passed out on the couch. "No thanks." I opened the car door and Toby leaped outside. I followed him up the driveway, pausing to wave good-bye to Charlie, who waited until I was safely inside.

Tonight had been full of surprises, not least of which was discovering my uncle still cared about me, a lot, and wanted me back in his life. No, he wasn't a magic wizard. He was better than that, because he was real. He'd given me a lot to think about.

And the sexy chauffeur? I'd definitely be thinking about him, too.

Chapter Six
September 26

BREAKING NEWS FROM TRI!UMPHANT! HARVEST INDUSTRIES—TRIUMPHANT TY MISSING; PARTNER ASSUMES CONTROL OF COMPANY

National Newswire BREAKING NEWS

J.J. Briggs, acting president of Tri!Umphant! Harvest Industries issued a press release from Denver headquarters today. Tyler Covington, the face of Tri!Umphant! Harvest, has not appeared at any of his scheduled engagements for the past month. Rumors have been swirling that Mr. Covington has abandoned both his business and his family, rumors that J.J. Briggs adamantly denied today at the press conference.

The text of Mr. Briggs' statement appears below.

"All speaking appearances for Ty Covington have been cancelled for the next two months. Mr. Covington is taking an extended leave of absence for health reasons. Ticket purchasers will be given free tickets to a future engagement upon his return. There is no truth to the rumors that Mr. Covington is missing or that Harvest is in financial distress."

"Ty is an inspiration to many of us and we know he will return reinvigorated with new words of wisdom to share. In the meantime, I am acting as the interim president of Tri!Umphant! Harvest Industries," Mr. Briggs stated. He did not respond to questions from the press.

Comment on this story:
Share your comments on this story on our website. Comments may be removed by the moderator if considered inappropriate.

"That Tri!Umphant! crap is such total bullshit. I saw that Covington guy speak and even bought his CDs. I listened to the first two but then I couldn't stomach any more of his vomit. What a SCAM!"
–DaveInDenver

"All that motivational stuff is a joke. Save your money and just get off your butt and get a job.

There, I said all you need to hear in one sentence. Where's my million-dollar speaking fee? HA HA!"
–JoeKnows

"Just because it didn't work for you DaveInDenver doesn't mean it doesn't work. Some of us have the attention span to listen to ALL the CDs and it was LIFE CHANGING!! Don't hate on something you don't understand." –MissKT

"MissKT you are a freaking MORON! Your hero is in hiding. Dude even bailed on his family. What kind of 'positive harvest' is he unleashing for them?" –DaveInDenver

"Even Jesus spent forty days alone in the dessert, DaveInDenver! Ty is coming back soon. I believe he will return to his fans and his family in TOTAL TRIUMPH!" –MissKT

"Learn to spell MissKT. Jesus spent time in the desert, not a cherry pie. You're an idiot to think Covington is coming back. He's on some island no one has ever heard of, with plenty of cash to live out his life in style. Cash that idiots like you shelled out!" –DaveInDenver

Comment removed by moderator.

Comment removed by moderator.

Comments no longer accepted on this story. Please visit our home page for more breaking news.

*M*om and I sat in the family room together with our laptops. We'd closed all the drapes on the first floor of the house. Vans from the local TV news stations lined our street. I'd snuck around to the back of the house, ducking behind hedges when I got home from school so that no reporters would spot me. Every so often, one of the reporters rang the doorbell and Toby barked until he was hoarse. I knew he sensed our anxiety. Our fear.

J.J. called Mom to ask if she wanted him to come over and make a statement to the local press to get rid of them, but she told him no, he'd already done enough damage, thank you very much.

"The cat's completely out of the bag now," Mom said, staring at her laptop. "No more pretending he's got laryngitis." She snorted in disgust. I'd tried to convince her to stop reading all the horrible rumors online but she ignored me. "I guess it's a good thing I've got a new job."

I gaped at her. "You do? Doing what?"

"Working for Pam Hendricks, as her assistant."

No way. Fake-Bake Pam? Chloe's mom? Crap.

"I'm going to help out in her office while I study for my realtor license. Do open houses once in a while." She shrugged. "It's a foot in the door, I guess."

Even the smallest seed can blossom into an unexpected harvest. I heard Dad's voice in my mind. *Tend to all your plants and opportunities, no matter how small.* Personally, I'd like to mow down this opportunity, or weed-whack it out of existence.

"So what about Harvest?" I asked, changing the subject from Mom's awful new job. "I don't understand why J.J. is in charge."

She closed her eyes and sighed, then set her computer on the coffee table. "I don't know. It was a decision made by the board."

"How is that possible? Dad invented Tri!Umph." I had a sudden craving for ice cream. I was turning into Pavlov's dog. As soon as I heard bad news, my mouth watered for Ben & Jerry's.

Toby pawed at my jean-clad leg, whining his unhappiness. I massaged his ears. "It's okay, buddy," I whispered. "Don't freak. Leave that to the professionals."

"It's a little more complicated than that," Mom said, answering my question with another sigh. "Your dad and J.J. both created Harvest. They each have different strengths."

This was news to me. As far as I knew, my dad *was* Tri!Umphant! Harvest. J.J. did boring stuff in the background like arrange Dad's speaking schedule and produce the DVDs. Dad called it "administrivia" so I had the impression it was grunt work anybody could have done, but my dad had picked his oldest friend. Sort of did him a favor.

I closed my laptop. "Mom, can we not talk about this for a while? I feel like I'm going to throw up."

Mom turned the TV to the classic movie channel. We watched Katharine Hepburn, Cary Grant, and a baby leopard while overdosing on Cheetos and peanut M&M's. I slugged down soda and Mom slugged down wine.

To each her own poison.

Sometime around nine o'clock, the reporters gave up and left. Toby collapsed in his dog bed, exhausted from his front door vigil.

"Do you think they're gone for good?" I asked hopefully.

"Let's hope so." She refilled her wineglass, which wasn't even empty. "Damned reporters."

"Maybe Brad and Angelina's secret quadruplets will be revealed and take the news focus off Dad. I hear they were born with Brangelina tattoos." I waited for her laugh.

"You can save the vulgar humor for your friends." Her eyes were slits. Back to non-swearing proper mom, just like that.

"Mom, I think our *Downton Abbey* days are over. Our lives are turning to crap. We've got to laugh at something."

She ignored me, flipping the channel from Cary Grant back to the local news. A perky reporter chirped into the camera. "No signs of life today at the Covington residence. If Tyler Covington is there, he's not coming out to talk to us."

Cut to shot of reporter on our front porch, ringing the bell. Toby's muffled bark sounded in the background.

"Now can I make jokes about celebrity offspring? And their tats?" I asked.

Mom rose creakily from the couch and tossed the remote at me. "Knock yourself out. I'm going to bed."

Whatever, Mom. Just go ahead and check out. Dad did; you might as well, too.

After Mom went to bed, I opened my laptop with Toby

curled next to me. After watching a few puppy videos that made me almost smile, I typed in a new search.

There he was. My dad, sort of blurry and poor audio quality, but that was definitely him. He paced the stage, lit by spotlights. I wasn't sure which arena he was in, but it was a big one. The camera cut to the audience where thousands of people hung on his every word. A picture of my old pink bicycle flashed on the screen behind him.

Dad told the audience how J.J. had taught me to ride a bike when I was six years old. My dad couldn't do it because he'd been very ill. So sick he almost died. This was the famous brush-with-death speech. He told the audience how his illness made him see what was important in life, how it inspired him to follow his dreams, and to teach others how to do the same.

I kind of remembered my sixth summer. J.J. visited often, and one day he brought me a Barbie bike with pink and white handlebar streamers. He ran behind me for days, holding onto the back of the bicycle seat until I mastered the sidewalk on my own.

"No training wheels," he'd insisted to my worried mother. "They're a crutch. She needs to learn to trust herself." That was part of Dad's spiel, too, how J.J. reminded him that we rely too much on training wheels in life, that we need to learn to balance on our own.

The camera panned the audience for close-ups. Most of the women and a few of the men were in tears, picturing me on my bike, my dad on his deathbed, J.J. reassuring my overwhelmed mother.

When I was younger, Dad dragged Mom and me along during his summer tours, and this was the point when he made me join him on stage. Unlike Dad, I looked petrified, and more than once I reached around to pull my underwear out of my butt crack. Those videos had done wonders for my social life. Not.

I stopped the video and leaned against a pillow. It was quite a story, at least the way my dad told it. I closed my eyes and remembered how proud I'd felt watching him from backstage.

What had happened? What had caused him to run away? To go against his own philosophy of facing life head-on, no matter what curveballs it threw?

I opened up Dad's Facebook fan page. I scrolled the page, reading all the gushing comments about how awesome he was, how his philosophy had changed lives in dramatic ways. I scrolled down to the entries from before he'd disappeared, looking for some clue about what was going through his mind.

"Is Ty okay?" Written by somebody named Bethany. *"I've seen him speak so many times,"* she wrote, *"but this last time he seemed off, somehow. The fire wasn't there."*

I sat up, propping pillows behind me.

"I thought so, too," someone named Li Wei had replied. *"It's like he wasn't all there. Like part of him was missing."*

A chill ran up my spine. I looked at the dates. Three months ago. I'd been busy hanging out at the country club over the summer, swimming and playing tennis. I hadn't thought about it since it happened, but now that I read these comments, I remembered coming home late one night and hearing a noise from Dad's office. When I'd peeked in, he was at his desk, head in his hands. He looked up when the door opened, wiping his eyes.

"Are you okay, Dad?" I didn't think I'd ever seen him cry before.

He'd flashed me his magazine cover smile. "I'm fine, sweetie. Just...tired."

I'd said good night and closed the door. And hadn't worried, because my dad was always fine.

How many other clues had Mom and I missed, or ignored, because we didn't want to see them?

I closed my laptop and tried to sleep, but my phone pinged with a text from Charlie. *"R u ok? Saw the reporters on your porch on the news."* Punctuated with a frowny face emoticon.

His concern was comforting, especially in light of Mom's cranky exit.

"I'm ok," I typed, then amended it. *"We both are."*

It was a lie, of course, but what else could I say?

CHAPTER SEVEN
SEPTEMBER 27

Sunlight woke me earlier than I wanted, especially for a Saturday. I'd begged for blackout window shades so I could sleep in, but Mom always refused since they wouldn't match the pastel and lace that covered every inch of my bedroom. Sometimes I felt like I lived inside a wedding cake.

I wanted to wallow in the few blissful seconds between asleep and awake, where I could pretend Dad wasn't a late-night TV joke, and Mom wasn't keeping the liquor store in business, but I couldn't. At least it was the weekend. I squeezed my eyes shut, picturing Chloe prepping the CNN report for my locker, maniacally waving her glue gun like a weapon.

Downstairs, Mom was already dressed and drinking coffee.

"Big day in the real estate world?" I asked, surprised to

see her awake.

She shook her head. "You and I are going to the cabin for the weekend. I don't want to be here if the paparazzi come back." She took a sip from her mug. "After everything that's happened, you and I could use a break."

I usually whined about going to the mountains, but right now running away sounded good. When I was younger I'd loved our cabin trips, because I got uninterrupted time with my dad, who ignored the phone and focused on Mom and me the whole time. But the past couple of years, whenever we were up there all I could think of was the fun I was missing in town, like shopping with Sal and stalking Ryan.

"Come on, Toblerone." I raced upstairs to throw clothes and a couple of historical romance novels into my Hilfiger duffel. Toby licked my hand and whimpered. He knew my packed bag meant fun for him and he was eager to go.

Mom was already in the Volvo with the engine running when Toby and I ran downstairs.

"Change of plans," I texted Sal as we drove, since she'd wanted to get together today. *"Headed to mtns for wknd."*

Her reply flew back. *"R U OK?"*

Okay? My world was tilting on its axis and there was nothing to grab onto. I was flying into space, with no one to catch me.

I was most definitely not okay.

I snuck glances at Mom and her white-knuckled grip on the steering wheel as we drove west on the highway, listening to a local band we agreed on. Toby let out an occasional bark when we passed other cars with dogs hanging out the window.

Sal texted me so many times that I resorted to turning off my phone. I kept hoping Mom's cell would blast out Frank Sinatra singing about being the king of the hill, Dad's signature ring tone, but her phone never rang.

We spent our weekend quietly: reading, hiking, and sneaking glances at our cells about every five minutes. I think we both thought Dad would call us. He had to know his absence had blown up in the media. On Monday, Mom called Woodbridge to excuse my absence, extending our escape from reality by an extra day.

On our last night, we ate dinner on the cabin deck in the glow of candles, wrapped in fleece jackets. Toby snored at our feet as we shared a frozen pizza that tasted like paste. I missed Mom's cooking.

"Darcy, we're going to make it through this. I promise you. I don't know how yet. But we'll survive."

"Please don't tell me we will Tri!Umphant!ly survive."

Mom sipped her wine. "A lot of people use your dad's philosophy to survive horrible situations and to turn their lives around."

I looked at my dirty Uggs. I really didn't want a lecture on the genius of "Thoughtful! Responsible! Initiative!

"But," Mom continued, "it's not the only way."

She had my attention.

"Before I met your dad my life was simple. I taught

kindergarten and lived in a small apartment with my best friend from college." Mom smiled at the memory. Her eyes stared off toward the hillside, a looming, dark shadow under a sea of winking stars.

"We lived on ramen noodles and the leftovers my friend brought home every night from her waitress job." Mom poured herself another glass of wine as I watched her warily.

"Who was your friend? Do I know her?"

Mom paused. "No. She was still in my life when you were very young, but then she moved to Tucson and we lost contact."

"You should see if she's on Facebook." I grabbed another slice of pizza. I was going to gain ten pounds through this ordeal at the rate I was eating. Stress = ravenous.

Mom shook her head. "You know I don't do Facebook."

"Yeah," I said around a mouthful of pepperoni. I was glad about that. I spent most of my screen time on Tumblr and Instagram, but the thought of friending my mom freaked me out. I followed my dad's Facebook fan page, but we definitely weren't FB friends.

"Anyway, I guess what I'm trying to say is, I was able to earn a salary, to take care of myself." She held my gaze. "I can do it again. I can help take care of us." She took another sip of wine. "But I'm sure Dad will be home soon and get back to work at Harvest."

"If you have to work, why don't you teach again?" I reached for another slice of pizza. Maybe this one would taste better. Toby looked up at me and whined. I snuck him a piece of pepperoni, which he inhaled without chewing.

Mom shook her head. "I don't think I have the energy. Plus,

I'd have to go back to school to renew my teaching license. I think real estate is the best choice." Mom sat up a little straighter and raised her chin, almost daring me to disagree.

The thought of Mom working for Chloe's mom killed me, but she'd already made up her mind. Maybe it would work out.

Mom's eyes brightened. "Darcy, I can do this. And you can help." I almost choked on my pizza crust, but she continued without noticing. "You're so good on the internet and with your digital camera. You can help me take photos of the houses for online marketing."

I stared at my mom. It was bad enough she was doing this real estate thing, but dragging me with her? No way.

"I don't think so. I don't know anything about real estate and—"

"You don't need to. You just take pictures of houses and put them on a website. It's probably just like what you do with all those online sites, right? We can start with the cabin." She stared down at her hands. "We might need to put it on the market soon. That's what J.J. recommends."

"Sell the cabin?" My stomach clenched. The cabin was Dad's favorite place in the world. We couldn't sell it.

Mom nodded, her eyes welling with tears.

I reached down to pet Toby. I'd give anything to trade places with him, to spend my time chasing squirrels and rabbits while the humans dealt with all this drama, which was getting worse by the minute.

I frowned. "Is this whole mess J.J.'s fault? Did he screw up somehow?"

She stared into her wine glass. "I don't know."

My heart pounded. "So what he said about Harvest going broke? It's really true?"

Mom's face sagged. "Oh honey, you have no idea how much I wish it wasn't. But I'm afraid it is." She poured herself more wine. "After meeting with the board, it sounds pretty bad." She forced a wobbly smile. "At least your tuition is paid through the year, so you don't have to leave your friends at Woodbridge."

Right. Friends like Chloe.

"What are we going to do?" I didn't recognize my own voice.

Mom swirled the wine in her glass, not meeting my gaze. "Right now, we just have to put one foot in front of the other."

I glared at her. "You sound like Tri Ty."

Her smile was wistful. "It's good advice, no matter who it's from." She shivered, rubbing her jacket sleeves. "Anyway. Dad's old truck is here. You could drive it back to town tomorrow. It's not fancy but at least it runs."

I thought of Charlie being car-free. I'd been so set on getting back my Audi, but now that felt selfish.

"Yeah," I agreed. "I think I remember how to drive that beast." Dad had shown me how to work the gearshift when I'd first learned to drive. "Because you never know," he'd said. "Life doesn't always have an automatic transmission." I smiled wistfully at the memory, at how my dad could turn anything into a "Tri Ty" cliché.

Suddenly I was completely blindsided by tears. It was like a cosmic hand from the universe smacked me upside the head and I suddenly knew deep in my soul that all of this was true and I couldn't stop it. I'd been living in some weird state of denial these past few weeks, but now I shook with sobs as reality sank in.

Mom knelt next to my chair and hugged me. "Let it out, honey, just let it out. It's the only way we're going to make it, by facing this head-on. And it hurts like hell, doesn't it?"

In spite of my tears, I almost smiled when I realized Mom had cussed. That was twice in one week. She was making progress.

"*M*om is *not* going to be some fake-baked realtor like Chloe's mom," I whispered into Toby's floppy ear. It was early Tuesday morning and I was sneaking in one last hike before we headed home. Toby wriggled out of my hug and took off, having caught the whiff of something much more interesting than me.

Dad loved our mini-Stonehenge. He and I had built it the summer I was nine. We'd spent a whole weekend arranging rocks into a circle, laughing and messing around. Every time we came up to the cabin we checked on it, fixing parts that fell down and adding new rocks. Even when I whined about being away from my friends, I still loved our Stonehenge hikes.

As I came around a bend in the trail, I saw the stones. Toby waited for me, panting happily. The circle was only about ten feet in diameter since the clearing was small. Rocks of all sizes balanced on top of each other. Dad and I had used a photo of the real Stonehenge as our guide, but our replica was hardly exact. I approached the circle and knelt to raise some of the fallen rocks.

"Stay, Toby," I commanded. He stayed, not venturing into the circle. He'd destroyed it once as a puppy, crashing into the circle and sending the rocks tumbling. He sighed heavily and flopped to the ground, sending up a cloud of dust while I busied myself with the stones.

It felt good to lift and move the rocks, to feel their rough surfaces anchoring me to a place where I felt safe. In the middle of the circle lay a small stone Dad and I had found years ago. It was a perfect skipping stone, flat and smooth, yet somehow it had morphed into almost a heart shape. Dad and I took turns holding it each time we visited, making wishes.

Today I hesitated to pick it up. It felt off somehow, doing this ritual by myself, but I needed to feel the smooth stone for myself. I held it in my hand and traced its shape with my forefinger. "Dad, please come home," I whispered. "You're the one who always says we can handle anything, as long as we face it together."

I closed my eyes and pressed the stone to my chest, stone heart to human heart, and sent a prayer, a wish, a plea to the universe, to God, to whoever or whatever was listening.

"Bring him home. Even if we lose everything else, please bring my dad home safe."

As I packed to leave the cabin, I glanced around my bedroom, at the bulletin board full of bumper stickers for Greenpeace, Wahoo Fish Tacos, and the Broncos, the posters of Phoenix, Snow Patrol, and my favorite movie stars. There were photos of Dad and me building a snowman, of Mom and me decorating a Christmas tree by the cabin's fireplace.

I zipped up my duffel and then ran my hands along my bookshelves full of all my favorite series, especially Harry Potter, which I re-read every winter break in front of the cabin's roaring fireplace. I didn't want to believe this was the last day I'd spend at Camp Covington, but I feared it was.

As we drove back to town, me following Mom in Dad's ancient Ford truck, I practiced visualizations like Dad told people to do on his DVDs. I imagined his BMW in the garage. I saw him closeted up in his office on the phone with J.J., somehow fixing this disaster. I pictured him greeting us with bear hugs, grinning like he always did under the spotlights.

I hoped that if I wished hard enough, my wish would come true.

Chapter Eight
September 30

The Grim Reaper, as I'd decided to call the truck, was a champ. We made it down the mountain with no problems. The only thing wrong with it was the sound system. My parents had actually driven that thing around listening only to AM radio? How had they survived? I mean, I wasn't expecting an MP3 jack but at least FM?

After listening to some political blathering on talk radio for a few minutes, I turned it off and looked at Toby. "Guess we'll just have to sing to ourselves, Toblerone."

And so we did. I sang most of the *Wicked* soundtrack, which I'd memorized during the hours spent listening to Sal rehearsing it. Toby chimed in with a howl every once in a while.

My dad had been so mad when I taught Toby to sing.

"Don't encourage that god-awful howling," he'd growled at my nine-year-old self.

"It's not howling, it's singing," I'd protested.

At the time, Toby and I were singing along to pop music Dad hated. Looking back, I think that was the problem. If we'd been singing to music Dad approved of, like the Rolling Stones, he might've cheered us on.

We must have been a funny sight driving down the highway, Toby and me singing in an old truck that belched an occasional blue puff of smoke with a BMPRCRP license plate. Dad said it meant "Bumper Crop" for Harvest, but in my mind it was always "Bumper Crap."

Once we hit civilization again, Mom and I pulled into a 7-Eleven to gas up our vehicles.

"I'm going into Pam's office for the afternoon," Mom said. "But you don't have to go back to school. Enjoy your mental health day."

"Thanks." I grinned at her. It felt good to play hooky on a school day, since I never did.

*B*ack in town, Toby and I stopped at the Chewybacca Boutique. My former allowance of one hundred bucks a week had dwindled to an occasional twenty from Mom. I'd saved enough to buy a bag of the good stuff for Toby. Next, I ran into the grocery store to grab some Doritos and fruit. Mom had said to buy healthy food, thus the fruit. Now I'd used up most of my cash. God, I needed money.

Charlie had texted me over the weekend, checking in

on us. His warmth and concern drew me like a magnet to his corner of town, plus I had more questions about my dad. And there was always the possibility of eye candy, if Lucas was working.

I drove to his shop, then parked a block away and sat debating with myself, suddenly overcome by shyness, remembering how I'd practically run out of the store last time.

"This is stupid," I muttered aloud. "Stop being such a coward."

Visor mirror inspection for food in teeth. Check. Cell phone ready in case anything weird happened and I needed to fake getting an emergency text. Check. God, I was so not my dad's Tri!Umphant! daughter. He'd walk into this store like he owned the place and sell a full set of his life-changing DVDs to anyone within shouting distance.

As I approached the store, Lucas nodded at me from the sidewalk where he leaned against the wall, smoking a cigarette. Too bad he smoked; that was the only problem with his otherwise perfect look. I tripped on the curb while fumbling with Toby's leash. Oh yeah, I was gonna *rock* this.

Toby dragged me toward Lucas, who flicked his cigarette butt into a trash can. "Nasty habit. One of these days I'll kick it." He bent down to rub Toby's ears. "So you got some new wheels?" He stood up, tilting his head toward the truck.

"More like old wheels. It's my dad's truck." I ducked my head, embarrassed. "Maybe it wouldn't be so bad if I lived on a farm." I glanced up to find him watching me curiously.

"I like trucks. Not just any girl can pull off driving one." What the heck did that mean? I was too flustered to ask.

He held the door open for me, bowing and flashing a grin. "Come on in, niece of Charlie."

Toby dragged me into the store, his nose seeking out the donuts. My uncle was nowhere in sight. "Where is he?" I asked.

Lucas put a hand in his front pocket and he pulled out his cell. My gaze followed his movement, straight to his crotch. I blushed and looked desperately around the store for something else to stare at.

"Hang on a sec." Lucas's fingers tapped on his cell. I assumed he was texting Charlie to announce my arrival.

My body felt turned inside out, all of my nerves skittering along the surface of my skin instead of staying inside where they belonged. What was wrong with me? Woodbridge was filled with hot guys but I never reacted like this. Not even around Ryan.

Lucas sauntered to the other side of the counter with Toby close at his heels.

"Toby!" Embarrassed, I snapped my fingers at my dog. "Get over here." Toby ignored me, watching Lucas with adoration.

Lucas laughed. "Looks like Toby's still in love with me."

"Apparently so." I returned Lucas's smile, forcing myself to maintain eye contact.

Get a grip Darcy. You're here to see your uncle. Your life is falling apart. This is no time for a hormonal meltdown.

"Water?" Lucas asked. "Coffee?" He grinned. "Just black coffee here; no hazelnut."

"Water please." I feigned interest in a stack of old magazines on the counter. Maybe if I didn't look at him, he'd go away.

A water bottle slid toward me on the counter, pushed by long fingers anchored to a perfectly sculpted arm.

Don't make eye contact. Don't do it. Where the heck was my uncle? I took a sip of water.

"Are you okay?" asked Lucas. "You look kind of stressed."

Water squirted out of my nose. I grabbed a napkin and wiped my face. Dad would be so proud. I took a deep breath and met Lucas's eyes again. He wasn't laughing at me. He wasn't laughing at all.

"I saw the Letterman show on YouTube," he said quietly. "With the Top Ten list."

Oh God.

I couldn't think of a thing to say, so I didn't say anything.

Lucas pulled a screwdriver out of his back pocket and started taking apart an old radio. I was grateful I didn't have to make eye contact anymore. Just watching his face as he concentrated on the radio was causing me plenty of internal havoc.

The weird "bwahahaa" noise sounded as the door to the store opened. Lucas glanced up and I swung around on my stool.

"Darcy." Uncle Charlie smiled at me like I was holding a lottery check. "I'm so glad you came back to see me." He glanced at Lucas. "Us."

I blushed. "Yeah, uh, s-sorry about last time," I stammered. "Leaving in a hurry."

"We're the ones who owe you an apology," Charlie said, shooting a cryptic look at Lucas. "We didn't mean to embarrass you."

Lucas looked up from the radio, meeting my eyes. "Definitely not," he said. "It sucks about your car." He held my gaze. "And everything else."

I swallowed and blinked nervously. Maybe I should have worn some of Sal's eye shadow, something sparkly to deflect all this intense eye contact.

"It's okay. I was the one who freaked out. I'm just kind of overwhelmed."

Charlie put a hand on my shoulder. If I closed my eyes I'd swear it was my dad. "Of course you are," Charlie said. "I've been thinking about your predicament, trying to think of some way I can help you and your mom."

Predicament. Ha. What a polite little word. I was calling it the Tri!Umphant! Shit Storm myself, but I wasn't going to tell Charlie that. Even though I felt surprisingly safe and comfortable with him, I didn't know him well enough for cussing. Yet.

"Yeah," I said. "That's kind of why I came by. I want to talk to you about my dad."

"Let's go for a walk," Charlie said. He hooked Lucas with a commanding gaze. "Hold down the fort, Captain Jack. And keep an eye on Toby for us while we walk."

Heat flooded my face. So I wasn't the only one who thought Lucas looked kind of like Johnny Depp? Only taller, and not at all scrawny, and with only one visible tattoo.

Charlie winked at me as we left the store. "That's Lucas's nickname. All the girls around here call him that."

My body betrayed me and I giggled like a middle-schooler.

Charlie laughed as we walked down the street. "Sounds

like you agree. That's part of the reason I hired him. My sales to girls have increased dramatically. That, and he's got magic hands that can fix anything."

I tried not to think of stalker girls flooding the thrift store waiting for some time with Lucas and his magic hands.

Charlie and I walked down Broadway. We passed a pawn shop and smoke shop before I worked up the courage to ask my question.

"So," I said. "About my dad. He's never done anything like this before. Just disappeared." I took a breath. "I wondered if he, you know, ever did something like this before? Maybe when he was younger?"

Charlie didn't respond right away. We walked by an antique shop and a weird store that sold only rubber ducks. It made me smile. If this place could make it, maybe some day I'd open a salt and pepper shaker store.

"No," Charlie said, answering my question. "He didn't. You don't have any idea where he is?"

I sighed. "He sends postcards. We never know where they'll be from."

"He's not answering his phone, is he? I've left him messages and texted him."

"No," I said. "Mom and I keep trying his phone, too. But he never calls back. He checks in with J.J., his partner, so we know he's okay." At least we hope he is, I thought.

"I can only imagine how scary this is for you, Darcy. But I want you to know your dad would never leave you and your mom forever. He'll come back." He let out a long, slow breath. "I don't know when. But he will."

I wanted to believe it. Hearing my uncle say it gave me

a tiny burst of hope.

We'd reached the end of the double block. Charlie turned around. "Let's head back. I want you to meet Liz."

We walked in companionable silence until Charlie stopped in front of a coffee shop. The sign on the brick wall overhead said "Tin Lizzy's" spelled out in metal script, with the dots over the "I's" shaped like coffee mugs. The barista behind the counter looked up as we entered, her face lighting when she saw Charlie. She was beautiful in the way only middle-aged hippie chicks can be, with long, thick brownish-gray hair, beautiful skin, and huge brown eyes. She was dressed like a granola, but on her it looked elegant. I had the crazy thought that I wanted to be just like her when I was forty years old.

"Charlie." Her voice was musical. "This must be Darcy." She turned her big doe eyes on me. Everything about her warmed me like some kind of cosmic hug.

"Darcy, this is Liz, owner of this marvelous caffeine emporium." Charlie and Liz shared a look so sizzling I realized they were more than just friendly business owners. Not a thought I wanted to dwell on.

"What can I make you?" Liz asked. She gave me a warning frown, though her eyes danced with laughter. "No foo-foo drinks, though."

So no strawberry frap. Got it.

"I'm not really thirsty right now. But thanks."

She gestured to the pastry case. "Hungry? It's on the house."

The croissants looked tempting, but then I thought of how sporadically I'd been running with Toby lately and shook my head.

Glancing around the store, I noticed a faded HELP WANTED sign in the window. *"Part-time barista needed: nights and weekends. Free drinks and food!"*

Liz needed a barista. I needed a job. Should I apply?

"Um, the barista job?" I said to Liz, trying to force the tremble out of my voice. "Is it still available?"

She and Charlie exchanged surprised looks.

She nodded. "Are you interested?"

I'd suck at customer service. I didn't know how to talk to strangers. I'd break the fancy espresso machine. Lucas would see what an idiot I was, when he came in for his high-maintenance coffee drink.

"Maybe," I said, answering her question. *Probably.*

Liz smiled. "You could apply right now." She gestured toward the gleaming copper espresso machine that looked like something from a steampunk movie. "Show me what you can do."

I swallowed. I made Mom a pot of coffee every morning, to chase away her hangovers, but that was the extent of my barista skills. "I should probably check with my mom first," I said. *Wimp.*

"I could use someone reliable," Liz said. "I've had to fire the past couple of people I've hired because they were so flaky."

Yikes. I'd never had a job before, because I hadn't needed the money. Listening to Liz, I realized this was a big deal. I thought of one of Dad's favorite lines: *never commit unless you mean it.*

"You can come by anytime to apply." She grinned. "I

practically live here. Just ask Charlie."

"I'll let you know," I said, and then turned to Charlie to say good-bye.

He pulled me into a hug. "Don't be a stranger, favorite niece." The hug intensified, reminding me of Dad. "I mean it," he whispered in my ear.

"Okay," I whispered back.

I left Liz and Charlie together in the coffee shop, since I was ready to get Toby and head home. What was it about this neighborhood? It was so unlike my part of town, but I wasn't scared. I felt…comfortable. Was it because it was so different? Because it was easier to hide here? It was highly unlikely I'd run into anyone from Woodbridge.

Maybe hiding out was a good idea. Dad obviously thought so. But I wouldn't hide 24/7 like him. If I got a job with Liz I'd just hide out here a few nights a week and some weekends. Plus I'd make money.

"So what do you think of Tin Lizzy's?" Lucas's low voice stopped me in my tracks. I was so lost in thought I hadn't noticed him standing on the sidewalk, a cigarette dangling from his fingers. Toby lunged for me, and I took the leash from Lucas, careful to avoid skin contact.

"It's great," I sighed. I thought again about working there, and pictured myself standing behind the counter, waiting on customers.

Lucas nodded. "Yeah, it's a cool place. And Liz is awesome." He exhaled smoke from his perfectly straight nose.

I crinkled my own nose as the cigarette smoke reached me.

He stubbed out his cigarette quickly and tossed it into a trash can. "I need to get back to work," he said. "Broken toasters are calling."

I stole one more glance at him, hoping not to forget any details. "Maybe I'll see you around," I said.

He nodded. "I hope so." He pushed through the door of the Second Hand Story, pausing briefly to glance over his shoulder. His lips quirked in a mysterious smile that made me half want to run away, and half want to chase him like a pathetic fan girl.

Instead I walked as quickly as I could to my truck, still trying to preserve a little dignity by not breaking into a full-on sprint.

Spending time on Broadway made me feel like the universe had cracked open a new door for me. I could see a tiny bit of light on the other side.

Did I dare open the door all the way?

CHAPTER NINE
OCTOBER 2

As I sat in study hall, my last period of the day, Mom's text intruded on my black thoughts. *"I have a great idea. R u there?"*

"No," I typed. *"I've been abducted by aliens. They have Dad, too."*

She ignored my black humor. *"Meet me after school. Bring your camera."*

Mom hadn't exactly been full of great ideas lately. I dreaded hearing the next one.

"???" I texted back.

She sent me an address. Sigh. Was she still thinking about me taking pictures of houses for a real estate website?

"C u later," I replied.

Mom texted back a row of smiley faces. Lately we did

better communicating via texts and notepads than in person, because when we were together in the evenings, she turned into someone else when she drank.

After school I waited until the parking lot was almost empty before I revved up the beast. It was my latest strategy to avoid stares and mocking laughter, especially since Sal had slapped on a "Save a horse, ride a cowboy" bumper sticker.

"It's true," she'd said when I busted her. "You need a cowboy, or any boy toy. Something to take your mind off all the stress."

"Not exactly my first priority," I'd replied, trying to block out the image of Lucas's face that popped to mind.

I found the house and parked my rusty truck behind a row of shiny, perfect cars: Mom's Volvo, Fake-Bake Pam's Mercedes, and a couple of BMWs. The place was immense, even bigger than our house, and that was saying something. Mom must have been watching for me or maybe the belching Reaper announced my arrival. She flung open the massive front door before I could ring the doorbell.

"Darcy, come in. You have your camera, right?"

I nodded and stepped into the enormous entrance hall. Suits of armor? Flags with coats of arms? Seriously? How pretentious could you get?

Laughter bounced off the stone floor, as did the clicking of high heels. Fake-Bake Pam and some other lady walked toward us with bright red lipstick smiles stretching their face-lifted cheeks.

Mom put an arm around me. "Darcy, this is Pam Hendricks. You know her daughter Chloe."

Fake-Bake Pam narrowed her eyes and gave me one of those wimpy girl handshakes that felt like a dead fish. I hated that. My dad always taught me that a woman's handshake should be as firm as a man's. Liz had a strong handshake, warm but firm. I gave Pam's hand an extra squeeze as I thought of the hell Chloe had put me through at school.

"Darcy," she said, wincing at my grip. "It's so cute of your mom to give you this little job."

Job? What job? I glanced at Mom, whose expression silently begged me to act like I knew what was going on.

Pam turned to the woman next to her, who apparently went to the same tanning salon she did. "Darcy, this is Dee Armstrong," said Pam. "She's an interior designer helping me get the house ready to be listed. You probably know her son Ryan from school."

My heart thudded straight down to my feet. I nodded and stuck my hand out to shake hers. Manners could over-ride shock, evidently. Good to know.

"Lovely, darling, lovely to meet you."

At least her hand didn't feel like a dead fish.

"So," Mom said, "Darcy and I will get started on the photos and get out of your way."

I frowned at her. Get out of their way? We weren't taking up any more space than the freaking suits of armor.

Mom tightened her arm around my shoulder and steered me out of King Arthur's court.

"What the—" I began, but she put a finger to her lips. We walked silently down a hallway and emerged into an enormous kitchen. I looked around, my mouth open in shock.

"Three stoves? Two refrigerators? Two dishwashers? For real?"

Mom crinkled her nose and shrugged. "They like to entertain."

"For the army?"

Mom laughed. "Maybe for a few generals. Not the whole army."

I crossed my arms. "So tell me about this job I'm supposed to know about."

Mom took a breath. "Well, I was thinking… Remember when we talked at the cabin? You taking photos for the real estate website?"

I'd hoped she'd forgotten.

"It's a perfect match. You can earn some extra cash. Spend a little time with me. Pam will pay you five dollars per photo."

I stared. Five bucks a photo? I could do better than that setting up my own photo booth at a preschool. But it wasn't the money so much as the neon "charity case" sign that seemed to be blinking over our heads.

"She doesn't need me to take photos, Mom. I'm sure she already has someone to do that, someone who specializes in that type of photography. I'm not some junior realtor wannabe."

Mom bit her lip and turned to look out the fifteen-foot windows. She was quiet for a long time. I stared at the black and white tiled floor. God, I could be such a bitch.

Her eyes were glassy when she looked at me again. "Damn it, Darcy. I'm doing the best I can. You can't blame me for Dad leaving." Her words stung like a spray of shattered glass.

I yanked my camera from the bag slung across my shoulder. "Where should I start?"

"Start here. I'm going to find Pam and Dee. After you finish the kitchen, we need photos of the entry hall, the great room, and wine cellar. Just poke around. You'll find them."

She was gone before I could form an apology. I supposed if I couldn't say I was sorry, at least I could take the photos. I looked around the room and started snapping. Zoomed in on one of the stoves. Panned out wide to show all three. Knelt down to shoot the window from my knees. The sun shone in like a sign from God.

After the kitchen was photographed more times than a movie star, I went in search of the great room. I tiptoed through the butler's pantry, stopping when I heard voices.

"Isn't she pathetic?" I recognized Pam's voice.

"Oh, I don't know, Pam. That's a bit harsh." That was Dee, mom of Ryan.

"She's not half bad as a potential realtor," Pam said. "But there is no way she'll be able to earn enough to stay in their house. Or deal with all the debt. I heard from a *very* reliable source that Ty's company is in real trouble." She laughed. "And that odd little daughter. She could be halfway attractive if she put some effort into it, though she definitely didn't get her parents' looks, poor thing. But she just slinks around, not even making eye contact with anyone."

"Ryan told me about the day her car got repossessed," Dee said. "Poor girl. From the school parking lot, can you imagine? I feel sorry for them. They've had their world turned upside down, Pam."

I hardly dared to breathe. Sweat freckled my arms and neck. God, Pam was a bitch. Just like her daughter.

Pam's voice echoed off the stone walls. "Ty must have already paid this year's tuition or else I'm sure Marilyn would have had to put Darcy in public school. I don't know how long she can keep up this charade." Pam pronounced the word: "<u>sha rahd</u>" like a Brit. I wanted to kick her in the teeth.

"Well, thank goodness for Darcy that she doesn't have to switch schools right now, with everything else going on," Dee said.

"True," Pam said. "I'm sure it's a comfort to have friends like my Chloe."

My hands shook. I gripped the camera as if it could transport me to another world. I couldn't listen anymore. I shoved the camera into my bag and texted Mom, my hands trembling. *"Gotta go. C u @ home."* I retraced my steps back to the stupid King Arthur entry hall and slipped out the front door.

My truck had never looked so good. I jumped in and threw it into reverse, squashing a row of innocent fall mums as I backed down the driveway.

Before I knew it, I was on the highway headed for the cabin. Eventually the truck bounced down the rutted road that led to Camp Covington. As I turned off the engine, I noticed the FOR SALE sign tied to the deck railing. Wow. Mom worked fast. I squeezed my eyes shut, resting my head against the steering wheel. Inhale. Exhale.

My phone pinged with a text. *"R u ok? Where r u?"* Mom. I sighed. I'd ignored my phone the entire drive but that hadn't stopped her from blowing up my phone with texts and voicemails.

I jumped out of the truck and headed down the trail to our Stonehenge. The aspen trees were a symphony of yellow and orange leaves shimmering in the fall breeze, surrounding our small henge. I stood at the edge of the circle for a long time, just breathing. I took a picture of the henge with my cell.

Then I reared back and kicked the tallest stone. It was like knocking over the first domino in a long chain. It only took a few seconds for our henge to collapse in on itself. As I stared at the destroyed henge, it was my turn to collapse, sinking next to the fallen stones, sobs overtaking my body.

*I*t was dark when I arrived at Tin Lizzy's because I'd sat crying in front of the destroyed henge for a long time. Eventually I'd stumbled down the trail to my truck and texted Mom to tell her I was okay, but I'd be home late.

I parked the truck across the street and slid out of the cab to the sidewalk, where the cozy glow from the coffee shop drew me inside.

Jazz music hummed under the gurgle of the espresso machine. Charlie and Liz both played KJAZ, the local public jazz station, in their stores. The place had been empty during my afternoon visit, but now three girls about my age huddled around a board game, laughing and hugging coffee mugs to their chests. An older couple sat on a sagging couch next to a bookshelf, reading quietly and sharing a single mug of something hot and spicy-smelling. A circle of women sat around a table covered with baskets of yarn, knitting needles clacking. It was nothing like the frenetic Starbucks attached to Barnes & Noble.

I loved it.

A flutter rose in my stomach. Was I crazy to be here? Could I possibly work here and not totally mess it up? I could never work for Fake-Bake Pam, because it hurt too much knowing what she thought of my mom, and me. And working close to my uncle, in Liz's cozy shop, was a job I wanted, not one being forced on me.

I heard Liz's tinkling laugh before she emerged through a curtained area behind the barista counter with a cell phone pressed to her ear. She scanned the store quickly and her eyes lit up when she saw me. She murmured a quick good-bye into her phone.

"Darcy! I'm so happy to see you." A few of the customers glanced our way, and then turned back to their activities. "Did you come back for that croissant?"

The open warmth of her smile felt like a hug. I took a deep breath and approached the counter. "Actually, I decided to apply for the job."

She nodded as she dried a coffee cup with a dish towel. "I've had a couple of people apply," she said, "but I'm still taking applications."

I had competition? Uh-oh.

She tilted her head and examined me thoroughly. I blushed under her appraising gaze. "Let's talk. But first you need something to warm you up. What's your favorite drink? And remember, none of those foo-foo Starbucks concoctions." She grinned.

"Uh...okay." I hesitated. "Tea," I said weakly. "Something with cinnamon, if you have it."

"Of course I have cinnamon tea." She handed me an enormous mug of steaming water and gestured to three brass racks overflowing with tea boxes. "Take your pick. Sugar and cream are on the counter against the far wall."

I stirred sugar into my tea and then followed Liz behind the barista bar, then through shimmering gold curtains to a hidden part of her shop. "Come sit down," she commanded.

Instead, I stopped with a gasp on the threshold. We had entered Fairyland.

Strings of firefly lights lit the tiny room. Two deep chairs nestled in a corner, a small table between them, overflowing with books and magazines. The scent of incense and the sound of jazz came from somewhere. The walls, painted deep lavender, were covered with vintage French ads and 1980s celebrity posters. The juxtaposition made me smile.

"It's perfect," I whispered.

"Thank you," Liz said. She sat in one of the cozy chairs and gestured for me to take the other. I did, and glimpsed a small closed-circuit monitor mounted unobtrusively in a corner, showing the café and its patrons.

Liz followed my gaze. "Lucas hooked it up for me. Every time a customer walks in the door, there's a bright blue glow on the screen, then it goes back to normal. I prefer that to that horrible Halloween noise when you open Charlie's door."

I laughed. "I can see why. This is great. If I were you, I'd never want to leave."

"Most days I feel the same way," Liz agreed. "It's taken me a long way to get the life I wanted. But I finally made it." She sipped from her pink cat mug and locked eyes with me. "Your dad might even say I reaped my harvest."

I flinched. I'd managed to forget about Dad since I'd arrived here. Liz bringing him up felt wrong.

She didn't miss my reaction. "Your dad's ideas have helped many people, Darcy. I can't speak to what he's doing right now, but there was a dark time in my life when his words were a guiding light. I wouldn't have this shop if it weren't for him."

I stared at her, shocked.

"Oh, I never met him personally. Your uncle Charlie gave me a set of his CDs several years ago. At first I thought Charlie was trying to get me to join a cult." She laughed and tossed her long braid over her shoulder. "But because I was falling madly in love with Charlie, I agreed to listen to a CD before I'd pass judgment."

Charlie gave Liz the Harvest CDs? Did Charlie believe my dad's stuff, too? I thought of all the times I'd heard Dad rag on Charlie's lifestyle, of how I grew up not knowing my uncle at all. My internal stress ball threatened to explode.

I squeezed my eyes shut. Damn it, I didn't want to feel angry again. Coming to Liz's was like finding an oasis in the desert. I didn't want it muddled up with my dad, and I didn't want even more reasons to be mad at him. I took a deep breath.

Liz squeezed my knee and I opened my eyes. "Let's not talk about that," she said. "We have more important things to discuss, like if you want to do a trial run tonight. We need to see if you can handle my Italian baby out there. Bella is temperamental, beautiful, and a real handful. But she makes the most amazing espressos in town."

All thoughts of my father fled. A temperamental Italian espresso machine that had probably cost Liz thousands of dollars? "Um...maybe I could just be the tea maker?"

Liz threw back her head and laughed a deep, throaty laugh that came right from her gut. "Oh honey. If you're the only person working here, what do we tell our coffee customers? No. You'll learn how to rule Bella. She's difficult but not impossible." She grinned. "Kinda like me."

I took a deep breath and stared at the giraffe painted on my mug. My dad's words floated to mind, unbidden. *"Try one new thing. Plant one new seed."*

"I have to warn you, I'm not mechanically inclined. I can barely make toast." So much for selling myself.

Liz laughed again and set down her teacup. "Neither was I. When I decided I wanted my own coffee shop, my biggest worry was how the heck to make a cappuccino."

"Really?"

Her glittering eyes held mine. "Really. I spent weeks visiting coffee shops all over town. I'd order something and sit down and lurk. I watched those baristas work their magic. And I realized something."

"What?"

"That anyone could do it. Kids younger than you, folks old enough to retire. I watched people who turned out perfect drinks one after the other while barely looking at the machine and serious artists who never took their eyes off the gauges." Liz reached behind her chair and pulled out a tin of butter cookies. She pried off the lid and held it out to me. "These are my weakness. Especially with tea. Take one."

I dipped the cookie into my tea while she watched approvingly.

"It's like dancing," she said. "Once you know the steps, you bring your own style to it. And the most important thing I learned?"

I waited, paying more attention to her than my cookie. My dad was going to have to pay for my liposuction when he got home.

"Each cup got easier. Each time I messed up a latte, I was that much closer to making a perfect one. You only become an expert at something by failing millions of times along the way. I wanted to master Bella the beast, so I did." She paused to chew her cookie. "What have you mastered?" she asked suddenly.

"Me?" The question startled me. "Nothing."

"Nothing? There's nothing you do well, maybe something you do every day so you don't even think about it?"

I thought for a few moments. Did running count? "I do run. A lot."

"There you go. And I bet you didn't start out running five miles at a stretch, did you?"

No, I definitely hadn't. I'd started by just running with Toby as a puppy, the two of us romping in the park, then trotting along the canal trail haphazardly. But somewhere along the way, it turned into something I was really good at. I made goals and met them every week, every month. I entered local 5k and 10k races that Dad never knew about, so he wasn't waiting at the finish line expecting me to win.

But I charted my progress and bettered my time each time I competed. Only I did it for me. Not for my school. Not for my dad. Just for me.

"Maybe I can do this," I said, more to myself than to Liz.

"Of course you can. Especially with our secret weapon." Her smile deepened.

"Secret weapon?"

"Lucas. He figured that baby out in five minutes. Every time she acts up or throws a tantrum, he's the one who fixes her. We have a deal—free drinks as long as I can keep him on speed dial for emergency repairs."

Magic Hands on speed dial? Oh God. How would I ever concentrate enough to learn to make an espresso?

As if on cue, the tiny TV screen glowed blue, then faded back to black and white, showing Lucas headed for the counter. The girls around the board game stopped chattering and watched him, elbowing each other and giggling.

"Hi, Lucas," one of them sing-songed, her voice tinny through the small TV's speaker.

He turned and shot them his sexy grin. "Hey," he said. "Who's winning?"

There was snorting and laughing and something that sounded like, "Whoever you want to."

Liz pushed herself out of the deep chair, shaking her head. "That poor boy. Girls follow him like rats and the Pied Piper."

At the curtain, she glanced back and shot me a devilish look. "Come out after you catch your breath. I know he tends to take it away."

She left me staring openmouthed. Maybe I should just

hide out until Lucas went back to Charlie's store. Or maybe I should just sneak out the back door to the alley and make my escape. If Liz had other applicants for this job, did I even stand a chance?

God, I wanted this job. But I was terrified I'd screw it up, if I were lucky enough to get it.

The TV screen flickered blue again. A frazzled-looking mom had come in with a bouncing child begging for a brownie.

Lucas had disappeared from the screen. Whew. He must have gone back to Charlie's store. I leaned back in my chair and closed my eyes.

"You can do it," I whispered. "Even McDonald's sells espresso now."

"Hey, Darcy," said a familiar, sexy voice.

I jumped, sloshing tea out of my cup and onto my shirt. My face flushed.

"Sorry. I didn't mean to scare you." Lucas pushed the curtains aside and walked toward me, a steaming to-go cup in his hand. "Do you need a towel?" He glanced at my chest. My wet chest.

"No, no. It's fine." I grabbed a napkin and dabbed uselessly at my shirt. At least it was a small stain so I didn't look like I was competing in a wet T-shirt contest, but that didn't stop me from wanting to disappear.

He sank into Liz's chair and grinned. "Were you talking to yourself?"

I leaned back in the chair. If I hoped to get a job where I'd be seeing this guy all the time, I'd better practice my coping skills. "No, I was talking to my friend about applying to work here." I tilted my head toward a David Bowie poster on the far wall. "He comes with me everywhere. But most people can't hear him." I lowered my voice. "Can you?"

Lucas burst into laughter. "I've met the other job applicants," he said. "They didn't talk to imaginary friends."

I returned his arch smile. "Then maybe I have an advantage."

Lucas's smile widened to a grin. "You might. Then again, it might depend on Bowie's conversational skills. That's an important part of the job."

I looked at the floor. I might be able to joke around in Fairyland, but Lucas was right. Conversation was an important part of the job. And strangers made me sweat.

"Are you worried about that?" Lucas asked. "The talking to customers part?"

"Yeah." I peeked at him from under my lashes, which weren't half as long as his. "That and the monstrous Bella. I don't think I can handle her." I glanced at the TV screen, where Liz stood at the espresso machine, working like a maestro.

He grinned and stretched out his long legs. "You can handle Bella. Liz and I can teach you. It's pretty cool to be able to make yourself any kind of coffee drink, instead of having to pay five bucks a pop."

"But I'm a total klutz."

He took a drink from his cup. "You should've seen Liz when she first got that machine. She was in here every day swearing at it. She'd get so mad, she'd tell Charlie she was going to close the store and give up. But we found some videos on YouTube that helped. And she called the guy who sold her the machine. She paid him to spend a day with her, making the same drinks over and over. Now she's a pro."

Ugh. She hadn't made it sound so grueling. "What about you?" I asked him. "How long did it take you to tame Bella?"

He dipped his head. "Not as long as Liz."

"Uh-huh. You figured it out right away, didn't you?" I accused, narrowing my eyes.

He shrugged and took another long drink, but when he lowered his cup his lips twitched like he was biting back a smile.

"I'm not sure what to do." I glanced at the TV screen again. Liz was talking and laughing with the reading couple. The girls had resumed their board game.

Lucas frowned. "If you do take the job, Liz isn't going to let you fail. She'll be here to help you and train you. And I'm usually around, too, if the machine explodes or something." He brushed back his hair and grinned.

I stared into my mug. Liz's shop was like nothing else in my life. Peaceful. Mellow. Fun. When I was here I forgot about all the other crap. Plus my uncle worked just a few doors down and I really wanted to get to know him better.

And Magic Hands would be on speed-dial.

"You're probably right." I took a deep breath and stood up. "Time for my trial run."

Lucas stood up, too. "I need to go. I've got a lot of homework."

"Where do you go to school?" I asked. He seemed older than the guys at Woodbridge.

"CU Denver. Engineering school."

Holy hotness, a college boy. Sal would totally freak. "Oh," I managed to say. "That's cool."

"It's my first year there. Last year I went to a community college because it was cheaper, but this year I transferred to CU." He shrugged. "It's intense but I'm doing okay."

I nodded wordlessly.

"Knock 'em dead, Darcy." He shot me another killer smile. "I'll see you around." He flipped me a peace sign, then disappeared through the curtains.

I didn't know what it was about him. Nobody had ever affected me with such intensity. If hotness was an app, Lucas would be a bestseller.

*B*ella was a beast. A shiny, noisy, scary beast. She belched steam and spewed burning liquid. She terrified me.

"Baby steps," Liz said. "Let's start with an espresso." She ground coffee beans and filled the filter cup, grinding and pushing with a metal tamper until the grounds were tightly packed.

"Here." She handed me a long black handle attached to the silver filter cup. "Slide and lock it into place."

I slid. I tried to lock it into place, but instead I dropped it, and fine grounds of espresso flew everywhere. "Crap. I'm sorry." I bit my lip. Inhale calm. Exhale stress.

Liz grinned. "You should've seen the mess I made my first day battling Miss Bella. Let's do it again."

And so we did. Grind, tamp, slide, lock. Steam, release, magic! Hot steaming espresso filled the tiny china cup under the spout.

"You did it!" Liz high-fived me and laughed. "One

down, a million to go."

We spent a long time together behind the counter. I watched her like a hawk, trying to memorize all the steps needed to make a latte, an Americano, a cappuccino.

I served tea and pastries and worked the register. I met some of the regulars, whose faces lit up when they discovered I was Charlie's niece. I tried to make up for my Bella incompetence by cleaning every cup and utensil the second it hit the sink. I bussed and cleaned tables before Liz even noticed they were dirty. I played *Candyland* with two little girls while their mom talked to Liz. I refilled the tea racks every fifteen minutes until Liz told me to take a chill pill.

I was the embodiment of Thoughtful! Responsible! Initiative! It was the best time I'd had in forever.

At ten o'clock, after everyone had packed up their knitting and laptops and said good night, Liz locked the door. She sank onto one of the couches and sighed. "Busy night." She yawned.

I stacked up board games and put them on a shelf.

"Sit down, Darcy."

I sat across from her and smiled tentatively, wondering how I'd compared to the other applicants. I looked around the shop, imagining working here regularly, daring to hope I would be.

"I know it'll take me a little more time to learn Bella," I said. Understatement of the century. "But I promise I'll work very hard. I'll do anything. Even clean the bathroom." I'd learned how to wield a toilet bowl brush, since we no longer had a housekeeping service.

Liz looked at me intently, not smiling. Her voice was quiet when she spoke. "There have been three total applicants—a guy who cranked death metal and scared away my customers, a girl with a permanent sneer and an inability to make change to save her life, and you."

Her face blossomed into one of her cosmic smiles. "No contest, Darcy. The job is yours. Can you start this week?"

"No way. I mean, yes! Of course!" I wanted to hug her but didn't want to freak her out.

"Good. Call me tomorrow after school and we can figure out this week's schedule." She rose from the couch. "Thank God you were the best applicant."

"Why?"

"Because it would've broken Charlie's heart if I didn't hire you. But this was a business decision." She smiled down at me. "You showed an excellent work ethic and you treated my customers with kindness, even the kids. I'd be stupid not to hire you."

"Thank you, Liz. I promise I won't let you down." I stood up and put out a hand to shake.

She ignored my outstretched hand and pulled me into a hug. "I know you won't. Now let's get out of here and tell your uncle the good news."

CHAPTER TEN
OCTOBER 3

The next day I barely focused on school. Mom had been passed out on the couch when I'd gotten home from the coffee shop the night before, killing my glow from Tin Lizzy's. I wanted to talk to her about my new job. About ditching her at the photo shoot. About Dad's latest postcard that had arrived yesterday. But how could I if she wasn't awake in the mornings and was hardly ever sober at night?

She wasn't home when I got home from school. After calling Liz to figure out my work schedule, I took Toby for a long run, listening on my phone to one of Dad's classic spiels on how to survive tough times. "The human spirit is indomitable," he said. "Just like gardens that lie dormant all winter and resurrect every spring. So do we, even when we're sure we can't."

His latest postcard wasn't so indomitable. The front of the plain black card said, *"This is a postcard from someone on the road."* How lame. On the back he'd scrawled, *"I'm still looking. Not sure when I'll find it. But I love you. –Dad."*

What was I supposed to do with that?

My stomach rumbled as Toby and I neared home. I hadn't eaten lunch at school because I'd forgotten my sandwich, and I didn't want to spend any cash. I thought of Mom spending her day with the evil Pam, and guilt washed over me as I remembered how I'd ditched the photo shoot and destroyed our henge.

Instead of microwaving junk tonight, I'd make her dinner, to apologize for everything.

But I had no idea what to cook. I'd never made anything besides cereal, Pop Tarts, and sandwiches. Maybe I could find something easy from one of her cookbooks.

I flopped onto the couch with a stack of cookbooks. Toby jumped up next to me, nosing the books. How did that crazy dog know I was reading about food?

French Cuisine for Special Occasions. Indonesian Delicacies for the Adventurous Cook. Whatever happened to *Cooking for Dummies*? I pulled out my phone and searched "cooking for idiots." Aha. Cookingfortheclueless. com.

Step one: what ingredients are on hand?

Hmm. I moved Toby from my lap, went to the pantry, and stared at the nearly empty shelves. Noodles. A jar of salsa. A can of tuna. A half-empty box of generic cereal. Two bottles of unopened dill pickles. A can of evaporated milk.

"Not even Mom could turn this junk into a meal," I told

Toby.

I looked at the website again. "Tasty meals on a tight budget." That was more like it. I clicked the link and scrolled through the choices. Tuna noodle casserole. Hmm. I pictured the pantry shelves. We had noodles. And tuna. What else did I need? Frozen peas, cream of mushroom soup. Sour cream. I had twenty bucks in my wallet.

When Mom got home three hours later, she almost fainted when she saw the casserole dish on the counter.

"Darcy? Is this… Did you cook dinner?"

I grinned. "Yes ma'am. It ain't fancy, but it's not too bad."

She gaped at me, then regained her composure. "Don't say— "

"Ain't. I know." I grabbed a plate from the cupboard and spooned a heap of tuna and noodles on it, then zapped it in the microwave.

"So." I crossed my arms over my chest and tried to give her the same assessing look she'd given me every day after school. "How's life? Aside from your photographer bailing on you?"

She laughed, then dropped her keys on the counter and walked over to give me a hug.

"My day sucked. But it just got a lot better." She held me tight.

"Mom, please. Only vulgar girls say 'sucked.'"

She stepped back from me and shook her head. "You

never cease to amaze me."

I rolled my eyes. "Come on, Mom. It's just tuna casserole, not the Nobel Prize." I opened the freezer and grabbed the pint of Ben & Jerry's I'd splurged on.

"How was your day?" she asked. "The truth, please."

I shrugged. "Like yours. It sucked." I pulled the lid off the ice cream and grinned at her. "But it's better now."

We sat together on the couch watching some show about hot aliens with supernatural powers. One of them kind of reminded me of Lucas.

"So," I said. "I have news. I have a job."

She almost choked on her food. "You're kidding. Where?"

I told her about Charlie and Liz, about how I'd made a mess with Bella but somehow gotten the job anyway. I didn't mention Lucas. I was keeping him all to myself.

"That's wonderful, sweetheart. I'm so proud of you."

Her pride made it that much harder to tell her the next thing. I swallowed over the lump that rose in my throat.

"After I left Pam's, I went to the cabin. And I..." I blinked my eyes against the tears. "I knocked down Dad's Stonehenge."

Mom didn't say anything for a long time, then she heaved a long sigh. "So you saw the 'for sale' sign?"

I nodded, still fighting back tears, and full of remorse.

"I was going to tell you. Eventually. But I knew you'd be upset." She gave me a sad smile. "Guess I was right about that."

"Honestly I'm not sure why I did it. I think it was everything. Hearing Pam—" I stopped. I wasn't going to tell Mom about Pam's insults. "Just being around her," I said. Inhale.

Exhale. "Just everything," I whispered.

Mom nodded and slowly chewed another bite of casserole.

"I'll go back and fix it."

She swallowed her food and shook her head. "Don't bother. I'm sure whoever buys it will get rid of the stones."

My throat burned and tears spilled down my cheeks as the reality of our losses overwhelmed me again. It wasn't just the stuff, like my car or the cabin. That sucked, but what I missed more than anything was my dad. I missed his strength, his booming laugh, his constant insistence that I could do more, be more. I even missed his platitudes and clichés.

Mom set aside her plate and reached over to hug me. "It's not always going to be this hard, honey."

I wanted to believe her. More than anything, I wanted to believe her.

But I didn't.

Chapter Eleven

The universe hit the pause button, granting me a blissful couple of weeks. There were no weird postcards from Dad, just texts from J.J. telling us Dad was okay but still on the road. I only found a few empty wine bottles in the recycling bin. Even the harassment at school had eased off, but I knew that would only last until Dad was in the news again. Girls like Chloe didn't just turn over a new leaf overnight.

Every day after school I headed straight for Broadway, even on the days I wasn't scheduled to work. The shops became my sanctuary. When I was there, I could breathe without reminding myself to exhale. On my days off, I hung out in Charlie's shop. I sorted through clothes and organized books. Lucas kidded me that I was trying to steal his job, but I told him I had no interest or ability in repairing broken appliances. Plus, as I reminded him, it wasn't really a job when I was working for free.

As I got more comfortable, I was able to joke around with Charlie and Lucas. Every time I made them laugh I felt like I'd earned the right to hang out a little longer. I could even make eye contact with Lucas without breaking a sweat. Laughing with him felt natural and easy. He'd nicknamed me Shaker Girl, since I was so obsessed with Charlie's collection. I contemplated getting the words tattooed on my thigh every time I passed the Inkheart tattoo parlor.

Charlie and I talked about everything. He told me stories about my dad from when they were kids. According to Charlie, my dad didn't always have a stick up his ass. He'd actually been fun sometimes.

"From the moment you were born, you became the most important thing in Ty's life," Charlie said one day while I sorted through a box of books.

I set aside a few regency romances to borrow later. Maybe it was because Mom had named me after a character in a Jane Austen novel, but I loved to immerse myself in a world full of gentleman callers with impeccable manners and dry wit. Guys who said all the right things and made a girl feel treasured.

I ran my hands over the worn cover of a paperback featuring a perfect couple dancing in a ballroom. Nobody was dropping by my house leaving calling cards or inviting me on carriage rides. Or texting to ask me to a movie. I couldn't even get my dad to return my calls. I sure didn't feel like the most important thing in his life.

"It's true," Charlie insisted, reading my doubtful expression. "I know Ty can be intense. But that doesn't mean he doesn't love you."

Of course he loved me. I just didn't know how much he liked me. I wasn't his dream daughter, I knew that. I'd rather curl up and read than prance around on the stage telling people to "plant their dream crop."

"I don't think I have any of his DNA," I said with a sigh. "At all."

"I disagree," said Charlie. "You're a natural with customers. Liz can't believe her good luck."

I flushed with pride. But still, making somebody coffee wasn't exactly comparable to standing on a stage inspiring thousands of people.

Charlie watched me closely, then tossed a dust rag at me and grinned. "Get busy, Shaker Girl."

*O*ne afternoon, Lucas and I were in the middle of a fake karate fight over a Pokémon T-shirt we both wanted when the Halloween cackle announced Aphrodite herself. Lucas froze mid-action move. I snatched the T-shirt away from him, declaring victory by forfeiture, but Lucas was in a daze.

"Hi, Lucas," said the girl. From the way she looked at him, and the way he suddenly forgot I was there, I realized she must be his girlfriend. How could he *not* have a supermodel for a girlfriend?

"Uh, um," he stammered. "Darcy, this is Heather. Heather, Darcy."

"Hi," I said, forcing a smile. I felt like a ragged shepherd in the Nativity play, standing next to a glowing angel.

She glanced at me, barely making eye contact. "Hi." Then she returned her focus to Lucas. They'd both forgotten I was there.

I headed to the back storeroom to calm my nerves and dig through boxes, looking for salt and pepper shakers, my comfort kitsch. The last thing I needed was to watch Lucas drooling over some gorgeous girl. I'd told Sal that Lucas and I were friends, nothing more, and I told myself that, too. Constantly.

As I dug through boxes of donations, getting newspaper ink all over my hands, Lucas poked his head in the storeroom. "I've gotta go," he said, sounding anxious. "Charlie should be back anytime. You got it under control until then?" He glanced toward the door and I knew he was dying to chase after the angel.

"Sure." I forced a smile. "Have fun."

He gave me an odd look, then grabbed his backpack and left without saying anything else.

I wondered what it would be like to have him chase me down like that. "Give it up, Shaker Girl," I whispered. I opened another box and my mood lifted when I spotted the Scooby-Doo and Shaggy salt and pepper shaker set. I might not get the guy I wanted, but there was always Scooby-Doo.

*L*iz told me I was free to read or do homework during slow times at her place, so one day I brought my backpack full of wire, beads, and my jewelry-making tools. I wanted to make something for her as a thank-you for hiring me. It was a quiet afternoon with only two tea drinkers sitting on a loveseat together. I set up my supplies on the rickety table that none of the customers liked. I'd just crimped on my first bead when a dark little head popped up at the table.

"Whatcha doin'?" An adorable little girl stared at me with enormous eyes that looked vaguely familiar.

"Where'd you come from?" I asked, wondering how I'd missed her.

"From outside." She parked her tiny body on the chair next to me. A small chubby hand reached tentatively toward my pile of beads.

"Can I touch one? Please?" She looked like her heart would break if I said no.

"Sure." I smiled and slid a few beads toward her. "Do you want to make some jewelry with me?"

Her eyes got even bigger and she nodded.

"What's your name?" I glanced around for her parental unit, not seeing anyone. Maybe her mom was in the restroom.

"I'm Pickles."

I cracked up. "Pickles? Really?"

She shrugged. "It's my good name. I don't like the udder one."

"It is a good nickname," I agreed.

"My name's not Nick!" she exclaimed with a huge grin. "It's Pickles!"

This kid was a born comedian. My dad should add her to his act. I tied a knot at the end of a piece of silver cord and handed it to her.

"I'm Darcy. Just Darcy. You know how to string beads, right, Pickles?"

She nodded again, watching me closely. "Why are you making an ouchy necklace?"

Frowning, I paused. "Ouchy?"

"It's all pokey." She pointed to the copper wire in my hands.

"The wire? It really doesn't hurt. I get rid of the ouchy parts before I wear it." There was no point explaining soldering to her since she was only three or four years old.

"My brudder uses the same tools," she said, pointing toward my pliers.

I laughed. "Does he make jewelry, too?"

"No, silly! He fixes stuff."

"Uh-huh," I agreed, more focused on the necklace pattern spread out on the table.

"I make my brudder a necklace," Pickles said happily, swinging her legs under the table. I hoped she had a brother who was cool enough to wear a necklace she made. We worked together in companionable silence, Pickles occasionally sneaking another bead from my pile as I pretended not to notice. I glanced around, wondering who she belonged to.

"Pickles? Is your mom or dad—"

"Uh-oh," whispered Pickles, interrupting me. She slid off the chair and hid under the table.

I peeked under the table. "Pickles? What's wrong?" She shook her head and put a finger to her lips to shush me. She pointed to the door. Lucas stood on the sidewalk, laughing with Homeless Harry. Harry had introduced himself that way when he stopped in for a free coffee from Liz.

"No sense sugarcoatin' the facts, darlin'. I am Harry and I am homeless," he'd told me.

"Gotta go," I whispered to Pickles. "Customer on deck."

"He's not a cussomer," Pickles whispered. "He's my brudder."

That explained the familiar eyes. And the gorgeous dark hair.

"I'm not here!" Pickles whispered vehemently, shaking her head.

I walked to the counter, trying to act casual. I didn't know why Pickles was hiding from Lucas, but there was a girl code to uphold. If a sister wanted to hide, I had to help her out.

As Lucas approached, I tried not to notice how good he made a plain T-shirt and jeans look. Yeah, we were becoming good friends, but my heart still sped up around him. But all I had to do was picture Heather to quash my palpitations.

"Hey, Lucas. What'll it be? Chocolate milk?"

He shot me his sexiest grin. "Triple-shot cappuccino. Extra dry. But I don't think you've achieved level three on the Bella skills barometer, Shaker Girl," he teased. "I'd better make it myself."

"Those are fighting words, Martinez. Come on, give me a chance."

He raised an eyebrow. "Somebody's feisty today. All right. Show me what ya got."

Ha. If he only knew what I'd like to show—

A loud crash echoed around the store, followed by the sound of hundreds of tiny bouncing beads skittering across the wooden floor.

"What the—" Lucas spun toward the noise. A tiny dark head popped up, then back down.

"Pickles? What did you do? What are you doing in here?" Lucas barked. He was next to her in a flash. I was right behind him.

Her frightened face made me step protectively between them. "It's okay. It was an accident. I'll clean it up." I had no idea how I was going to retrieve all those beads, but I'd figure that out later.

The tea drinkers set their mugs on the table and left quickly.

"You knew she was in here?" Lucas looked surprised and slightly pissed off.

I crossed my arms defensively. "Yes, of course." I glanced down at the tiny girl sandwiched next to me. "Necklace-making one-oh-one. Today was our first class."

Pickles stuck out her tongue at her brother.

Lucas leaned back on his heels, his narrowed eyes taking us both in. "Well, pardon me, ladies." He leaned over and righted the table. "I thought my little sister was helping Charlie organize socks by color. Like she promised." He shot her a dark look. "She forgot to tell me she had other plans."

"Lucas, don't be mad," I pleaded. She was so adorable I didn't want her to be in trouble. "She's fine. We were having a great time together."

He looked at me doubtfully, pinning me with those hypnotic eyes.

"Really," I insisted. "Pickles and I have a lot in common."

He cocked an eyebrow. "Like what?"

"You wouldn't understand," I told him. "It's girl stuff."

"Yeah," agreed Pickles. "Girl stuff. Go 'way Lukie. I'm

staying with my friend."

Lukie was not amused. "You made a huge mess, Pickles. You need to help us clean it up."

"I'll help. You go." Pickles fumed.

Choosing to steer clear of the sibling love fest, I knelt to pick up the scattered tools, and wires…and the beads…so many beads. Lucas whispered something in Pickles' ear. She stomped to the other side of the store and plopped onto a couch, chubby arms folded over her chest, as she glared at her brother.

Lucas knelt next to me, looking contrite. "I'm sorry about the mess. And about Pickles being in here bothering you. She was supposed to stay in the shop." He took a breath. "I didn't mean to get angry. I just freaked out when I realized she was here with you and I didn't even know it. If anything happened to her…"

"She's great," I said. "She can come in here anytime I'm working." I paused. "Liz must love her, too."

Lucas nodded. "Yeah, totally. I'm sure that's why she snuck over here. Liz fills her up with cookies and hot chocolate."

We piled my tools and wire on the table. "You make jewelry?" Lucas asked.

I nodded.

"Cool." His gaze swept the floor. "This bead situation sucks. I'll go get the broom." He turned to glare at his sister. "Pickles, don't move."

She stuck out her tongue again. "You not my boss," she said, still glaring. "I like Darcy more dan Heather." She looked at me, and then turned a frowning gaze to her brother. "Why don't you like Darcy instead? You could kiss her instead of Heather."

"Pickles." Lucas's voice was low. "Don't say another word."

I stood frozen with embarrassment as I imagined Lucas sweeping me into a passionate kiss while Heather and Pickles looked on.

"Sorry, Darcy." Lucas laughed and shook his head, keeping his eyes on his sister. "Sometimes she says stupid stuff. Don't pay any attention to her."

The idea of kissing me was stupid? I glared at him, too. "She's a good kid, Lucas. Don't call her stupid." I turned away and stalked to the counter to make his crappucino.

Lucas went to sit with Pickles on the couch, talking to her in a low voice. She slid off the couch and walked over to me.

"Sorry for making a mess, Darcy," she said, looking pitiful.

I handed her a chocolate chip cookie. "Accidents happen, sweetie. Maybe we can try again another day."

Her face brightened as she bit into the cookie.

"I'm taking her back to Charlie's," Lucas said, coming up to take her by the hand. "I'll be back to clean up the beads for you, but I can't stay too long because I have to get to class."

My hand was steady as I gave him his drink. "Don't bother."

He frowned. "Did I... Are you...upset with me?"

Pickles glared at him. She was clearly the smarter sibling.

I looked down to wipe the spotless counter. Think of

Heather, I told myself. Goddess of beauty, lover of Lucas. And who was I? Niece of Charlie. Duster of shakers. The girl next door. Literally.

Of course what Pickles had said about him kissing me instead of Heather was stupid. So stupid that he'd laughed at the idea. I raised my eyes and let out a long breath. "It's been a long week."

He hesitated before speaking, as if holding something back. "You're sure about the bead clean-up?"

"Positive." I forced a smile.

Lucas and Pickles left, but as the door squeaked behind them, I heard her clear voice.

"I still like Darcy better dan Heather."

CHAPTER TWELVE
OCTOBER 25

Dear Darcy

My journey continues. Not sure when I'll be back.
Still following the Stones.

Love,

Dad

This one was postmarked Rolla, Missouri. "*Greetings from the Middle of Everywhere.*"

Rolla? More like the middle of nowhere.

"The Stones? He's following the Rolling Stones?" I asked Toby. We leaned against the pillows on my bed. He stretched and yawned, then closed his eyes.

Dad's card didn't make any sense. Even if that ancient

rock band was touring, they wouldn't be playing in the middle of nowhere. But just in case, I googled it. Nope, not touring.

What was in Rolla that could possibly interest my dad? I looked at one of the town's visitor websites. A university. Lots of outdoor activities and an abundance of trout streams. My dad hated fishing. I scrolled down to the bottom of the page and my breath caught.

"Stonehenge revisited."

I clicked the link. Photos of a partial replica of the original Stonehenge filled the page. I skimmed the description. The henge was on the university campus, built by engineering students back in the 1980s. Holy shiz. *Still following the Stones.* I grabbed my cell and called Mom.

"Darcy, what is it? I'm in the middle of showing a house. I'll call you back."

"Mom, I think I know what Dad's doing. He's chasing Stonehenge."

There was a long pause. "What are you talking about?"

"His latest postcard, from Missouri. There's a henge replica at a university there." I ran down the stairs, nervous energy shooting through me like fireworks. "I bet we can find him. I'll look online to see where the other replicas are." I yanked open the pantry and grabbed a box of crackers.

"Darcy, you're not making any sense. I need to go. We'll talk later tonight."

"But I—"

The call disconnected. Damn it. Why wouldn't she listen to me? This was a huge freaking clue about what Dad was doing. I tore into the box of crackers. Toby padded into the kitchen and looked up at me with hopeful eyes.

"Fine, you greedy dog." I grabbed the box of Scooby treats and tossed him a couple. "But this means no skipping our run tomorrow." I was proud of myself that I'd resumed my goals. For a while I'd slacked off, especially on the mornings I found Mom passed out on the couch. But lately, on days I didn't want to run, I heard Dad's voice and his stupid quote about even the slowest runner still crossing the finish line.

Lame. But I still ran.

I spent the next hour scouring websites about Stonehenge replicas. They were all over the country. I found one in Ingram, Texas, which explained Dad's first postcard. I needed to plot the henges on a map. Dad had a whole shelf full of atlases in his office.

Opening the office door, I looked around the room, feeling his absence more keenly here than anywhere else. I grabbed the biggest atlas and ran upstairs to my room, threw the oversized book on the bed, and opened to the U.S. map. Using a red pen, I starred all the states with henges. Kansas, Kentucky, Michigan. New Hampshire, Virginia, Washington.

How could I possibly figure out where he'd go next?

My phone alarm beeped and I realized I was due at Liz's in an hour. I needed to leave now to catch the bus, since the Reaper guzzled so much gas and I was trying to save money.

The sleuthing would have to wait until later.

Sal called me as I waited at the bus stop. "You're working tonight, right?"

"Yeah." I couldn't contain my excitement at the first hope I'd had in forever. "Sal, I think I found out something about my dad. I might know what he's doing."

"You're kidding!" she exclaimed. "What?"

Bus exhaust fumes filled my nose. "I'll have to call you later. It's a long story."

"I never see you anymore." She sounded like she would be pouting, if she were a pouting kind of girl. "There's a party tonight. You should come after work. You can tell me all about your clue, Dr. Watson."

"Actually, the correct reference would be Sherlock."

"Whatever, brainiac. Will you come to the party?"

The bus shuddered to a stop in front of me. "Maybe. Text me later."

"Ciao."

*L*iz untied her "Kiss me, I'm over-caffeinated" apron and hung it on a hook. She wore the necklace I'd made for her. She wore it often, and had been bugging me to make more jewelry to sell in the coffee shop, claiming that customers kept asking where they could buy a necklace like hers.

"You're in charge, darling," she said. "Time for Charlie and me to hit it."

It was my first night to close the shop by myself. I'd logged enough time with Liz and enough solo afternoons that she'd decided I was ready. Still, she assured me, "Lucas will come over to help you lock up and make sure everything's okay."

My stomach tightened. I hadn't seen him since the bead incident. I still felt a little hurt and embarrassed that he'd laughed at the idea of kissing me. Some tiny part of me still hoped that someday he'd see me in a kissable light, but more likely I was another sister to him, just taller and snarkier than Pickles.

"Do I really need his help?" I asked.

Liz raised an eyebrow. "Trouble in paradise?"

I blinked at her in confusion. "What do you mean?"

She packed up her tote bag, watching me curiously. "You two get along so well. I thought you'd be happy to have him swing by to help."

"Uh, yeah." I paused to breathe. Exhale stress. Inhale calm. "It's fine if he helps. I just…just wanted to do it on my own. You know?"

She smiled at me and tossed a loopy, hand-knitted shawl around her shoulders. "I trust you completely, if that's what you're worried about."

"I know you do, Liz. And thanks for asking Lucas to stop by. I'm sure he'll be…helpful."

She waved good-bye and zoomed out of the store like a whirlwind. Charlie met her out front and enveloped her in a hug. They waved to me and then disappeared into the night.

Lucas showed up about nine thirty. I glanced at the Eiffel Tower wall clock. "You're early. We close at ten." I was irritated that he was such a distraction, much as I tried to ignore his effect on me. I wanted to think about my Dad, and I was anxious to get home to look online for more henges. I'd already texted Sal that I wasn't coming to the party. She was bummed, but she'd get over it.

Leaning against the counter, Lucas watched while I washed plates and cups. "I know when closing time is, Shaker Girl. But Charlie's shop closes at nine, so I've got time to kill." He grinned. "I thought I'd grace you with my company."

I rolled my eyes. "Make yourself useful. Take out the trash. Sweep the floor. I'm still finding beads everywhere."

His smile faded. "That sucks. You should've let me help clean up that day."

"I'm kidding." I narrowed my eyes. "But you should let Pickles come see me again for a jewelry lesson. We'd have fun."

"You're serious, aren't you? You realize that little kids are terrorists in disguise? They just wait for the right opportunity, and then wham! They'll take you right out."

"Chicken," I accused. "Afraid of your own sister?"

He wandered behind the counter and grabbed a dishtowel, then took a wet cup from my hand and dried it. I was surprised I wasn't electrocuted by his fingers touching mine. He, of course, was completely unfazed.

"My sister is going to run her own army someday," he said. "Meanwhile, she's got me to boss around."

I handed him another cup to dry. "You just have to know how to handle little kids," I said. "They aren't that complicated. The boys, especially, are easy to manage since they aren't as smart. Even when they grow up."

He flicked the towel at me and I jumped out of the way, laughing.

By the time ten o'clock rolled around, I'd forgiven him for not falling in love with me. Maybe it was better being friends. We probably had a lot more fun that way.

Lucas was in the alley taking out the trash when the front door swung open. Damn. I'd forgotten to flip over the

CLOSED sign and lock the door.

"Good evening."

I looked up to see an older man in a tweed blazer and matching cap. He brushed snow off his shoulders and smiled at me. "The snow just started and I see you're about to close. Can you make me a quick double-shot cappuccino, extra dry, and I'll take it to go." He looked around the café. "Where's Liz tonight? She's the best barista in town."

"She left early." I paused. He must be a regular, so I turned on the charm. "I'm Darcy. I started here a few weeks ago."

"Ah. I'm Herbert. I'm sure you must be a fabulous barista, too, if you're working for Liz." He rocked back on his heels and waited for his drink, smiling like a kid at Disneyland.

Thanks to Lucas and his extra dry obsession, I wasn't freaked out by Herbert's order. I held the pitcher of milk under the steaming rod and cranked up the frother, releasing more steam. The milk bubbled noisily.

Would I be able to predict Dad's route, if I mapped all the henge towns? Could I figure out where he was going based on where he'd already been?

The steamer sounded like a train whistle, jarring me back to where I was, but not before the milk boiled over, scalding my hand.

"Damn!" I dropped the pitcher, hot milk spilling all over my shoes and the floor.

"What happened?" Herbert peeked over the counter, alarmed.

Tears burned in my eyes as the hot milk burned my skin.

I ran to the sink to put my hand under cold water.

"Darcy? Are you all right?" Lucas was at my side, his hand on my shoulder. I looked up to see his beautiful eyes raking over me with concern.

I shivered at his touch and closed my eyes, dying of embarrassment. "I will be." So stupid. My first screw-up in weeks and it happened when Lucas was there to witness it.

"She burned her hand," said Herbert. "I'm not sure what happened. I just heard her yell and then she dropped the pitcher."

Lucas leaned over the sink to look at my bright red skin. "That's a bad burn. You might need to see a doctor."

"What? No. Absolutely not." This was mortifying. "It's not a big deal."

Herbert cleared his throat. "Any chance I could still get my cappuccino? Already paid for it, you know."

Lucas glanced at Herbert, then at me. He rolled his eyes. "Sure," he said, "but then we really need to close up."

"Double shot, extra-dry crappucino," I muttered to Lucas. His sideways smile stopped my heart.

He zoomed around like Super Barista, cleaning up the mess I'd made, preparing and handing Tweedy his drink in a few efficient moves, then escorting him to the door. Lucas locked the door behind him and flipped the OPEN sign to CLOSED.

"I can't believe that guy," he said, shutting off the overhead lights. Only a dim glow behind the counter remained.

My hand was raw and red. I turned off the faucet and wrapped a towel around it. "Me either. I wonder if he would've still wanted his drink if I'd chopped off a finger."

Lucas laughed. "Probably. 'Paid for it already, you know.'" He walked behind the counter and took my hand. "Let me see it," he said softly.

I stood there trembling, whether from the shock of the burn, the embarrassment of my espresso disaster, or my proximity to Lucas, I didn't know.

He unwrapped the towel and I winced. "I don't need to go to the ER. It's not that bad."

"I'll be the judge of that," he said, glancing at me from under those disgustingly long eyelashes.

"Oh really? Are you in med school, too?"

He smirked. "No. But I've taken first aid classes. And I've seen Bella do damage before."

"On Liz?"

"Yeah. When she first got this machine." He shook his head.

"The emergency drawer," I said. Liz had mentioned it before, but I'd never looked inside it. "Maybe there's a first aid kit in there."

Lucas frowned. "Emergency drawer?"

I pointed to the red skull and crossbones painted on a drawer under the counter, and was baffled when he dropped my hand and burst out laughing.

"What?" I tingled from his touch and the burn.

Lucas yanked open the drawer and pulled out a hand-lettered sign which read, *"Beautiful Bella is having a time-out. Regular coffee and tea only today. Sorry. Try us again tomorrow. We hope she'll be in a better mood then."*

"Liz used this a lot when she first opened up." Lucas slid

the sign back in the drawer. He shot me another sexy smile as he headed for the back of the store. "I'll go to the real emergency drawer and get the first aid kit."

God, now I felt like a total idiot. I sighed and put away the clean cups with my uninjured hand. I just wanted to get home and talk to Mom about what I'd discovered about Dad, and show her the places I'd already marked on the atlas.

Lucas reappeared quickly with the first aid kit, housed in a vintage jewelry box, not a plastic tub with a giant red cross on the lid.

"What's that?" I asked, as he removed the cap from a slender silver tube.

"This is some burn gel Liz got when she was first taming Bella. It's the same stuff chefs use for burns in the kitchen." He waved a white roll at me. "And this is gauze. Maybe you've heard of it?"

"Ha." I glared at him and muttered, "I'm not in a joking mood."

He looked up from the gauze as he unwound it. "Why not? Now seems like a good time for a joke. It'll help take your mind off the pain."

"The pain is the least of my worries," I said. "I've got a lot on my mind."

"Yeah? Like what?" Lucas took my hand in his and smoothed cool gel over the burn. The sensation blocked out all rational thought for a few seconds, until he reached for the gauze and wrapped it gently around my hand.

"Earth to Darcy," he said, letting go of my bandaged hand and looking into my eyes. "So what's on your mind besides the pain, which I just totally eliminated for you?"

He'd taken away the pain, all right, but not in the way he thought. I kept my eyes lowered while I composed myself before answering him.

"It's some stuff I figured out today. About my dad." I raised my head, blinking quickly, hoping he couldn't see any evidence of me swooning over him.

He leaned against the sink. "You want to talk about it?"

I hesitated. In some ways, it was easy to talk to him. But the person I really needed to talk to was Mom. "Maybe later," I said. "Right now I need to get home."

"Will you be able to drive okay with your hand like that?" he asked as he packed up the first aid box.

"Not an issue. I took the bus."

"What about the truck?" He glanced up.

"I'm trying to save gas money. That thing gets like ten miles to the gallon. Plus, it's been blowing more blue smoke lately."

"How long is your bus ride?"

"About forty-five minutes from my house to here. I've got one transfer. I don't mind, though. It gives me time to read and listen to music."

"Buses don't run as often this late," Lucas said. "When were you supposed to catch one home?"

Oh crap. I looked at my watch. 10:33. I'd missed the 10:19, plus we still had to finish closing up. I pulled my phone out of my pocket to check the schedule app I'd downloaded.

I'd be lucky to catch the 11:21. Great. I sighed heavily.

"I'll give you a ride," Lucas said.

I stared at him. Ride home with Lucas? Just the two of us?

"Uh...I'm on the other side of town. It's okay. I'll just wait in here until it's time for the bus."

"No way," he insisted. "The later it gets, the weirder the bus passengers get."

"Worse than the Harry Potter Knight Bus?"

He grinned. "Yeah. Besides, Charlie would kill me if I let you wait here by yourself for the ghost bus. Let me help you close out the register, then we can blow this pop stand."

Liz had left me written notes, but I sat back and cradled my hand while Lucas pushed buttons until the register spewed out a long tape showing all the day's sales. We counted all the cash and then added up the credit card receipts.

Lucas grinned. "Now let's see how much free stuff Liz gave away."

"Huh?"

"Pay attention," he commanded.

The register tape said we had sold $179.45 worth of food and drink. The cash and credit card receipts added up to $159.37.

"Net loss of $20.08," Lucas said. He sighed. "I don't know how she does it."

"Does what?" I was confused.

"Gives away stuff for free and still manages to keep this place open." He shrugged. "Charlie says the rent for these places is really cheap. Somehow the two of them manage to pay it each month."

"Does Charlie give away stuff, too?"

Lucas grinned. "Are you kidding? Of course he does. He's a total sucker. So is Liz. Guess they're made for each other that way."

"That's pretty cool." A bitter laugh escaped me. "Maybe if things hit bottom for Mom and me, we can get free food from Liz. And some clothes from Charlie." I wanted to snatch the words back as soon as I said them.

Lucas gazed at me for what felt like forever. "How bad is it, Darcy?"

The directness of his question made me wince. "So bad I don't even know how to talk about it," I said, my voice barely above a whisper.

"Then maybe you *should* talk about it." He crossed his arms over his chest. What would it feel like to have his arms around me? To have him hold me while I spilled out all my fears?

I turned away and shrugged. "Denial is working pretty well so far."

"Maybe for a while. But the truth beats the crap out of denial. Eventually." He sighed heavily. "Believe me, I know."

I looked at him, surprised. "Yeah?" Curiosity consumed me. What skeletons lurked in the closet of Mr. Magic Hands? What truths had he run from?

He turned back to the register and busied himself locking the cash and credit card receipts into a small metal box bedazzled with purple and pink rhinestones. "I'll show you where to hide this, then we should go."

The hiding place was in Liz's fairy cave, under a table covered by star-and-moon patterned fabric. The table looked like it might tip over from the weight of the haphazard stacks of books.

"Very secure," I observed.

Lucas looked up from where he knelt on the floor, grinning. "It works for Liz. You are now only the fourth person who knows the secret location of Ft. Knox."

"Hmm…Liz, Charlie, you and me?" I guessed.

"Yep." He stood up and brushed his hands on his jeans. "Let's roll. My car's in the alley."

After double-checking the front door to make sure it was locked, we turned off the lights in Fairyland. We emerged from the back door into the alley, which was shrouded in darkness.

"Did Liz give you a key?" Lucas asked.

"What? Oh yeah, she did." I dug in the pocket of my jeans, glancing over my shoulder nervously.

"Are you scared?" There was a hint of laughter in his voice.

I glanced at him and saw his perfect lips curve into a mocking smile. Stubbornly, I jammed the key into the lock, once I managed to find the keyhole in the dark. So what if I was scared? Any normal person would be nervous in a dark alley. Just because Magic Hands was used to it didn't make me weird.

"She definitely needs a light back here," I muttered.

"Yeah. But she and Charlie always leave together. Plus she knows everybody in the 'hood. She feeds most of the homeless guys so I don't think she worries about it."

The lock clicked into place. "Ready?" I asked. My eyes had adjusted well enough to the dark to see that he was still grinning. So what if I was jittery and wanted to get out of the dark alley? I wasn't as brave as Liz.

"Don't worry, Shaker Girl," Lucas said, and before I

could respond, he slung his arm over my shoulders. "My car is right over there. I think we'll make it there in one piece. Plus you've got those badass, shirt-stealing ninja moves if anyone jumps us."

I went completely mute. How could I expect to keep up a witty convo with him so close, with the warmth of his arm and the proximity of the rest of him driving all thoughts out of my head? Neither of us spoke as we walked down the alley toward a black car. It was awkweirdly awesome.

Lucas dropped his arm to unlock the passenger door of his car. The physical contact had been way too short, and I sighed.

Out loud.

"You okay?" he asked, leaning on the door, waiting for me to get in.

"Oh yeah. I'm just…um, tired." How lame. I sank into the passenger seat of his muscle car.

When Lucas slid into the driver's seat, my senses went into hyperdrive and I told myself to get a grip.

"I just need to let someone know I'm running a little late." He had his phone out, fingers flying over a text.

Stomach plummet. Of course. The goddess Heather was waiting.

"I really don't mind taking the bus," I said. "You have plans and—"

"Don't be stupid," he cut me off. "I'm giving you a ride. My plans are flexible."

He started the car and we rolled slowly down the alley.

"Do you remember where I live?" I asked.

He shrugged. "Basically. You can direct me when we get

close."

I nodded, then he plugged in his iPod and a familiar song flooded the car.

"You like Phoenix?" I asked, surprised. That was twice he'd played some of my favorite music.

He glanced at me, then back at the road. "I can change it to something else." He reached for his iPod, but I stopped him with my bandaged hand, then yanked it away like I'd been shocked.

"No, don't change it. I love this song."

Lucas smiled in the blue glow from the dashboard and we drove without talking, just listening to the music. If I closed my eyes and filtered out most of reality, this could be a perfect night, a perfect date. Except for the small detail of Lucas already having a girlfriend and my life completely falling apart. Oh, and my dad being MIA on some sort of crazy clonehenge quest.

"Do you want to talk about it?" he asked. Even with heat pouring out of the car vents, a shiver slid through me.

"Talk about what?"

"Whatever was worrying you earlier. Whatever distracted you enough to make you burn yourself."

I watched his profile. "You think that's why I burned myself?"

He shrugged. "You said you had a lot on your mind. Something about your dad."

I huffed out a sigh. "It's a long story. And it's…just weird. I'm still trying to figure it out."

Lucas was quiet for a few moments. "I'm a good listener," he said. "Just ask Pickles. I listen to her ramble all the time."

I laughed. "Her stories are probably much more interesting than mine."

He didn't smile. "I doubt that." He glanced at me. "Seriously, Darcy. If you ever want to talk about…all that's going on…" He paused, and then spoke again. "My mom left, too. Like your dad."

My stomach twisted. "She did?"

He looked at me, then back at the road. "Yeah. So I know what you're going through, sort of. Though my mom wasn't famous, so the whole country wasn't making jokes about it. That must be hard."

He'd opened a door, but I wasn't ready to walk through it, so we drove the rest of the way without speaking, the music filling our silence.

"Tell me where to turn," Lucas prompted me as the houses we passed increased in size. I guided him to my address.

He turned toward me. "You shouldn't be taking the bus and walking home this late by yourself. If you can't afford to gas up your truck, I can give you rides home on the nights you work late."

"But…it's completely out of your way."

He ran a hand through his hair and shrugged. "I like driving."

I sat there, speechless, until he shifted the car into park, leaving the engine running. "Come on." He opened his door. "I'll walk you up."

"I'm not going to get jumped," I joked, though secretly I was thrilled when he actually walked around the car and opened my door, like a gentleman in one of my favorite books. No Regency duke would've dropped off his date and stayed in his carriage texting.

He smiled at me, but didn't say anything as we walked quickly up the cobblestones Mom had imported from England. We stood in front of the massive double doors while Lucas dug into his pocket and the wind bit through our coats.

"Here." He handed me the silver tube and roll of gauze from Liz's first aid box. "Put more gel on your burn tomorrow and rewrap it."

I took the first aid supplies, impressed by his thoughtfulness. "Oh, wow. Thanks." I didn't know what else to say. His kindness rendered me speechless.

The universe needed to spread out its gifts a little more evenly instead of dumping them all onto one person. Lucas had his act together in a way I never would. Smart, composed under pressure, thoughtful, not to mention smoking hot. I sighed and unlocked the door. Toby waited, wriggling and whimpering. He launched himself at Lucas.

Lucas grinned and bent down to pet him. "How's my Toby?" Toby slobbered all over him.

"I think he *is* your Toby," I remarked. Add *beloved by dogs* to the list of his attributes. "Even I don't get that kind of greeting."

He laughed and stood up. "I'm sure you're his favorite. But I could definitely rob your house if I wanted to."

Another gust of wind blew snow around us. I hesitated. Should I ask him in? Was my mom in a wine coma yet, or would she be awake enough for me to tell her about the henges? And what about his "flexible plans?"

"Do you want to come in? For a minute. To warm up

before you head back across town," I said quickly. I thought of one way we could warm up and immediately wished I hadn't said that.

He shook his head. "That'd be great any other time, but I'm sort of running late."

I knew my face burned with embarrassment. Hopefully he'd just think it was windburn.

"Sure. Well, thanks again." I stepped inside, ready to slam the door so that I could collapse in private. He'd churned up all sorts of emotions tonight that I didn't want to deal with.

"I'll see you soon," Lucas said. He held my gaze for a moment, his eyes hooded in the darkness, and then hurried down the steps to his car.

I raised my hand in a half wave. He saluted me with a grin, then slid into the car and drove away into the night, taillights disappearing too quickly.

There went my dream guy. Who happened to be unavailable. Not to mention completely unattainable.

I slammed the front door behind me, as if that would keep my feelings for Lucas outside, too. I had way too much else going on in my life to be distracted by him. I needed to focus my energy on Dad, and Mom. I was the sanest of the three of us. I had to do something to keep us from crashing, because I was pretty sure we were careening out of control down a twisting road that dropped into nowhere.

The house was silent. No late night TV noises. After checking to make sure all the doors were locked and lights were out, I trudged upstairs with Toby at my heels.

I paused at Mom's door and heard her snoring. Great.

The more she drank, the louder she snored. So much for telling her what I'd figured out from Dad's postcards and my online research.

"Come on, Tobester," I whispered. "It's time for bed."

Exhaustion overwhelmed me. I didn't have the energy to look up more clonehenges tonight. I'd do it tomorrow. Maybe then Mom would be in a better condition to listen to me.

Toby and I snuggled together under my covers, listening to the wind howl outside. I closed my eyes. "I'm going to find you, Dad," I whispered. "I don't know how, but I will."

CHAPTER THIRTEEN
OCTOBER 27

"*N*ow!" Mom screamed into the phone. "You get over here right now, J.J. You can tell me in person what the hell this is." Mom held a stack of papers in her trembling hand. She ended the call and threw her phone against the wall. Plastic bits went flying, making Toby cower and slink away.

I reassembled Mom's phone while she disappeared into the wine cellar. Maybe tonight she'd let me have a glass. I shuddered and shook my head. That wouldn't solve anything; she was living proof of that. I picked up the papers, pages and pages of legalese, but one word jumped out at me.

Eviction.

My runner's legs morphed from muscle to liquid in seconds. I sank onto a kitchen barstool, my eyes blurring with tears as I tried to decipher the document. Mom came back into the kitchen, clumsily juggling three bottles of wine. My stomach clenched as I looked at her.

"Please, Mom. Not now. Can't you go without drinking for just one day?"

She glared at me. "You see what that says? They're kicking us out, Darcy. Kicking us out of our own fucking house."

"Mom!" She'd never dropped the f-bomb. Ever.

She sneered at me. "It's not like I'm offending you. And if there was ever a time for me to get drunk, it's now."

Tears streamed down my face, but I shook with anger. "Damn it, Mom. You have to stop this. J.J.'s on his way over. You can talk to him. Convince him to change his mind."

"That's what I'm planning to do, Darcy."

I took a deep breath. "He's not going to take you seriously if you're drunk."

"I don't need you lecturing me. You have no idea what I'm going through. Go upstairs, Darcy."

"No."

Her eyes widened. "No? Who do you think you are?"

"I'm Tri Ty's daughter," I said flatly. "And yours. And I'm not going anywhere."

We stared at each other, not moving or speaking.

Toby broke the tension with a bark when the front doorbell rang. I felt Mom's glare like an icy wind on my back as I went to answer the door.

J.J. looked startled to see me instead of Mom. "She's in the kitchen," I said. "Come on."

He followed me, footsteps heavy on the tile. When we reached the kitchen the three of us stood like points on a triangle, watching each other warily.

J.J. spoke first. "You can't hide out anymore, Marilyn," he said. "If we don't have Ty, we don't have a product to sell. By disappearing, he's completely ruined Harvest." His face was haggard, but I saw no compassion in his eyes. "The eviction was a board decision. I can't change it."

"How can you do this, J.J.? Kick us out of our home?" Mom's face showed only fear, no traces of her earlier anger.

J.J.'s frustration snapped at us with each word. "The company owns the house. It's one of the only assets we own free and clear. The board is seizing it."

Mom's face crumpled. "But I thought it was our house. Mine and Ty's."

J.J. scowled. "It used to be. But Ty signed the house deed over to the business."

"What?" Mom reached out for a chair to steady herself. She looked as fragile as a lost child, and all of my anger at her dissolved. I crossed the kitchen and wrapped an arm around her waist.

"Why would he do that?" Tears streamed down Mom's face. "I don't understand."

J.J. looked at the floor as he spoke. "I told you about the bad investment decisions. Maybe he felt guilty about that."

My anxiety swelled to enormous proportions. This didn't make sense. The one thing Dad would never do was leave Mom and me without a roof over our heads. Didn't J.J. know that?

Mom sank slowly into a chair. She pulled a crumpled tissue out of her pocket, wiped her eyes, then spoke again. "We need more time. This eviction notice doesn't even give us a month to get moved." Her voice was pleading. "J.J., at least give us more time."

J.J. shook his head sadly. "Can't do it, Marilyn."

"He's coming back," Mom whispered. "He has a plan. He must. He wouldn't let everything fall apart. Not after all these years. Harvest is his life."

"Where is he, Marilyn?" J.J. pushed.

"I told you I don't know. He never calls. He ignores his emails. I don't have any way to reach him." Her voice quivered.

"What about the postcards he was sending?" J.J.'s voice had turned cold.

Goose bumps prickled my skin. Mom had told J.J. about those?

I didn't know how much I could believe J.J., but he and Mom needed to know what I'd discovered about the clonehenges. If there was a hope of finding Dad, if we could figure it out, maybe the board would change their mind, or at least give us more time. I had to say something.

"I might know where he is." My voice echoed in the quiet kitchen.

"Darcy." Mom's voice held a warning.

J.J. took a step toward me. "If you know where he is, you have to tell me."

This wasn't the old J.J., the one I'd known forever. This J.J. was threatening, angry, and full of desperation. I wanted to back away from him, but I held my ground. "I'm not sure. But I think I might know what he's doing."

Mom closed her eyes and shook her head. "Don't listen to her, J.J. She's grasping at straws."

"No I'm not." I met J.J.'s hard stare. "I think he's on a quest. He's traveling the country looking at Stonehenge replicas."

J.J.'s mouth opened in surprise. "He's what?"

Mom had risen from the chair to open a bottle of wine while I spoke. She poured two glasses and handed one to J.J., who took a long drink.

"Darcy, have you talked to your dad?" J.J. asked. "Do you know for sure that's what he's doing?"

"No. You're the only one he's talking to. Isn't he telling *you* what he's doing? Where he's going?"

J.J.'s eyes narrowed and his lips thinned. "No. He only lets me know he's okay. I can't get him to tell me anything else. He doesn't even have his cell anymore, or doesn't turn it on. He calls me from random places on the road."

"But you're his best friend," I said, not quite believing him. "At least he's calling you. Can't you tell him what's happening with the house? I know he'd come home if he knew." My pitch rose as I fought back tears. "You must know something, J.J."

He flinched like I'd hit a nerve, and a ripple of suspicion went through me. I darted a glance at Mom, wondering if she'd seen what I had, but she was refilling her damn wineglass.

I didn't know what was going on with him, but J.J. was our only link to Dad. Maybe if I showed him my map, he'd tell us more. "I have his postcards. I'm plotting them on a map. Do you want to see it?"

J.J. looked at Mom, who shook her head again. I bit the inside of my lip in frustration. Why didn't anyone believe me?

"I don't know." J.J. hesitated. "That sounds…desperate. Like you're searching for a method to his madness."

"He's not crazy." Even as I said it, fear tingled my scalp.

J.J. sighed. "I'll look at your map, if it'll make you happy."

I frowned. "Don't patronize me, J.J. Just forget it if you don't believe me."

He glanced at Mom, who said nothing as she drank more wine.

"Would it change things," I asked, hating the way desperation weakened my voice, "if you could tell the board that we can find him? Could we keep our house?"

J.J. rubbed his forehead. "I don't know, Darcy. It would take a miracle at this point."

"Just look at it. Please." I turned and headed for the staircase, willing them to follow me as readily as Toby did. I was almost to my bedroom door before I finally heard their steps on the stairs.

"Here goes nothing," I whispered to Toby.

The map hung on the wall over my desk, covered in red stars and post-it notes. I'd traced a black dotted line showing his travels so far. The line made a loopy infinity symbol across the bottom right quadrant of the map, running south then east, then north, then west and dipping down south again.

J.J. and Mom stared at the map. He stepped closer to read my post-its, which listed the date of each card's postmark He turned toward me. "Is there a Stonehenge route he's following? Like in those 'roadside attraction' books? Why would he go to *these* places?"

I looked at my feet. That was the burning question,

wasn't it? And I couldn't answer it.

"Darcy?" Mom prompted me.

They didn't believe me. When I looked up all I saw was pity for the poor deluded girl trying to find a clue in random patterns. I turned away from Mom's doubt and J.J.'s condescension. "Forget it. You think it's wishful thinking. Childish. Desperate." Mom put a hand on my shoulder but I shrugged it off. "Just go," I whispered. "Please. Just leave me alone."

They left my bedroom quietly, but Toby stayed. I collapsed next to him on the floor and buried my face in his fur. Maybe they were right. Maybe I *was* desperate. Delusional. Following a fantasy.

Like Lucas said, eventually truth beat the crap out of denial.

I had to face the fact that Dad was gone.

CHAPTER FOURTEEN
OCTOBER 28

"We have to move," I told Sal over cold French fries in the cafeteria. "I've been trying to think of a way around it, but I'm stumped. I don't know where we'll go. Or what we'll do with all our stuff."

Sal blinked worried eyes at me. "What about those big storage lockers? You could rent a few of those."

I shook my head. "Those cost money. Lots of money."

"Oh." She dipped a French fry in ketchup, then left it on the plate. "Maybe you could have a sale?"

"A garage sale? Sell Mom's antiques for pennies on the dollar?"

"No," said Sal, "a what-do-you-call-them. An estate sale."

Wait... That was actually a good idea. I'd seen those

signs in our neighborhood, like a rich person's alternative to a garage sale. We had expensive stuff. Maybe if we could get some decent money for it, that would tide us over until Mom could get a better job and get out of Fake-Bake Pam's clutches. I whipped out my phone and texted Charlie. *"R U around today? 4:00?"* I was due at Liz's at four thirty.

His reply pinged within seconds. *"Of course. C U then."*

Sal watched me closely. "Who was that?"

"My uncle. He'll know the names of estate sale companies."

Sal raised her eyebrows. "Do you think your mom is willing to part with all her stuff?"

I hugged myself, feeling suddenly chilled even though I wore a bulky sweater and jeans.

"She doesn't have much choice. We can't afford to store it. And we have to move by the end of the month."

Sal shook her head. "You continue to amaze me, girl-friend. Darcy to the rescue."

I frowned at her. "Somebody has to. Dad's gone. Mom's a wreck." I shrugged and tried to smile.

She sighed. "Too bad there's nobody around to rescue you. Somebody with a big heart and a hot body."

"Please." I rolled my eyes. "That only happens in romance books, or movies."

"Speaking of…" She waggled her eyebrows. "What about that Lucas guy? You haven't mentioned him lately."

I snorted. "Where do I start? One: he is totally out of my league. Seriously, you have to meet him sometime and then you'll see what I mean. Besides, I told you, we're just friends. We spend most of our time joking around with each other."

I paused to steal one of her fries, ignoring her doubtful look.

"Two," I continued, "he has a girlfriend who looks like a supermodel. Three: I have way too much stuff going on in my life to even think about getting involved with anyone."

"Joking around, huh?" A tiny smile curved her purple-glossed lips. "In the movies, friendship leads to romance all the time."

I snorted. "My life is not that kind of movie." I stole another fry and pointed it at her. "Trust me. It's better this way. I've gotten used to just hanging out with him. He makes me laugh. And sometimes when I'm with him, I even forget about everything else that's going on."

She narrowed her eyes at me. "I rest my case."

"Sal, you aren't listening to me."

"Au contraire, my friend. I am listening to your voice and watching your face. And getting two very different messages."

I shoved away the plate in frustration. "Salena. Listen to me. When I'm working at Liz's, or hanging out with my uncle and Lucas, it just…just feels better. I can be myself with them. They know all about the Tri!Umphant! Shit Storm and don't judge me. Or mock me. Or ask prying questions."

She looked hurt. "Are you saying that I'm prying? That you don't feel like yourself with me?"

"No, damn it. But you and Mark are the only people at Woodbridge who don't see me as Loser Repo Girl. I feel like I'm suffocating here. I'm surrounded by people who have no clue what it's like for me and my mom right now. Everyone is just going about life as usual. Pretty soon they'll be going skiing every weekend. Hooking up and partying all the time."

How could I make her understand how different I felt from everyone else? And how normal I felt when I was with Liz and Charlie. And Lucas.

I sighed. Sal probably did see through me when I talked about him; I couldn't deny the way I felt around him. But all I'd told her was true. Just friends. Goddess girlfriend. Life a disaster zone. I pushed away the memory of the night he'd driven me home. I'd thought I'd felt a spark flicker between us then, but it had to be wishful thinking on my part.

"Look," I said with an apologetic sigh. "I don't mean to bite your head off. I need to take Toby for a run, so I can burn off some stress. Trying to figure out what to do is making me nuts."

She nodded, as subdued as I'd ever seen her. "Just remember I'm always here, right? To talk. Or, you know, take a break and just hang out." She winked. "Or check out hot guys on Tumblr."

I shook my head, smiling. "I miss you, too, DQ." I stood up. "Thanks for the suggestion about the sale. It's a really good idea."

She gave me a sad, halfhearted wave as I walked away. I felt unsettled, too. Sal was my only friend left at Woodbridge. I didn't want to lose her, but all I could think about was the next problem, and the next, and hope that someday things would be normal again. Not like they used to be, but a different type of normal, one where there'd be time for Sal and hanging out. I just hoped she'd still be there for me when that day finally came.

I called Mom during a free period, shivering on the empty soccer field because I didn't want anyone to overhear my conversation.

"Mom, I've got an idea. A way for us to get money."

"Money? What are you talking about?"

Her voice sounded slurred. God. It was only one forty-five. On a Tuesday. Working for Pam was a crap job but it wouldn't last if she kept drinking during the day.

I pushed that worry away and concentrated on the one I could do something about. "We could sell our stuff at an estate sale. Most of it anyway. I bet we'd make a lot of cash."

Silence.

"Mom?"

Her sigh was long and shaky. "I don't know, Darcy. That sounds…overwhelming."

I paced along the edge of the field. "I know, but I'm going to talk to Charlie about it today. Get some names from him. Will you at least think about it?"

She sighed again. "I guess so. But even if we do it, I'm not going to have time to deal with it."

So it was going to be my problem? How would I pull off an estate sale by myself?

"Mom, I don't think I can do it alone." I hesitated. "Will you be home tonight? After I get off work I'll make dinner. We can talk about it."

"You don't have to cook."

"I know." But if I didn't, who would? Besides, I was getting better at it. I'd found an old cookbook in Charlie's store that didn't require twenty ingredients for every recipe.

I wasn't a gourmet chef like my mom, but the stuff I made was edible. Usually.

"I'm not sure how late I'll be working." Her voice was distant. "And I might just go to bed when I get home."

I held my breath, anxiety overtaking me again. *Exhale.* "Okay. Can you call me though? Let me know when you're home."

"I'll try to remember."

How hard was it to remember to call your own daughter? And who was the mom, anyway?

I knew the answer to that, even if it made me sad and anxious. But if I had to be the parent, then okay. I was going to make this happen, because I had no other choice.

*C*harlie grinned as he looked up from behind the counter. "So what's the emergency? Donut deficiency?" He lifted the lid of his donut case and handed me my favorite. He never ran out of pink frosting and sprinkles.

I took a huge bite, then plunked onto a swiveling stool and dropped my messenger bag to the floor. "I wish that's all I needed." I brushed crumbs off my shirt. "Mom and I have to move. By the end of the month."

Charlie's grin faded. "Oh God, Darcy." His eyes filled with sympathy and sadness. "Oh, sweetheart, it's just too much. It's not fair."

I frowned. "Honestly, Charlie, I can't get distracted feeling sorry for myself." It was true. I'd thought about it on the bus ride. We needed money desperately. I had to do what I could to get Mom to face reality somehow. *You can't control the storms that tear through your crop,* Dad said. *But it's up to you what you do after the storm moves on. You can give up, or clean up.*

"I need names of estate sale companies. People you know, honest people who won't screw us over." Charlie regarded me soberly and I continued, "And we've got to find an apartment, too. Somewhere cheap, but not too scary."

"I might know of a few places." Lucas startled me as he emerged from the curtains hiding his fix-it area.

My hormones did a happy dance at the sound of his voice. I was glad Sal wasn't there to say "I told you so."

"We can't afford too much." I dropped my eyes, embarrassed, then remembered who I was talking to. Lucas was hardly a rich kid. He would understand. His gaze fixed steadily on mine as he waited for me to speak.

"Depending on how much we make on the estate sale, I'm guessing we can afford about six or seven hundred a month. We need two bedrooms. And somewhere that takes dogs."

"Duh. Of course you need to bring Toby." His mouth quirked up, but I thought I saw a trace of pity in his eyes, and my jaw tightened.

"If you know of some places, that'd be great," I said a little stiffly. "We don't have much time."

The two of them stared at me without speaking. I looked from Charlie to Lucas, bothered by their silence. "What is it?" I asked. "You both still speak English, don't you?" I tried to joke, but I needed to keep my momentum, just like when I ran. I slid off the stool and headed toward the furniture section. "We're probably going to need a small kitchen table. No way can we take our gigantic one to a small apartment."

Lucas stood between me and the furniture. My shoulder brushed against his chest as I stepped around him, and I tried to ignore the sparks shooting through me from the brief touch.

"We should probably keep the good stuff we already have, right? Like the espresso maker, the toaster, that kind of stuff." My words tumbled over each other. *Keep moving. Gotta keep moving.* I turned back to Charlie. "Mom always bought the best." I glanced at Lucas and smiled shakily. "Anyway, I know a guy who can fix those things if they break." My heart didn't race. Too much. My pulse stayed steady. Mostly. This "just friends" thing was working great.

Lucas tilted his head at me. "What's funny? God, Darcy, you're talking about moving and losing all your stuff. Why are you smiling like that?"

I shook my head. "Never mind." I paused to compose myself. "You guys are awesome. I'm going to need all the help I can get." I held out my hand. "I need a pen." Lucas stared at me like I was nuts, but grabbed a pen from his back pocket.

"Give me your hand," I said. He did and I wrote my cell number quickly on his palm, then I dropped the pen into it. I even managed not to blush too much. "Text me if you hear of any places we can afford."

"Uh, yeah. Sure. Absolutely." He slid his pen back into his pocket and ran a hand through his hair, frowning slightly. I tried to read his expression, but he dropped his gaze, hiding it from me.

I returned to the counter. "Charlie, do you think one of your estate sale connections will sign a contract with a minor?"

He blinked at me. "Your mom will need to sign it."

I sighed. Surely Mom could do that, at least, even if I was going to be stuck doing everything else. "Okay. But I'll probably have to do all the meetings myself. Mom's…um… really busy with work. Will you vouch for me?"

He looked like he might cry. "Of course I will."

My shoulders sagged with relief. Maybe I could make this work. Maybe I could move a few mountains, with a little help. *"No one does anything truly alone. We're all standing on the shoulders of those who came before us, or leaning on those walking next to us, sharing our load."* Dad's Greatest Hits, number 1,834.

"What time does your shift start?" Charlie asked.

"Four thirty. Why?"

"I'm calling in a favor from the lovely Liz. You and I are going to get something to eat first." He glanced at Lucas. "Hold down—"

"—the fort. Got it, boss." Lucas smiled at both of us, though his eyes were troubled as they lingered on me.

*I*n a booth at Pinky's Panini World I gorged myself on the most decadent sandwich ever invented—stuffed full of feta cheese, kalamata olives, roasted chicken, and sundried tomatoes. Charlie ate a salad. I didn't know how he maintained that vegan thing, but he said it was easy. He'd even set up a vegan section in his store, where people could buy shoes and purses that weren't made out of leather.

"The pile of crap on your plate just keeps getting bigger, doesn't it?" he said, putting down his fork.

I almost choked on an olive, hearing my Zen uncle swear. He must be serious. I didn't want to talk serious business, so I kept stuffing my face so I could get away with just a nod.

Charlie fiddled with his straw wrapper for a moment, then reached into his pocket and placed a set of salt and pepper shakers on the table. "These are for you." One was a black ninja with a white sword; the other was its mirrored twin: a white ninja with a black sword.

I stopped chewing long enough to smile. "Wow, Uncle Charlie. These are cool."

"They made me think of you." He resumed eating his rabbit food.

"Me? Why would ninjas make you think of me?"

"Because you're stronger than you realize. And you have the potential to be heroic."

Since when did my uncle turn into Samuel L. Jackson and decide to recruit me to join the Avengers? Even worse, he kind of sounded like my dad when he was in hyped-up motivational mode. "I'm not exactly a superhero, Charlie. Not even a sidekick."

The corners of his eyes crinkled. "You underestimate yourself, Darcy. I hate to see that."

Wouldn't I know it if I were special, or amazing, or heroic? Did Superman need a memo to remind him that he could fly and crush steel with his bare hands? No, he didn't.

I was just plain old Darcy. My dad was the amazing one. Or at least he used to be. Not me.

I picked up the shaker set. They were cute baby ninjas, not exactly threatening warriors of the night. "They're a great addition for my collection. Thanks, Charlie." I chewed on my thumbnail. "Why do I get both of them? Don't you want to keep the salt shaker?"

He smiled and shook his head. "I don't need to anymore." He almost looked embarrassed. "Kind of silly, I guess, but I hoped if I kept sending you shakers all those years, one day you'd want to track down their mates. And the guy who had them."

I wanted to jump across the table and hug him, but I kept it under control because I knew I'd start crying if I did. "Your strategy worked," I said, tearing up anyway. "I found you."

Charlie nodded, smiling. "Now tell me about your dad's latest postcard."

I thought my fabulous panini might just come right back up. "How did you know I'd gotten one?"

"It's been a couple of weeks since you mentioned getting one. I just assumed he was due to send another."

How much could I tell him? Would he think I was overreacting if I told him I thought Dad was losing it? I fished the card out of my bag and slid it across the table. The others were still in my drawer at home. I carried this one with me because I was still thinking about it. Obsessing, maybe.

Charlie read the card, rubbing a hand thoughtfully across his beard. It seemed like hours before he looked up.

"Well?" I asked, when he finally did.

He shook his head. "I'm not sure what to think."

A spark of anger flared in my chest. What was wrong with the adults in my life? Was I the only person who could read between the lines?

"It's impossible to live up to my reputation. **(Translation: I can't do this Harvest BS anymore.)** *People have made me larger than life. I'm just a man. A regular man. I don't have all the answers.* **(Translation: I am a total fraud.)** *I don't know if I have any answers at all. People are better off following their own advice, not mine.* **(Translation: I am quitting. And I'm not coming home. Ever.)***"*

"What's not to understand?" I snapped. "He's bailing." I glared at Charlie. "He's not coming back."

Charlie leaned against the booth and sighed loud enough to make Pinky glance at us. "I don't know what he'll do, Darcy. I don't think even he knows what's next."

Outrage fanned the anger spark to a furious flame. "So my mom and I are supposed to just sit around waiting, while our lives get worse by the day? We're supposed to wait for him to decide we're worth coming home to?"

Charlie flinched. "You and your mom are worthy of a lot more than you're getting right now." He reached across the table and clasped my hands. He had Dad's hands, only not. Charlie's were rough with calluses. Dad's were always smooth and manicured. "Will you let me help you, Darcy?" Charlie asked, his eyes full of love and concern.

I stared at Dad's loopy handwriting on the postcard. What could Charlie possibly do to fix any of this? Send a tractor beam out to find my dad and plunk him back into his Harvest offices, raring to go? Find an extra million bucks lying around the thrift store to bail us out?

The fire in me sputtered and died. Charlie was one of the only good things in my life right now. It wasn't fair to take out my anger on him.

"Just hanging out with you and Liz is enough," I whispered. "It's more than enough. It's keeping me going right now."

Charlie's hands squeezed tight around mine. "I want to do so much more." He swallowed. "I've called your mom a few times. She hasn't called me back."

Did you call in the evening? I wanted to ask. She was probably passed out drunk or hadn't bothered to listen to her voicemail.

Out loud I said, "She's working a crazy schedule with the real estate business. I never know when she's going to be home." *Or awake. Or sober.*

Charlie nodded. "I'm sure she's overwhelmed by everything and doing all she can."

I fiddled with my side salad, not daring to look at Charlie. I didn't want to talk about Mom. "Charlie, there's something I don't understand. Something I've been wanting to ask you, but I'm not sure how."

"I hope you know you can ask me anything."

I nodded. "It's about my dad. And you. I don't understand how…" I took a breath and started again. "You don't seem mad at him at all. But he rejected you. He stopped inviting you to our house when I was just a kid, but you made Liz listen to his CDs. You've even said you like some of his Harvest stuff. If I were you, I'd be really angry. And hurt."

Charlie rubbed his beard, then met my gaze. "You certainly have a right to ask all this, Darcy." He gave me a small smile. "I'm glad you did. It just confirms something about you."

"What's that?"

"You have a seeker's soul, Darcy. Like me."

"A seeker? Me?"

He smiled again. "Yes. You want to know *why*. You don't like easy answers."

I nodded. "I don't have much patience for BS. Especially now."

He chuckled. "So I won't give you any." He steepled his hands, watching me closely. "Your dad and I were very different as kids. We were both smart. But he was the popular one. The athlete and the scholar. I was the hippie." He grinned. "You probably figured that out."

I laughed softly. "Yeah."

"So when it was time for college, your dad headed off in a glorious blaze of scholarships and big dreams. I was a year behind him. After I graduated high school, instead of going to college I took some time off. I stayed in a monastery. It was a silent order, so I didn't talk for three months."

My eyes widened. "No way."

"Way." He grinned. "Then I spent some time in a Buddhist retreat center. I learned how to meditate. I still do it every day."

"Maybe I should try that," I muttered, thinking of my anxiety balloon.

"I highly recommend it," Charlie said. "What I'm trying to say is that I understand the desire to go on a quest for meaning, which is what I think your dad is doing."

I stared at Charlie for a long time. I thought of the many hours Dad and I had spent in the sacred space of our personal Stonehenge. *That I'd destroyed.* Was he trying to regain that sense of peace? Had he stopped believing in Harvest? Was he looking for a new lodestar to follow?

"But what about when I was a kid?" I asked. "All those years we never saw you? Aren't you mad at him for practically disowning you?"

Charlie took a long breath. "I forgave your dad long ago, Darcy. I've always believed that some day he and I will reconnect. I still think we will." He paused. "Especially now."

He looked at his plate. "The thing about Harvest," he said quietly, "is that I agree with most of what your dad says." He looked up and grinned at me. "Your dad and I believe many of the same things. We just have different ways of living what we believe."

That was an understatement. I thought of my dad jetting around the country and hanging out with famous people. Then I thought of Charlie hanging out behind his counter, listening to anyone's story in exchange for a donut. Charlie was the listener. My dad was the speaker. But maybe they weren't so very different underneath the surface.

"You should've been a priest," I said, taking another bite of my sandwich.

His eyebrows rose. "Almost did that," he said. "But then I ended up with the store. And I met Liz."

I thought of all the people Charlie helped, the clothes he gave away, the homeless who found warmth in his store on cold days, telling him stories for free donuts. "Your store is like your church," I said.

He reached across the table to squeeze my hand. We sat quietly, just looking at each other. Finally I picked up the ninjas and waved them between us. "I should head back to Liz's. It's time for my badass ninja self to kick some espresso butt."

Charlie laughed as he put cash on the table to pay our bill. As we left the restaurant, he wrapped his arm around my shoulders and smiled down at me. "Remember when I said you were my favorite niece?"

"And your only niece," I reminded him as we fell into step together.

He ruffled my hair. "You'd be my favorite even if I had a hundred nieces."

*M*om was already passed out in her bed when I got home close to eleven. Judging by the state of the kitchen, she'd had wine for dinner.

Toby slept next to me on the couch as I watched a rerun of *Friends*. In the middle of an episode, Mom staggered into the family room rubbing her eyes.

"What time is it?" she asked.

"Almost midnight. You never called." She stared at me glassy-eyed so I went on in the same level voice, "I had an early dinner with Charlie so I didn't cook. But there's still leftover meatloaf from last night in the fridge."

"Ugh. Disgusting. I hate meatloaf."

I glared at her. "Well, pardon me, madam chef, but it's the best I could do. And it's better than a crummy frozen dinner so I think you should thank me."

She sank into the chair across from me. She was still in her work clothes. Her slacks were wrinkled and her blouse dotted with red wine stains. "Give me a break, Darcy. I've had a long day."

I stared at her in disbelief. I could tell by the way her words slurred that she was still drunk, even after sleeping. "*You've* had a long day?" I asked. "What about me?"

"It's not the same thing. You're just a kid."

"Not anymore I'm not. Thanks to Dad." I paused. "And you."

Her eyes narrowed to slits. "Don't you dare blame me for this."

My chest heaved. "I don't blame you for Dad leaving. I don't. But I do blame you for not being around anymore." And for being drunk all the time, but I was too scared to say that out loud.

"I have to work, Darcy," she whined. "I have to do whatever Pam tells me to. The money she's paying me is the only thing keeping us going."

I took a calming breath, because I needed her onboard with the estate sale idea. I *wanted* her to act like a grown-up, to be her old self, to take some of the load off my shoulders. But maybe that was too much to ask. "That's why I called you this afternoon about selling our stuff. What do you think?"

She stared at the television for a long time, then shifted her gaze to me. "It's too much for me, Darcy. But if you're willing to do it, go ahead."

Just because it was the answer I'd expected didn't make it hurt any less. "You'll probably have to sign the contract," I told her. "I'm sure I'm too young."

She closed her eyes. "Fine. Whatever. Go ahead and set it up."

I shut off the television and went to bed without saying good night.

CHAPTER FIFTEEN
OCTOBER 29

The next day I called the first estate sale company on Charlie's list. I'd worried about it all day at school and tackled it first thing when I got home.

"Family Solutions," said a tinkling voice.

"Hi, I'm Darcy Covington. My uncle, Charlie Covington, recommended that I call you."

"Yes?" The woman on the phone was hesitant.

I tried to lower my voice so I sounded older. "My family needs to have an estate sale." I took a breath. "My mom will sign all the paperwork, but I'll be coordinating it." I tried to sound bossy, like Sal, and give her no chance to say no. "Charlie assured me that you'd be happy to work with me, with our family, but if you'd rather not, he's given me some other names to call."

"Oh, well, of course I can help." The woman sounded perkier. "Since Charlie recommended you."

"Great." I smiled into the phone. "When can you come to our house? We're moving at the end of the month so we need to do this sale right away."

"Oh my. That's tough, with a holiday next month. Let me look at my calendar." I heard the clicking of a keyboard. "My next opening is December fifth."

Crap. We had to be out by the end of November. "Is there any way you can do it sooner?"

"I'll put you on my calendar for the weekend of December fifth, but you might want to check with the other companies Charlie recommended. Call me back to let me know either way."

My little bit of optimism took a hard hit. I'd been sure this was the answer, but I should have realized a good agent would be booked far in advance. I spent the next half hour calling Charlie's other referrals, trading voicemails, and pacing the kitchen floor, my stomach getting tighter and tighter with anxiety. We were out of luck. No one had openings before the end of the year. Family Solutions was our only option.

I only needed an extra week, or two. Could I persuade the board of directors to give us a break? J.J. hadn't given us much hope, but if I went to them myself, showed them I was working on the problem...

Toby snored from the middle of the kitchen floor. I sank next to him and rubbed his stomach. "What should I do, Toblerone?"

Persuade the board to give us extra time. Make a speech

in front of all of those people who thought my dad was a criminal. Just the idea of it made me sweat.

"I don't know if I can do this," I whispered. Toby opened an eye to look at me as if wondering what I was so worried about. He had a lot more confidence in me than I did.

I needed to prepare. To practice. It was going to be like debate class, only a million times worse. "But this is different," I told Toby. "This time there's a lot more than a grade at stake. I have to win."

I arrived at Charlie's shop an hour before my shift started at Liz's, grateful to see him behind the counter. I'd brought Toby with me since I sometimes left him with Charlie or Lucas while I worked in the coffee shop.

"How'd it go?" he asked. "Did you find someone to do the estate sale?"

I nodded and grabbed a donut. "Family Solutions. The only problem is she can't fit us in before we have to move. I don't know what to do."

Charlie frowned. "Is there any way you can push back the move date?"

I stared at my lap. "Maybe," I said quietly, "if we ask the board for more time."

"Hasn't your mom asked?" Charlie asked, his voice soft with concern.

I still hadn't told my uncle about Mom's drinking, and I didn't want to now. He already worried enough about me. "I'm sure she will," I lied, knowing I was the one who had to do it. Even though I was terrified.

He frowned. "What can I do to help you, Darcy?"

I forced a smile. "Keep supplying these donuts."

He reached across the counter and squeezed my hand. I held his gaze, so grateful to be with him, yet seeing so much of my dad in him that I had to fight back tears.

Toby jumped up and raced for the door. I turned to see Lucas standing outside, laughing with Eddie from Inkheart. If I were a dog, I'd be panting at the door, too. Lucas saluted Eddie then pushed through the door. He bent down to pet Toby, then looked up and grinned. "Hey. What's up?"

"Not much." I focused on my donut. He looked exceptionally delicious today, wearing a tight, dark green thermal shirt that outlined his muscles and made his eyes look like sparkling jewels. God, I was pathetic. What was I doing, designing a romance book cover in my head?

He perched next to me on a stool and grabbed a donut. "Put it on my tab," he told Charlie, who just winked at him.

"Hey!" I pointed accusingly. "The pink ones are mine."

He raised an eyebrow, watching me intently while he licked the pink icing with his tongue. Holy hell. I turned away and gulped my water. There weren't enough ice cubes in the city to cool me down right now.

"I'm taking Toby for a walk before my shift starts," I said, sliding off my stool to avoid looking at his eyes or his mouth...or his tongue, still working on the icing.

Lucas stood up, wrapping his donut in a napkin. "I'll go with you." He glanced at Charlie as he slid the donut toward him. "Save this for me. Okay if I take my break before my shift even starts?" He grinned.

Charlie looked back and forth between us. "Go ahead," he said, a funny little smile on his face.

Toby danced around us as we headed for the door. Lucas held it open and then fell into step next to me as we walked down Broadway. My heart hammered as I tried to think of something to talk about. We always seemed to have lots to talk about in the shops, but we hadn't done this before, just the two of us.

"Truth, Darcy," he said. "How's everything going? For real."

I stumbled and he put out a hand to steady me, which didn't help since the sudden warmth of his touch made me even more klutzy.

"I'm okay," I said, once I'd figured how to walk again.

"You're lying," he said conversationally, like he'd asked me about the weather. He tossed his long dark hair out of his eyes and I swallowed, trying to maintain my composure. "You're worried about something. More than usual, I mean."

My lips parted in surprise. "How can you tell?"

He shrugged. "I just can." I gazed down at Toby, whose tail wagged at warp speed. "It might help to talk about it," Lucas said, his voice soft.

I glanced at him, startled at the intensity I saw in his eyes. I turned away, pretending to be interested in the jumble of model airplane kits in the window of the run-down hobby store.

His hand brushed mine, lacing our fingers briefly, but before I could catch my breath, he released my hand and took hold of Toby's leash. He cleared his throat. "That's what friends are for, right?"

Friends. Right. Of course. I let go of the leash, letting
Lucas take over. "Yeah," I said, my voice a little wobbly.
We walked in silence and I wondered if I'd hallucinated the
whole almost-held-my-hand thing.

"If you don't tell me what's up, I'll just ask Charlie."

I took a deep breath. Inhale calm. Exhale obsessive need
to analyze potential hand-holding event. "I found someone
to do the estate sale. Mom said she'd sign the paperwork,
but left me in charge of it all. But there's a scheduling issue."

He was quiet for a bit, but the back of his leash-free hand
brushed mine again as we walked. "When my mom left," he
finally said, "my dad kind of checked out for a while. He
spent all his time fixing his car, or working late doing repairs
for the property management company he works for." He
took a deep breath and suddenly I wanted to reach out to
squeeze his hand. But I didn't have the guts to do it. "I took
care of Pickles all the time." He turned to grin at me. "I even
changed her diapers."

"Wow." I laughed at that image. "That's what I call
brotherly love."

"Right? I'm just that awesome."

Without thinking, I shoulder-bumped him. "Shut up."
Crap. Had I actually just touched him on purpose?

"So, um, anyway." He shot me a sideways glance as he
tucked his hair behind his ear. "I guess what I'm trying to
say is, I've sort of been there. Doing the stuff parents are
supposed to do, because they can't. Or won't."

We ended up in a neighborhood park. "When did you,
I mean *how* did you get your dad to…to start functioning
again?"

He stopped, forcing Toby to stop, too. He stared down at me as we stood on a small wooden bridge, the breeze ruffling his hair, focusing on me so intently that I could hardly breathe.

"I didn't, Darcy. That's the thing. You can't make your mom change. She has to do it for herself."

I swallowed. I knew what he said was true, even though I wanted him to give me some sort of magic key that would unlock the door to my mom's closed heart.

He took a step toward me. A muscle in his jaw twitched, and the blue-green ocean color of his eyes seemed darker than usual. Then Toby spotted a squirrel and took off at full speed, yanking Lucas after him. I exhaled and grabbed the bridge railing for support as I watched Lucas run behind Toby, laughing and yelling at him to heel.

Had he almost kissed me? Or was I losing my mind?

We walked back to the shops together, talking and joking about unimportant things, the sparking tension between us gone. Maybe I'd imagined the whole thing.

I was glad to be working by myself tonight. My mind was a jumble of worries about the estate sale, anxiety about persuading the Harvest board for more time to move, punctuated by images of Lucas gazing at me on the bridge, his eyes burning with intensity.

My shift was almost over when the door swung open. A gust of bitter cold wind whooshed in along with the last person I expected to see.

"Ryan? What are you doing here?" I stared at him, stunned.

He brushed snow out of his hair and smiled at me. He wore his Burton snowboarding jacket and swung his Range Rover key on a long lanyard, looking like an ad for a ski resort.

My heart thudded, but not with excitement like it did for Lucas.

"So this is where you work, huh?" He looked around the shop. The place was empty since it was almost closing time. "Sal told me about this place."

I would kill her. Painfully.

"You want something to drink?" I asked, wondering what the heck he was doing here.

"Sure," he said. "Make me your specialty." He moved close to the counter, watching me work Bella.

"Soo," he said, drawing out the word. "I was wondering. Does your dad still have that box suite at the football stadium?"

My hand slipped on the filter holder and I almost spilled espresso grounds everywhere. Was he seriously angling for tickets? I stared at him, wondering why I'd ever thought he was hot, when he was so shallow.

"Uh, I guess," I said. "I mean, technically it's owned by his company." Unless J.J. had sold it already.

"Cool."

I handed him the finished mocha, not bothering to put whip cream and sprinkles on it. He took a sip and raised his eyebrows. "This is good."

Of course it is, I wanted to say, because I'm a kick-ass

barista. Instead I just shrugged. "Thanks." I heard the back door open and close, then familiar footsteps and the jingle of Toby's collar. Lucas stopped short when he saw Ryan.

"Hi," I said to him, willing Ryan to leave. Like *now*. Toby moved behind me, licking up crumbs from the floor.

Lucas looked between Ryan and me, his eyes narrowed. "Hi," he said, his stare settling on Ryan.

"Hi," said Ryan, oblivious to the tension crackling around him.

"Um, we're just about to close," I told Ryan, pointing to the Eiffel Tower clock that indicated 9:55.

He glanced at the clock, and then turned back to me. "Cool." He hesitated. "Do you need a ride home?"

"She drove her truck," Lucas said next to me, before I could reply.

I glanced at him, startled, but Ryan just shrugged again, still clueless. "Okay." He took another drink of his mocha. "So, uh, maybe you could let me know about the tickets. The Seahawks game is coming up. It should be awesome."

I had no words, so I just mimicked his shrug.

He took a step back. "Guess I'll head out." He glanced around the coffee shop. "It's not Starbucks, but this place is all right." He shrugged again. "Kinda run-down, but I guess it's just this neighborhood."

Lucas stiffened next to me, his hands clenching into fists. I bustled past him, store keys in hand, gesturing for Ryan to leave. "See you later," I said, practically slamming the door. I locked it and flipped the sign from OPEN to CLOSED then took a deep breath before turning around.

Lucas stood with his arms crossed, glaring at me. I flicked

off the main lights, which only made him look scarier, like a gorgeous, angry statue bathed in the soft lights behind the counter.

"Who was that?" He bit out the words.

"Just some guy from school." I busied myself picking up empty coffee mugs and plates, but nervous energy jangled through me, making me clumsier than usual.

"Is he…" Lucas's voice trailed away, then he cleared his throat. "Are you…dating him?"

The tray of empty mugs wobbled as I glanced at him. His hands were in his pockets now, but he still looked angry. Or maybe not angry, exactly, but…something. Something not happy.

"Uh, no. He's just…" I could hardly say Ryan was a friend, since he only showed up when he wanted a favor. He still had never asked me how I was doing. Not even once. Not to mention, "just friends" was what I always said about Lucas, and what I had with him was special, in its own way.

"Just what?" Lucas prompted, his voice low.

I set the tray on a table and looked at him. "Just a guy who has no clue about what's really going on in my life."

Lucas crossed his arms again, still watching me. "So what was he doing here? Besides insulting Liz's shop and my neighborhood?"

Ouch.

I picked up the tray and walked toward him slowly, my gazde on the floor so I didn't trip again. "He wanted something from me."

Lucas reached out and took the tray from me, his fingers brushing mine and zapping me like they always did. "What did he want?"

I turned away to wipe down the counter. "My dad's company has a box suite at the football stadium. Ryan wanted tickets to the Seahawks game." I tried to force a laugh. "At least, they used to have a box. J.J.'s probably selling it. Like he's selling our house."

The tray slammed down, sending cups and plates clattering. I whirled to look at him. He bent over the counter, picking up the spilled cups, his hair hiding his face.

"Are you okay, Lucas?" I didn't know what was happening, or understand the energy rolling off of him in waves. I could practically reach out and touch it.

He ignored me as he washed dishes in the sink.

"I used to think I was in love with him," I said, surprised by my confession. "If you can believe it."

Lucas stilled, then straightened and turned to look at me. "I can believe it. Girls are suckers for a pretty face."

"You would know." Oh my God. I'd said that out loud. And I couldn't take it back.

He watched me silently, waiting. I turned back to the counter, scrubbing hard, wishing I could erase my words the way I erased the coffee stains.

"But you're over him," Lucas said from behind me.

I nodded, but didn't turn around. "There's not much to be over," I muttered. "He never really knew me. And he's not very...aware of what other people are going through."

Unlike you, I wanted to say, but this time I kept my mouth shut.

We cleaned up and avoided eye contact. After I closed out the register and hid the cashbox in Ft. Knox Fairyland,

we left together. Lucas waited while I locked the alley door,
Toby nudging his hand for petting.

I really wished for a light in the alley tonight, because
the dark made me want to walk closer to Lucas. But I didn't.

He held the truck door open while Toby jumped inside
and I climbed in after him. I started the Reaper and Lucas
closed the door, then gestured for me to roll down the
window.

"Sorry," he said. "I didn't mean to be a jerk earlier. But
that guy…" He shrugged and turned to look down the dark
alley.

"It's okay." I swallowed over the lump in my throat.
Where had that come from? I reached over to pet Toby.
"Thanks for the walk today. For telling me about your dad."

"I'm always here for you, Darcy." His voice was quiet.
"Whatever you need."

I nodded, unsure of how to reply.

He stepped away from the truck, pulling up the collar
of his leather jacket against the wind. "See you later, Shaker
Girl."

Then he turned and walked away, disappearing into the
darkness.

When I got home, I found Dad's latest postcard on the
kitchen counter.

This one was from New Mexico with only the state flag
on the front. He hadn't written a single word on the back.
Instead he'd sketched a man sitting cross-legged on the

ground. All around him swirled images of angry faces. The man's eyes were closed and a single tear rolled down his face.

The drawing worried me more than anything that had happened so far. Was this how my dad felt? What made him run away?

I thought of Lucas, telling me he was there for me. I had the urge to call him, to share this latest burden with someone I knew would listen.

But instead, I trudged slowly up the stairs and collapsed on my bed, closing my eyes and praying for sleep.

CHAPTER SIXTEEN
NOVEMBER 4

I'd been to the Harvest offices many times before, but never by myself. Dad's personal parking spot in the underground lot was empty. I pulled the rumbling truck into it, grinning at the idea of J.J.'s face if he saw this crappy truck where Dad's BMW usually parked.

I was halfway across the lot before a voice stopped me.

"Young lady? You can't park there."

I turned around to face Don, the security guard who'd known me since I was a little kid.

His eyes widened as he recognized me. "Darcy? What are you doing here? Shouldn't you be at school?"

Great, my own personal truant officer. I hesitated. "I have a message, for J.J. and the board."

Don shook his head, his gaze softening. "I sure do miss

your daddy. I hear all kinds of rumors about him." He narrowed his eyes. "And I don't believe any of that crap on the internet about him ruining the company. Your daddy ain't that type."

Some of the tension eased out of me. "Thanks, Don. That means a lot." I adjusted the messenger bag slung across my body. "I need to get in there before I chicken out." I glanced at the silver Jaguar in J.J.'s parking spot.

Don followed my gaze and grimaced. "You want me to back you up?" He slapped his hip. "They don't let me pack more heat than a Taser, but it could come in handy up there." He grinned at me.

I laughed. It would be nice to have a semi-armed sidekick, but I had to do this on my own. "Thanks for the offer, but I'm good." I took a few steps away, then turned back. "If I have to make a fast getaway, you can keep the dogs off of me."

Don laughed and raised his hand in a mock salute.

I pushed through the steel door and waited at the bank of elevators. Breathe. Inhale calm. Exhale stress. All I was asking for was time, not money.

When the elevator opened onto the penthouse suite, Dad's secretary looked up. She looked even more shocked than Don. "Darcy?" she whispered, then glanced over her shoulder to the long row of offices behind her. "What are you doing here?" Mrs. Hamilton looked like a scary high school principal, but she was as sweet as cotton candy.

"I need to see J.J and the board," I said. "I'm guessing they're meeting? Freaking out about my dad?" I knew Dad always had board meetings on Tuesday mornings, and hoped the day hadn't changed. I hadn't even thought twice about ditching school to do this. I looked down the hallway toward the conference room and swallowed hard.

"Yes. In fact the whole board is in there right now," she said, watching me warily.

Dreams die every day because people are afraid to take the first step. Dad's words propelled me to take one step, then two.

Just do this, I told myself. Don't stop. Don't think. Just do.

"Darcy, wait!" Mrs. Hamilton called after me, but I didn't stop.

Photographs lined the walls—enormous framed photos of my dad with athletes, rock stars, and internet millionaires— brass plaques attached with quotes from the clients. *"I owe my success to Ty's philosophy." "Tri!Umphant! Harvest turned me from a star into a superstar."* And on and on.

The conference room door was closed, but I heard yelling on the other side. I closed my eyes, imagining Dad's face. I pictured him coming home, enveloping Mom and me in bear hugs. Visualized him standing here instead of me, throwing open the door, confronting J.J. and the board. Telling them it was all a mistake. Demanding apologies. Firing J.J.

My hand shook as I reached for the doorknob, but I tried to channel some of Dad's strength. What did I have to lose? We were already losing everything.

I opened the door.

The voices stopped. A sea of unknown faces stared at me, some of them openmouthed.

"Darcy, what are you doing here?" asked J.J., the only person I recognized.

An older woman sitting at the head of the table spoke. "You're Darcy Covington? Tyler's daughter?" She glared at me from behind enormous eyeglasses.

I nodded. My courage was fading fast.

"What do you want?" Her voice was like steel.

I swallowed over the lump in my throat. "One week. No, make that two weeks."

She frowned at me. The others gathered around the table whispered to each other, darting looks at me. "Two weeks?" she asked. "Two weeks of what?"

"Time," I said. *Breathe.* "We need two more weeks to move. Two weeks beyond what you've given us as the eviction date."

The whispers grew louder.

"Darcy, you shouldn't have come here." J.J.'s voice was low and closer than I expected.

I turned toward him. "Why not, J.J.? You wouldn't listen to us. What else could I do?" I turned to the woman who'd spoken, since she looked like she was in charge. "You're taking everything from us. We don't have any money. Now we're losing our home. Selling everything. Don't you people have any heart?" I looked around the table. No one spoke.

"My dad built this place!" I flung out my arms. "If it weren't for him, Harvest wouldn't exist. None of you would be on this board. Don't you owe us some compassion?"

"We don't owe you anything, Darcy." J.J.'s voice was soft but dangerous.

Suddenly everyone was talking and yelling, gesturing

and pointing.

"Silence!" The woman banged her hand on the table. Everyone turned to look at her. "Is this true, J.J.? Mrs. Covington asked for more time to move?"

J.J. blanched but said nothing.

I glared at him, furious, then turned back to the woman. "Yes," I said. "It's true. But J.J. told my mom he couldn't do anything about that. He said it was a board decision." I took another breath. "That's why I'm here. To ask you to…to… please reconsider."

The woman lowered her glasses on her nose, looking at me, then at J.J. "Based on everything else we've heard from you today, J.J., I'm inclined to believe this young lady."

The whispering started again, but the woman held up her hand to silence it. "It seems the least we can do is give them more time to move." Her eyes pierced mine. "God knows they've suffered enough already." Her gaze swept the table. "I move to amend the eviction notice to allow the Covington family an additional month to vacate the house."

An extra month? My knees threatened to buckle with relief, but I forced myself to stand straighter.

"I second the motion," a voice called from the far end of the table.

My imperious savior scanned the board members, her eyes narrow behind her glasses. "All in favor?" A chorus of ayes filled the room but J.J. stayed silent.

"Very well, Miss Covington. The attorneys will amend the paperwork and messenger it to your mother."

I nodded, swallowing tears. "Thank you," I mumbled, not trusting myself to say more.

Her eyes fixed on mine. "I wish we could do more. But we have stockholders to answer to." She gestured to the door. "We need to resume our meeting now."

As I backed toward the door, I forced a grateful smile to those sitting closest to me. A few smiled in return, but most sat as still as statues. As I turned the doorknob, the woman's voice stopped me. "Miss Covington."

I met her eyes.

"Your father would be proud of you." She paused. "Very proud." She pushed her glasses up her nose. "That's all." She nodded and returned her attention to the stack of papers in front of her.

I left the room, closing the door behind me, and floated down the hallway, feeling disembodied. Mrs. Hamilton waited at her desk, her hands twisting nervously. "Darcy, what happened?"

I gave her a thumbs-up as I continued floating toward the elevators.

She frowned. "What does that mean?"

"It means I got what I came for."

The elevator door swooshed open and I stepped inside. Maybe I'd inherited some of Tri Ty's DNA, after all.

*M*om and I ate tacos while watching *American Idol.* I was usually working when it was on, so I recorded it to watch late at night. It was a perfect distraction from our family's disaster, watching other people bomb on national TV. The tacos were pretty good, too. I'd even splurged on a couple of out-of-season avocados and made us guacamole to celebrate. I hadn't told Mom the good news yet. I was waiting to see how much she'd drink. So far she'd only had one glass of wine, so I decided now was as good a time as any.

"So," I said casually, "I got the Harvest board to agree to an extra month. We have until the end of December to move out. You'll get new paperwork from the attorneys. So this means we can have the estate sale, then we'll have plenty of time to sort through what's left. We can move what we want to keep. The rest can go to charity." I took a bite of taco. "It will give us more time to find a new place to live, too."

Mom gaped at me. "You what? How in the world?" She still looked like hell. Rumpled. Wrinkled. Exhausted.

"I went to the office today and sort of crashed a board meeting." I grinned. "I didn't have an appointment, but they didn't turn me away."

Mom's mouth dropped open. "Oh my God. Darcy. You shouldn't have done that."

I stiffened. "Why not? Were *you* going to ask them?"

Mom lowered her eyes. "No, I wasn't. But you shouldn't have gone down there. J.J. is so angry at your father. Everyone at Harvest is."

I thought of Don the security guard, and Mrs. Hamilton. And the lady with glasses who'd given us the extra time. "Not everyone is," I said.

She fell back against the couch cushions. "I'm amazed they agreed to that." She looked at me. "What about J.J.? When I call to ask if he's heard from your dad, he's always so difficult over the phone."

"Well, fortunately the decision was put to the board, and J.J. was outvoted." I smiled at her, but she just shook her head.

"Sometimes you remind me a lot of your father."

"Really?"

She nodded as she bit into a taco.

This was the first conversation in a long time where she was mostly sober. I decided to take advantage of it. "Mom?" She watched me, eyebrows raised expectantly, and I went on. "I've been thinking about Dad. About how at first I couldn't believe he just…just left us. But I've been remembering stuff. Like over the summer when he missed an appearance in Salt Lake. Remember that?"

Mom put down her taco. She nodded, wiping her hands on her napkin. "He said he had a really bad stomach bug."

"But I read some stuff online, from over the summer. People who went to his shows said he didn't seem like himself." Mom didn't say anything so I pressed on. "And he'd been sleeping a lot. There were some days he didn't get out of bed until dinner time."

He'd told us he was just exhausted from work and travel, but it had been completely unlike him. Dad was invincible, so I'd taken his word that he was okay, but I'd been thinking about all of this when I lay awake at night, trying to put the pieces together.

"I should have done something," Mom said, her voice barely a whisper. "Called his doctor. Asked J.J. for help. But I wanted to believe him when he said he was just tired from working too much."

We sat in silence, focusing on the tuneless girl on TV. It

hadn't occurred to me that Mom might be feeling as guilty as I did about missing the clues. But I couldn't shut down. I'd learned that about myself. I was learning that I could make things happen. People listened to me. They helped when I asked them to, like Charlie and Lucas. They even changed their minds, like today at the board meeting.

"The estate sale lady is coming tomorrow at four," I reminded Mom. "Can you be here?"

Mom ran a hand across her eyes. "I don't think so. I'm working on a special project for Pam. On the computer." Mom lowered her eyes. "I get the feeling she doesn't want me meeting with clients right now. I can't blame her." She raised her eyes, pooled with tears.

"Oh, Mom." I pushed aside my TV tray and scooted closer to her on the couch. I held her hand. "Pam's an evil bitch. So is her daughter Chloe."

Mom laughed. "Maybe so, but she's paying me right now so I have to do what she asks."

I sighed. "Can't you find a better job, Mom? Someplace where you're not treated like a slave?"

Mom leaned against me. "It's been so long since I've worked, Darcy. I don't have many marketable skills."

"You have lots of skills, Mom. You just can't recognize them right now."

She laughed. "You're my daughter so you have to say that." She squeezed my hand. "Maybe after we get moved I'll look for something else."

I wanted to believe her. "I almost forgot," I said, anxious to change the subject. "I'm going to look at apartments soon with Lucas. Do you want to come with us?"

Lucas had texted me during school to say he'd found several places that fit our criteria. He'd also sent me a photo of a *Toy Story* salt and pepper shaker set: Woody and Buzz Lightyear. *"Yes or no?"* he'd texted.

"Yes," I'd replied, grinning at my phone until Sal kicked my foot so I didn't get busted texting in class.

Mom shook her head. "I'm doing open houses the next few Saturdays."

"I thought you said Pam didn't want you meeting potential clients."

"These are foreclosures. I don't think she cares who sees me there."

So it would just be Lucas and me. Together. I bit my lip. No big deal. He was helping me as a friend. Sal's skeptical face loomed in my mind, but I shook my head to get rid of the image. I didn't have time for wishful daydreams. We had to get ready for the estate sale, pack, find a place, and move. Plus school, which I wasn't focusing much energy on. At all.

The guidance counselor had called me into her office a few days ago to tell me she'd met with my teachers and because of my "situation" I was being given a reduced workload for now. That was a relief, but I didn't care about my grades as long as I passed. I knew my Ivy League dreams were dust, but I didn't want to give up on the idea of college completely.

We watched the rest of *American Idol*, and Mom even laughed out loud a few times at some of the contestants. Reality television had its uses.

Sal called me just as Toby and I were drifting off to sleep.

"What's up?" I mumbled.

"Just checking on you. How's everything going?"

I expelled a sigh of relief. "Better, believe it or not. We've got some extra time to move."

"That's great. How'd that happen?"

I smiled into the phone. "I asked. And I received."

She was silent for a few moments. "That's awesome, Darcy. Good for you."

"Thanks." Pride washed over me again, a pinprick of daylight in my darkened state of mind. "So anyway, I'm going to be busy getting everything ready. I hope you aren't calling to invite me to a party, 'cause you know I can't come."

"I know how busy you'll be," Sal said. "That's why I'm calling. Mark and I want to help with the move. You've seen those muscles of his. He can lift anything." She giggled. "And I can help pack. Provide moral support. You just let us know when and where, okay?"

My eyes misted. "Thanks, soul sister. You dress like a train wreck, but you have some redeeming qualities."

"And you need a makeover and a boy toy, but we'll deal with that later."

"G'night, DQ."

"G'night, Darce."

Sometimes your garden surprises you. Dad's voice was strong and clear in my mind as I snuggled under the covers. *You don't remember planting strawberries or mint, but there it is, rising up in the middle of the carrot patch. Maybe the seeds blew in from the neighbor's garden. Or maybe they were buried in the dirt and you unearthed them when you tilled the soil. Or maybe you're reaping what you've sown. However it happened, you now have unexpected bounty. Accept it with gratitude.*

CHAPTER SEVENTEEN
NOVEMBER 6

*C*hloe pushed against me in the hall. Hard. My books tumbled to the floor.

"I don't have time for this, Chloe," I said as I knelt to gather my books. "Don't you have somewhere to be? Isn't Satan lonely without you?"

"You're the one who can go to hell, Darcy," she said. "I don't know what Ryan ever saw in you."

Nothing, other than a potential stadium suite ticket. But I didn't care. That crush was part of my past. Even if Ryan didn't see anything special in me, I was starting to see myself differently. I saw myself standing in the boardroom as J.J. must have, eyes flashing with determination. I saw myself laughing and joking with customers in the coffee shop. I saw myself making dinner for Mom and me, even on late nights when she was already drunk when I got home from work.

It didn't matter what anyone else saw in me. For the first time, I felt like I was seeing myself.

My teachers were sympathetic, all of them telling me some version of the guidance counselor's story. I could make up my homework later. Or skip some of it entirely. My academic track record made them willing to accommodate me, but I didn't want special treatment.

Chloe backed off, making me wonder if I should've stood up to her a long time ago. I fought a smile and plowed through the rest of my classes.

Sal caught up with me after school. "What's on the agenda today?"

"Meeting with the estate sale lady," I answered.

"Sounds scary. Do you want company?"

"Thanks, but I'll manage."

Sal grinned. "She's large and in charge, that's my Darcy."

"I am not large."

"It's a metaphor."

I laughed. "I know. But as much sugar as I'm eating lately, sometimes I worry."

She rolled her eyes. "Please. You look great." She narrowed her eyes. "Actually you do. You're almost glowing." Shock filled her face. "God, you aren't pregnant, are you? You haven't hooked up with Lucas and not told me?"

I gaped at her. "Absolutely not. My God, Sal, how many times do I have to tell you—"

"Yeah, yeah, you're just friends." She frowned at me. "So why are you glowing like a fire goddess?"

I laughed. "Maybe I am on fire. It feels that way. There's

so much to do, and I need to do most of it. But I have all this energy just bursting inside of me." I bit my lip. "It's a good thing I do have all this energy. Mom is just…overwhelmed."

"She's still drinking too much?"

Leave it to Sal to cut through the bullshit. "Yeah. Not always. But most of the time."

Sal looked worried. "Maybe she needs professional help."

"Maybe." I hoped I wasn't making excuses for her, but I wanted to see what happened when we were more secure. "I think she's just doing it to cope. It's not the best choice. But I'm hoping once we're moved. Once Dad comes back…"

Sal blinked in surprise. "Have you heard from him?"

I shrugged. "Another postcard. Cryptic as usual. This one was from Georgia."

"Georgia?"

"Who knows?" I'd plotted this one on the map, too. The stones were called the Georgia Guidestones. One of the stones was engraved with ten New Age-y guidelines. Dad had circled the last one: *"Be not a cancer on the earth— Leave room for nature."* And he'd only signed his name, nothing else.

I thought about telling Sal about my map, but after my mom and J.J.'s reaction, I wasn't sure I wanted anyone else's opinion on my theory about Dad's clonehenge quest. Except, maybe I could tell Lucas. I had a feeling he'd listen.

"Well, call me later," said Sal. "I've got to get to rehearsal."

"Break a leg."

She frowned. "You don't say that before rehearsal.

You're supposed to tell me to bomb."

"Theater people are so weird."

She tossed her hair out of her eyes. "Whatever. Are you working Friday night?"

"Yep. Liz texted me today to see if I can close up. She has plans with Charlie. Wanna come by for coffee?"

"Yeah, I'll stop by on my way to Derek's party."

"Hope rehearsal sucks!" I laughed, waving as I ran to catch the bus.

*M*s. Hetherington from Family Solutions stood in our foyer and looked around with wide eyes. "This is Tyler Covington's home? I didn't make the connection that Charlie is his brother."

"Yes," I said simply. "I'm Ty's daughter."

She tilted her head. "I've followed the news. So he's not coming back?"

I swallowed. "He is. Eventually. In the meantime, we need to move. And we need cash. Lots of it." There was no sense beating around the bush. This was her business and I needed—we needed—as much money as we could get.

"I do wish your mother was home."

"She's working. But I promise she'll sign the contract. She wants this done."

Ms. Hetherington nodded. "Then let's get to it."

We spent two hours walking through our house, talking about every item we owned, Toby trailing at our heels. She wanted to know the names of the artists whose work Mom collected. Fortunately Mom kept a careful journal with that information. Ms. Hetherington's eyebrows raised as she flipped through it. "We may be better off working through some art dealers I know."

"Fine," I agreed.

"Your mom doesn't want to keep any of it?"

"We've kept a few things aside. They're in the master bedroom." I'd had to force Mom to make those decisions, plying her with coffee and dragging her to each room in the house to tell me what she wanted to keep and what could go.

Ms. Hetherington nodded and made notes on her clipboard. "We'll need to put stickers on everything you want to keep," she told me as we stood in the kitchen. "I'll have my crew with me to price everything. We'll come the Tuesday before the sale. It will take us a good three days to price it all and display it properly. The sale will start on Friday and go through Sunday." She eyed me, businesslike but kind. "It's probably best if you and your mother aren't here. It can be…difficult…to watch strangers haggle over your things. To see them carted away."

I swallowed. "If you think that's best."

"I do."

She prepared the contract while I made us tea. It seemed appropriate somehow. I felt like a character in one of my regency novels, at the whim of strangers who controlled my "estate."

"Because I know your uncle so well I'm trusting that your mother's signature will be authentic." Ms. Hetherington eyed me over the teacup.

I blushed. I had thought of forging it, but there was no need. Mom would sign. "It will be. Should I fax it to you?"

"That will work temporarily, but I'll need the original when we come to get things ready." We shook hands and said good-bye.

I sank onto the foyer floor after closing the front door. Toby plopped down next to me. "We did it, Toby." We lay on the cool tiles, just breathing. Once my heart stopped racing and my breathing calmed, I sat up. "We deserve a reward." Toby panted in agreement. I headed for the freezer, intent on ice cream, but I veered toward the garage instead. I grabbed Toby's leash from the hook. He danced with excitement.

We ran awkwardly at first. I'd gone too long between runs. My breathing was ragged, but I pushed through. My body protested but eventually settled into a familiar groove. "Better than ice cream," I said to the stars winking above us. Sometimes I hated how early it got dark in the winter, but as we jogged through our neighborhood, the blanket of stars above us felt familiar and comforting. Toby jogged alongside me, his dog grin splitting his face.

And it *was* much better than ice cream.

CHAPTER EIGHTEEN
NOVEMBER 7

*S*al came by Liz's on Friday night, true to her word. I'd just made her a triple-shot mocha with extra whip cream when the door opened and everything switched to slow motion.

It was like a scene from a movie. Everyone in the coffee shop turned to the door. How could they not? Lucas and Heather belonged on the big screen, though 3D IMAX could hardly do them justice. He was stunning in his tux. She'd cause car crashes in her strapless red dress and stiletto heels. They stood just inside the doorway, talking to some regular customers who'd recognized Lucas.

"Who the hell is that?" Sal whispered. She'd visited me at Liz's before, but never when Lucas was around. I'd described him to her, but obviously I hadn't done him justice.

My heart felt shattered as I watched him put his hand

on Heather's lower back, steering her into the shop. That day we'd walked together, when he'd almost held my hand, I must've been imagining the connection. I'd definitely hallucinated the part about him wanting to kiss me on the bridge.

I leaned in close so only Sal could hear me. "That's Lucas. And she's the reason he'll never look twice at someone like me. Her name is Heather."

Sal turned to me, her eyes huge. "That's Lucas? Holy shizballs, girl. No wonder you're spending all your time here."

I blushed. "Shut it, DQ."

Liz flitted around the cover model couple, forcing them to pose while she snapped photos. I'd wondered why she hadn't left for the concert when I arrived. I busied myself washing clean cups, trying not to stare, while my heart shattered even more.

Sal leaned over the counter, talking under her breath. "Darcy, honey, when it's time for you to finally pick your boy toy, he's the one."

"Shut up," I hissed.

"Oh, come on, sweetie. He's unbelievable. I didn't know they made them like that in this neighborhood or I would've moved here years ago."

"You're obnoxious."

"Yet still you love me."

I threw a towel at her just as Lucas and Heather approached us. Sal dodged the towel, which hit Lucas in the chest. Just kill me now. I was already dying inside anyway. "Sorry, Lucas," I muttered, mortified.

He bent down to retrieve the towel, and then tossed it to me, a tense smile on his movie star face. I stuffed the towel in the hamper under the sink as Heather watched us, annoyance wrinkling her tiny, perfect nose.

"Darcy, you remember Heather," he said, his jaw tight as he inclined his head toward her.

I wiped my hands on my apron. "You look amazing," I said to Heather, forcing a smile. I glanced at Lucas. "You both do." Lucas ducked his head and I thought I saw his neck redden slightly, but Heather nodded, as if I'd only stated the obvious.

"I didn't think you were working tonight," Lucas said, looking up, his brow furrowed.

I cleared my throat, noticing that Heather was antsy, obviously ready to leave. "It was last minute. Liz asked me to close up so she can leave early for a concert with Charlie."

He raised his eyebrows. "Closing solo?"

"Sure." I forced a smile I didn't feel. "I'll be fine. I know where the first aid kit is."

His answering smile looked forced, too. I missed his easy, sexy grin. Heather tugged on his arm. "We should get going, Luke. Our reservations are at seven thirty." Luke? I'd never heard anyone call him that, unless I counted Pickles calling him Lukie.

Lucas glanced curiously at Sal, who'd been watching our exchange intently.

"Sorry," I said. "Forgot my manners. This is my friend Salena. Salena, this is Lucas."

I paused. "And this is Heather."

"Call me Sal," she said, offering her hand to Lucas,

batting her eyelashes while ignoring Heather. Heather's eyes narrowed. "So is this just a regular Friday look for you two?" Sal asked.

Lucas laughed nervously. Heather didn't. "It's, uh, Homecoming," he said, turning away from me to face Sal. "We're on our way to dinner." He glanced over his shoulder at me. "I told Charlie and Liz we'd stop by. Photo op. They insisted."

I nodded. "They would."

Sal tapped a finger on her chin. "No offense, Lucas, but you look a tad old to be a high school dance escort."

His eyes widened, then he laughed. "You think they won't let me in? I graduated from Sky Ridge two years ago."

"I'm a senior at Sky Ridge High," Heather piped up. "Luke and I met last summer." She looked up at him, dreamy-eyed.

Liz rushed back into the store, an out-of-breath Charlie trailing behind her. "Oh, thank goodness you're still here. I ran next door to borrow Charlie's video camera."

"Looks like you borrowed Charlie, too," I said. Liz bopped around like Lucas was her son.

Lucas briefly closed his eyes, looking embarrassed as Charlie zoomed in on him with the camera. "You guys are too much." His voice sounded strained.

Heather giggled. "I want copies of the video." Behind her, Sal stuck a finger down her throat, pretending to puke.

One of the knitting ladies circled around the paparazzi hubbub and asked me for a latte. I was never so happy to wait on someone in my life.

"Have fun tonight," I heard Charlie say over all the

chattering. "You can party all night, Lucas. You've got the day off tomorrow."

I tried not to imagine Lucas spending all night with Heather. They finally left, Heather waving to everyone like she was on top of a float. Lucas looked distracted, nodding a curt good-bye to Liz and Charlie, not even looking my way as the door closed behind them.

Sal turned to me, looking like the Cheshire cat. "My, my. How very interesting."

My heart ricocheted wildly in my chest. Lucas thought of us as friends. But seeing him with Heather made me realize how much I cared. How much I wanted something more.

Give it up, Darcy. It doesn't matter how much you want it.

Guys like Lucas were destined for girls like Heather. It was an unwritten law of the universe.

"Don't you have a party to go to?" I slammed coffee mugs into the sink.

Sal shrugged. "I do. But I'm glad I didn't miss all that drama."

Liz joined us at the counter, bubbling like a shaken-up soda can. "Weren't they something? My goodness, she was so beautiful. And Lucas…" Her voice trailed away as she looked at me. She cleared her throat and some of the fizz went out of her voice. "Darcy, thanks so much for closing up tonight. Charlie and I are so appreciative."

I nodded, not trusting myself to speak. I imagined Liz and Sal examining me like a lab specimen, wondering how the sight of Lucas and Heather together had affected me. I couldn't let them know how much it had.

"It's fine," I told Liz. "I'm happy to do it." I forced a

smile even as my eyes brimmed with tears. "Not like *I* had a big date tonight." Sal stared at me, sudden realization dawning in her eyes. I dropped my gaze.

Liz squeezed my shoulders. "You sure you're okay by yourself tonight?"

I nodded, willing the tears to dry before they fell. I had to keep it together.

Liz said good-bye to Sal and her regulars, the fizz bubbling up in her again as she left the store, encompassing all of us in her good-bye wave. Why was that type of wave endearing from her but annoying as hell from Heather?

"You really should go," I told Sal, not looking at her. "I know your drama posse is expecting you." I knelt down and busied myself under the sink, wiping away tears while I pretended to look for something.

"I know when I'm not wanted," Sal said. "And I also know what you're hiding from, Darcy."

I stayed on my knees, refusing to look at her.

"It doesn't work, you know. Denying your feelings. Especially for you. Your heart is huge."

I looked up at her in surprise.

"It's why we're friends." She shrugged. "You have an enormous heart, but you keep it hidden. Because you're afraid of it getting broken." She glanced at the door as if she were looking for someone. "I see it, Darcy. I always have, because you let me." She took a deep breath. "But I think…I think maybe he sees it, too."

My knees popped and cracked in protest as I stood up. "What are you talking about?"

"Just a feeling I have." She wiggled her eyebrows. "I'm

very sensitive to male energy. And Lucas's energy was whacked out tonight."

I walked around her to shove tea into the tea racks. "Whatever, Sal. Lucas and I are friends." I sounded like a glitching MP3 track. "He was just nervous with everybody making such a big deal with the photos and video." It was true that I'd never seen him act so weird. So distracted. He must really like Heather. Maybe he even loved her.

Ugh.

I had to bury my feelings for him. I didn't know how, but I had to figure out a way.

Sal nodded at my excuse. "Maybe. Maybe not."

"You really need—"

"—to go," she finished, grinning. "I am, right now." She hugged me good-bye and was out the door.

Whatever energy had been keeping me upright faded away. I sat down at one of the tables and rested my head in my hands. What was that prayer about accepting things we couldn't change? There was so much in my life right now I couldn't change.

Lucas saw me, all right. As a friend. So what if we liked the same music? So what if our walks with Toby had become a regular thing now? So what if I'd finally told him about my map, and about the henge at our cabin? So what if he hadn't made fun of me or dismissed my ideas, but had listened and asked questions?

So what if we couldn't stop laughing when we redid Charlie's store window, with Pickles' help, arranging the squirrels into a ridiculous Christmas morning scene, complete with coal-stuffed stockings? That was nothing compared to how he was with Heather tonight. She was so incredible he couldn't even relax around her. I definitely didn't impact him like that.

It was time to put my feelings for him in the same place with all my other impossible dreams, like Dad coming home to rescue us and Harvest, like Mom snapping out of it and becoming herself again. Like life going back to what it used to be.

I could make some things happen, like getting the board to extend our moving date, but making someone fall in love with me? That wasn't something I could control.

Love was mysterious that way, surprising us when we least expected it. And I did love Lucas, I realized that now. But I'd keep that secret safe inside me, next to all my other impossible dreams.

CHAPTER NINETEEN
NOVEMBER 9

The Grim Reaper belched blue smoke as I drove to Charlie's early Sunday morning to pick up moving boxes. My chest tightened when I saw Lucas's car in the alley. What was he doing here? Shouldn't he be home recovering from his wild dance party weekend? I pushed away images of him entwined with Heather. Unlike Lucas, I hadn't had a wild weekend. I'd drowned my sorrows in ice cream and a weepy old movie, *The Way We Were*, one of the best doomed romances of all time.

Charlie had given me a key to his store and I went in through the back, heading straight for the storeroom to avoid Lucas. But he was already there, stacking and shoving things around with a vengeance. His hair was messy, like he hadn't bothered to shower. Maybe he hadn't. Maybe he'd spent the past thirty-six hours with Heather.

He whirled to face me, his face tensing when he saw me. "What are you doing here?"

He sounded so angry that I took a step backward. "I, uh, I came for boxes. I just—" I took a breath to calm myself. I didn't know what he was mad about, but whatever it was, I had a right to be here, too. "We're starting to pack. And we need more boxes."

He held my gaze then looked away. "Of course." His voice was rough. "I can help you break some down."

I walked toward the stack of cardboard in the corner of the room. "That's okay," I said. "It looks like you have other stuff to do."

He appeared next to me and took a box from the stack. Our eyes met, then we both looked away. He still looked furious, but I had no idea why.

I picked up an X-acto knife from the table and sliced through the packing tape holding the box together. It was going to be a long morning if he stayed there with me. "Do you want some coffee?" Liz wouldn't be opening the store for another couple of hours, but I knew she wouldn't mind if I let myself in and made us drinks. Maybe caffeine would improve his mood.

He shrugged. "Maybe. I don't know." He focused on the box, not looking at me.

What was his damage?

I finished disassembling the box, then collapsed it and started a pile. I'd tape them back together at home. As I sliced through the tape on another box, I wondered what I could say to shake Lucas out of his black mood. I thought of the movie I'd watched last night.

"'Your girl is lovely, Hubbell,'" I quoted.

He looked up from the collapsed box he was folding. "Who's Hubbell?"

"It's a quote from a movie. One of my favorites."

"What movie?" He wasn't smiling yet, but he didn't look quite as angry.

"Just google what I said. You'll find it."

"Why not just give me a straight answer?" He frowned and grabbed another box, dismantling it with more energy than necessary.

"Maybe you bring out the worst in me," I teased. Almost there. I'd get him laughing any minute.

"Whatever," he said. "I know you're bringing out the worst in me this morning."

I didn't know what to say to that. Surprised and hurt, I turned away and focused on another box.

He sighed behind me. "Sorry, Darcy. I'm just…tired. So tell me, what's the point of your obscure movie quote?"

I turned to face him. Was he dense or what? "'Your girl is lovely.' As in, Heather, your girl, is lovely. Spectacular, in fact. You two must have made quite an entrance Friday night." If this friendship thing was going to work, I had to get comfortable talking about his girlfriend, even as my heart broke just saying her name.

Lucas sighed again and brushed his hair out of his eyes. I'd never seen him like this…wrinkled and disheveled and unshaven. I didn't think it was possible he could look even sexier than usual.

"I don't really know what to say to that," he said. "It's

not like I had anything to do with her looks." He took the collapsed box I was holding and tossed it on the stack.

I struggled for a funny comeback but didn't have one, so I spoke my thoughts aloud. "Most guys can only dream of dating someone like Heather. I was paying you a compliment." I shrugged. "Never mind."

Lucas grabbed another box and sliced through the tape as if it were his worst enemy. "Most guys aim too low," he said, so softly I thought maybe he was talking to himself. Then he looked right at me. "Girls like Heather are a dime a dozen."

I choked out a laugh. "Dime a dozen? Where are you shopping, dude?"

He grabbed his water bottle off a shelf and took a long swig. I watched his Adam's apple bob up and down, hypnotized. He capped the bottle and leaned against the wall, arms crossed over his chest. "Anyway, she's not *my girl*."

I almost sliced right through my finger. I dropped my gaze, focusing very carefully on my cutting. I didn't dare ask what I wanted most to know. I had to think of something else to say.

"She's not? Maybe you should let Pickles know. I don't think she's a fan."

Finally he graced me with a laugh. "Pickles has way too many opinions about my personal life. I don't need to give her any more ammo."

Some of the tension eased between us. At least it eased out of him and I hoped I faked it.

"Just wait 'til Pickles is older," I said, taking advantage of the lightened mood. "She won't approve of anyone you bring home. Ever."

He threw a flattened box onto the growing pile. "You never know. She might."

I was dying to know about Heather. This time the words blundered from me before I could stop them. "So…if she's not your girl, then Homecoming was…?" The question hung in the air for an eternity.

"What those dances always are. Homecoming, prom, all that crap. Overpriced dinner. Dirty dancing. Drunken puking all over my tux and my car."

"Oh," I breathed. "I'm sorry, Lucas. That sucks."

He loomed over me, his expression impossible to read. But any echo of laughter was gone, thanks to my inquisition. Why did I always talk too much around him? His hand grazed mine as he took the box I'd forgotten I was holding. He sliced into it while he spoke. "It wasn't the first time. That's why she's not my girl. But I promised her I'd go to Homecoming a long time ago, and I didn't want her to end up without a date."

Like she wouldn't be able to find another date. I wanted to roll my eyes at him, but restrained myself. I'd already done enough damage.

He tossed the box on the pile and tilted his head. "So, Darcy. How was your weekend? What did you do besides watch sappy movies about guys named Hubbell and their lovely girls?"

A tiny smile quirked his lips. I took it as a peace offering.

"There was puking in my weekend, too. But it was just Toby. He got into some moldy garbage."

"Is he okay?"

At last my eyes were free to roll. "Your dog is fine."

His smile returned. "Good. I'd hate to have to call the authorities. Or the vet."

"Ha. No need for that. Most of the time Toby has a cast iron stomach."

Lucas glanced at me. "So do I."

"So you're like Iron Man?"

He shook his head in disgust. "Iron Man had iron in his chest, not his stomach. I know you don't read comics, but didn't you see the movie? C'mon Shaker Girl, keep up."

"You think you can out-geek me?" I challenged.

He pointed to his retro Ninja Turtles T-shirt. "No contest. I win."

I pointed to his pocket knife as he cut into another box. "Speaking of geeks, is that Boy Scout issued?"

He grinned. "Salvation Army store. Way cooler than Scouts." As he leaned over to grab more boxes, I snuck a glance at his butt. I couldn't help myself. "My weekend wasn't a total loss," Lucas said, tossing me another box, which I caught one-handed. "Nice catch."

"What was the good part?"

"Yesterday I took Pickles to see some weird movie about punk fairies packing pink swords."

I gasped. "You saw the Fierce Firestorm movie?"

He laughed. "You *are* a geek. So you're a Firestorm fan?"

"Duh."

"Wish I'd known."

I raised an eyebrow. "So I could've taken her and spared you the agony?"

"No," he said. "So we could've gone together and shared

the pain."

What was happening here? This wasn't flirting, was it? No, it couldn't possibly be. Just because Heather wasn't his girl didn't change anything. This was what we always did. Witty repartee was our thing, like Tony Stark and Pepper Potts, speaking of *Iron Man*. Minus the kissing.

Lucas put his hands on hips and cocked his head. "I think I'd like that coffee now."

I searched his face for signs of any new feelings toward me. What the heck did I think I'd see? Cartoon hearts instead of eyeballs? I was being idiotic. If he'd wanted to ask me out, he could have done it any time since he and Heather broke up. I tossed my box on the pile. "One extra dry, triple-shot coming right up." I wiped my hands on my jeans as I left the storeroom.

Liz's shop was quiet and peaceful. I made our drinks quickly but took a moment to calm my nerves before I went back. I spotted a few beads on the floor. I still found them sometimes when I swept, even though it had been ages since the Pickles incident.

I bent to pick them up. One was small, perfectly smooth and dark green. The other was a mosaic, a riot of colors. They rested in my palm. I was the green one, understated and easily overlooked. Lucas was the blast of colors, drawing admirers like moths to a flame.

I shoved the beads in my pocket, reminding myself I needed to keep my feelings for Lucas tucked safely away. I had to focus on reality. There were boxes to pack. Dogs to feed. Moms to sober up.

*L*ucas and I spent the next hour breaking down boxes and joking around. Coffee perked him up, and by the time the last box was on the pile, all traces of his earlier irritability had vanished. As he tossed the boxes into the back of my truck, he caught me eyeing his tattoo. I'd never been able to get a full view of it, since only part of it peeked out from under the sleeves of his T-shirts. With the change in weather, he normally wore long sleeves these days or covered up with a fleece jacket. The T-shirt showed off those biceps and his ink.

He leaned against my truck, looking very bad-boy cool. "You're wondering what it is, right?" he asked, as he pushed up his sleeve.

So much for me trying to be subtle. "It's…uh…it's none of my business…"

"It's okay, Darcy. It's not a gang symbol." He hesitated. "Or a naked girl." I heard the smirk in his voice and laughed nervously, leaning in to study the tattoo, careful not to look at his face.

The characters looked like Japanese calligraphy. "What does it mean?" I asked quietly. I had a desperate need to reach out and trace the ink. I raised my eyes to his, hoping they didn't betray my desire.

"It's the Kanji symbols for 'live for today.'" He paused, smiling. "At least, I hope that's what it is. I hope Eddie at Inkheart didn't mess with me."

I nodded, willing myself to relax, be witty. "Right," I agreed. "Maybe it says 'I love Hello Kitty.'"

He grinned. "But I do love Hello Kitty. Pickles can

vouch for me."

We laughed together. I swallowed and glanced down the alley, needing to break eye contact.

"Anyway," he said, his voice low. "I got it after my mom had been gone for a year, to remind myself I couldn't live in the past anymore, hoping for what was. To remind me that all I've got is today." He pulled his sleeve down and shrugged, almost embarrassed. "Some people think it's lame."

I frowned at him. "I don't think so. I think it's... meaningful."

"Thanks," he mumbled. He tossed the last of the boxes into the back of the truck.

I climbed in and started the engine. He frowned as the Reaper roared to life.

"You need to get this beast worked on," he called to me over the roar of the engine. He pointed to the blue smoke coming out of the tail pipe.

"I know," I said. "After the estate sale. I'll have money then."

I started to roll up the window but stopped when he stepped closer, his face even with mine. "I can work on it now. You can pay me for parts later."

"You don't have to do that," I said, swallowing nervously.

He rested his arms on the doorframe, a hint of a smile on his sexy lips. "I know I don't have to. But maybe I want to."

"Oh." I swallowed again, wishing I'd grabbed a water bottle from Charlie's fridge.

He stepped back, slapping the door of my truck like a quarterback slapping a receiver after a catch. "Let me know if you change your mind, Darcy. You can call me anytime. If this breaks down or whatever."

"Right. Like you'd come running at three a.m." Oh crap. I'd used my outside voice, hadn't I? Damn, damn, damn it. I bit my lip, watching him nervously, wishing I could take it back.

He looked startled, but then he smiled in a way I'd never seen before. "For you? Yeah."

Then he turned away, disappearing into Charlie's store before I could even catch my breath.

CHAPTER TWENTY
NOVEMBER 11

I'd barely started my shift at Liz's on Tuesday when Lucas showed up.

"Hey, Shaker Girl," he said, leaning on the counter while I cleaned coffee mugs.

"Hey." I glanced up and smiled. I wanted to give him a nickname too, but the only ones I came up with I'd never say out loud. His Royal Hotness, Lord Lucas didn't have quite the same bounce as Shaker Girl.

"So." He cleared his throat. "Are you doing anything after work tonight?"

The mug slipped from my hands, clattering into the sink but not breaking. I reached for it, trying to compose myself before I dared to look at him.

"Because Pickles needs a babysitter," he continued,

"and I, um, have plans. And my dad actually has a date, which is good. Weird but good. He's waiting 'til I get home before he leaves."

I looked up. The butterflies in my stomach turned into an angry knot. He wanted me to babysit while he went on a date? And his dad, too? That teeny tiny flame of hope I'd had about us snuffed out.

"How late are the Martinez men going to be out on the town?" I asked, trying to sound snarktastic, like I didn't care that he only saw me as babysitter material.

We stared at each other and I was proud of myself for keeping my gaze locked on his. I didn't blink, but he did. "I, uh…" He reached up to run a hand through his stupidly perfect hair and glanced away. "I'm not s-sure."

It was fun watching him stammer. I was glad he could tell I was pissed, and that it rattled him.

"I don't know, Lucas. This is really last minute." Asking me to babysit was like him throwing me an eighty-yard pass, pushing me so deep into the friend zone I'd never get out.

His frown faded, but he didn't smile. "Yeah. I know it's a lot to ask but—"

"But you have a hot date," I said. "And so does your dad." And of course it wouldn't occur to him that I might, since I never did.

He pushed off the counter, shoving his hands in his pockets. He stared at the floor. "No, I don't," he said. "But I have to do something after work. I'm not sure how long it will take." He looked up at me and swallowed. "Look, I shouldn't have asked. You've probably got plans—"

"I don't." Somehow him not having a date changed

everything. "I can do it."

He blinked again. "You can? Really?" I wondered how many girls said yes to him because of those damn eyelashes.

"If I can leave by one, it's probably okay," I said. "Pickles and I can make jewelry together."

His lips quirked. "She's usually asleep by eight thirty."

Oh. My turn to feel stupid. "Of course," I said, reaching for another cup to wash. "So I'm just hanging out at your house? In case of a secret ninja attack? How much do you pay?" His shocked expression made me laugh. "I'm kidding, dork. I don't expect payment. I've got a book to read." I cocked an eyebrow. "And I assume you have a TV?"

"Books. TV. We have one. Both, I mean. Books and TV." He stepped back from the counter, stuttering and staring at me like I was an alien. Or a psycho. Possibly both.

I frowned, confused. "You okay, Lucas? You're acting sort of weird."

He nodded. "I'll meet you after work. You can follow me to my house."

To the ends of the earth and back, Your Royal Hotness, that's how far I'd follow you. But all I said was, "Sure. See you then."

"Guess where I am?" I said the second Sal answered her phone.

"Paris? Rome? Somewhere with a sexy guy?"

"Close. I'm in Lucas's bedroom."

"What?!" Her shriek almost broke my eardrum.

I giggled into the phone. "Check it out." I snapped a quick photo of his bed and texted it to her.

"Oh my God, Darcy! What the hell are you doing?"

"Babysitting."

She snorted. "I haven't heard it called that before."

"Honestly, that's all I'm doing. Lucas and his dad are gone, so I'm here taking care of his little sister." I paused. "Except she's sleeping, so there's nothing to do but snoop around."

"That's just wrong, Darcy. What if he catches you?"

"I know it's wrong but I can't resist. And he won't. He said he'd be a couple of hours."

She sighed in my ear. "So he's out hooking up with some other girl and you're being a pathetic stalker taking pictures of his room."

I leaned back in his desk chair, looking around. His room wasn't a total disaster. The bed was made, and there was just one small pile of clothes on the floor. So far I'd resisted the urge to bury my nose in it.

"He's not hooking up. He told me he had something to do, but it wasn't a date."

"Wait a minute. He *specifically* told you he didn't have a date?"

"Yeah." I spun his chair around to examine his desk. Lots of fat textbooks. A pile of notebooks. A stick-figure drawing by Pickles. A stack of comic books.

"Interesting," Sal said, her voice full of innuendo.

It was my turn to snort. "He only told me so I'd do this. At first I thought he had a date, and I freaked him out because I let my claws out." I spun the chair again, surveying his walls. I propped my feet on his bed. A couple of muscle car posters and all the Denver sports teams, but no half-naked girls. Maybe Mr. College Boy had outgrown that phase.

I considered Pickles sleeping in the next room. Or maybe he was just a really good guy, who thought about what his sister would see when she busted into his room, which I assumed she did, probably every day.

"This has got to be the weirdest first date ever," Sal said.

My feet slammed to the floor. "Wait, what?"

She laughed in my ear. "Okay, it's not a date. But it's something."

"Yeah. It's called babysitting." I glanced at his bookcase, which held way more video games than books. A couple of framed photos claimed the prime spot: center shelf. I stood up to go inspect them.

"Anyway," I said. "You always give me crap for not doing anything fun. I thought you'd think this was funny, me being in a guy's bedroom minus the guy." I leaned in to examine the photos. A much younger Lucas. A guy who must be his dad. And a pretty woman who had his eyes. His mom. Him and Pickles with Santa, looking ridiculously adorable together, especially because he was taller than the Santa.

"It is funny," Sal said. "I'm glad you called." She paused. "Where does your mom think you are?"

"With you, of course." I'd texted Mom that I was with Sal, but she hadn't replied. I knew she was already in her wine coma.

"I got your back, girl," Sal said, then laughed suggestively. "I bet if you wanted to, you could end up in that bed later tonight. With him."

"Sal!" I gasped and straightened, scurrying out of the bedroom as if that would somehow undo what she'd said. "You're totally misreading the situation," I insisted. I went back to the small living room and flopped onto the couch. I wondered where Lucas always sat. Was it in the corner I'd chosen? Or maybe the other one. God, I was insane.

"How 'bout you call me tomorrow?" she said. "Let me know how this bizzaro undate night ends up."

I took a deep breath, looking around the cozy living room, so unlike our enormous one we never used. "Yeah, sure."

After we hung up, I pulled out my novel. Reading a romance in Lucas's house felt weird. Sort of risky. But also exciting. I kicked off my shoes and wrapped myself in a faded afghan, burrowing into it. I was tempted to sniff it to see if I could catch his scent, but decided I'd already gone Stalkers R Us by taking a picture of his bedroom.

I read for a long time, flinching occasionally as unfamiliar creaks sounded throughout his house. The wind howled outside, but I felt safe, like he was there with me. Ridiculous. I refocused on my book boyfriend, pushing away thoughts of Lucas and whatever non-dating activities he was up to.

My eyes grew heavy as I read the same paragraph over and over. I curled deeper into the blanket. Maybe I'd take a catnap...just for a little bit...

"*D*arcy." A voice trickled into my dream. I danced in an elegant ballroom, the light from hundreds of crystal chandeliers glinting off the charming duke who spun me around. I danced like I'd been born to do it—graceful and light on my feet, no tripping or stumbling.

"You're beautiful," said my dance partner. Lord Martinez was regal in his evening clothes. I knew I was the luckiest girl in the room.

"Thank you," said my dream self. Not, "Shut up!" Or "As if!" I smiled into his eyes and he leaned closer. "I want something, Darcy," he whispered, his breath tickling my dream ear. "Something only you can give me."

I felt something on my cheek. On my hair. Something warm. Solid. That didn't make sense; we were dancing. He had one at my waist and held my hand with the other. Who was touching my face, my hair?

"What?" I asked, twisting and turning. I lost my footing, stumbling against the duke. "What do you want from me, Lucas?"

"Darcy?" The hand moved from my hair to my shoulder, shaking me gently. "You need to wake up."

My eyes flew open. Lucas sat next to me on the couch. Like right next to me. Somehow while sleeping I'd stretched out my legs, and he sat on the middle cushion, my body almost wrapped around him.

I leaned into the back of the couch, trying to put space between us. He dropped his hand from my shoulder. How long had he been sitting there watching me sleep? Was it his hand I'd felt on my face? In my hair? Or was that part of the dream?

He smiled down at me and I wondered if I was still dreaming.

"What did you mean?" he said. I looked at him blankly and he added, "You asked me what I wanted."

Of all the nights to talk in my sleep. Crap.

"Um, what?" I feigned confusion and rubbed my eyes. "I guess I was dreaming."

He shifted on the couch, clearing his throat. "You were dreaming about me?"

I peeked out from under my eyelashes. "Um, maybe? I don't really remember." I threw the blanket off my burning body. "I should go."

He leaned over and grabbed something from the floor. "I think you dropped this." A smile played at his lips as he looked at my book cover.

Perfect. Because I hadn't embarrassed myself enough talking to him in my sleep. I reached out to snatch the book from his hands.

He smirked at me. "Good book?" His body still had me penned in, whether I liked it or not. Of course I liked it, while simultaneously hating that I couldn't just get the heck out of there.

"What time is it?" I looked around the room for a clock but didn't see one.

"A little after midnight." He raised an eyebrow. "You going to turn into a pumpkin?"

"It would be my truck that would turn into a pumpkin." I tried to look exasperated at his fairy tale ignorance, but it was impossible, not with his eyes smiling at me.

"Right." He grinned. "And what happens to Cinderella?"

"Her fancy ball gown turns back into rags." That had almost happened, when I woke up. I was in my jeans and fleece shirt, not the gorgeous gown I'd worn in my dream.

His eyes skimmed down my body, then came back to rest on my face. "I wouldn't say rags," he said, his voice husky.

I sat up, trying to pull my legs up next to me. He moved just enough so I could do that, but apparently he wasn't going anywhere.

"It's snowing pretty hard," he said. "I'm not sure you should drive, especially with those tires. I checked them out; they're almost bald." He frowned at me. "You should get snow tires."

"Tires can go bald? Do they get beer bellies, too?" I attempted to joke rather than focus on the fact that he was being all…protective, or whatever it was he was doing.

He shook his head but I saw laughter in his eyes. "How about I drive you home? After my dad gets home? You can get your truck next time you're working."

I fiddled with the afghan fringe and thought of what Sal said about this being an undate. Right now everything felt "un." Uncomfortable. Un-relaxed. Un-normal.

"You did me a favor, staying here with Pickles. It's the least I can do." He stood up suddenly. "You hungry? I am." Then he walked out of the room before I could answer. What was up with him tonight?

I checked my phone to see if Mom had texted. Nothing. I shoved my feet back in my shoes and went to peer out the front window. Snow whirled under the streetlights and trees bowed under howling gusts of wind.

Lucas came back into the living room with two soda cans and a bowl full of chips. He set everything down on the coffee table then plopped on the couch. In the corner where

I'd been sleeping. I *knew* it was his corner. I bit back a smile, looking out the window again.

"Come sit down," Lucas said, snapping open his soda can. He picked up the remote and turned on the TV. When I didn't move, he tilted his chin at me. "I'm not going to turn into a rat, like in Cinderella."

I rolled my eyes and moved to the couch, sitting next to him but putting lots of space between us. "The mice turn into horses, not guys." I shook my head in fake disgust.

"Somebody turns into the driver. Was it the dog?" He grinned. "I guess that's me, since I'll be driving you home tonight. Unless Toby knows how to drive and can come get you."

Was this the part where we went from undate to date? I had no idea what was happening. I took a handful of chips. "I don't need you to drive me home. I'll just drive slow."

"Nope," he said, keeping his eyes on the explosions on the screen.

My back stiffened. "You're not the boss of me, Lucas."

He turned toward me, laughing. "You've been spending too much time with Pickles."

"Whatever." I knew I was blushing. "You know what I mean. You can't make me do something. Or not do something."

"I've figured that much out," he said, glancing toward a screen explosion, and then back at me. "You're almost as stubborn as my sister." He took a bite from a chip, chewing slowly, watching me.

"Almost?" I tried to look threatening, which just made him grin.

"Stubborn works for you," he said, pausing to drink from his soda. "It's how you get what you want. Setting up the estate sale, getting more time to move." He muted the TV, turning to face me on the couch. "You don't need a fairy godmother." He ran a hand through his hair, a frown furrowing his forehead. "Sometimes I wonder if you need anybody. You're like a one-woman tornado, knocking down everything that gets in your way."

Whoa. I flinched as if he'd slapped me. He made me sound like a freak.

His frown deepened as he took in my reaction. "Darcy. What'd I say?" He leaned forward, reaching a hand toward me, but I brushed it away, turning so he couldn't see my face.

Damn it. What the hell was going on? He was sending me all kinds of mixed signals. Sort of flirting but sort of not. Trying to compliment me but making it sound like an insult.

"Shit," he whispered. He powered off the TV. "Darcy. Look at me."

I shook my head.

"Please."

Slowly, I turned toward him. Everything about him screamed maximum frustration. I closed my eyes, hating what I saw. I wanted to see so much more from him.

"What do you want from me, Lucas?" I asked, keeping my eyes closed.

He was quiet so long that I opened my eyes. His gaze was scorching. So was this angry Lucas? Or was that heat in his eyes something else?

"I could ask you the same thing," he said, his voice so low it made me shiver. "What do you want from me, Darcy?"

I heard Sal's voice in my mind. *"It's not a date. But it's something."*

There were so many ways this could blow up in my face. I was pretty sure telling him I wanted him to whisk me away in a carriage was the wrong answer. Telling him I wanted him to kiss me? To see me as more than a babysitter? That was the honest answer, but one I'd never admit.

I took a long, deep breath, thinking about how he'd said I didn't need anyone.

"It's not true, what you said about me not needing anyone," I said, keeping my eyes on his. "I do need people."

He waited, still as stone.

"I need...my dad."

He flinched, and I saw pity flash in his eyes, but he stayed silent as I went on. "And I need my mom. My uncle. Liz. My friend Sal."

We stared at each other, both of us waiting for me to say it. But I was so afraid. Confronting the Harvest board of directors had been child's play compared to this.

Then he said it for me. "And me? Do you need me?"

I couldn't look at him, because I knew I couldn't hide what I felt for him. I might as well have it tattooed on my face. I tucked my hands under my thighs, digging my nails into the denim of my jeans.

"What I feel for you is..." I couldn't believe I was doing this. I wasn't ready.

I thought of how he'd looked at me that first day we'd walked Toby together, of what I thought I'd seen in his eyes. How I'd been sure he'd wanted to kiss me, then wondered if I'd imagined it. How he'd said I could call him at three a.m., and he'd come running.

"Complicated," I finally said, still not looking at him. "My feelings for you are…confused. You're such a…a great friend."

"Friend," he repeated, his voice sounding grim.

I finally looked up. His jaw was clenched, his eyes slits. He turned away from me, reaching for the remote, but I put out a hand to stop him. As my hand rested on his, he shifted his body to face me again and I saw it.

All of it.

Everything I wanted to see. What I thought I'd never see from him. For me.

"Oh," I whispered.

"Oh," he echoed, the corner of his mouth lifting slightly. "Still confused?"

It was all there, waiting for me. All I had to do was claim it.

Claim him.

Or was it? The possibility I was imagining this was overwhelming, terrifying. I jumped up from the couch, hurrying toward the closet where he'd stashed my coat. I tore it off the hanger and tugged it on, then grabbed my messenger bag.

He stood up, crossing the small living room in just a few quick strides, just like a duke on a mission.

"Where do you think you're going?" He sounded like a demanding duke, too.

"H-home," I stammered. Because I'm a coward. Because I can't handle what's happening here. Or not happening. Whatever. I had to escape.

"It's not safe," he said, trying to block me as I moved toward the front door. "Let me drive you."

I pulled the keys from my bag. "Let me go, Lucas. I'll be fine."

He stared down at me so intensely I half expected him to pick me up and throw me over his shoulder. But then something shifted. His shoulders dropped and he stepped back. "If this is what you want. To leave."

We stared at each other. We both knew he was talking about more than me driving home by myself. I swallowed and reached for the doorknob. "Good night, Lucas."

He crossed his arms over his chest, narrowing his eyes. "At least text me when you get home." A muscle in his jaw twitched. "Please."

"You said I'm a one-woman tornado. I'm sure I'll make it there in one piece."

He grimaced. "I never meant to hurt your feelings." He stepped toward me. "If that's why you're leaving—"

"It's not that." I tugged on my fleece hat and my gloves. "Well, maybe a little. It's… I just…" Some part of me knew I was crazy, walking away from what I wanted. But the rest of me knew it was a survival tactic. I couldn't take one more punch to the heart.

He reached out, his finger trailing down my cheek, stopping under my chin. "I'm not going to stop you, Shaker Girl," he said, his voice soft. "But I want you to remember something."

"W-what?" How could I say actual words with him touching me?

"When we were tearing down boxes the other day?"

I nodded. He'd moved his hand, now tracing down my other cheek.

"I said most guys aim too low." His lips curved into a sensual smile. "I want you to remember that I aim high."

He dropped his hand from my face and opened the front door. Snow and wind swirled into the house, chasing away the warmth he'd just flooded me with.

"I'll remember," I managed to say, before I turned away and rushed down the steps to my truck.

I texted Lucas once I was home. Mom was asleep on the couch as usual. Toby and I burrowed under my comforter, the light from my phone like a tiny flashlight in our blanket cave.

"I made it."

His reply flew back instantly. *"Good."*

I hesitated, then sent another message. *"You never told me what you were doing tonight, while I was sleeping AKA babysitting."*

I watched the dots as he typed his reply. *"Helping out a neighbor."*

"Mr. Good Samaritan."

"That's me. Always at your service."

Just one more reason I'd fallen so damn hard for him.

I closed my eyes. Wishing. Praying. Hoping.

That maybe, just maybe, I could trust what I'd seen. That he was falling for me, too.

And I promised myself that next time, I wouldn't run away.

CHAPTER TWENTY-ONE

Denver Daily News
November 21

The Secret Scoop from the Street
by "Crystal Ball"

Tyler Covington Spoils Harvest

While his wife and daughter live in seclusion in their country club mansion, refusing requests for interviews, Chief Operating Officer and acting President Jonathan James (J.J.) Briggs shoulders the burden of running the motivational speaking empire while its star is missing.

"It's been rough," J.J. says from his office on the fourteenth floor of the downtown headquarters of Tri!Umphant! Harvest Industries. His face is haggard. He needs a haircut. "Ty was the face of Harvest, but he was the brains, too. He guided the ship. Made all the decisions. I'm just picking up the pieces right now, hoping to satisfy our investors."

Rumors have been flying on the internet about Covington's disappearance, including speculation that he left the country with millions, abandoning his family and his business.

Someone must know where this guy is. I press J.J. for an answer. He runs his hands over his weary face. "I think his family might know something. But if they do know, they're not telling anyone." He shrugs. "They have a lot to lose if he doesn't come back. We all do."

Rumor has it the Harvest board of directors has frozen all accounts and assets of the Covington family and seized their home. I ask J.J. what will happen if Mr. Covington doesn't return. He shakes his head. "Ty decided to diversify our investments some time ago. Harvest owns a lot of corporate real estate. But this isn't a great time to have most of your assets in property, as you know." J.J. sighs. "I tried to talk him out of it, but he was running the show."

So if Ty doesn't come back?

"The board will need to make some hard decisions," J.J. told me. "We may need to liquidate most, if not all, of those assets to satisfy our investors. Without Ty here creating new motivational product..." J.J. is too overwhelmed to finish his thought and ends our interview.

It will be fascinating to watch this story play out. Tyler Covington has been a pillar in the local business and philanthropic communities. Everyone I spoke to had good things to say about him and expressed shock and disbelief that he would abandon his family and his business.

Coach Hook of the Broncos said, "We miss Ty. A lot of the guys leaned on him both on and off the field. We hope he comes back soon."

Personally, I have known Tyler Covington for many years. He always struck me as intense and genuine. I hope he returns, but even if he does, it sounds like his Harvest will be ruined.

I sat in Liz's fairy cave, drinking tea and eating cookies. A copy of the newspaper's gossip column rested on the table between Liz and me. Charlie leaned against the wall, stirring his coffee.

The article had blindsided me, deflating the tiny bit of hope and confidence I'd built up after the board meeting. It had devastated Mom.

"How's your mom?" Charlie asked.

"Comatose." I didn't look at him.

"I don't believe a word of that article. I think J.J.'s lying about Ty making the investment decisions." Charlie's voice was harsh.

I shrugged. "I don't know what to think, Charlie. It doesn't matter anyway. What matters is that everyone else will believe what they read."

Charlie and Liz exchanged worried looks.

"What are you doing for Thanksgiving?" Liz asked.

"Thanksgiving?" I blinked at them.

Liz shook her head at my cluelessness. "It's next Thursday."

Wow. Mom wasn't acting like she usually did when a holiday loomed. She wasn't in a baking frenzy. She hadn't taken the silver out of the china cabinet for polishing. Mostly she was drinking herself to sleep every night.

"You'll come to my house. You and your mom." It was a command from my uncle, not a request.

"I don't know…it's probably best if we spend the day at home, just the two of us."

"You need to be around people who care about you," Liz said.

"Come at four. You don't need to bring anything except your mom and Toby." Charlie sounded just like Dad when he gave orders.

I shrugged and then nodded. It wasn't like we were doing anything other than hiding in the mansion. And eating frozen pizza on Thanksgiving sounded awful.

Chapter Twenty-Two
November 22

Thanksgiving dawned clear and cold. I spent the morning arguing with Mom about going to Charlie's. She didn't want to, but I did. I was desperate to get out of our house and be with people who made me feel wanted.

At three thirty, I emerged from my bedroom wearing a dress. I'd put on more makeup than usual and attempted to curl my hair, even though it fell right back to straight boringness. I added a couple of sparkling barrettes Sal had given me. I had to at least put forth some effort since I knew Mom wouldn't.

"The train's leaving the station," I announced as I walked into Mom's bedroom. She sat on the bed in her bra and underwear staring into space. "God, Mom. Can't you even try?" I stomped to her closet and yanked out a dress.

I tossed it to her. "Hurry up. We need to leave, like now." I prodded her until she was fully dressed. I dug out jewelry from one of her many jewelry boxes. I made her sit at her vanity table while I brushed her hair.

"I don't know why you're going to all this trouble."

I stared at her reflection in the mirror. "Because I care about Charlie. And Liz."

Mom dropped her eyes. "It's not like we have anything to be thankful for."

I stopped brushing her hair. "That's not true."

"Name one thing," she said.

"We have each other."

She sighed and reached out to touch a perfume bottle. "That's what people say when they're desperate. When they've lost everything."

Tears welled in my eyes. "But I mean it," I said.

We didn't speak as I drove us to Charlie's. Her depression terrified me. I wanted to turn it off with a switch, but didn't know how.

Charlie's house wasn't far from his store. It was small and tidy, with funky metal sculptures sticking out of dormant flowerbeds. The sculptures made me laugh, but Mom just frowned at them.

Lucas opened the door. I caught my breath when I saw him. I didn't know he was invited. Things had been awkward between us since the night at his house. We acted like polite strangers. We didn't tease each other anymore, and we hadn't taken Toby on any walks together. I thought about him constantly, about what he'd said about aiming high, wondering if he meant me. God, I hoped so, but part of me still couldn't believe it.

Mom glanced back and forth between us. He looked almost as good as he had on Homecoming night, though he wasn't in a tux. But he had on nice pants, and a dress shirt and tie.

"Wow," I said, recovering as well as I could. "You almost look like a grown-up."

"So do you." His eyes skimmed over me. "I didn't think you owned any dresses."

He held the door open for us. My arm brushed his, waking up every nerve in my body. I stepped away from him.

"Lucas, this is my mom, Marilyn."

He put out his hand. "It's great to meet you, Mrs. Covington. I've heard so much about you."

Mom raised an eyebrow. "I can't imagine you've heard anything good."

"Mom." I glared at her. *Way to go, Mom.* We hadn't even sat down to eat yet.

A dark-haired man about Mom's age joined us in the living room. As he stood next to Lucas I realized who he was.

"This is my dad, Alejandro," Lucas said. "Dad, this is Darcy and her mom, Marilyn."

Alejandro shook our hands. As I looked into his eyes, I noticed they danced with amusement, just like Lucas's did when we kidded around.

"A pleasure," Alejandro said. He offered his arm to Mom. "Should we go supervise the cooks in the kitchen?"

Mom surprised me by going with him, resurrecting some of her manners. Then Lucas and I were alone. I felt shy around him, almost as much as when he'd shown me his tattoo. Maybe it was the dress. And the tie. And getting caught dreaming about him.

"I didn't know you'd be here today," I said.

He tilted his head. "Would you have stayed home if you'd known?"

I blushed. "No, of course not. I just—"

"Darcy!" Pickles ran into the room at top speed, screeching to a stop in front of me. Her eyes were huge. "You look so pretty!" She turned to Lucas. "Doesn't she?" She turned back to me. "Way prettier dan Heather." She frowned. "I hate Heather."

Lucas picked her up like she was a sack of flour and tossed her over his shoulder. "We all know how you feel about Heather," he said, walking out of the room. "I think you can stop announcing it like the town crier."

"I'm not a crier!" she protested as he tickled her.

I followed them into the kitchen, laughing, and grateful for Pickles' interruption.

We spent the afternoon eating turkey and tofu. Charlie and Liz had cooked enough food to please the carnivores and the vegans. I watched Mom closely as she drank wine, but she stopped after two glasses. I sighed with relief when she switched to coffee. Maybe she didn't really have a drinking problem. Maybe it was just the stress. Maybe if she spent more time with people like Charlie and Liz...

Jazz played on the stereo while Alejandro and Charlie bantered like old friends, which they obviously were. Liz turned her cosmic rays on full blast for Mom, who responded by relaxing and laughing in a way I hadn't seen in forever. Lucas and I debated whether it was better to watch Studio Ghibli movies subtitled or dubbed. I'd missed arguing with him, joking with him. I'd missed him, period.

When none of us could eat any more, Pickles wormed her way onto my lap and played with my necklace, one of my own creations. Toby snored under the table, full of the scraps people had been sneaking him. No one mentioned Dad or the gossip column in the paper.

I wanted to freeze time at this table, with these people who'd become so important in my life. Mom had said we didn't have anything to be grateful for, but the gratitude that swelled in my heart brought tears to my eyes.

Pickles stopped playing with my necklace when I reached up to brush a tear away.

"Why are you crying?" she whispered. She darted a suspicious look at Lucas, as if ready to blame him. He settled his gaze on me. My heart raced but I didn't look away this time. There it was again—what I'd seen that night at his house, what I'd seen on our walk with Toby.

I finally broke eye contact to answer Pickles. "Did you ever cry because you were so happy it just sort of spilled out?"

She considered this seriously. "Maybe. When I got lost in the grocery store, then Lukie found me." She patted my cheek with her chubby hand. "I love you, Darcy," she whispered. "Don't cry."

I wiped another tear from my face and kissed her nose.

Lucas slid his chair away from the table and left the room. He returned a few minutes later with pie and dessert plates.

"What kind of host forgets about dessert?" he teased Charlie.

Everyone laughed, and Pickles slid off my lap. Lucas cut the pie and Pickles delivered plates to each of us. Charlie raised his wine glass and cleared his throat. "I'd like to make a toast." Everyone raised a glass and waited for him to speak. I was relieved that Mom held up a water goblet. Charlie turned his gaze to me. "To my niece," he said.

Uh-oh.

"When Darcy walked into my store the first time, I remembered the little girl I'd known long ago. But now she's an amazing young woman who's brought so much heart to our little corner of Broadway." He smiled, and I saw Dad looking back at me. "In spite of all she's dealing with, she makes us laugh every day. She's always there when we need her. She has a quiet strength that informs everything she does." He paused and shot a grin at Liz. "Not to mention, now I get to have date nights since Darcy's there to close up shop on the weekends." He lifted his glass. "To Darcy!"

Everyone echoed his words. "To Darcy!"

Mom beamed at me, her eyes bright with tears. I didn't dare look at Lucas. I'd heard him toast me along with everyone else, and that was enough.

"To family and friends, old and new," Liz said.

They went on like that for ages, toasting and laughing.

Eventually Lucas started to clear the table. I stood up to help him.

"That's why you need kids," Alejandro said to Liz and Charlie. "To do the dirty work."

Their laughter followed us into the kitchen. Lucas scraped the plate scraps into a trash can while I stacked glasses on the counter. Charlie's kitchen was exactly as I'd imagined, complete with a dozen sets of salt and pepper shakers lining the windowsill over the sink.

"Are you glad you're here today?" Lucas asked, turning from the sink. His sleeves were rolled up and his hands dripped with soapy water.

I nodded. "Very," I said quietly.

"Me too," he said. "I've missed you. Missed us."

My body forgot how to breathe, and I couldn't even draw enough air to agree.

He cleared his throat and turned away, drying his hands on a dishtowel. "Did Charlie embarrass you? With his toast?"

"Yeah." My voice was croaky, but at least it worked. "His toast surprised me. But it was nice."

"It was also true."

I stared at my shoes, afraid to look at him. One minute we were joking and debating about books and movies, then the next thing I knew he said things that made me tongue-tied and breathless. Just when I thought I could relax around him, he put me off balance.

Pickles bounced into the kitchen. "Charlie says there's more pie! A chocolate one. Daddy says I can have a piece." She looked at her brother with pleading eyes. "Where is it?"

Lucas laughed as he ruffled her hair. "In the fridge."

I yanked open the refrigerator to retrieve the pie box, grateful for the distraction.

"Let's take it to the dining room, Pickles," I said, side-stepping around Lucas. "I'm sure other people will want some, too."

*M*om yawned and stretched as we drove home. "That was wonderful, Darcy. Thank you for dragging me out."

"They're awesome people."

"They are," she agreed. "So…" She hesitated. "You and Lucas? Is there something going on I should know about?"

I squeezed the steering wheel. "We're friends. That's all." *For now*.

"Hmm," she said. "We'll see how long that lasts."

"What do you mean?" Had my mom seen the way he looked at me? The way I looked at him?

She chuckled softly. "Nothing." She patted my knee. "I owe you an apology. Earlier today you said we had each other to be thankful for. I said some things that weren't kind. Or true."

I glanced at her and then looked back at the road.

"Darcy." Mom's voice was soft. "You've grown up so fast…with all that's happened. I'm so proud of you."

"Thanks," I whispered.

"Your dad would be, too." She swallowed. "He will be, I mean. When he comes home."

"I wonder what he's doing tonight," I said.

She shifted in her seat. "I wonder, too." Her hand reached for mine and I took it, leaving one hand on the wheel.

We drove the rest of the way hands gripped together, each of us sending wishes and hopes to Dad, wherever he was.

Chapter Twenty-Three
November 29

Lucas called me on Saturday morning as I was getting dressed to go apartment-hunting with him. I'd been staring in my closet, debating what to wear. Boring sweatshirt and ratty jeans because we were just friends and I didn't care how I looked? Or cute sweater and nice jeans because I did care? Especially after what he'd said at Thanksgiving about missing me. Missing us.

It felt like something had shifted again that night, and it wasn't just my ever-hopeful imagination or all the romances I'd been reading. Which reminded me, Charlie still hadn't found the stack of regencies I'd set aside in his store, and I was desperate for new books to read. I could ask Lucas if he'd seen them, but that was too embarrassing.

"So," he said on the phone. "I was thinking it'd be easier

if I picked you up. That way you don't have to take the bus down here to meet me."

My heart sped up. Pick me up? Like a date?

"But it's out of your way. Aren't the apartments down by Charlie's store?"

There was a moment of silence. "Yeah. But still. It's not that far. And I was thinking I could check out your truck like I suggested before."

"Did Charlie put you up to this?" I demanded.

His laughter sent a shiver down my neck. "No. I thought of it all by myself. Imagine that."

I smiled into the phone. "Well, in that case you can pick me up. Do you need my address?"

"I remember where you live. I'll see you in an hour."

I compromised and went with the cute sweater and ratty jeans. And a tiny bit of mascara. And lip gloss. And earrings.

While I waited for Lucas to arrive, I stared at my map. Ingram, Texas. Rolla, Missouri. Alliance, Nebraska. Santa Fe, New Mexico. Laguna Beach, California. There weren't any henges in Laguna Beach. Dad's postcard had been of a sunset over the ocean. Dad loved the ocean. Maybe he'd just headed west after leaving Santa Fe.

The doorbell startled Toby awake and he tore down the stairs, barking like mad. I stopped at the mirror over my dresser. No, I was nothing like Heather. But that didn't matter. Like Sal said, I was on fire. Lit from the inside.

"Get your butt in gear," I told my reflection. I ran a brush through my hair one last time, then hurried down the stairs to calm Toby.

"Hey," said Lucas when I opened the door, as relaxed as

if he came over every day. Toby became a wriggling ball of pathetic dog suck-up-ness. Lucas laughed and bent to play with him.

"God, my dog is a useless protector. What if you were a crazy serial killer?"

"Then I wouldn't have rung the doorbell." He looked up and grinned at me.

"Good point. Let me just grab my bag." I turned away so he wouldn't see me blushing. My body was so over this "just friends" delusion.

"Hold on," Lucas said. "What about your truck?"

Oh yeah, that. I turned back to him. "Do you really have time for that?"

"Got the whole day off. Charlie was cool with it since I'm helping you."

"So helping me is a way for you to suck up to your boss, is that it?"

He rolled his eyes. "You figured it out. My ultimate evil plan is to rule the empire of Broadway. First, the Second Hand Story. Then Liz's store. Then Homeless Harry and I are taking over Inkheart. Harry's got wicked ink skills."

I burst out laughing. "The truck is in the garage," I called over my shoulder as I led the way. "Come on."

Lucas followed me through the dining room. "Do you want something to drink?" I opened the fridge. There wasn't much, but we had a few store brand colas left. "Lucas?" I turned around to see an empty kitchen. I returned to the dining room to find him staring up at the chandelier, Toby sitting patiently next to him.

"That's one killer chandelier," he said. "If anyone ever

did break in, you could use it as a weapon."

"I hate it," I said, "but my mom loves it. It's definitely a conversation starter for dinner parties. Or it used to be, when we had them."

Lucas took the soda from me. "Thanks." He snapped open the top and drained half of it in one swallow. "Take me to the Reaper."

"How did you know I called it that?"

"You told Charlie." He grinned. "Sometimes people forget I'm working behind the curtain. I overhear a lot of interesting conversations."

Oh God. My mind raced, wondering what other embarrassing conversations he might have overheard. He laughed at the expression on my face. "Don't look so freaked. You haven't given away any state secrets. Nothing worth turning you over to the Feds, even though I hear the reward money's pretty good."

"That's a relief." I started to punch him on the shoulder but stopped myself just in time. *Must not make physical contact.*

"Can I have the key? I want to back it out to the driveway." Lucas held out his hand. I grabbed the key from the hook and tossed it to him.

Toby ran after Lucas as he headed into the garage.

"No, boy," I said. "You're not going for a ride."

Toby looked at Lucas hopefully. Lucas opened the truck door and Toby hopped in.

"Way to undermine my authority, dude," I said.

Lucas slid into the truck and grinned at me, starting the engine and revving it loudly. Blue smoke filled the driveway as he backed out of the garage. He turned off the engine and hopped out, then buried himself under the hood while I tried to convince Toby to come out of the truck. My dog wasn't budging.

"I'll need to spend more time," Lucas said from under the hood. "But it might be your transmission."

"Is that bad?"

He stood up and shrugged. "It could be. Or it could be a fluid change will fix it." He glanced around the garage, apparently not seeing what he needed. "I'll have to fix it at my place. I'm going to wash my hands before we go."

"Can you grab a Scooby snack from the kitchen counter?" I called through the mudroom. "It's the only way Toby will come out of the truck."

I heard Lucas laugh from inside the house. He emerged without the dog treat.

"You forgot the snack."

He waggled his eyebrows at me. "Watch and learn." He leaned into the truck and within seconds Toby had jumped out, eyeing him with devotion.

"That's disgusting," I said, glaring at him with resentment.

"Just call me the dog whisperer."

"Can we go now? I can't take much more of this. Next thing I know, Toby will want to go home with you."

"I'd love that but my dad's allergic to dogs. And cats."

"That's too bad."

"Yeah, it sucks, especially for Pickles. She loves animals."

"Poor Pickles. She's so awesome."

He stared at me in mock horror. "What is wrong with you?"

"Just call me the kid whisperer."

He pointed a finger at me. "Touché, Shaker Girl, touché."

While Lucas pulled the truck back into the garage, I ran into the bathroom by the kitchen. My face flushed and my eyes shone with excitement. I hoped Lucas wouldn't notice, since it was all because of him.

"So tell me about these places we're looking at." I buckled myself into his immaculate car. "How'd you find them?"

"Lots of people in the neighborhood come into Charlie's store. I asked around." He handed me his iPod. "Pick something you like."

I jerked my arm away as our arms brushed, wondering if he felt the same electricity that I did. I glanced at him, but saw no change of expression in his face.

Paging through his music, I was surprised to see a lot of the bands I liked. I thought Ice Krystal and Phoenix had been a fluke.

"You like Passion Pit? And Snow Patrol? What's with all the emo music?"

He laughed. "What did you think I liked? Death metal?"

"I don't know. I just didn't expect that you'd like—"

"Chick music?"

It was my turn to laugh. It was easier to laugh than say what I was thinking, which was that it was one more way I felt connected to him.

He was quiet for a few minutes, then spoke. "The first place is an apartment right on Broadway. It's above the panini shop."

"No kidding?" I turned to stare at him. "Does it smell

like onions?"

"And garlic."

"Really? I don't know if my mom could deal with that."

He grinned at me. "Honestly, I don't know what it smells like. You know Pinky, the owner? He called Charlie when he saw one of the signs."

"What signs?"

Lucas looked embarrassed. "I put up a few signs around the neighborhood."

I hesitated, surprised. "You mean like, 'apartment wanted for two weird chicks and their spastic dog'? Something like that?"

Lucas shot me a grin. "Just like that. With a photo of two zombie chicks."

"Excellent." I forced a lightness in my voice, but inside I was a quivering mess of churning emotions. His Royal Hotness had put up signs? For me?

We parked in front of the panini restaurant, just a few blocks down from Charlie's.

Pinky must have been watching for us because he met us on the sidewalk, wiping his hands on his apron. He shook Lucas's hand, then reached for mine. His grip felt like a bear's.

"You tell me what you think, honey. If you like it, you bring your mama back to see it."

He unlocked a door I'd never noticed, tucked into the brick wall next to the restaurant. At the top of a flight of stairs, we entered a bright apartment flooded with sunlight. A large window looked down onto Broadway. I wondered if the sound of traffic would bug my mom. The bedrooms were small. There was one bathroom with a tiny sink. I tried to imagine Mom and me sharing a sink and a shower. The kitchen was small, but there was a newer gas stove and a tiny dishwasher. A window ringed by white curtains let in cracks of sunlight. I looked out to the alley below. It was hardly the view we had now, looking out at our pool and gardens.

"It's nice," I said, trying to sound enthusiastic. "Very clean. And bright."

Pinky nodded eagerly. "And you can have your dog here, too."

I imagined having to walk Toby downstairs every time he had to do his business. That would get old fast.

"Since you're Charlie's niece, I can give you a deal. Five hundred a month. No security deposit."

That was a killer deal. But the place was so small. And it did smell a little bit like onions.

"This is the first place we've looked at," Lucas said. "So I don't think Darcy is ready to make a decision yet."

I smiled at Lucas gratefully. I'd gained some people skills lately, but I didn't want to hurt Pinky's feelings.

"Yes, yes, of course. I understand." Pinky's head bobbed up and down. "You go look at the other places." He looked at Lucas. "You have my number? Call me later, okay?"

Lucas nodded.

We trooped back down the stairs, but this time I brought up the rear, not so I could check out Lucas's butt or anything.

"Next?" I said, after Pinky had gone back inside his restaurant.

"Do you want to walk? It's only a few blocks away."

"Yeah, let's walk." We fell into step together easily, like we always did.

"So that wasn't exactly what you were looking for?" Lucas asked.

"It was nice. Really it was. But it's just…I can't picture my mom…"

"It would be a big step down. But from what Charlie tells me, your mom will adjust."

I almost tripped. "What did Charlie say about my mom?" I heard the defensiveness in my voice.

Lucas put his hands up. "Nothing bad. He likes your mom a lot. I guess he knew her pretty well, back when she and your dad were first dating." It was hard to imagine Charlie and my mom and dad hanging out together, but they must have, once upon a time. "He said she was down-to-earth." Lucas paused. "Or she used to be, anyway."

That wasn't a phrase I associated with my mom.

"She used to be a teacher," I said. "She and my dad didn't have anything when they first got married. Dad used to say they lived on love, not money." He also said he preferred having both money and love, but I didn't mention that.

Lucas laughed. "That sounds like something from one of those lame books you read."

"I guess." I stared straight ahead, feeling heat bloom on my cheeks. "And they're not lame. Guys just don't get them." I felt Lucas's gaze on me, but he didn't say anything. I walked faster, forcing him to catch up.

We headed a few blocks east of Broadway, into a neighborhood full of old trees and tiny houses. Some of the houses looked like fairy cottages, with picket fences and gardens. Others weren't so well-kept, overgrown with weeds and paint peeling from the shingles.

"It's a mixed neighborhood," Lucas said, watching me closely. "But most of the people who live around here are pretty cool. Not much crime. Occasional car break-ins, but that's about it."

"Are you sure? It looks kind of, um, sketchy."

He inclined his head. "I'm sure. You realize we're just a few blocks from my place, right?"

"Oh." I hadn't realized, since I'd followed him home blindly that night. Where were my witty comebacks when I needed them?

He pointed to a tiny blue house surrounded by towering trees. "We're looking at that one. It's seven hundred a month but I thought you might still want to see it."

He was right. It looked like an illustration from a storybook.

The elderly woman who opened the door flashed a bright smile at Lucas. "Hello, sweetheart. It's good to see you." She turned her watery eyes to me. "And this is your girlfriend who needs a place to live? She's very cute, Lucas."

"I'm not his—"

"She's not my—"

"Girlfriend," we said in unison.

"Oh my. Pardon me, dears. I misunderstood. When Lucas asked me, I just assumed..." She stepped back and opened the screen door. "Where are my manners? Come in, both of you." She held out her hand to me. "I'm Mrs. Sandri. Would you like something to drink? I made tea."

"No thanks." I shook her hand, staring at the floor and

willing it to swallow me up.

"Yes, please. That would be great," Lucas said.

Of course his composure was better than mine. He was as poised as my dad.

"I'll be right back. Feel free to look around." Mrs. Sandri left the small living room, disappearing under an archway. The place was like a dream cottage. I wondered if Snow White lived here, too.

"It's pretty cool, isn't it?" Lucas asked.

I nodded, still unable to look at him after the misidentification. His voice echoed in my mind. *"She's not my girlfriend."*

The living room was small, but there was a fireplace in one corner. Looking through the archway, I saw a tiny dining room with a non-scary chandelier. I heard cups clinking and guessed the kitchen was beyond the dining room. I followed the narrow hallway off the living room and found two bedrooms, both decorated with ruffles and flower-printed fabric. There was a bathroom between them. It was small, but not as small as the one in Pinky's apartment. The house reminded me of Liz and her fairy cave.

Returning to the living room, I found Mrs. Sandri settled in a wing chair by the fireplace. Lucas sat on a small sofa across from her, drinking from a teacup. The delicate china balanced in his strong hand made me suddenly imagine him dressed in breeches, sitting in a drawing room, waiting to call on his lady. God, I was deranged.

I took a breath and sat next to him. The couch was so small that our thighs touched. The contact felt like fire shooting up my leg. I scooted over, leaving a few inches between us, and reached for my cup. Too bad it wasn't iced tea so I could dunk it over my head to cool my burning face.

"So tell me, honey, do you think my little house might work for you and your mom?" Mrs. Sandri smiled at me.

"It's a lovely house. But don't you live here?"

She sighed and shook her head. "Not for much longer. I'm moving to a home for seniors next week. That's why almost all the furniture is gone." She took a sip from her teacup. "The house is just too much for me to keep up on my own, even with Lucas doing the yard work for me and fixing everything that breaks." She winked at him. "He even came by late one snowy night when my washing machine overflowed and flooded the laundry room."

I glanced at him, raising an eyebrow, remembering his text the night I'd babysat. *Helping out a neighbor.*

He mirrored my eyebrow lift, then focused again on his teacup. But he was smiling.

"I don't want to sell it just yet," she continued. "And my sons don't want me to, either. So we're hoping to find some good people to rent it out. At least a year, maybe longer. Someone steady and responsible, which Lucas assures me you are. He speaks quite highly of you. Tells me you're in quite a pickle with your dad on the run. And all that nasty business about him on the news." She shook her head and clucked her tongue. "And your mama working so hard she doesn't even have time to come look at places with you. You poor dear."

I shot him a look. He was still fascinated by his teacup.

"And of course I adore your uncle; known him forever. So if you think you're interested you'd be at the top of my list. Though I would need to meet your mother, of course, since she'd be the one to sign the lease."

I set my cup on the table with a shaking hand. "Yes, of course. Mom would need to see the place first." I shot Lucas another look. "And we have a few other places to look at, don't we, Lucas?"

He set his cup on the table next to mine. "Yes, we do. Mrs. Sandri, may I use your bathroom please?"

"Of course, dear. You know where it is."

After Lucas left the room, she turned toward me with a conspiratorial smile. "Honey, I'm sorry I mistook you for his girlfriend. But I just assumed, because I know he has a girl. Of course he does, a handsome, sweet boy like that. And when he came around asking about the house, the way he talked about you and your situation... He just seemed so worked up that naturally I assumed..."

Worked up?

"It's okay, Mrs. Sandri." Something about her chatty concern made me feel I should reassure her. "Trust me, if you saw the type of girl Lucas dates you'd know why it was so, um, funny you thought I was his girlfriend." I swallowed as I forced a smile, because it wasn't really funny.

She frowned at me. "What do you mean, sweetheart?"

I sighed, then gave voice to all my insecurities, the ones that drowned out the memory of the night at his house. "You should have met his last girlfriend. She looks like a supermodel. The two of them were like a perfect matched set. Trust me, when she was in the room, Lucas didn't even know I existed." I took an unladylike gulp of tea. "Anyway, Lucas and I are just friends."

"Friends who need to get to their next appointment," Lucas said from the hallway.

I looked up, horrified. How long had he been standing there? His eyes seemed to bore into my very soul. I dropped my gaze, wishing once again that I hadn't used my outside voice.

I jumped up from the couch. "I'll take the cups to the kitchen." Lucas's eyes followed me like I was his prey and he was about to pounce. I could feel his anger all the way into the kitchen. Why was he angry, anyway? I was just speaking the truth about him and Heather.

Damn it. This was going to make things awkward again. I could have apartment-shopped on my own, but it was hard enough that we were moving. Doing this part with Lucas made it much more bearable.

"Please don't get up," Lucas was saying to Mrs. Sandri when I returned to the living room. "We'll let ourselves out."

I took a breath. "Thank you so much, Mrs. Sandri. You have such a lovely home. I'm sure my mom will like it. I'll be in touch with you soon."

"You have my number?"

"I'll give it to her," Lucas said, smiling through gritted teeth.

As soon as we were on the sidewalk, Lucas took my elbow. "What the hell was that?"

I shook my arm loose from his grip. "Don't grab me like that. What was what?"

"You're way too smart to play dumb with me, Darcy. Knock it off. You know damn well what I mean." His beautiful eyes were practically shooting sparks.

"The perfection part? About you and Heather looking like you belonged on top of a wedding cake?" If I was going down, I might as well do it in a blaze of glory.

He closed his eyes and his nostrils actually flared. Then his eyes snapped open and pinned me with a fierce gaze. "Not that, but yeah, that was idiotic, too. I meant the other thing you said. About me being so...so distracted by Heather that I didn't notice anyone else if she was around."

I spoke quickly, determined to figure out once and for all what he felt for me. "You can't deny it, Lucas. When she was around, the aliens could've landed and taken all of Broadway hostage and you never would've noticed."

He glared at me, his lips drawn in a thin straight line. His intensity made my stomach flutter. "Okay, so maybe you'd have noticed if the aliens took Pickles. Maybe." I waited for him to crack even the tiniest smile, but he didn't.

Instead, he stalked down the sidewalk. I hurried to catch up with him. At least we'd changed the subject. Painfully so, but at least we weren't talking about the utter humiliation of him overhearing me go on and on about how perfect he was. And how invisible I was.

And he hadn't denied what I'd said, about not noticing anyone else when Heather was around. Maybe I really had misinterpreted everything, like what he meant when he said he aimed high. Maybe he didn't mean me at all.

"Let's just get this over with, Lucas. How many more places do we have to look at?"

He stopped and pinned me with the spark-shooting glare again. "So you want to leave? I'm so full of my... perfection...that I'm a pain in the ass to spend time with?"

I felt like he'd sucker-punched me. How had things gotten this twisted around? One minute we were practically best friends and the next minute we were fighting like alley cats.

"God, you're so—" He ran a hand through his hair.

"I'm so what, Lucas? So annoying? So clueless? A one-woman tornado of craziness? Quick, pick one before you lose a turn."

"Stop it," he said, his voice low.

"Stop what?"

"Stop doing that. Getting snarky. You do it when you're upset."

I gaped at him. He had no idea how snarky I could be. I narrowed my eyes. "Come on, Lucas. You know you're only doing this to win points with Charlie. You don't really care where my mom and I end up."

The words hung there between us, like the slow-motion bullets in an action movie. But no one was dodging these bullets, and I wanted desperately to snatch them back. His hands clenched into fists. I had the feeling that if I were a guy I'd be lying on the grass, writhing in pain. That sounded preferable to enduring his frozen stare.

He spat out his next words. "If we actually are *friends*, Darcy, then guess what? I'm going to be honest with you." He laughed, but it was bitter. "You've already been honest about your opinion of me." He paused. "When I picked you up this morning, I didn't think we'd end up fighting. I was hoping maybe—" He stopped and ran a hand through his hair. He blew out a frustrated breath, then his eyes latched onto mine. "I was stupid enough to think we'd hang out like we always do. Maybe even have fun, while you're trying to figure out what to do next." He looked away from me, his jaw tight. "God only knows where I got that crazy idea."

My eyes filled with tears. If this *were* a romance novel, this was when he'd sweep me into his arms and kiss me passionately, telling me he loved me.

But this was real life. This was the twenty-first century, not the nineteenth. Hip hop music blared from the house across the street. Little boys played basketball in the driveway next door. Mrs. Sandri peeked out the front window, watching us argue. Across town, my mom sat in some dingy, abandoned house hoping someone would make an offer so she could redeem herself in Pam's eyes.

I'd insulted Lucas with a cruel, untrue accusation, so now he was lashing out at me.

I turned away so he wouldn't see my tears because he was the kind of guy who'd feel terrible if he made a girl cry, even if he was supremely pissed off with her. Even if she'd hurt him first.

His hands gripped my shoulders and whirled me around to face him. His eyes darkened, hiding emotions I couldn't pin down. Muscles twitched in his jaw.

"We're going to finish this," he said, glowering at me.

"Finish what?" I could hardly speak, hardly breathe.

His hands fell off my shoulders and he stepped away from me. "We are going to finish looking at places for you to live. Today. So that you can decide and bring your mom back to the place you like best. Follow me," he commanded. His Royal Hotness was channeling his inner duke again, barking orders. All he needed was a whip and some hunting dogs yapping at his heels. We walked six blocks without speaking to each other, and then he stopped suddenly in front of a duplex.

"This one is only $550 a month. It has two bathrooms." He spoke to me like I was a stranger, breaking my heart. Lucas poured on the charm for the guy who opened the door, but none of it spilled over onto me. I went through the motions with perfect politeness, but my mind was reeling.

How much time had Lucas spent trying to find me a place to live? And those signs he'd put up, that he'd joked about? He was freaking amazing. And I was acting like a brat. Like the spoiled rich kid he'd thought I was the first day I met him. What was wrong with me?

I shook the duplex owner's hand when we left, not even remembering his name.

"What'd you think about that place?" Lucas asked, his voice carefully neutral.

We were like two bombs wired to explode at the slightest expression of emotion.

"It was fine." Truthfully, I couldn't remember a thing about it. I'd been too distracted by my thoughts, by my regret at lashing out at him.

"Did you like it better than Mrs. Sandri's house?"

"What? No. I mean, I like that place the best so far. How many more places?" Desperation leeched into my voice.

"Just one."

"Good."

He sighed next to me as we walked to the last place.

We stopped in front of an apartment house. It was small, only four stories high. The building formed a U-shape and each apartment had a balcony overlooking the swimming pool below.

"Some people really like pools," Lucas said. "I wasn't sure if you and your mom did." He sighed again. "Then I saw the pool in your backyard today. I know this doesn't quite measure up."

My eyes swam with tears again. "Please don't," I whispered. "Please stop."

"What is it?" He stepped in front of me. He blocked out the sun. "You're crying." He looked down at me, his expression stormy.

"No shit, Sherlock," I said, wiping my eyes. "Don't worry, it's not contagious."

He stuffed his hands in his pockets. "Do you want to skip this place?"

I nodded.

"If I was one of those guys from those damned books you read," he mumbled, "I'd have a monogrammed handkerchief in my pocket. But I don't."

I laughed shakily as I wiped my eyes with the back of my hand, picturing the HRH monogram on his imaginary handkerchief. "So are you secretly reading regency romances, Lucas? Is that why I can't find the stack I saved at Charlie's?"

His eyes widened, but then he dropped his gaze and I would've sworn I saw the hint of a blush creep up his neck.

"It's nothing to be ashamed of." I had to choke back a giggle at the mental picture of him reading about rogues and wallflowers. "I have lots more I can lend you—"

He shrugged, running a hand along the back of his neck. "Okay, so I read one. It was awful."

"Then you picked a bad one. Next time I'll pick for you."

I thought of some of the books I could lend him, especially some of the sexier ones, and it was my turn to blush.

"No thanks," he said. "I'll stick to my textbooks. I don't have much time for other reading, anyway."

I pictured the comic books on his desk and smiled. I felt awful about lashing out at him, especially after all he was doing for me. I took a breath. "I'm sorry, Lucas. For saying that you don't care what happens to me or my mom." I glanced at him. "Because I know you do."

His jaw clenched and he looked away.

"Lucas?"

Sighing, he stared at the ground. "I'm sorry, too. For getting upset about what you said about Heather and me. But it's not true…" He ran a hand through his hair.

"What's not true?"

He still wouldn't look at me. "Never mind."

I sighed and pulled my jacket tighter around me. "We're quite a pair, aren't we?"

His finally raised his head, a ghost of a smile on his lips. "Like a buddy movie gone really bad."

That made me laugh for real. "Lucas?"

"Yeah?" He watched me, his expression wary.

"I don't even know how to thank you. The places were great."

"Not all of them," he said. "But you're welcome."

"I loved Mrs. Sandri's house. I want my mom to see it."

His shoulders sagged. Was that relief? "I thought you'd like that one best."

"See?" I blinked in the sun and smiled at him for real. "Maybe you do know me pretty well."

He dropped his gaze again, but not before I saw something indefinable flicker there.

"I'll take you home." He fished his keychain out of his pocket, still not looking at me.

"No."

"No?" He looked up, his eyes shooting angry sparks again.

"I'll take the bus. You've spent enough of your day with me already. I'm sure you have better things to do."

"Darcy. Don't be a—"

"Don't you dare call me a martyr."

His eyes widened. "How'd you know I was going to say that?"

I tapped my head. "I'm psychic."

He almost smiled. "Warn me next time. I'll bring my tin foil hat."

"Those never work. My wicked mind-reading skills penetrate right through that stuff."

"You're a mind reader, huh?" He swung his keychain around his finger, watching me through narrowed eyes. "Tell me what I'm thinking right now."

I swallowed. There were so many things I hoped he was thinking. "You're thinking you can't wait to drop me off and go do guy stuff. Fix cars, watch ESPN. Watch a dude action movie instead of hanging out with a girl who watches sappy movies and reads awful books."

He shook his head, his cryptic smile making my heart flutter. "You're a lousy psychic. Not even close."

"Food," I said. "That should've been my first guess. You're always hungry."

"True, but that's not what I'm thinking about right now." He took a step toward me and suddenly this wasn't a game anymore. "Guess again." His voice was soft, like a caress reaching out to me even though his hands were in his pockets. "Tell me what I want."

You want to kiss me. You're going to kiss me. I see it in your eyes. I wasn't psychic, but I wasn't blind, either. Oh. My. God.

"Crapuccino," I croaked. "Extra dry."

"Wrong," he said, taking another step toward me. "Try again, Shaker Girl." We stood inches apart, breathing in each other's air.

The sharp ring of my cell sounded, making both of us jump and shattering the tension. Frustration shot through me as I pulled my phone out of my pocket and stared at the caller ID.

"It's my mom. I need to answer." Why oh why hadn't I put it on silent?

"No worries," Lucas said, stepping back. His gaze had lost its heat and intensity, and I missed it already. We started walking, and he hung back a few steps to give me privacy.

The raw pain of Mom's sobs pushed away all my fantasies about Lucas. "Mom? What is it? Is it Dad?" Please, God. Don't let him be dead.

Lucas caught up to me. I barely registered his hand on my shoulder.

"Not Dad, me. It's me. Oh, Darcy, I've failed us," her voice wailed in my ear.

I turned away from Lucas, afraid he'd hear her. "Mom, just tell me what happened."

"Pam fired me today. She said I was…un(hic)reliable. And un(hic)professional. She said I looked like something the cat dragged in."

I closed my eyes and sagged against Lucas, dimly aware of his arm encircling my shoulders. "Oh, Mom," I whispered. "I'm so sorry."

"Where are you? When are you coming home?"

"I'm with Lucas. Looking at apartments, remember?" Oh no. How could we rent a place now, without any income? Oh my God. Don't think about it. Just do the next thing… do the next thing. Breathe. "I'll be home soon, Mom. I'm almost at the bus stop."

"I'll come get you," she said, slurring her words.

"No, Mom. You've been drinking. You can't drive."

Lucas took the phone from my hand. "Mrs. Covington? This is Lucas. I'll drive Darcy home. We'll be there as soon as we can." He paused. "Yes, ma'am. Good-bye."

He handed the phone back to me then tightened his grip around my shoulders.

He put a finger on my lips. "Don't argue. I'm driving you home."

"But…but." What could I say? That I didn't want him to see my mom drunk? That I wanted him to see me as…not perfect, exactly, but maybe…acceptable?

That hardly mattered now.

*L*ucas drove fast, but not so fast that I worried. "Should we bring food to your mom?" He hesitated. "If she's drinking, she should eat."

I leaned my head against the passenger side window, closing my eyes, relishing the feel of the cool glass on my skin. "We have leftover enchiladas. I made them last night. And some burned rice."

"Sounds great. Is there enough for me, too?"

I opened my eyes to stare at him. "What?"

His eyebrows knotted. "I'm not going to just drop you off, Darcy. I'll come in to help. Stay for a while."

"You know what? You're really taking this rescuing-the-damsel-in-distress role way too seriously. Stop reading my books."

He shot me a hooded glance. "Is that what you think I'm doing?"

"Isn't it?"

"Be careful. You're veering away from buddy-flick territory back toward mortal-enemies-locked-in-combat territory."

"Maybe I'll just be quiet."

"Excellent choice." He picked up his iPod and the sounds of one of my favorite indie bands filled the car.

"Maybe you're the one who's psychic," I said, my eyes closing again as I rested against the window.

"How so?"

"This is my de-stress music. It chills me out." I sighed, pulling my jacket tight around me. I wanted to stay in his car forever, eyes closed, music playing, just driving.

"It's going to be okay, Darcy," he said softly.

"How do you know?"

"Because you're strong. You'll get through this."

I opened my eyes to watch his profile as he drove. "Tough girls always finish last."

He glanced at me with that smile that turned me to jelly. "You're watching the wrong movies." He paused. "Maybe you should read more of your lame romances. Don't they always have happy endings?"

"They do. But life doesn't always tie up in a pretty bow at the end like it does in those books."

He nodded. "Life's messy," he agreed. "But sometimes amazing things can happen, even when it seems like it's all falling apart."

He couldn't possibly be talking about us. He was just trying to distract me from the nightmare that was my life. "Ah, Master Martinez," I said. "You speak such words of wisdom. Grasshopper can only hope to learn from you."

He shot me a dark look. "You should stop talking now."

I wished he'd just kiss me to shut me up, like in the movies, but instead we kept driving in silence, while I prayed my mom wouldn't be a total wreck by the time we got home.

Chapter Twenty-Four

Mom was lying on the couch when we walked in, surrounded by the clutter of our messy family room. I'd been meaning to clean it, but there just wasn't time with school and work and starting to pack for the move. Besides, we never had company anymore so what was the point?

Lucas was gracious, as always. "Hello, Mrs. Covington. It's good to see you again."

She stared up at him, her eyes unfocused. Pam was right. She did look like something the cat had dragged in. It was amazing she hadn't been fired sooner. I blinked back tears. I could *not* fall apart. Not in front of Lucas.

"Well, look who's here." Her words slurred as she tried to focus on me. "I knew there was something going on with you two."

"Mom. Please." I shot her a pleading look.

"Well, it's true. Darcy never brings guys home, but I'm not surprised to see *you*." She pointed a wobbly finger at Lucas.

I thought I would faint or hurl, or both. I hated how alcohol did this to her. I didn't dare look at Lucas, who'd busied himself gathering up the dirty plates and glasses scattered over our coffee table. Toby danced around him, thrilled to see the dog whisperer. Lucas caught my eye as he walked toward the kitchen.

"I'm sorry," I mouthed, using every power in me to keep my tears at bay.

He shook his head. "Nothing to be sorry for," he whispered.

Once he'd left the room, I tried to get Mom to sit up. "You've got to get to bed. You're completely wasted."

"Damn straight," she said, her stinking breath blowing in my face. "I have every right to be. That damn Pam had no right to fire me. She knows how much I needed that job."

"She's running a business, Mom. Not a charity." I couldn't believe I was defending Fake-Bake Pam. I stood up, pulling Mom to her feet. She swayed and leaned into me. Suddenly Lucas was there, propping her up from the other side.

Our eyes met as we supported her. I wasn't sure what I thought I'd see. Disgust maybe. But that wasn't it. His eyes burned with all sorts of emotions, too many for me to untangle. I looked away.

"Upstairs, Mom. You need to sleep it off."

She laughed bitterly, leaning most of her weight on Lucas. "Why? 'Cause everything will be perfec' in the morning? Darcy thinks she's gonna find her dad and drag him home.

Thinks he's gonna come riding in on a white horse with a bag full of money. Gonna stand on his stage and turn this pile of shit into a pile of gold."

"Mom. Don't." I couldn't stop the tears now. I shook with anger and fear.

"Darcy, go sit down," Lucas said, adjusting Mom so that he bore all her weight. "I'll get her upstairs."

"Mine's the biggest bedroom. Can't miss it, kid." Mom cackled like a crazy woman. "Ty always had to have the biggest everything. And look where it got him."

I remembered Lucas telling me about Heather puking at the Homecoming dance. I prayed my mom wouldn't complete my humiliation by doing that.

Lucas pinned me with his eyes again. "I've got her, Darcy. It's okay."

Tears streamed down my face as I watched them leave the room. It was a relief having someone else here, but it shouldn't be Lucas helping her up the stairs. It should be Dad. But if Dad were here, none of this would be happening.

Toby hovered at my feet, tail wagging.

"Come on, boy. At least I can take care of you." He followed me into the kitchen where I fed him. I loaded the dishwasher and cleaned off the counters. I heated the leftover enchiladas in the microwave, wondering if Lucas would be so appalled by my mom that he'd leave without eating.

"How often does that happen?" Lucas's voice startled me from the doorway.

I spun around to face him. "What do you mean?"

He walked toward me slowly, watching me as if I were

a trapped animal ready to flee. "How often do you come home to that? How often do you have to help her to bed?"

I focused on Toby, who'd rushed to Lucas as soon as he'd heard his voice.

"Darcy, look at me."

That was the last thing I wanted to do, but he closed the gap between us and tilted my chin up. "Tell me how often you come home to this."

"A lot," I breathed. Tingles ran down my jaw to my neck from his touch. I couldn't look away from him. "Especially lately."

He let go of my chin and shoved his hands in his pockets. "She needs help, Darcy. So do you. You can't do this by yourself."

"I know," I whispered. "I just keep hoping..."

"I don't want to be the one who tells you to stop hoping. But you have to deal with what's right in front of you."

"But I *am* dealing with it." Anger flashed through me. "I got us extra time to move. I set up the estate sale. I'm going to get us moved." Tears pushed away the anger and I was crying again. "Once we're out of here, maybe she'll stop. When she's not surrounded by all these...reminders... of what life isn't anymore."

His arms were around me before I could say anything else. "I know," he whispered into my hair. "I know."

I let myself be held. I'd imagined him holding me a million times, but not for this reason. He still felt amazing. The universe had a cruel sense of irony.

The microwave pinged. I was reluctant to step out of his grasp, but I did. "Dinner is served," I said, grabbing a dishtowel to wipe away my tears. "Unless you want to blow this pop stand, which I'd totally understand."

He looked surprised. "Do you want me to go? I thought you wouldn't want to be alone."

I focused on using hot pads to pull the casserole dish out of the microwave. "You've pretty much spent your whole day dealing with the Covington shit storm. I'm sure you have somewhere else to be on a Saturday night."

"I chose to spend the day with you. And I'm choosing now to have dinner with you."

I shrugged like it didn't matter, but relief washed over me. I didn't want to be alone. Having him stay was like having a net stretched under the tightrope of my screwed up life.

He found plates and silverware. "Do we eat under the scary chandelier?" He tilted his head toward the dining room.

"No." That was the last place I wanted to sit. "We could watch a movie or something." I forced a smile. "Something with lots of explosions."

"Sure," he said. "After we eat. I want to talk to you first." He set the plates on the granite counter in front of the barstools.

Panic washed over me. I didn't want a serious chat right now. Experiencing my reality was bad enough; we didn't need to talk about it.

"What about that buddy-flick situation we discussed earlier?" I said, forcing a lightness I didn't feel into my voice. "I'd rather we didn't end up in another fight."

"Not my first choice, either. But we're still going to talk."

A huge sigh gushed out of me. "Sometimes I wish I did drink. Now would be a good time."

He frowned at me. "You don't really mean that."

I slid onto the stool next to him, hyper-aware of his closeness. "No, I don't." I took a long gulp of water. "How about a smoke instead?"

He almost choked on his water. Once he'd swallowed, he shook his head at me. "You're not very observant. I quit smoking weeks ago."

Huh. He was right; I hadn't noticed. In my mind, he was often leaning against the old brick wall of Charlie's store, smoking and talking to whoever wandered by. The thought flitted through my mind that he wouldn't taste like an ashtray. If a person were to kiss him. Not that I'd ever know.

"That's good," I said. "One less cancer to worry about when you're old and gray."

He narrowed his eyes. "The sooner we get this over with, the sooner we can watch your buddy flick."

Inhale calm. Exhale stress. "Explosions and car crashes. No buddy flicks tonight. But by all means, let the lecture begin."

He closed his eyes briefly, frustration etching his perfect face. "I don't want to lecture you. I just had a suggestion. Maybe a couple of them."

"Can I ask you something, Lucas?"

He sighed. "Go ahead. I knew you couldn't just sit there and listen."

I pointed my fork at him. "I could if I wanted. But what I'm wondering is, are you one of those guys who needs to feel like they're Lancelot coming to the rescue all the time?

Like on the daytime TV shrink shows? Those guys who pick women who…" My voice trailed away as I realized I'd just implied he was my knight. And that he'd picked me as his lady to rescue. My cheeks flamed.

His lips compressed into a thin line. I couldn't tell if he was biting back a laugh or an argument.

"I didn't mean that you and me… What I meant was…" Oh God. Why couldn't I just keep my mouth shut? Someone needed to shove me back into my mousy Darcy shell.

"Please keep talking," Lucas said, his eyes fixed on mine. "I can't wait to hear more."

I shook my head and took a huge gulp of water so I wouldn't be tempted to keep babbling and make things worse.

He put his hands on his legs and shook his head, laughing a little. "You're a piece of work, Darcy Covington."

I stayed quiet, staring at my plate but sneaking glances at his denim-clad thighs.

"No, I'm not one of those guys," he said, sighing. "I'd never get anything done if I rescued everyone who needed it." He paused to drink a sip of water, then turned to face me. I heard him take a deep breath. "But I do like to help people I care about." He reached out to cup my chin, raising my face to look at him. "That's why I'm here with you right now." His hand moved to brush a loose hair behind my ear, then came to rest on my shoulder. I stopped breathing, staring into his beautiful eyes, wondering if my brain would ever form a coherent thought again.

"This isn't how I planned to tell you how I feel," he said softly. His hand drifted slowly down my arm, lighting a trail of fireworks on my skin. His strong fingers laced through mine, and his thumb drew slow circles on my palm, making me glad I was already sitting, since I might have lost my balance otherwise. "But I'm so tired of waiting." He took a breath, then dropped his eyes, looking at our entwined hands.

I knew I should say something. Anything. But I was afraid that if I even breathed too loudly, the spell would break and he'd disappear in a puff of smoke.

He raised his eyes to mine, and his lips twitched. "Are you actually speechless, for once?"

I blinked at him. Two blinks for yes.

His smile was slow, and sexy. "Come on, say something. Tell me more about the TV shrink's bullshit theories about rescuing people and falling in love." He paused and took a deep breath. "But I have my own theory about that, if you want to hear it."

I stared at him, still afraid to breathe, to move. If this was a dream, I didn't want to wake up.

His grin faltered. "You have to say something, Darcy. Because I think… I hope…you feel about me the way I feel about you." He looked at me from under his ridiculous eyelashes. "But I-I'm not sure."

I was stunned when I heard the nervousness in his voice. I breathed out slowly, finally finding my voice. "You aren't sure how I feel about you?"

He shrugged and ran his free hand through his long, dark hair. "Sometimes. But then you pull away. Like that night at my house." He sighed. "I know my timing sucks. You're dealing with so much crap right now. I was going to wait until you moved." He ducked his head, looking even less sure of himself. "I had a whole evening planned." This time his smile was shy and sweet, and it took my breath away even more than his usual sexy grin did. "I was hoping to sweep you off your feet. Like those guys in your stupid books." His neck reddened. His Royal Hotness was blushing. Big time.

I couldn't believe I impacted him this way. Me, queen of the mice. I wanted to freeze time so I could come back to this exact moment whenever I thought I didn't have the strength to keep going. I took a deep breath. "You already did," I whispered.

The look he gave me made my heart do cartwheels. He slid off his stool and pulled me into his arms. Maybe I wasn't psychic, but I felt like I was reading his mind, and he was reading mine, confirming all the feelings I'd been hiding from him.

"Just to be sure," I said, my voice shaky as I wrapped my arms around his waist, "this isn't like a pity thing? No Lancelot complex?"

His lips grazed my forehead. "Not even close." He pulled me closer. "You said I never noticed you, when Heather was around." His fingers moved through my hair, sending shivers up my spine. "I always noticed you, Darcy. Always." One hand stayed in my hair, the other moved down my back, stopping just above my waist, the warmth of his hand burning through my sweater.

"Heather was like a carnival. Loud. Crazy. Too much. I never cared about her...like that." He moved his hand, letting his fingers drift underneath my sweater, the warmth of his hand on my back setting my skin on fire. "With you, it's… I don't even know how to say it. It's like you're a work of art. Every time I'm with you, I see something new. Something beautiful."

My head rested against his chest, and I felt his racing heart. I had to say something, if only I could rouse my vocal cords from their swoon. I cleared my throat. "You're, um, not so bad yourself."

He laughed, the rumble in his chest vibrating against me. "And you always make me laugh. No matter what kind of crap's going on in your life." He leaned back slightly to look down at me. "I don't know if you're ready to hear this, but I need to say it."

He took a breath and my heart beat so loudly I was sure he must hear it. His fingers stroked my back and I suddenly knew why fainting couches had been invented. His gaze roamed over my face, and I suddenly believed him. He saw me, the real me. And he thought I was beautiful. The realization was so powerful, so true, that I gasped.

He nodded as if he'd read my mind. "Yeah," he said, his voice low, caressing. "I love you, Shaker Girl. I love the way you do what scares you. I love that nothing stops you. I love that you care so passionately about everyone." He grinned at me. "I love how goofy you get about salt and pepper shakers. I love how you can't control Toby." His grin faded as he took a shaky breath. "That first day I picked you up…" He sighed. "I thought you were just a spoiled rich girl." His expression changed, surprising me with its fierce intensity. "I had no idea how wrong I was. Or how much my life was about to change." He rested his forehead against mine. "I'm so sorry about all you're going through, but I'm not sorry that it brought you to me."

What could I possibly say in response? *Dude, I love your eyelashes?*

I wanted to tell him how much I loved him, but a tiny part of me was afraid to jinx things, by telling him how I felt. Besides, he'd said enough for both of us.

"Lucas?"

"Mm?" he murmured, his lips inches from mine. One hand still stroked my back, the other still played with my hair.

"Is this the part where you kiss me?"

"Right," he chuckled, just before his mouth claimed mine. "Like I'd forget that part."

He kissed me gently at first, waiting to see how I responded. I reached up to run my fingers through his hair and it was even better than I'd imagined. His grip tightened around me and I felt the muscles in his arms flex as he deepened the kiss, his lips hungry against mine.

I tugged at his hair, pressing into him. He groaned deep in his throat and his tongue swept into my mouth, making my world tilt. Then both of his hands were underneath my sweater, his callused hands on my smooth back, making me melt against him, caressing yet insistent as his tongue plunged even deeper, making me stagger against the bar counter.

He broke the kiss and whispered in my ear, "Just so you're clear, that wasn't a pity kiss."

I swallowed, struggling to find my voice. "I don't know. I might still need some convincing."

He laughed softly against my hair. "I'll see what I can do."

And he did.

Chapter Twenty-Five
November 30

Lucas spent the night.

But not with me.

He slept on the couch in the family room, after the two of us spent a couple of hours on the couch not watching the buddy movie he insisted on putting in the DVD player.

When the sunlight woke me, happiness washed over me like a river. I could hardly believe last night had happened, but when I looked out my bedroom window, his car was in the driveway.

I showered quickly and took more time getting dressed than usual. When I sat at my vanity and looked in the mirror, I grinned. Maybe I wasn't a supermodel, but Lucas said he loved me. And he'd somehow managed to fall in love with me during the worst time of my life.

"But that's why," I whispered. Because somehow, all of this drama had made me blossom into someone I didn't know I could be. I looked at the pepper shakers scattered across my dresser. It was because of them that I'd found Lucas. And Charlie and Liz. That I'd found a way to cope with everything.

Suddenly I remembered Mom passed out in her bedroom. My happy bubble popped instantly. Crap. What was going to happen with her today? Now that she didn't have a job, what would happen to us?

I so badly wanted to rent Mrs. Sandri's house and move, the sooner the better. The reporters wouldn't be able to find us anymore. We'd be away from the country club witches who didn't speak to Mom. I'd be where I now felt at home. I hoped Mom would eventually feel that way, too, about our new neighborhood.

I peeked in on Mom, who snored loudly. She wasn't getting up anytime soon. I tiptoed in and checked the room for puke. Nada. That was a relief.

Downstairs, Lucas was already awake making us espressos. My heart swelled, seeing him shirtless and barefoot at the counter, yawning as he looked out the window. He'd fed Toby, too.

"Are you sure you can work that contraption? She's a beast."

He turned around, looking so sexy with his messy bed head that I thought I might melt. "Hey, Shaker Girl. Sleep well?"

I nodded. I loved the way he looked at me.

"Good. I'm glad one of us did." He glared at Toby

accusingly. "Your dog insisted on sleeping on the couch with me. He slept great but I didn't."

"The hazards of being a dog whisperer," I said. "Plus, I'm not so sure he's my dog anymore. He seems to have transferred his allegiances."

"He was easy to win over." He gave me his sexiest smile. "His owner took a while longer to convince."

I raised my eyebrows. "I'm a much better actress than I realized. You had me at hello."

He groaned. "Is that another old movie reference?"

I grinned wickedly. "You watch too many action movies. With not enough kissing."

He pointed at me. "And you need to watch movies from the twenty-first century. There's this thing called Netflix. Maybe you've heard of it?"

I clucked my tongue. "And here I thought you were a romantic."

"Oh I am," he said. "I can prove it." He shot me a sexy smile. "Come here and I'll show you."

So I did.

Long after the espressos were cold, we sat down to eat generic cereal. Lucas frowned after he took a bite. "You need to buy the good stuff."

"We're on a budget, cereal snob."

"You gotta watch for the sales. Pickles is great at that. She's in charge of cereal choices, but she can't spend more than three bucks a box."

I laughed. "I'll take her shopping with me sometime."

He sighed. "That reminds me. It's going to suck having a four-year-old gloat about my love life. She's been wanting us to get together since that day she spilled all the beads at Liz's."

I ducked my head. "She has excellent taste."

He took a bite of cereal and nodded. "Except for the Firestorm Fairies."

"You have a lot to learn, Grasshopper. We'll start with season one, Fire Force Revealed."

"It can't be any worse than the ancient stuff you watch." I threw my napkin at him.

He slid off the barstool. "Come on," he said, reaching for my hand. "We have to finish our conversation." He pulled me into the family room and we plopped on the couch. He pulled on his shirt, which was probably a good thing, if he wanted me to focus. I waited while he tugged on his shoes.

"Last night, before we got...distracted...I told you I had a few suggestions."

I opened my mouth and he put a finger on my lips. "Please. Just this once. Listen."

My lips closed and he dropped his hand.

"Okay, so, it's none of my business, yet it is. Especially now." His eyes locked on me, brimming with emotion. "I think Mrs. Sandri's house would be perfect for you and your mom. But now your mom doesn't have a job."

"I've been thinking about that, too," I whispered, blinking back tears.

"I'm sure the estate sale will pull in a decent amount of cash. But you need to put down a deposit and first month's rent now." He took a breath. "Don't you dare accuse me of rescuing you. It would be a loan. You'd pay me back when you could."

"No—" I began, but he put up his hand.

His eyes pleaded with me. "God, Darcy. It's not like you're stealing from me. And I mean it about being a loan. Because I know that's the only way you'll accept help."

A few traitorous tears escaped. Lucas reached over to wipe them away with his thumb, his touch making me shiver.

"I've got to get to class, then I'm due at Charlie's at two. Are you working after school today?"

"No, but I need to come by for more boxes."

Lucas nodded. "Good. You need to bring your mom so she can sign the lease. I'll arrange to meet Mrs. Sandri. How about four at her house?"

"Lucas. You're so incredibly..." There weren't enough superlatives for me to say what was in my heart.

"Zip it." He grinned at me. "You had me at hello."

We stared at each other, then he stood up suddenly. "I can't stay here, or else I'll start kissing you again and I'll never make it to class." He put out his hands and pulled me to my feet. "One last thing, Darcy." He paused and ran a hand through his hair.

"I know what you're going to say. About my mom and her drinking. She needs help." He looked relieved that I'd said it and he didn't have to. I stared at his shoes as I spoke. "I just haven't been able to confront her yet." But last night was the last straw. I had to talk to her. Maybe losing her job would make her face the truth.

Lucas tilted my chin so I was looking at him. "Do you want me here when you talk to her? Or maybe Charlie?"

I shook my head. "It's really between her and me." I put my hand on his chest, feeling his heartbeat. "But thank you."

His jaw twitched as he covered my hand with his. I felt his heart speed up. "I'll see you later today. Text me if you can't make the four o'clock."

"Okay," I whispered. I stood on my tiptoes and kissed his cheek. "That one doesn't count. Now get out of here."

"Your wish is my command, Shaker Girl."

After he drove away, I dragged Toby back into the house. He'd chased Lucas's car halfway down the driveway.

I knew just how Toby felt.

Chapter Twenty-Six

I carried a steaming mug of coffee into Mom's bedroom and perched on the bed, rubbing her back. She mumbled and rolled away from me, pulling the covers up to her neck.

"Mom," I spoke quietly. "It's time to wake up."

She mumbled again. I set the mug on the nightstand and pulled the covers back. She rolled over and glared at me. "What the hell do you think you're doing?" Her face was smeared with makeup. Her hair hadn't been washed in forever.

"I'm waking you up. In more ways than one."

She hoisted herself onto her elbows, glaring at me. "You're not in charge, Darcy."

I almost laughed. "Actually, I kind of am. Have been for some time now. So I'm telling you to get up. We have a lot to do today. We have boxes to pack. A lease to sign."

Her mouth opened and shut like a ventriloquist's dummy.

"This isn't you, Mom." My hand swept around the room, which was a disaster zone of piles of clothes and unwashed plates. She fell back against the pillows. I picked up her hand and held it tight. "You're still in there, my perfect mom. The one who doesn't get drunk and drop the f-bomb. The one who never leaves the house without looking like a glamour photo." I smiled down at her. "Actually, it's okay if you tone that down. We can't afford the tanning salon and hair maintenance anymore. But you could at least take a shower." I pushed the limp hair out of her eyes. "I've been doing your laundry, but you keep wearing the same stuff over and over."

A tear rolled down her cheek, and into her ear, but she didn't say anything.

"It sucks that you got fired, but you needed to get free of Pam. I know you can find a better job. I believe it, even if you don't." I put my hand on her heart. "But most of all, I need my mom back. Because I've been trying to do it all by myself." My voice caught. "And I can't…can't keep doing it. I need you, Mom. So much."

Her eyes closed and tears streamed down her face. I lay down beside her and held her hand in mine as we breathed together.

Inhaled. Exhaled. Just breathed.

*M*om called school, excusing me to leave at noon because she wanted me to go with her to a recovery meeting. I was nervous, but proud of her. I stood at my locker, which was a disaster, not organized the way it used to be. Somehow I'd hardly noticed its disintegration. I guess it reflected my state of mind. Or it used to, anyway. But today my mind was clear, focused. Hopeful.

I knelt on the floor, digging through the mess, pulling out papers to be recycled or filed. Shoved in a corner, I found a typed list: The Top Ten Reasons Chloe Hendricks Sucks.

I'd actually come up with way more than ten reasons when I'd made the list. I scanned the reasons, some of them mean and petty, some sort of funny. After the Letterman locker defacing, I'd wanted revenge, so I'd created this list and planned to use it, but then I'd chickened out.

Reading it now, all I felt was relief that I hadn't done to her what she'd done to me. I didn't want to be that person. I tore the list into pieces, bursts of gratitude shooting through me with each rip. I tossed the shredded list and the rest of my old papers in a recycling bin and headed for my truck.

The parking lot was full of people since it was lunch break. Chloe and Ryan leaned against his Range Rover, kissing. As I walked by them, I smiled because all I felt was lightness, like a weight I didn't even know I'd been carrying floated away. They had their lives. I had mine. And in spite of the Tri!Umphant! Shit Storm, I wouldn't trade with them in a million years.

Plus, there was amazingly epic kissing in my future, too. In just a few hours, if I was lucky.

Mom and I pulled up to Mrs. Sandri's house right on time. Charlie was there, too, talking to Mrs. Sandri and Lucas on the porch. My mom froze when she saw everyone.

"It's okay, Mom. They're here to help us. They care about us."

She didn't want to get out of the car. "I don't think I can do this. I'm so embarrassed." She looked at me, panicked. "And your boyfriend is here, too. I know I said awful things to him last night. I'm so sorry, honey." She dropped her gaze. "They care about you, Darcy, not me."

I tilted her chin up, just like Lucas did to me. "Then let that be enough. Anyone who cares about me gets you, too." I smiled at her, but she was crying again. "Besides, you know that's not true. Uncle Charlie cares about you, too."

"I've let you down," she said. "What if I do it again?"

"What did they say in that meeting today, Mom? You have to take it day by day. And today you haven't let me down. You're here, where I asked you to be. Now it's time to do the next thing."

I got out of the car and walked around to open her door. I held her hand as she stepped out. She was pale, but her hair was shiny and she wore clean clothes that weren't wrinkled. I handed her a handkerchief to wipe her tears.

She laughed. "Where'd you find this?"

"In your dresser." I glanced up the sidewalk toward Lucas and Charlie. Lucas jumped off the steps and jogged over to us. He bent down to kiss my cheek, laced his fingers through mine, and smiled shyly at my mom.

"Hi Mrs. Covington," he said. "I hope you'll like this house."

Mom blushed. "Lucas, I need to apologize for last night—"

Lucas put up a hand. "Please don't. I know you've been under a lot of stress."

She shook her head, eyes downcast. "That's no excuse," she muttered.

"Come on, Mom," I said, tugging her after me. "Mrs. Sandri is waiting for us."

Charlie hugged Mom and spoke softly to her. I couldn't hear what he said, but I could tell Mom was fighting back tears.

Mrs. Sandri ushered us into her house, fluttering around, offering tea and cookies. Lucas and Charlie waited in the living room while Mom and I toured the house.

"What do you think?" I asked her when we'd reached the back bedroom.

Mom looked at the lace-curtained windows and doily-covered nightstand. "It's like a dollhouse," she said.

"I know. Isn't it great? It's just right for the two of us."

Mom looked at me, her eyes filled with sadness. "It could work for three people, too."

I nodded but said nothing.

"Charlie's offering to loan us the deposit and first month's rent to tide us over until after the estate sale," she said.

"Lucas offered, too," I said.

Mom frowned. "I hate being a charity case."

"It's a loan, not charity. You know we'll make enough money at the estate sale to pay them back. And you'll get a better job, Mom. I know you will. Plus I'm earning money. I can still help with groceries and gas."

A deep sigh shuddered through Mom. Her eyes looked clearer than they had in weeks. "It wasn't supposed to be like this. Your life. My life. It was supposed to be—"

"I don't know anymore what life is supposed to be,

Mom. I'm just dealing with what it is."

Mom gave me a tight-lipped smile. "Planting new crops?"

"Yes. Sometimes you have to start over. Like Dad says… sometimes acts of God, or acts of people…mess everything up. I'm not going to sit and rot, and I'm not going to let you, either."

"I don't know if I can do this, Darcy," she whispered.

"The universe threw us a huge curveball, Mom. But we're still here. We can't give up." My voice sounded stronger than I felt.

She stared down at the flowered rug. "I wish your dad was here."

"Me too. But he's not." Frustration welled up inside of me. I knew this was hard for her. Moving out of our home meant that life would never be the same. It was literally closing the door on our old life.

Mom took a deep breath. "All right. Let's sign the lease."

I hugged her tightly, not wanting to let go. "It's going to work. I know it is."

She held my hand as we walked down the hallway. "When did you get so strong?"

We signed the paperwork with Mrs. Sandri, who insisted we eat her cookies to seal the deal.

Afterward Charlie and Mom went outside, to talk about the money, I assumed. Mrs. Sandri took the empty plates to the kitchen while Lucas and I sat on the small sofa, our legs in full contact this time. He leaned over to kiss me, but I pushed him away.

"What?" he laughed as I held him at arm's length.

"Mrs. Sandri will be back any second."

"So? She figured out you were my girlfriend before you did."

I shoved him back against the fluffy cushions. "Very funny."

He pulled me into him and kissed me before I could argue any more.

"I knew I was right about you two," said Mrs. Sandri as she walked back into the room. Her eyes danced, and she smiled at me when we pulled apart. "One of the advantages of old age, dear. I know love when I see it."

Chapter Twenty-Seven
December 5

Sal and I ate lunch together in the back of the cafeteria. Her fierce glares scared away all the drama groupies. She knew today was the estate sale, but she also knew I didn't want to talk about it. Instead, she prattled on about rehearsals, interspersed with stories about Mark's creative bedroom skills. "Speaking of," she said, pausing to suck down soda, "what's up in that department with you and the smexy college boy-toy?"

I smiled but shook my head. "Nothing to spill."

Sal had been deliriously happy when I'd told her about Lucas and me. She'd gloated about how she was right about him on Homecoming night. "You've got to be kidding me. If I were you, by now I would've—"

"Stop. I don't need you to spell out what you'd have

done by now." I stole one of her fries. "I'm moving at my own speed with Lucas. And he's fine with that."

Her eyes narrowed. "I don't get you, Darcy. That's like having dinner in a gourmet restaurant but skipping dessert."

"Drop it, Sal. He's not just a boy toy. He means a lot to me."

Sal rolled her eyes. "Like I don't know you're madly in love?" She paused, giving me one of her mind-reading glares. "Did you tell him yet? That you love him?"

I sighed. "Not yet. I will. Soon." He knew. How could he not?

"You have to say it. Especially since he said it to you first. It's like a rule."

"It's not a rule."

She snorted. "Whatever. Subject change. Give me some juicy details. Please tell me he's an awesome kisser."

I shook my head, laughing at her, but I felt my cheeks burning as I thought of Lucas's kisses. He was most definitely awesome. Epic. Off-the-charts.

She grinned, pointing a fry at me. "I knew it. Details. Now."

"No." I reached for another fry but she pulled them away.

"No details, no fries."

*M*om picked me up after school and we went to a movie, then dinner, something we hadn't done in ages. When we got home, it was clear that the estate sale lady was right about not being around to watch the vultures. Our house was almost picked clean of small items. Sold tags were on most of the furniture. I was grateful my room was off-limits, since I was bringing everything with me.

"You okay?" I gripped Mom's hand as we walked into the kitchen, where the cupboards were open and almost bare. We'd saved a set of dishes and glasses, some pots and pans, but all the fancy china and crystal was gone.

She bit her lip as she took it all in. She squeezed my hand. "I will be."

We watched a Hugh Grant movie, since Mom loved him, nestled on the couch together like when I was a kid. She drank herbal tea and I ate popcorn. We even managed to laugh a little when Hugh's friends all crammed into a tiny car to race across London so he could declare his love to Julia Roberts.

"We're going to be okay, Mom," I whispered, as the movie credits rolled.

"I hope so, honey. I hope so."

*L*ucas texted me as I was falling asleep. He'd gone to a basketball game with friends.

"How's my girl?"

"Sleepy. But ok."

"How's your mom?"

"Sad. But sober."

"That's good, right?"

It was.

Darcy and Marilyn,

Houses built on sand collapse. Empires built on lies cannot stand. I pray for forgiveness.

-Ty

Chapter Twenty-Eight
December 6

*M*om and I stood in the driveway ready to go our separate ways on Saturday. A line of people snaked down our sidewalk, anxious to get into the sale. They watched us curiously as we stood by our vehicles.

Mrs. Sandri had given us a key and told us to clean and paint, whatever we needed to do. Mom had decided to paint. She looked determined, wearing an old Tri!Umphant! T-shirt and sweatpants. I didn't even know she owned sweats.

"Come by on your lunch break," she said, since I was scheduled to work all day at Liz's.

I nodded, my throat tight around unshed tears. I was so proud of her and so relieved she hadn't relapsed. I'd been terrified she would. I took a breath and smiled. "Don't paint the living room puke green. Or princess pink." I crossed my eyes, making her laugh.

She did her best Fake-Bake Pam impression. "I think you know I have much better taste than that."

We laughed and hugged each other tightly.

I was glad to be working by myself for the first part of the morning. The smell of brewing coffee relaxed me, reminding me that I was in a safe place. His Royal Hotness was my first customer, entering through the alley door before I'd unlocked the front door. Unlike the front-door customers, he greeted me with a kiss that set me on fire, chasing away my worries with his touch.

"I didn't think you were working today," I said, when we came up for air.

"I'm not," he said, his eyes drinking me in like he hadn't seen me in a year. "But I wanted to see you." I leaned against his chest and sighed without words. He held me, running a hand through my hair. "What's wrong?"

"The house is practically empty. It's so hard being there when it doesn't feel like home."

"You're almost out of there," he whispered against my hair.

"I know." I raised my head to smile at him. "Mom's at Mrs. Sandri's today. Painting. But I don't think she knows how."

"I can go by the house to help her."

I rolled my eyes. "How many times must we discuss the

hero complex? You're not in charge of rescuing us."

His jaw tightened. "Stop psycho-analyzing me. I happen to be an experienced painter."

I stepped around him to go unlock the front door. "Of course you are," I said over my shoulder, flipping the CLOSED sign to OPEN. "You also leap tall buildings in a single bound."

He ignored me, instead busying himself at the espresso machine. "I have a ladder. Paintbrushes. I even have painter's pants."

"I have a better idea. If you really have nothing to do today, how about fixing my truck?"

His smile faded. "Is it acting up?"

"No, just the blue smoke you already saw. But I'd like to know it's in good shape."

He frowned at me. "Are you planning a road trip?"

"No." My cheeks flushed under his penetrating stare.

He narrowed his eyes suspiciously. "What are you up to, Shaker Girl?"

I turned away, filling the pastry case. "I'm not up to anything. You know I want the truck fixed. And we'll have the estate sale money by the end of the week. So I can pay you for parts." I shot him a sideways glance. "And labor."

"My labor costs are high." He took the pastry box and set it on the counter, then pulled me into his arms again. "Very high. But I'll consider giving you a discount." He bent to kiss me again, tasting like coffee.

The front door whooshed open and we pulled apart. His eyes danced as he looked down at me, holding out his hand. "Give me your truck key."

I fished my keys out of my pocket and handed them

over. Lucas glanced toward the guy in bike shorts who'd paused to pick up a copy of the daily paper I'd set on a table.

"I'll see you later," he whispered, kissing me quickly on the top of my head. I heard the alley door close as I turned to take the cyclist's order.

Lucas returned at five o'clock, just as my shift ended. He'd texted me earlier, telling me that he and Mom decided I had to wait until the end of the day to see their handiwork, because it was a surprise. True to his word, he wore painter's pants, a torn T-shirt, and a bandana tied around his forehead. There was grease on his arms and paint splatters on his nose. It was surprisingly sexy.

"Wow," I said. "How much is this day going to cost me?"

"You have no idea," he said. "Even with your girlfriend discount, you'll probably have to take out a loan." He slanted me a wicked grin. "Or maybe we can work something else out."

Liz emerged from Fairyland, a stack of books in her hands. She stopped short when she saw Lucas. "Oh my. What have you been up to?"

He shrugged. "Not rescuing people. Not helping out people I care about. Not much of anything, really."

Liz looked between us and laughed. "I'm not sure what's going on here," she said, "but I'd recommend a shower for one of you. Dinner for both of you." She stage-whispered to me, "Somewhere romantic. With lots of candles."

"What a genius idea. Darcy, you can drive." Lucas tossed

my keys over the counter and I caught them, barely.

"What about the shower?" I said.

"Go check out your new purple living room. Then pick me up at my place in an hour." Lucas turned and headed for the front door. He stopped to look at me over his shoulder. "Don't be late. I turn into a monster if I'm not fed regularly."

"Maybe I prefer vampires."

"You disappoint me," he said, shaking his head in mock disgust. "I thought your tastes were more original."

The door slammed behind him, but I knew he heard my laughter.

The living room wasn't purple. The pale gray walls were soft and welcoming, and the molding and baseboards gleamed white. The colors made the pale pink stone around the fireplace glow, beckoning people to gather around it.

"This is amazing," I breathed, looking around.

"We did good, didn't we?" Mom agreed. I raised my eyebrows at her grammar. She giggled, brushing her hair out of her eyes. Her T-shirt and jeans were covered with paint splatters and her grin was huge, and proud.

How could I ever thank him? I knew he was kidding about payment, but I wished I could show him how much his time meant. I knew that I would've done the same for him, if I could. Maybe someday I could return all the favors I owed him.

I looked out the window to the barren trees outside. When something was given out of love, was it really a favor? Or was it simply a gift, given without expectation of anything in return? I knew the answer.

"He helped me paint for several hours." Mom smiled at me. "He's quite entertaining. And very sweet. I'd say you're a lucky girl, but I think he's lucky, too, to have found you."

I blushed. "I don't know about that."

"I do," Mom said.

"What are you doing for dinner?" I suddenly felt guilty and anxious about leaving Mom alone tonight. "You could join us."

Mom shook her head. "No way. You two deserve a night out without your pathetic mom tagging along. Besides, I have plans."

That was a surprise. "Plans? With who?"

"Some new friends from my meetings. We're having Thai food, then going bowling."

My mouth dropped open. "Bowling? You? Do you even know how?"

"I think there's a stick involved, right? And beanbags?"

Laughing, I tossed a rag at her. "You're doomed."

We washed the paintbrushes in the utility sink in the basement and left them to dry.

"I brought clothes and toiletries so I could shower here," Mom said. "Since the sale goes until seven tonight."

That was a good sign, Mom planning ahead. But I was still anxious. "You sure you'll be okay tonight?" I asked. "Call me after bowling when you're heading home. I'll meet you there, so we can face the vulture pickings together."

Mom pulled me into a hug. "Don't worry. I feel like a new person today. This was what I needed, to get busy. You just enjoy your night with Lucas." She released me from her hug. "Darcy, we haven't talked about this for a long time, but make sure you're using protection, okay? If you are having sex, I want you to be safe."

"Mom!"

She frowned at me. "It's my job to look out for you. I don't mean to embarrass you, but—"

"Mom, stop. We're not. Trust me, okay?"

Her eyebrows rose in surprise. "You're not? Really?" God. She was worse than Sal.

"This conversation is over. I have to pick up Lucas in half an hour." I sighed and tugged at my hair. "You're right about him, Mom. He's very sweet. We're not rushing things."

She sighed, with what I assumed was relief. "Well, when the time does come—"

"Bye, Mom," I hollered as I shot up the basement stairs like a rocket. "We'll finish this conversation in our next lives."

Chapter Twenty-Nine
December 13

It was dark by the time Lucas and Mark drove away with the last load in my truck. Charlie drove the U-Haul, while Sal and Mom's new recovery friends followed in their overflowing trucks and cars. We'd survived moving day, with the help of our new tribe.

Mom and I stayed behind to do one last sweep of the house to make sure we weren't forgetting anything. We stood in the dining room, arms wrapped around each other, looking up at the chandelier no one had bought at the estate sale.

"I still feel like someone's going to stab me whenever I look at it," I said.

Mom laughed softly. "It wasn't one of my better decisions."

"But you like it," I said. "That's what matters. Are you bringing it with us?" I couldn't see it in Mrs. Sandri's cozy dining room.

Mom shook her head. "It stays with the house. It belongs here."

I nodded. We both jumped when the doorbell rang, its chime echoing off the empty walls and floors. Toby ran to the door, skittering across the tile floors, his paws not used to the lack of rugs.

J.J. stood on the porch, his features harsh under the bright porch lights. I was shocked to see him. He was such a part of my old life that seeing him was like stepping back in time.

None of us spoke for several seconds.

"May I come in?" he asked.

Mom gestured him into the foyer.

"I know it's a bad time," he said, looking around at the empty rooms. He turned to Mom, his eyes full of sadness. "I'm so sorry, Marilyn. I never thought it would come to this."

Mom nodded. "None of us did. But here we are." She took a shaky breath and reached into her pocket, then held out a keychain. "I guess you're here for these."

He frowned. "That's not why I'm here." He sighed, running a hand through his hair, which was peppered with much more gray than a few months ago. "I wanted to warn you before you see tomorrow's news."

"Is it Dad?" I whispered. "Have you heard from him?" Mom reached out for my hand. We gripped each other's fingers tightly.

J.J. shook his head. "No. It's Harvest. We're officially declaring bankruptcy. Everyone is being laid off. A trustee will take over what little funds are left."

I looked at Mom, who stood as still as a statue.

"So you've given up," Mom said. "All of you have."

J.J. sighed. "Haven't you, Marilyn?" He threw out his arms, encompassing the empty house with his gesture. "There's nothing left to hope for."

Mom dropped her head.

"That's not true." The anger in my voice surprised me. "We can't give up hope. He's going to come home. Someday."

J.J. shook his head, his face haggard and drawn. "Even if he does, what's left for him now?"

Mom's head snapped up. "*We* are, damn it. We're still here."

"Don't you think he would've come home by now, if that was enough?"

The cruelty of his words shocked me. How could Dad's friend say something so awful? "You should leave," I said. "Now."

He held out his hand and Mom dropped the keys into his upturned palm. His fingers closed around the keys and I felt like he'd just slammed the door on all our history together. The shared family trips to our cabin, to the Harvest company ski condo, the hours of babysitting I'd logged with his kids. All of it meant nothing to him.

"I'll have our secretary call you for your new address, in case we need to send any more legal documents."

"You do that," Mom said, her voice falling like ice chips.

We watched him get into his Jag and drive away. Mom sagged against me and I wrapped my arm around her shoulders.

"He's scared," I said. "And angry. He's lashing out at the wrong people." I'd heard that from the TV shrink reruns I still watched when I couldn't sleep. I'd learned some things besides the Lancelot rescue-hero complex. Like the signs of depression. I was pretty sure we'd missed or ignored all of them with Dad.

"I know," Mom said, "but what if he's right? What if we're not enough?" She turned to face me. "I know I dismissed your idea of Dad chasing Stonehenge, but I've been hoping you were right. Hoping he was on some bizarre quest that would lead him home. Eventually."

"I wanted to talk to you about that," I said. "About where I think he is, and where he might go next."

Mom bit her lip. "You really think you know where he is?"

"I'm not sure, but I think I have a decent guess."

She swallowed, her hand at her throat. "Maybe…maybe I can hire a private investigator to find him, if you're sure. You can't go, Darcy. You can't."

I frowned but didn't argue. The only person going on a hunt for my dad was me. But now wasn't the best time to plead my case with Mom.

"Let's go, Mom. We'll talk about this later. Everyone's waiting for us." I forced a smile. "They probably already ate all the pizza."

She took a deep breath and looked around one last time, her eyes drinking in the emptiness.

"Come on, Toby," I called. He charged out the front door and down the steps toward Mom's Volvo.

Mom walked through the doorway, tears glinting in her eyes. She squeezed my shoulder, then followed Toby.

I pulled the door closed behind us and didn't look back.

Chapter Thirty

December 17

National Newswire BREAKING NEWS

Tri!Umphant! Harvest Industries held a press conference today from headquarters in Denver, Colorado. Acting president J.J. Briggs began the conference by reading the following press release:

"The board of directors voted today to file bankruptcy. A trustee has been appointed by the court to liquidate all assets and pay off all debts. All employees will be terminated as of the end of December."

Mr. Briggs was asked to comment about the continued absence of Tyler Covington, the face of Tri!Umphant! Harvest.

"He's not coming back," J.J. said. "We had

no choice but to file bankruptcy. We don't even know if he's still in the country."

Mr. Briggs was asked if the return of Mr. Covington could change the board's decision to file bankruptcy.

"That's a moot question," said Mr. Briggs. "Ty's gone. For good."

Mr. Briggs declined to answer any more questions.

Comments:

Share your comments on this story on our website. Comments may be removed by the moderator if considered inappropriate by NN.com.

"I knew it! I knew that guy was a total fraud. Good luck getting refunds on your Harvest tour tickets." –DaveInDenver

"He helped me through awful times. I don't know what happened to him, but I'll always love Ty." –MissKT

"You true believers are nuts, MissKT. The guy might as well have held a gun to your head and robbed you." –DaveInDenver

"I'm not going to argue with you, Dave. You can't change my mind and I can't change yours." –MissKT

*L*ucas texted me as I unpacked a box in our new kitchen. *"Can I come by your house tonight after work?"*

Like I'd say no.

"Make sure your mom's home, too."

So much for the hot and heavy kissing session I was hoping for.

"Sure. C U tonight." I wondered what he was up to. I tore open another box. I'd find out soon enough.

*I*t was after ten when Lucas rang the doorbell. Mom had made hot chocolate and actually baked cookies when I told her he was coming over. She even used her snowman cookie cutter. I couldn't remember the last time I'd seen her bake. The sight of her standing sentry over our professional grade Kitchen Aid mixer made me deliriously happy.

Toby barked when he heard Lucas calling to him from the other side of the door. Disloyal dog.

I flung open the door and my mouth dropped open. Lucas and Charlie stood on the top step, balancing a Christmas tree between them. The smell of fresh-cut pine filled my nose, flooding me with memories. Liz stood on a lower step, smiling up at me and holding shopping bags overflowing with wrapped packages. Pickles bounced up and down next to Liz, waving to me and giggling, wearing a headband full of jingle bells.

"What... Why..." My brain stopped computing.

"Can we come in?" Lucas asked. "Or do you just like watching me show off my muscles?"

Laughing, I stepped back and opened the door wide. The room filled with voices and laughter as Lucas and Charlie set up the tree next to the fireplace. Mom directed Lucas to the basement for the Christmas decorations. He returned with an enormous box of ornaments and cobwebs in his hair. Charlie queued up an Ella Fitzgerald holiday album on his iPod while Pickles stuffed herself with sugar cookies and hot chocolate.

Lucas pulled me into the darkened hallway for a deep, toe-curling kiss. I brushed cobwebs out of his hair when his kisses drifted down my jaw to my neck.

"Lucas," I whispered. "There's a parent and sibling here. Plus an uncle and my boss."

"So?" he murmured, working his way back up my neck to my earlobe.

Pickles bounced into the hallway. "Presents!" she exclaimed. "We're putting them under the tree right now!" She stared at us as Lucas came up for air. "Why are you eating Darcy's ear?"

"I'm hungry," he said. I whacked him on the chest.

Pickles wrinkled her nose. "You're gross, Lukie."

I shot him a warning glare but he just pulled me in close again.

"Go away, Pickles," he growled. "We'll be there in a minute."

Pickles drifted back toward the living room but we heard her loud voice. "Lucas and Darcy are kissing. Because he's hungry."

Oh God.

We laughed against each other's lips, but we kept kissing.

Later we all sat around the tree. As she hung ornaments on the tree, Mom told stories about all of the lame ones I'd made over the years. Lucas took the popsicle frame with my brace-face sixth grade photo and hung it from his shirt collar.

"I'm keeping this one." He grinned at me.

"I bet you have one just like it."

"Nah. I never needed braces."

I rolled my eyes. "Of course you didn't."

A pile of wrapped packages spilled around the base of the tree. Just like on Thanksgiving, my heart overflowed with the love I felt from everyone. Lucas retrieved a small box wrapped in reindeer paper. He sat down next to me on the loveseat. "Open it," he said.

I glanced around the room self-consciously but no one was watching us. "It's not even Christmas yet."

"Haven't you heard of the twelve days of Christmas?" His eyes danced in the glow of the fire. "There's more where this came from. Open it."

"Okay." I felt myself blushing with anticipation. I'd never had a present from a guy before, except for the stuffed Elmo my kindergarten crush had given me, then taken back at nap time.

I unwrapped the package slowly, savoring the moment. Inside was a tiny box that said *"Build Your Own Stonehenge."*

I flipped it over to see a picture of a tiny green mat and tiny stones, a miniature replica of the original henge in England.

"I hope it's okay," he said softly. "It made me think of you. And your dad."

"It's perfect," I whispered. "Just like everything else tonight."

He leaned over and kissed me softly on the cheek. I leaned against his shoulder, absorbing his warmth, wishing we could stay like that forever. But with everyone there, I knew it was time to tell them about my plan.

Mom and I had run the gauntlet and survived. We'd left our old life behind and were starting a new life together. But while I'd spent the past few days unpacking, I'd had a lot of time to think. And all I'd thought about was Dad. About all the signs and clues we'd missed. About the appearances he'd skipped last summer, or the ones where he showed up but dialed it in.

I'd remembered one day in the summer, hearing J.J. and Dad screaming at each other in Dad's office and slinking away from confrontation rather than asking what was wrong. Holding the tiny Stonehenge model, I turned the box over and over in my hands. If the last few months had taught me anything, it was that I could deal with all kinds of crap, and survive.

"Hey, Pickles, come here sweetie." She'd been lying on the floor with Toby, using him as a giant pillow. She scrambled over to me and I wrapped an arm around her. "I need to have a grown-up talk with everyone right now, so I'd like you to go play in my bedroom for a little while." She gave me a sour look, earning her nickname. "I have some new beads, and a sparkly gold cord to string them on. You can make a Christmas necklace. Come on."

Lucas's penetrating stare hooked on me when I returned. "You all right, Shaker Girl?"

"Yeah," I said. "Just do me a favor. I need you to rein in your inner Lancelot, okay?"

He frowned at me. "What?"

Ignoring him, I spread out my map on the coffee table as everyone stopped talking to watch me.

Mom set her mug down and worry creased her face. Charlie and Liz watched me with concern and curiosity. Lucas sat up straighter. I could practically feel him reaching for his imaginary sword. So much for reining it in.

There was silence for a few moments as everyone stared at the map. I'd marked all of Dad's postcard locations with yellow post-its, and potential next stops with red stars.

"What is this?" Charlie asked.

"It's Dad's route, where he's been so far." I looked into his worried eyes. "And my best guess of where he's going next."

"No way," Lucas said next to me, his words clipped and angry. "No freaking way. You are not doing this, Darcy."

"Doing what?" Liz asked.

"Going on a damn rescue mission," Lucas snapped. His nostrils flared and in spite of my frustration, I had to suppress a giggle because I could practically see him storming through his castle, barking orders.

"What?" Mom sounded panicked. "Rescue mission? Darcy, we've talked about this. Honey, you can't do this. Not now. Not after we…" Her voice broke and she started to cry, making me feel terrible. But I couldn't give up.

"See, this is exactly why I warned you to rein it in." I turned on Lucas. "If you'd let me explain rationally—"

"I agree with your mom, Darcy," Charlie interrupted. "You can't possibly go off on some sort of crazy road trip based on random post—"

"This is why you wanted the truck fixed, isn't it?" Lucas's voice was low and angry. "How long have you been planning this?"

I looked into his stormy eyes, and knew I had to press on, no matter how upset he was.

"I can do it, Mom. I can find him. I know his path looks random, but he's chasing clonehenges. I'm pretty sure he's—"

"Pretty sure?!" Lucas exploded next to me. "You think you're going to just hit the road and—"

I whirled on Lucas. "I told you about this before, Lucas. About my map. Why are you acting like this?"

"Because you think you don't need anybody!" He was pissed. "You think you can fix everything by yourself."

"Not everything. But I can do this by myself."

"I'll go with you," Charlie said softly. "If you're determined to do this, you can't do it by yourself."

"No," Mom said. "Let's call the police, or maybe a detective."

"No one's coming with me!" Frustration surged through me. After all I'd done, everyone was treating me like I really was a damsel in distress who couldn't do anything by herself.

I turned back to Lucas. "You need to stop. I mean it. I'm not asking you to go fight dragons for me, so just back off." He opened his mouth to argue but I kept talking, turning my attention to Charlie. "Charlie, I love you and everything, but you have a store to run."

"Maybe I could go…" Mom said, her eyes on the floor.

"No, Mom. You need to stay here. You need to go to your meetings and be with your new friends." She raised her eyes and I smiled. "I'll only be a couple of days."

"I'm going with you," Lucas said, his voice low and full of ominous tones, like he was trying to hypnotize me with his superhero powers.

I turned on him again. "Okay, dude? The Lancelot thing? Not happening this time. You have a job—"

"So do you," he shot back.

"—and a sister to take care of."

We glared at each other, breathing heavily.

"Where do you think he is, Darcy?" Liz's voice was calm, controlled. I turned toward her, grateful she was treating me like an adult.

"I'm guessing Idaho, or Montana. He was in Washington, at a clonehenge in Maryhill. He sent us a postcard from there. But there aren't any other henges between there and Montana that I can find. I think he's headed to southern Montana. Some crazy rich guy built a private clonehenge on his property north of the Wyoming border."

Liz glanced at Charlie. "That's what, maybe an eleven or twelve hour drive from here?"

Charlie rubbed a hand across his forehead. "About that, depending on weather and traffic."

Liz gave me a slow smile. "You can take a couple days off work. I've got you covered."

Charlie looked at Lucas. "If you can run the store for a

couple of days, I'll go with her. Even if you can't, it won't kill us to close for a day or two."

I leaned back against the couch and sighed heavily. I didn't want to hurt Charlie's feelings, but I worried that if I found Dad he'd totally freak if I had his hippie brother with me. The brother he'd disowned and hadn't seen in years.

"Fine," Lucas snapped. "Whatever." He stood abruptly and left the room.

Crap. I hadn't meant to hurt him, but I knew I had. Why couldn't he see this was about me, not him? It didn't mean I thought any less of him just because I wanted to do this by myself. It wasn't his job to fix everything for me.

"Maybe we should talk about this tomorrow," Mom said, her voice still quiet. "Let everyone get a good night's sleep, then talk about all our options."

Charlie nodded. "Fine with me." He gazed at me, his expression full of compassion and worry. "It's a lot to consider."

I heard Pickles arguing with Lucas before I saw her. "I don't wanna go, Lukie. I'm making my necklace."

"You can finish it later."

Lucas grabbed their coats from the coat closet by the front door, not even looking into the living room. My heart ached. I wanted to go to him, to try to explain what I was doing. I hated that our night was ending like this, after he'd brought the tree and made everything so perfect for Mom and me.

Charlie and Liz stood up to leave, shooting worried glances at Mom and me.

"Thank you for everything," Mom said from her chair.

"The tree is wonderful. And the presents…you really didn't need to do that."

The front door slammed, shutting off Pickles' loud protests. Charlie and Liz both flinched.

I busied myself rolling up my map.

"You know it's because he cares about you so much," Charlie said softly. "He's worried."

"I know." I slid the rubber band around the map. "But he doesn't always have to be the hero."

Liz laughed softly. "It's who he is, Darcy. Especially with you."

I looked at Charlie. "Remember when you gave me the ninja shakers? And you said you thought I was heroic?"

Charlie nodded.

"Well, now it's time for me to prove it."

*L*ucas ignored my texts and my phone calls. I lay in my bed, staring at the ceiling. It sucked that we were fighting. We never had before. I was pretty sure he'd forgive me, after he calmed down and thought about what I'd said.

But right now I had more important things to figure out, like finding my dad. I knew no one was going to change their minds overnight. Charlie would still want to go with me. Mom would still want to call the cops, not that they'd listen to my crazy theory. Lucas would still insist he should go.

I rolled over and grabbed the mini Stonehenge kit. In the light of the full moon spilling in my window, I unwrapped it.

I set up the tiny stones on the tiny green mat. Tears filled my eyes as I remembered how I'd destroyed Dad's henge. I rested my head on my pillow, staring at the tiny henge on my nightstand, glowing in the moonlight.

"I'm coming, Dad," I whispered. "I promise."

CHAPTER THIRTY-ONE
DECEMBER 18

I tiptoed quietly down the hall, not wanting to wake Mom. In such a small house, it was a lot harder to sneak out undetected. In the kitchen, I filled a trash bag with dog food while Toby danced with excitement, his nails clicking on the linoleum.

"Shh, Toby. Sit." He sat, tail swooshing silently across the floor. "You've never gone on a road trip like this, buddy. I need you to be my copilot, okay?" Leash, Scooby treats, a giant Tupperware bowl for water. We were ready.

Writing a note was difficult. Whatever I said, Mom would flip out. So would Charlie and Lucas. Liz might be the only one who wouldn't. Guilt overwhelmed me, especially as I looked at our Christmas tree lights twinkling in the early morning darkness. But Dad's absence had hit me harder than ever last night. I couldn't face going into a brand new year without him.

Somehow I knew I could find him. I believed it deep in my soul, as much as I'd ever believed anything. It was like I could feel him calling to me. But I had to go by myself.

I feared that if Dad saw Charlie, who he hadn't spoken to in years, or Lucas, who he didn't even know, or Mom, whose life had fallen apart when he left, it would be too much for him. Seeing anyone but me could crack whatever shell might be protecting him. I imagined him as a terrified child, hiding somewhere, waiting to be found.

> *Dear Mom,*
>
> *Please don't freak. Don't call the cops or send out a search party. I'm safe. I have Toby with me for protection. I'll be back soon, and Dad will be with me when I return. I'll call you from the road.*
>
> *Love, Darcy.*

I wandered into the living room for one last look at the tree before I left. I knelt down and inspected the pile of presents. I looked for Lucas's handwriting on the gift tags. He wasn't kidding about the twelve days of Christmas; it looked like half the packages were from him to me. A heavy weight settled in my chest as I remembered how he'd stormed out of the house last night, too angry to even say good-bye. I picked up a small jewelry-sized box from him, hesitated, and then shoved it in my pocket.

Toby nudged me and I rose to my feet. In the kitchen, I grabbed another grocery bag and filled it with granola bars, chips, crackers, and a jar of peanut butter.

Toby squeaked out a "Let's go!" bark.

"Hush!" I whispered. "Don't wake Mom."

This was it.

The full moon lit up the truck bed as I tossed in our supplies. I craned my neck to look at the stars, sending a wish to the universe. After I slid into the truck, I glued the ninja salt and pepper shakers to the dashboard. Like I'd told Charlie, it was time to prove my hero potential. Plus, I figured a good luck charm couldn't hurt.

Popping the truck into neutral, I rolled the truck quietly down the driveway so Mom wouldn't hear us leave. Toby hung his head out the window, tail beating furiously against my arm.

I drove by Lucas's duplex, which was dark. "Forgive me," I whispered. "I love you. But I don't need a knight in shining armor with me this time."

I drove in the dark, listening to country music on the pathetic AM radio. I wanted to plug my headphones into my iPhone and listen to my playlists, but I knew I'd be inundated with calls and texts once everyone woke up. So I stuck with the radio, leaving my phone powered off.

By the time I got to Casper, Wyoming, it was a little after nine a.m. My stomach growled with hunger and nerves. I pulled off the highway to gas up the truck and get food.

I'd sent an email to Charlie, Liz, and Sal before I left since I hadn't wanted to wake them with pinging text messages. The email said, *"Sorry to do it this way, but I need to do this by myself. I'll be fine. DO NOT call the police. I have food and money. The truck is in great shape, thanks to Lucas. Also I have Toby to protect me."*

Lucas received a separate email: *"Thank you for everything. You're amazing. I'm sorry to leave this way, but I have to do this alone. I don't know if you understand why, but I hope I can explain it better when I get home. I love you, Lucas. So much it hurts."* It was the first time I'd actually said the words to him, even though he'd said them to me, more than once. I hoped this counted, even though it was virtual instead of face-to-face.

Toby scarfed down his food and water in the truck bed while we waited for the gas tank to fill. I sat on the edge, swinging my feet and rubbing my gloved hands briskly to warm up. It was oddly peaceful sitting in the cold wind. Dad always said the "W" in Wyoming stood for windy. I watched cars fly up and down the highway. I felt free. I'd never traveled anywhere alone. Even though I worried about what kind of shape Dad would be in once I found him, it was still liberating to be doing this on my own.

He'd be okay. Whatever fog he was under would lift as soon as he saw me. I had to keep telling myself that, even though J.J.'s words echoed in my mind: *"Don't you think he would've come home by now, if you were enough?"*

After a quick pit stop in a McDonald's bathroom, I bought Egg McMuffins and we hit the road again. I planned to make it to Montana today. It was about two hundred miles from Casper to the henge just across the Montana border. I hoped the truck was up to the challenge. My plan was to drive no more than the speed limit. However, the speed limit was fast up here—seventy-five miles per hour— and the Grim Reaper preferred about sixty miles per hour. Maybe I'd putter along in the right lane and let everyone pass me.

We'd been driving for about an hour when I counted the third Ford F-150 truck about the same age as mine. That was an unexpected bonus; we were even less conspicuous than I'd hoped, just in case Mom totally freaked and put out an APB.

The wind buffeted the truck as we passed oil rigs and cattle. Clouds had chased away the sun and light snow glanced off the windshield. I hoped I wasn't heading into a storm. Maybe I should've checked the weather forecast before I left town.

The clouds darkened and the snow increased in intensity the farther north I drove. My sweaty hands gripped the steering wheel. Lucas had said the new tires were in good shape; I hoped he was right. I turned on the radio and a staticky voice told me that parts of Wyoming and Montana were under a winter storm warning until eight p.m. Up to eight inches of snow was predicted, with gusting and blowing blizzard conditions on the highways.

Crap.

While newer SUVs and trucks continued to pass me, I drove slower and slower. This sucked. I tapped the brakes to test them, and the truck started to skid into the next lane. I needed to stop. There was a town coming up called Buffalo on the map, but I wasn't going to make it that far. I looked anxiously for the next exit sign.

*T*he Sleepy Side Motel had one of those cheesy neon arrows that flickered sporadically. The hand-lettered sign read *"$35.95/night."* The motel looked old and worn, not scary, but like it had suffered through the Wyoming weather for many years. Warm orange light spilled from the office windows onto the snow. "Friendly dogs can come on in," read a sign taped on the front door.

"I think we're in luck, Tobes."

A tiny old woman sat behind a counter, watching the news on a small TV. She peered up at me over her bifocals. Immediately I thought of Mrs. Beasley, a funny-looking old doll of my mom's with yellow hair, rectangular wire-rimmed glasses, and a blue polka-dotted dress.

"Hello, honey," she said, slowly straightening up from her chair. She peered over the counter at Toby. "And who have we here?" She reached into a fishbowl of dog treats and tossed one to him. "Hope that's okay," she said, after he inhaled it.

I smiled. "Sure, it's fine. I'm so happy you take pets here."

"I do believe we've done so since the first day we opened back in 1959. My husband always insisted dogs were part of the family. He'd get so sad when families came in telling us they had to board their dogs while they went on road trips." She paused for a breath, but not long enough for me to agree. "Sometimes we get a cat, which we aren't as partial too, but as long as they stay in their little travel cases, we don't mind."

I waited to make sure it was my turn to speak. "So, can I

get a room for the night? For me and Toby?"

"Well, of course, sweetie." She blinked her Mrs. Beasley blue eyes behind her glasses. "Are you traveling alone? Or do you have a parent who can sign in?"

What could I say? That my mom was standing right here under Harry Potter's invisibility cloak? Crap and double crap. Toby whined restlessly, his eyes fixated on the treat fishbowl. Mrs. Beasley tossed him another treat.

"You on your own, honey? Just you and your dog?"

I nodded.

She tapped her cheek with a ballpoint pen with a red feather taped to it. I wondered if it tickled.

"As a rule, I don't let out rooms to minors. Had some trouble with that in the past." Her eyes squinted, examining me for signs of trouble-making ability. "You sure you aren't hiding a boyfriend out there in that truck?"

Lucas and me in a motel room? My whole body flushed. I knew I looked guilty even though I wasn't. "No ma'am." I hesitated. "I'm…on my way to meet my dad."

"Well, then. It's a bad storm out there. Of course you can stay." She turned around and took a key off an old peg board. "Room twenty-three, around the back. Make sure the windows are locked; that wind's blowing mighty hard."

I paid her and took the key gratefully. I was surprised to see my hand trembling. The impact of what I was doing was starting to hit me. Once we were safely in our room, I let myself crumple. I fell on the bed and cried softly, all the stress leaking out through my tears. Toby jumped on the bed next to me and licked my wet face. This made me laugh, which totally freaked me out. Was this what hysteria felt like? Did I inherit the insanity gene from my dad? How could one crazy person rescue another?

"He's not crazy," I whispered out loud. "He's not. He just needs to come home."

Fortunately, all it took was a giant bag of salt and vinegar chips and a can of soda to restore my sanity. Now for the phone. How many voicemails and texts would I find?

"Courage," I whispered as I held down the power button. Toby sighed next to me on the bed. I rubbed his belly while I watched the screen fill with notifications.

Where to start? I wanted to start with Lucas, but knew I should start with Mom. I'd look at text messages first.

There were a dozen texts from Mom. *"Darcy how could you! Why didn't you wait until we talked? You shouldn't be alone."* And on and on.

From Sal: *"What the hell? You did this without telling me, your BF? I am done with you Darcy. D.O.N.E."* That hurt. But twenty minutes later she'd texted again. *"Please call me. Let me know you're alive. Just tell me u r safe. And call Lucas. He is totally manic."*

From Charlie: *"I wish you hadn't done this. Please turn around and come home. I'll go with you and we'll do this together. Your mom needs you."*

Of course she needed me. She needed me to find Dad.

Finally, I looked at the single text message from Lucas. *"Damn it, Darcy. I can't believe you did this. Not cool."*

The one person I wanted to call didn't sound like he wanted to hear from me. I knew he'd be mad, but somehow I'd hoped that his concern for me would override the anger, that his feelings for me were strong enough to forgive me for ditching him.

So much for that.

I looked at the list of recent calls. Eleven calls from Mom. Five from Charlie. Four from Liz. Seven from Sal. Zero from Lucas.

I called Mom, who answered on the first ring. "Darcy! Where are you? How could—"

"Mom, please just let me talk. I'm okay. I'm perfectly safe in a nice motel. It's run by a sweet little old lady who likes dogs. For real."

"You have to come home. Turn around right now. I swear if you don't—"

"Mom, please calm down. I told you, I know where Dad is, or where he's going to be. I should get to him today." I looked out the window at the blowing snow. "Or tomorrow. Then I'll come home. You have to trust me, Mom. I promise I'll stay in touch, but don't keep calling me or texting me every five minutes, or I'll turn my phone off. I swear I will."

She didn't speak. I heard sniffling. Then another voice spoke into the phone.

"Darcy? Are you all right? We're all so worried." Charlie. The one person I couldn't be tough with. I sighed into the phone.

"Charlie, I'm okay. Honest. It's kind of...exciting. A little weird. And like I told Mom, I'm in a perfectly safe motel." I took a deep breath. "Can you keep Mom from calling out the cavalry? Buy me some more time? I swear I know exactly where I'm going." I swallowed. "I know where he is, Charlie. I can feel it. I can feel him." It sounded crazy, but if anyone would understand, it'd be Charlie, the priest of Broadway.

Charlie's sigh was deep and drawn out. It sounded just like Dad when he was disappointed in me. "I wish you had waited. Let me come with you."

"I know," I whispered. "But I had to do it by myself."

He sighed again. "What if you're wrong, Darcy? What if you don't find him? How long are you going to keep looking?"

I'd been fighting away that worry ever since I made my plan to leave. How long would I look?

"If he's not in Montana, I'll come home." He'd be there. I could feel him calling to me.

"You promise?"

"Yes."

"You have enough money?" Charlie's voice hummed with worry.

"Yes."

He sighed again. "I know the truck is running fine."

I winced. "Yeah. Not great in the snow, but Lucas was… wonderful."

"You should call him." It was a command.

"I don't know. He's sort of mad."

"We're all 'sort of mad' at you, Darcy. That doesn't mean we don't want to know that you're safe."

I pulled at the threads on the bedspread. "Maybe you could tell Lucas I'm okay? And that I'm sorry?"

"I'll tell him you're okay. You can tell him the rest."

If he ever talked to me again.

"Is he with you?" I pictured Lucas pacing in front of the Christmas tree, watching my mom freak out.

"No, he's not here. But you know how to reach him."

It was time to disconnect. I needed to sleep. I was exhausted from leaving so early, the stress of sneaking out of town, and then driving in the snow on an unknown highway. Mostly I was panicking that I'd actually done it. What if it was a wild goose chase, like everyone thought? What if I was just as crazy as my dad?

"You need to check in often." I'd never heard Charlie so serious, so commanding. "If not, we *will* call the police, Darcy, to find you and make sure you're okay. Your mother can't take much more of this."

"I'm sorry. Charlie…" I hesitated, afraid to ask the question I needed to. "Is she drinking again?"

He sighed into the phone. "No, fortunately. She's doing okay. Some of her recovery friends came by to be with her."

If guilt were water, I would've drowned. "I'm sorry," I said, my voice barely above a whisper. "For all the worry I'm causing. But I promise this is going to end well. You'll see."

"I hope so, Darcy. I hope so."

*T*wo hours later I was still wide awake, even though fatigue overwhelmed me. I drew the curtains across the window, blocking out the white skies, but I still couldn't sleep.

I wanted to call Lucas, but I was too chicken, so I texted him. *"I'm sorry. So sorry. Forgive me? Some day?"*

He didn't reply. I leaned over the side of the bed and grabbed my jeans from the floor. I pulled out the present and slowly unwrapped it. When I saw the heart-shaped stone suspended from a silver chain, my heart danced inside my chest. I secured the clasp behind my neck and finally fell asleep, dreaming of the real Stonehenge in England, of finding my dad performing there to an audience of druids while I danced around in cowboy boots.

I woke up in a cold sweat with Toby planked out next to me on the bed, snoring. All my confidence from earlier had evaporated. What if I didn't find my dad? What if someone ran me off the road and killed me? Why hadn't I brought someone with me? What if…what if…

As I watched the hours on the clock tick by, my mind played out worst-case scenarios. I'd been so determined to do this alone, but now I regretted it. I'd pushed and pushed myself these past few months, doing what I had to for Mom and me, but I suddenly wondered if I had enough fuel to keep going.

"One last push," I whispered. I thought of all the races I'd run, and how sometimes the last few meters were the hardest.

I couldn't give up, not now, not with the finish line in sight.

CHAPTER THIRTY-TWO
DECEMBER 19

It was almost nine in the morning when I woke up from my sleep coma. I couldn't believe I'd slept that long.

"You're a lousy alarm clock," I told Toby, who yawned himself awake as I pushed back the bedspread. His ear flipped inside out as he rolled around the bed, and he grinned at me upside down.

I flung open the drapes. The snow had stopped. A white blanket sparkled in the sunlight, covering the fields as far as I could see. Assuming the roads had been plowed, I should cross the Montana border that afternoon. Then I'd have to sneak onto the private land to find the henge.

And then what? Camp out and wait for Dad? I hadn't really thought about the details. I'd focused all my energy on sneaking out of town without any unwanted company.

"I need food," I told Toby. "So do you."

I was tossing my duffel in the truck when Mrs. Beasley called across the parking lot.

"Sweetheart, come here!" She leaned on her cane in the office doorway.

Toby trotted toward her, tail wagging. He'd trust anyone with dog treats. I caught up to him quickly. She handed me a crumpled paper bag. "There's a donut in there. And some treats for your dog."

My eyes widened in surprise. "Thank you." I opened the bag. Pink icing with sprinkles. What were the odds? It had to be a sign.

"Good luck, honey."

I smiled tentatively. How did she know I needed luck?

She tilted her head toward my truck. "I saw your license plate. And the logo on your sweatshirt." I completely forgot I'd worn a Tri!Umphant! shirt yesterday. "I watch his PBS shows. I thought I recognized you from somewhere."

Stunned, I reached for the heart stone necklace resting against my collarbone.

"I hope you find him," she said. "He's a good man. I have all his books."

"Thank you," I whispered. Then, impulsively, I hugged her.

Toby and I ran for the truck. I waved as we drove away and she raised her cane in a good-bye salute.

As I crossed the border into Montana, I sagged with relief. "Almost there, Toby." I reached for my phone to call my mom, but there was no signal. I'd have to keep trying; the last time we'd talked had been over an hour ago.

The article I'd found on Clonemaniac's website, my favorite reference site, said the henge was on private property and the owner hated trespassers. He even had security guards. But it was supposed to be a spectacular replica. Clone freaks from all over the country risked getting arrested by sneaking onto the property. It was like a badge of honor to post photos and videos of their successful trespassing.

Clonemaniac claimed he'd snuck onto the property three times. He'd described his route in detail; I'd brought a print-out of his directions. Toby and I took an unmarked exit, then parked the truck on the shoulder of the road and found the mile marker where Clonemaniac had begun his trek.

"Maybe I should leave a trail of breadcrumbs," I told Toby. Though that would be pointless since Toby would eat them. We found the tree stump carved with a small "c" and an arrow pointing the way. Clonemaniac said the property owner tried to paint over the directions that clonehengers painted on trees, but the hengers were always one step ahead of him.

Toby ran like a possessed dog through the woods, thrilled to be out of the truck and able to chase critters. I worried he'd be spotted by security. Clonemaniac said that security was out in full force during full moons and solstices, but the rest of the time it was hard to predict.

Tonight was both.

The wind whipped around us. I zipped my coat up tighter and wished for the hundredth time that Lucas was with me.

He still hadn't responded to my text asking for forgiveness.

I wanted to call him, but reception had been crappy for miles.

Another small "c" and an arrow on a fallen tree pointed up a hill. Toby took off as if he knew where he was going. I slogged up the hill, grateful for my hiking boots. Clonemaniac said the henge was visible from the top of a hill. Snow and mud made the climb tricky, but once I crested the top of the hill, my breath caught.

The henge loomed about two hundred yards ahead of us. Someone had cleared out all the trees, leaving a huge open space in which the stones soared toward the sky like arms worshipping the heavens.

"Oh my God," I whispered. If Dad had found this, I wondered how it made him feel. Had he found what he was looking for? Did the stones hold some imaginary key that unlocked something inside of him?

Toby ran down the hill, heading straight for the henge.

"Toby, wait!" I called after him, then followed as quickly as I could, stumbling down the hill, grabbing at branches for support. Once on mostly flat ground, I ran after Toby. He hadn't gone more than thirty yards when he stopped. We were still too far away from the stones for me to see if anyone was there.

"What is it, Tobes?" A barbed wire fence stopped our progress. It looked like miles of fence penned in the henge, keeping trespassers far away from the stones.

"Electric fence," said a sign. *"Cross if you want to be crispy."*

Clonemaniac hadn't mentioned the fence. The pictures

he'd posted online had been from right inside the circle of stones. No way could anyone get that close now, unless they risked electrocution.

Toby sniffed around the base of the fence, hackles up, tail straight out behind him.

I looked at the stones. Even from a distance, they were spectacular.

No one else was here. What exactly had I thought I'd find, anyway? A guest book with Dad's name in it?

Now what? Should I wait? Maybe Dad hadn't made it yet. Or maybe he had, and been dissuaded by the fence. I could sleep in the truck, keeping vigil on the side of the road, waiting for him to show up. The wind picked up as I stood there staring at the stones, waiting for a sign from the heavens, or the druids.

Footsteps snapped twigs behind me. I froze in shock when I heard the click of a gun. A voice spoke, low and threatening. "Hold it right there. Don't move."

Toby charged toward the owner of the voice, barking and growling.

I spun around to see Toby growling at a man dressed all in black. His beard hid most of his face. He pointed a gun at me, then at Toby, then back at me.

"Call off the dog, or I'll shoot!"

Fear paralyzed me but I had to do something. "Just let me grab him," I said. "He's not dangerous. He's just protecting me."

"Ha." The man kept his gun leveled at me. "Grab him, then. And get the hell off my property."

I lunged for Toby's collar. He pulled the other way,

determined to go after the threat.

"P-p-lease. Lower the gun. It's freaking him out." And me.

The man glared at me, but lowered the gun halfway. "You another of those hippie nuts comin' to howl at the moon?"

"What? No. I'm just looking for someone."

"Yeah? Who ya looking for?"

Honesty was my only hope. "My dad. He's...sort of a clonehenge follower."

The man snorted. "He and a million other nuts." He kicked at the ground. "Never woulda built this if I'd known how many idiots there were."

My eyes widened. "You built it? You're the owner?"

"Yep."

I forced a quavering smile even though I was still shaking. "It's beautiful. Amazing. I've never seen anything like it."

"Thanks," he said gruffly. He raised the gun again. "You still need to get the hell off my property."

Toby started barking again. "Quiet, Toby!"

"Well, God tear it all. Damn dog is smart. Knows when I'm pointin' the gun and when I ain't." He lowered the gun and Toby stopped barking.

"Can I please..." I took a shaky breath. "Before I go can I show you a picture of my dad? Maybe you've seen him."

The man tilted his head. "What's the matter, kid? Your dad run away from home?"

I swallowed over the growing lump in my throat. "Yes."

The man scratched his head. "Well, I'll be. I thought I'd

heard all kinds of stories, but that's a new one." He rubbed his beard. "All right then. Show me the picture."

I grabbed my cell from my pocket and pulled up Dad's photo, one of his many glamour shots. I waited, trembling. I didn't know what to make of this guy. Clonemaniac said he was a hermit nutcase and to run like hell if you saw him.

Too late for that.

The man pushed my phone back at me. "He looks like one of them TV preachers. And no, I ain't seen him. So you and your dog need to pack it up and get outta here. Normally I'd call the sheriff, but you don't seem like a troublemaker."

I felt tears gathering in my eyes. "You haven't seen anyone come through here lately?"

He frowned. "Just a bunch of hippies I chased off yesterday. But there was nobody like your dad with them. Just a bunch of kids. They were chasing henges, too. Probably off to the next one on their list."

I wondered where they were headed. Maybe I could find them and show them Dad's picture. If they were traveling around looking at henges, they might have seen him.

He gestured with his gun. "Go on, now. I'll follow you out to where you parked. You're in that truck, ain't ya?"

I had no choice but to do as he said. It took forever to hike back to the truck, but Toby pranced around us happily since the gun was holstered. The man watched as Toby and I climbed into the truck.

"Don't even think about staying, or hiding somewhere thinking you'll sneak back later and wait for your dad. I got my security guard coming to take over for the rest of the day, and the night. And he ain't near as nice as me."

My shoulders slumped over the wheel. How had he guessed my plan?

I started the engine and pulled away slowly. He watched me from the road, arms crossed over his chest. I watched him in the rearview mirror until he was a small dot.

Why the hell had I come up here? What had I been thinking? Everyone was right. I had to accept that Dad wasn't coming home. Mom needed me. And I needed her. I'd been an idiot to think I could read Dad's mind and find him based on random postcards. I had to get somewhere with decent phone reception. I wanted to hear Lucas's voice and remind myself of all the reasons I had to go home.

I crossed the border back into Wyoming. As I got closer to Sheridan, my cell signal came back. I pulled off to the shoulder of the road and called Mom. "I...I'm on my way home, Mom." I swallowed over the lump in my throat. "By myself."

"Oh honey," she said, tears choking her voice, "it's okay. It's okay. You've done all you could. You were chasing a dream, sweetheart, but it's time to come home."

The words hurt, but I knew she was right. It was time to stop chasing dreams. I reached over to pet Toby, taking comfort from his solid bulk.

"How far away are you?"

I paused to calculate in my head. "I won't get home until maybe eight or so tonight. Maybe later."

"Is it still snowing?"

"Not really. Just a little dusting here and there. Will you call Charlie for me?"

"Of course, honey." She paused. "Check in at least every

hour."

"Promise."

"And Darcy? Will you please call Lucas and convince him you're okay? That boy is going to drive me to drink, and that's the last thing we need." She laughed a little. I could hardly believe she was joking about that, but in a way it felt good. Normal.

And maybe by the time I got home, Lucas would have forgiven me.

"I will. Love you, Mom."

"Love you too, honey."

When I called Lucas, he didn't answer. I listened to his outgoing message, but hung up instead of leaving a voicemail. He might be worried about me, but he still wasn't ready to talk to me.

*M*y eyelids grew heavy as I drove under the gray skies. I pulled off an exit in the middle of nowhere. Now that I'd given up my search, all the adrenaline that had been fueling me was gone, replaced by overwhelming fatigue and sadness. I set my phone alarm for thirty minutes. Maybe I'd feel better after a quick catnap.

I've heard that messages come to people in dreams. It always sounded cool but I never believed it. As I tried to nap, my dreams woke me over and over. I dreamed of Dad, J.J., Mom, Lucas, Charlie, Liz, and Sal. It was like a parade of everyone in my life, each coming by with something important to say. But in my dreams their mouths moved silently. I begged them to speak up, but they couldn't hear me and I couldn't hear them.

I'd been dreaming of Dad when my phone alarm jerked me awake. He'd sat cross-legged in the middle of the Stonehenge at our cabin, dressed in a suit, in full stage makeup.

"I've been looking everywhere for you," I'd raged at him. *"Everywhere!"*

He'd smiled up at me, blissful and unperturbed. *"I've been here all the time, Darcy. Listening. Just listening to the stones."*

Chapter Thirty-Three

As I drove, I couldn't shake my dream. I couldn't stop thinking of the hippies the nutty henge guy had mentioned. What if I could catch up to them somehow and ask if they'd seen Dad? But who knew where they were by now, or which direction they'd headed?

"It's the people who get up one last time who make it across the finish line," Dad's voice whispered in my mind. *"The ones who are fallen, broken, even bloody. Everyone else passes them by. It's often the fastest who give up first. The slow, wounded traveler in the back of the pack keeps going. He passes those who sprinted too fast. In the end, persistence pushes him across the finish line."*

I pulled off to the highway shoulder again and opened Google on my phone. I searched for "Stonehenge in Wyoming." Nothing. I pulled up the Clonemaniac site and typed in Wyoming. If anyone would know about it, he would.

"Blue Spruce, Wyoming. This henge is pretty cool, considering it's in the middle of nowhere outside a dead town. It's on private property but my sources tell me the owner doesn't really care. It's probably worth a stop if you're in the area."

My heart sped up. I'd seen a sign for Blue Spruce on the highway when I'd been heading to Montana. I pulled up my map to see where it was. It was only about fifty miles south of here, and it was right on my way home since it was just off the highway.

I revved the engine and pulled back onto the highway.

"One last stop, Toby," I said. "I've got to try it."

*B*lue Spruce, Wyoming, was a sad little town, if it could even be called a town. Half the shops were boarded up with For Lease signs in the windows. The shops that were open looked like they shouldn't be. Even the wind blew more fiercely here.

There was one restaurant in the center of the tiny town, Daisy's Diner. An enormous white-petaled flower with a yellow smiley face center was painted on the window, shining like a beacon in the midst of the other dingy, gray buildings. Someone in there had to know about the local henge.

When I walked in, all the customers looked up. A Christmas tree decorated with glinting lights and paper daisies stood next to a long counter lined with backless stools, most of which were occupied. It reminded me of Charlie's, except for the three-tiered rack of pies instead of a covered tray of donuts. How I wished I was sitting at Charlie's right now, listening to jazz and joking around with Lucas.

Most of the men at the counter looked like farmers, wearing denim and work boots, cowboy hats and baseball hats. A few of them nodded at me, and I smiled shyly.

Daisy bustled over. There was no question it was Daisy since everything on her was a daisy of some sort. Dangling daisy earrings, a huge daisy necklace, hairpins with tiny daisies, and a yellow apron patterned with rainbow-colored daisies.

"What can I do for you, sweetie?" She glanced out the window to my truck. "Are you eating here or getting food to go?"

"Actually, I just need directions to somewhere. But first, could I please use your bathroom?"

She pointed to a narrow hallway running parallel to the kitchen.

I slid off the stool and hurried down the hall. It was a one-holer, thank God. I locked the door and stared at myself in the mirror over the sink. I wondered how the motel lady had recognized me from Dad's anniversary specials. I looked nothing like that girl. My skin was pale and dark shadows made me look like a raccoon.

After washing my hands, I returned to the counter and slid onto a stool. Daisy was talking to a large sheriff who looked like a sausage stuffed into a too-small uniform.

"What's our favorite crime fighter up to today?" Daisy

asked.

He sank onto a stool. "Oh, not much. Just heading up to Bill Paxton's property. He wants me to run off a bunch of hippies camping on his land."

Daisy clucked her tongue. "Well, it's his own fault. If he hadn't built that ridiculous Stonehenge, those crazy kids wouldn't be camping there."

I gripped the edge of the counter and turned my stool so I could hear better.

The sheriff laughed. "I know. That's what I told him." He took a long drink from the bright yellow coffee mug covered with daisies. "I'm not in a hurry to get out there. The kids aren't causing any harm. Probably just smoking dope and howling at the moon."

I peeked up at the sheriff, surprised at his laid-back attitude.

Daisy handed him a donut oozing red jelly. He took an enormous bite, then walked over to a table of farmers, who laughed boisterously at something he said.

"Excuse me," I said to Daisy.

She turned to me, smiling as she wiped her hands on her apron.

"Um, about that Stonehenge? The one the sheriff was talking about. Is it far from here?"

Her smile faded. "Oh, sweetie. You don't want to go out there. The sheriff might think those kids are harmless but you never know."

She glanced out the window at my truck. Toby was licking the hand of a lanky man in a cowboy hat who'd reached through the cracked window to pet him.

"I don't know how much protection that dog will be," she said.

I thought of the gun pointed at me earlier. "You'd be surprised."

She wiped the counter with a rag. "Where are you headed, honey? I know you're not from around here."

I dropped my gaze.

"I don't mean to pry," she continued. "But I worry about a young girl traveling alone."

"I'm not alone. I've got my dog. And I'm heading home. I just need to…um…pick up my dad."

She smiled again. "Oh good. I'm glad to hear that." She glanced out the window again. "I've got a ham bone to get rid of. Let me get it for your dog. No charge."

Blue Spruce wasn't pretty, but it felt like I'd ended up in an old black-and-white TV show where everyone wanted to help out the pathetic stranger. Daisy came back with a bone wrapped in plastic.

"Thanks." Toby was going to be in heaven. "So about the Stonehenge? I just like to take photos of interesting stuff I see on the road. You know, the world's largest rubber band ball. Fake jackalope fossils. Stupid stuff like that." I shrugged, hoping she'd buy it and give me directions.

She crossed her arms, her eyes searching mine. "All right," she acquiesced. "It's about a half-hour drive from here, off the county road." She grabbed a paper placemat from the counter and drew a daisy flower to indicate her restaurant. She drew a straight north-south line and wrote I-25 next to it. Then she drew a squiggly line running parallel to the highway then jutting off to the west. She drew a star and slid the paper toward me.

"The ranch is right off the county road. You'll see a sign for Paxton Ranch, but you can't miss the Stonehenge. You'll see it from the road. You can take a photo if you pull off the road, that way you don't have to trespass." She frowned a warning at me.

I folded the map in half and shoved it in my bag. "Thank you." I smiled, lifting the ham bone to my forehead in a salute. "For everything."

"You're welcome. You be careful, honey."

I tossed the ham bone into the truck bed so that Toby wouldn't drive me crazy destroying it while I drove.

"If you had fingers, I'd tell you to cross them for luck," I told Toby as we drove away.

*D*aisy was right. It was impossible to miss.

The sight took my breath away. This wasn't a silly replica like the Carhenge I'd seen online. This was the real deal. I couldn't believe that Clonemaniac hadn't made a bigger deal of it on his website. I needed to post a comment on there. Maybe he'd seen so many replicas he was jaded. Yeah, the one up in Montana had been a lot bigger, but this one was every bit as impressive to me, especially since I could walk right up to it without getting electrocuted.

I ignored the KEEP OUT signs and drove through the open gate under the PAXTON RANCH sign. I parked near a post sticking up out of the ground, next to an ancient VW van. A wooden sign swung from the post. *"Do not disturb!"*

The words had been burned into the wood. *"Private Property! Stay out!"*

Someone had taped a cardboard sign under the warnings that said, *"Druids welcome. Vandalizers be warned. This place protected by magick."*

I shivered. "Ridiculous." I snorted. "Druid magic, my butt." But before I got out of the truck, I touched the ninja shakers for luck, just in case.

Toby and I struggled against the wind and I shivered in the quickly dropping temperature. I watched the sun slip below a ridge of red sandstone. The T-shaped granite sentries formed a ring at least thirty yards in diameter. It was awe-inspiring. I didn't care that it was a replica.

I shivered and pulled my parka tightly around me. I'd come this far, I might as well go all the way. I walked between two of the T-stones, emerging into the middle of the circle. Inside the circle were two enormous flat rectangular stones, each about five feet high. Someone had placed groupings of candles on the flat stones. I craned my neck to look up at the massive creation, brushing hair out of my eyes. If I believed in magic or powers unseen, this would be the time and place to make my request.

"Help me find my dad," I whispered to the looming towers.

No wonder people were in such awe of the original Stonehenge. Today we had the technology and machinery to create this. But how had the original builders done it thousands of years ago?

Voices sounded from the other side of the stone circle. The hippies. Toby reached them before I did.

"Hey man, check out this dog."

"Where'd you come from, buddy?"

"Let's give him some food."

"We ate it all, dude. That weed packed some serious munchies."

Great. At least they sounded harmless.

Several people huddled around a small campfire. The smell of burning wood reminded me of nights at the cabin, nights Dad and I had camped on our property instead of sleeping inside.

I approached them tentatively. Of course they were stoned; they had to be to even consider camping in this weather. They'd shoveled away snow and set up their tents on tarps, but I still couldn't see how they'd stay warm.

A skinny guy with a mop of curly dark hair and a spotty beard laughed as he wrestled with Toby. A girl with long red braids and an earflap hat grinned up at me. "Hey. Welcome to Druid Central." She offered me a hand-rolled cigarette. "Wanna hit?"

I shook my head. "No thanks."

"Wassup?" asked another guy lying in a sleeping bag. His head was shaved and he had enormous earlobe gauges. Dinner plates would practically fit in those holes. "You here for the ritual? It should be awesome. Claire's gonna start soon."

"Yeah," Claire said. She handed the joint to Mophead. "It's a powerful time, you know. The solstice. A time to release old stuff."

I had plenty of old crap to release. Maybe I should stay for the ritual.

"Is this your dog?" Earlobes asked from his prone position. "He's cool."

"Yeah. His name's Toby."

"Sit down," said Claire, patting the ground next to her.

I sat on the cold ground. Now what?

"So," I said, "I'm looking for someone. A guy who likes Stonehenges. I'm wondering if you've seen him."

I pulled my phone out of my pocket and brought up Dad's glamour shot.

Claire bent over to look into the phone. She laughed. "He looks like a movie star."

Small screen, I wanted to say. Strictly small screen.

"Have you seen him?"

"No," Claire said. "I'd remember somebody like that."

Mophead took the phone and shook his head. "Nope."

Earlobes held my phone above his head while he lay on the ground. "Nah. I ain't seen him. But we should ask Preacher. He might've."

He rolled over and yelled toward the tents. "Preacher! Come out here."

I saw the shadow of a figure moving inside the smaller tent. A hand reached up to unzip the tent flap. A man emerged, tall and scruffy. He walked toward the fire, his body buried under a thick black parka, his face hidden under a hoodie. He looked older than the others.

Toby stopped wrestling with Mophead. He froze, pointing his front leg, ears cocked and nose sniffing the air. Oh crap. Maybe they weren't as harmless as they seemed.

"Preacher, this girl's looking for someone," said Claire.

The man stopped next to the fire. My heart thudded in

my ears. I hoped he wasn't armed. I couldn't handle anyone else pointing a gun at me. Maybe I should've listened to Daisy.

He pushed the hoodie off his face and looked directly into my eyes. His beard was full, and limp, dirty hair grazed his shoulders.

Even in the dim light of the campfire, he looked a lot like his brother.

Chapter Thirty-Four

Lights from the dancing flames threw shadows on us, and onto the stones looming behind us. I made the first move. I ran to Dad and threw my arms around him, but he didn't hug me back. Instead he pulled away, his eyes wide with panic.

"Am I dreaming?" he whispered.

"No, Dad. It's not a dream. It's me." I loosened my grip and stepped back. My throat tightened as tears rolled down my face.

I'd done it. I'd found him.

Toby had gone into super spaz mode now that he knew who was hidden under the dirty clothes. He pawed at Dad's jean-clad legs, whimpering, his tail wagging furiously.

"Dude," said Mophead. "Your daughter? Wicked."

"It's a sign," said Claire. "From the universe."

Dad looked down at Toby as if he'd just noticed there was a spastic animal attached to his legs. "Toby?" He frowned at me. "The dog. His name is Toby, isn't it?"

Fear streaked through me like a rocket, lighting every nerve on fire.

"Yes," I said weakly. "Of course it's Toby."

He tilted his head, examining me closely. "You shouldn't have come, Marilyn."

Marilyn? He thought I was Mom? Oh my God. Oh my God. Had he gone completely bat-shit crazy? Oh my God.

"Dad." My voice was strangled by tears. "Dad, it's me. Darcy."

His eyes widened. Then it was like a light switched on from the inside. "Darcy! Oh God. Darcy. What are you doing here?"

"I'm—I'm rescuing you. Bringing you home. You have to come home. Dad, please. We need you." I swallowed. "And you need us."

"That's intense," said Earlobes.

We had to get out of there. I grabbed Dad's arm. Toby danced around us, barking with excitement. "Come on, Dad. Let's go." I tried to smile. "I have the truck. Your Harvest truck."

He looked at me like I spoke a foreign language.

I looped an arm around his waist and took a step. He didn't move. I took another step.

"Come on," I urged him. "We have to go. Get you some food." His body odor overwhelmed me. "A shower. Clean clothes."

I took another step. This time he stepped with me.

"Hey Preacher!" Mophead called after us. "You staying? Or going home with your daughter?"

"Home." Dad whispered so quietly only I could hear him. "Home."

We sat in the truck with Toby sandwiched between us. Dad wrapped his arm around Toby, petting him rhythmically. I leaned across Dad to hand-crank the window down. He really, really needed a shower.

Hands shaking, I pulled out my phone. Mom answered on the first ring.

"Mom. I found him."

Silence. Then a scuffling noise, and another voice.

"Darcy! What is it?" J.J.'s voice snapped.

My heart pounded. What was he doing there? I thought he'd given up on Dad.

"I found him, J.J. We're coming home."

"What?" he bellowed into the phone. "You found him? Where? Tell me where you are."

No freaking way.

"Let me talk to Mom, J.J."

More scuffling noises, then a new voice.

"Darcy. How is he? How are you? Do you want me to come meet you?" Charlie. Just the sound of his voice calmed me a little. Yes, I wanted him to meet me. But I'd come this far by myself. The hard part was over. Now I just needed to point the truck south and drive as fast as I could.

"No," I said, forcing strength into my voice. "I think

we'll be okay."

"Where are you?" Charlie asked.

"Blue Spruce. It's a small town in Wyoming. I think it's about three or four hours from home."

Charlie groaned. "How about if I meet you halfway? Or Lucas?"

"No." I'd made it this far. I wasn't about to call in the rescue squad now.

"Your mom wants to talk to him," Charlie said.

I looked at Dad. He stared out the window at the stones, which glowed white under the full moon. I lowered my phone and whispered, "Dad? Mom wants to talk to you."

He turned to me. His face was dirty, his skin red and chapped where it wasn't covered by his beard. His eyes watered as he shook his head. I wondered if he was on drugs right now. Maybe that was the problem. Once he sobered up, would he be my normal dad again? Was I going to have two parents in rehab? God.

I closed my eyes against the waves of emotion racking my body. I had to keep it together. Get us food. Drive hundreds of miles. We just needed to get home, then everything would be okay. Breathe, I told myself. Just breathe.

"He's exhausted," I told Charlie. "I'll call you back after we eat."

Charlie sighed. "All right. Promise you'll call as soon as you've had food."

I forced a lightness I didn't feel into my voice. "He kind of looks like you right now. His hair is longer and he has a beard."

Charlie whistled. "I can't wait to see that."

"J.J. will freak out," I said.

"I'm looking forward to that, too," said Charlie, in a threatening voice I'd never heard before.

I swallowed. "Charlie? Will you tell Lucas that I found Dad? And that I'm okay?"

The phone rattled with static. I hoped I hadn't lost the connection.

"Hey, Shaker Girl."

I closed my eyes, wishing I could swim in the warmth of his voice. God, I wanted to be home. To be with him. "Lucas," I breathed. "You're at our house?"

He chuckled. "Unfortunately. That J.J. guy is a trip. I want to punch him but Charlie won't let me." He sighed and his voice dropped. "You sure you can handle this? Driving him home by yourself?"

"Yes," I whispered. I glanced at Dad, who didn't appear to be listening to my conversation at all. Toby lay stretched across his lap, blissed out to be with alpha dog again.

I turned away from Dad, facing out my window. "Lucas. I'm so sorry about the way I left."

"Me too," he said. "Sorry I went all King La'ul on you."

I laughed as I pictured the temperamental king in the Firestorm Fairies world throwing a tantrum. "You did, didn't you? Storming around and slamming doors. All you were missing was smoke shooting out of your head."

He sighed in to the phone. "Yeah, well…I guess it's the Lancelot thing. I'm sure your TV shrink has a theory about it." He lowered his voice. "So why haven't you called me? You called everyone else."

"I tried once but got your voicemail. Reception sucks

up here. Besides, your text didn't sound like you wanted to talk to me."

He snorted. "You should've seen the ones I typed but didn't send."

I bit my lip. "So...am I forgiven?"

"Maybe," he said. "Depends on what you got me for Christmas."

I laughed and Dad jerked next to me.

"Look, I need to go," I said. "The sooner I do, the sooner I'll be home."

"I'm worried about you driving that truck in the snow. You didn't bother to check the forecast before you took off, did you?" I heard the struggle in his voice as he tried to mask his frustration and worry.

"Is smoke shooting out of your head, King La'ul?"

He snorted in my ear. "You're the most stubborn person I know."

"More stubborn than Pickles?"

"At least she lets me help her."

It was my turn to snort. "She's four years old, Lancelot, of course she does. Just give it a rest. I'm on my way home, I promise."

Lucas's voice faded as he talked to someone in the background, then he returned to our conversation. "Charlie says to call again as soon as you and your dad eat."

"I will."

Silence stretched between us, then, "Drive safe, Shaker Girl."

"I will. Promise."

I hung up and looked at Dad, who still stared out the

window while petting Toby. "Be right back. Don't move." I jumped out of the truck and ran back to the campfire. "I forgot to tell you guys. The sheriff's on his way to chase you away. You need to get out of here. Fast."

Claire tilted her head at me. "Awesome. Thanks."

Earlobes saluted me from where he still lay on the ground. "Preacher's got a cool kid."

I ran back to the truck and peeled out onto the road.

CHAPTER THIRTY-FIVE

As we headed back toward the main highway, the sheriff's SUV passed us going the opposite direction, lights flashing. I watched in my rearview mirror as he pulled off toward the henge.

"I hope they put the fire out and got out of there in time. They seemed pretty cool," I said.

Dad didn't say anything.

"How long were you traveling with them?"

Silence.

"We're going to get some food. You must be hungry." His face was so much thinner than normal. What had he and the hippies been living on, anyway?

"What happened to your car?" Maybe if I asked the right question, he'd respond.

"Sold it. In California. That's where I bought the van.

And met the kids."

We were back on Main Street. Most of the storefronts were dark, but light spilled onto the street from Daisy's.

"I'll stay in the car," Dad said when I turned off the engine.

Maybe that was a good idea. He did look and smell like a bum. "Okay," I agreed. "You stay here with Toby. What do you want to eat?"

He looked like I'd asked him what flavor poison he preferred. "Not hungry."

"Not hungry? But Dad, when's the last time you ate?"

He ignored me, dropping his head to focus on petting Toby. Whatever. I jumped out of the truck and slammed the door behind me. He wasn't making this easy.

Daisy looked up when I walked in. "You're back." She smiled. "How was the Stonehenge?"

I plastered a smile on my face. "Cool."

"Did you run into any trouble with those hippies?"

Only one of them. "Nope. They were harmless."

She nodded. "Good." She looked out the door toward my truck. "Is that your dad out there? Why don't you tell him to come inside?"

I pretended to look for something in my bag. "He's tired. We'll just take our food to go." I ordered two club sandwiches and sat on a stool to wait. My appetite had returned with a vengeance.

This rescue mission wasn't going as planned. Once I found Dad he was supposed to take charge. Even though his postcards had been worrisome, I'd still convinced myself that once he saw me, live and in person, everything would fall into place. He'd snap out of his fog, and Tri Ty would take over. But instead I'd found someone who barely resembled the dad I knew. He was in no condition to take charge of anything. I shredded a napkin while I waited for our food. I couldn't wait to get home. To see everyone.

Everyone but J.J.

Daisy plunked a bag down in front of me. Her siren red lips shot a puff of air toward her bangs. "You want drinks? Pie?"

Pie. Dad loved pie. His favorite was coconut cream, which Mom made for him on his birthday. "Do you have coconut cream?" I asked.

Daisy grinned. "Must be your lucky day, doll. Just made one yesterday and I still have a few slices left. You want two?"

"Just one please."

The cold air blasted me in the face when I went back to the truck. I banished Toby to the truck bed while we ate. I hated leaving him in the cold but it wouldn't be for long.

Dad took a bite of pie. "Delicious," he said. He glanced at me and smiled. It was quick, but it was still a smile. My heart pinged.

"It'll be so great to get home," I said.

Dad stared at the sandwich in his lap. He hadn't even unwrapped it. "Home," he whispered.

"Home," I echoed. I didn't dare tell him it was a different home now. We'd deal with that soon enough. He stared out the window again, looking like a caged animal.

"Mom will be so glad to see you. We've been so worried." I choked out the last word. I was determined not to cry, but it was like trying not to breathe.

Dad turned to face me. He looked feverish, his eyes burning with emotion. "I am so sorry, Darcy. I caused so much pain. Terrible failure. Failed at everything." He spat the words at me as if they tasted bitter.

"No!" I exclaimed. "You're not a failure. You just…just needed a break. Everything will be…better when you come home. You can figure it out…" I took a deep breath, unsure if I should tell him everything.

He was blinking very fast. "No. Can't do that. No. It's over."

"Over? What's over?" My body flooded with adrenaline.

"Me. I'm over." He stared at me, as if willing me to read his mind, to understand all the thoughts he couldn't seem to voice.

It was like all the stress and fear of the past few months exploded, and suddenly I was sobbing. All the strength and adrenaline that had fueled me faded away. I was six years old again, begging my dad to fix everything. I choked the words out between the tears.

"Dad. We've been…lost without you. Mom completely fell apart. She was drunk almost every night. She had a job selling real estate, but it blew up in her face."

His eyes brimmed with tears but he didn't speak.

"But she's better now. She stopped drinking. She doesn't have a job but I know she'll find one. And we have some money now, from the estate sale, and I'm working in this coffee shop, thanks to Uncle Charlie and—"

"Charlie?" Dad's voice was sharp.

"Yes, Charlie. He's been the most stable person in my

life since you left. He's amazing—"

Dad put up his hand. "I don't want to hear any more."

My jaw unhinged. "You what?"

His eyes were angry slits. "I do not want to hear another word. Damn it, Darcy. Why did you have to find me? Why can't you just let me go?"

Let him go? What was he saying? "But you need us! And we need you. You can't just leave us, throw us away like garbage. We're your family. You can't just walk away."

"You'll be fine. J.J. will take care of you. He promised me."

Hadn't he heard anything I said? "Dad, J.J. is not taking care of us. I know you probably haven't heard any news in forever, but he says you made some really bad investment decisions." I grabbed his hands, focusing on his eyes that so reminded me of Charlie's. "Dad, Harvest is bankrupt. Laying off all its employees." I swiped away tears. "We had to move. The board took our house."

Something flickered in his eyes. Was I finally breaking through his cloud of confusion?

"I don't believe it. J.J. wouldn't do that. We had a deal."

I dropped his hands. "I can prove it." I grabbed my phone from my pocket and pulled up the internet browser. He had to face reality, had to snap out of it. Tri Ty had to come back. "Tyler Covington missing," I typed. There were so many links to choose from. I clicked the top link and handed my phone to Dad.

I glanced in the window of the diner as Dad's fingers flew over my screen as he read. His breath came in short gasps. "No," he whispered to himself. It was like he'd forgotten I was there. "No."

He looked at me, his eyes wild. He dropped the phone and threw open the truck door. He jumped out and took off running down the dark road. Toby leaped over the side of the truck, pausing only briefly before racing after Dad.

"Dad, wait!" I yelled. "Damn it." I jumped out of the truck, but my jacket caught on the ancient window handle. I wrenched free of it, oblivious to the cold as I ran. Dad was a dark blur ahead of me. I didn't know he could run that fast. Toby ran after him, a smaller blur running as fast as I'd ever seen him go.

"Toby! Heel!" As if he would stop. Running was what he lived for. As far as he knew, this was a game, chasing Dad and being chased by me.

Headlights swerved around a corner, blinding me, bouncing up and down as the driver hit a dip in the road. Where were Dad and Toby? I'd lost sight of them in the glare of the headlights.

A ferocious squeal of tires and brakes froze me in place.

Chapter Thirty-Six

"Run," I told myself, so I did, as fast as I could through the snow-packed streets.

A car had spun out in the middle of the road. The driver stood in the road looking confused.

"What happened?" I was breathless and frantic as I stopped next to him.

He turned to me, his face worried. "I'm not sure. I was driving and suddenly this guy appeared out of nowhere, right in front of me." He swallowed. "If I hadn't swerved, I would've hit him for sure."

"Did you see a dog?"

He looked at me, his eyes still wide with anxiety. "A dog? No. Just the man."

"Which way did he run?"

"That way." He pointed toward the highway.

Crap. I took off, fear making me run like the wind.

There was no traffic where the road met the entrance ramp to the highway. "Dad!" I screamed at the top of my lungs. "Toby!" Soft whimpering met my ears. Toby. Oh God. I turned toward the sound.

"Toby? Toby!"

The whimpering grew louder. I ran down an embankment next to the highway. Dad lay on the ground not moving. Toby lay next to him, licking him, whimpering and scared. I sank down next to them.

Crap, crap, crap.

"Are you hurt? Dad, what happened?"

He rolled over and looked up at me. "Not hurt." He closed his eyes. "Leave me, Darcy. Just leave me here. Take the dog and go."

Like a match thrown into kerosene, my fear morphed, roaring into a raging fire of anger. "God damn you! No, I will not leave you here. I just found you! Who the hell do you think you are? Do you have any idea what we've…been through…" Sobs racked my body again. Toby scooted next to me and licked the tears from my face. I grabbed him and pulled him close.

"You are coming home. With me. Now. Don't you dare move. I'm going to get the truck." I stood up and pointed at Toby. "Stay, Toby. Don't move." I glared at Dad. "You either."

I ran as fast as I could back to the truck and drove like I was possessed back to the highway entrance. I pulled off onto the shoulder and ran down the embankment. Neither of them had moved.

"Come on." I leaned down and tugged on Dad's arm.

Toby nudged him, whimpering.

He struggled to a sitting position. "Christ, you don't give up, do you?" He looked up at me, scowling.

"Got it from you. Come on. Mom's waiting."

He dropped his eyes. "I can't face her."

"You can and you will." I tugged harder. Finally, he staggered to his feet. I pulled his arm around my shoulders and had a vision of Lucas helping my mom stagger through our house.

"One step at a time. The truck's at the top of the hill."

We climbed slowly, not speaking. Toby panted with anxiety, running back and forth from us to the truck. Once we were settled into the truck, I turned to face him. "Don't think of trying that again. I'm not even stopping to let you pee, Dad. We're going straight home."

He closed his eyes and leaned back against the seat, saying nothing. Toby collapsed across his lap again as we drove.

"It's a lie, Darcy. All of it." Dad's voice startled me after miles of silence.

"What are you talking about?"

"Harvest. My big inspirational story, my brush with death. It never happened."

My hands shook on the steering wheel. I turned to look at him. His eyes met mine. They pooled with tears, but they were focused. He looked like my dad again.

"It was J.J.'s idea to...to pump up the story. I was sick, but we always knew I'd recover. Death was never breathing down my neck. But it made a better story."

I slowed the truck to fifty miles an hour. It took all my energy to drive and listen to him at the same time.

"J.J. said it didn't matter as long as people were still inspired by the Harvest message, and it helped them." Dad cried quietly next to me, then he spoke again. "It was last summer. June maybe? I can't remember. I went to the children's hospital in Omaha, after my show there. The director was in the audience. He called, asking me to visit some of the kids."

Toby shifted in Dad's lap. Out of the corner of my eye, I saw Dad's grip tighten around Toby as he rubbed his ears. It was like watching myself when I was scared.

"So I went," Dad continued. "The director took me on a tour." Dad's voice caught. He choked out the next words between sobs. "I'd done hospital visits before. But something was different this time. There was this little girl…" His voice trailed away, then he looked at me. His voice was a whisper. "She reminded me of you. Something about her eyes."

I swallowed, not daring to interrupt him.

"He…he…told…those kids that I'd been where they had. That I'd almost died. But that I'd made it." Sobs racked his body. "He told them to…to listen to me." His whole body heaved next to me. "But when I…when I was supposed to talk…I couldn't…couldn't think of anything to say. I couldn't tell any more lies."

I eased the car onto the shoulder of the road and turned on the hazard lights so no one would crash into us in the dark.

"Dad." I reached out to touch him, but he pushed me away.

"Don't you see, Darcy?" His face contorted in fury, in shame. "It was a lie. Here I was standing in front of these kids who were really sick. Some of them had actual brushes with death. Most of them were on chemo. Like the girl who reminded me of you." He stopped, taking deep breaths to compose himself.

My mind reeled with what he'd told me, but I knew I had to reassure him and keep him calm. He was like a rubber band stretched to the point of breaking and I was terrified of what would happen if he snapped.

"But Dad," I whispered. "Your Harvest message…it's still true. It still helps people."

Dad spoke so softly I had to strain to hear him. "All these years, I told myself it didn't matter. I let myself believe J.J. even though deep down I knew I should come clean." His hands rested on Toby. "I'm a fraud, Darcy. Harvest deserves to fail." He looked at me. "But I didn't want you and your mom to be part of my failure. Last summer…I tried to explain to J.J. that I wanted to quit, retire, whatever. I couldn't do it anymore. But he wouldn't hear of it." His body shuddered. "He told me to follow my own advice and keep pushing. Never give up." He turned to stare out the window. "J.J. was supposed to take care of you. He promised."

My pulse thudded in my ears. "J.J. knew? He knew why you left?" All this time he'd known and hadn't told us? He'd watched us agonize over Dad's disappearance. He'd read some of the postcards but hadn't told us what they really meant? He'd watched Mom fall apart. All this time, he knew.

Dad spoke again. "I thought maybe I could figure out a way to tell the truth, but still keep Harvest going. That's why I left. To be by myself and work it out."

I stared into the night, watching the red glow of fading

tail lights pass us. I had to keep Dad calm until we got home.

"Harvest helped me, Dad."

He shifted in his seat to look at me. I turned to meet his eyes. He didn't speak.

"I'm not just saying that." I leaned against the back of my seat and closed my eyes. "I used to hate it, you know. All your platitudes about planting crops and reaping what we sow."

"I know," he whispered.

I opened my eyes and took his hands, no longer smooth and manicured but rough and chapped. "But the thing is, you were right. We can't just sit around waiting for someone to save us, or fix everything. We have to do it ourselves." I thought of Charlie. And Liz. And Lucas. "But other people can help, too." I took a breath. "I heard your voice, Dad. All the time. When I talked to the board. When I applied for my job, and got it." And when I'd told Mom she had to get help with her drinking. And so many other times these past months I'd been guided by his wisdom without even realizing it. "I think people will still listen to you, Dad. If you want them to."

Tears rolled down his cheeks and fell onto Toby's fur. "I don't know what I want, Darcy."

I let go of his hands, placing them gently on Toby. "Don't you want to go home? To see Mom?"

He didn't answer, so I started the truck and eased back onto the highway. I glanced at the gas gauge, knowing I'd have to stop at some point to fill up. What would I do then, chain Dad to the steering wheel?

We drove in silence. Eventually my hands stopped

shaking. My emotions fluctuated wildly. I wanted to kill J.J. but at the same time I never wanted to see him again.

All I wanted was peace in my life. I didn't care where we lived or what job Mom could scrounge up or if Dad worked in a 7-Eleven for the rest of his life. I just wanted to come home at the end of the day and find them there, laughing and talking like they used to. I wanted Dad to be strong again. I wanted Mom to stop crying, to stop worrying. To let go of the past.

The highway was a blur of trucks and cars flying past us. Light snow glanced off the windshield. Dad fell asleep, snoring softly. We stopped for gas and he didn't wake up. I sent a silent prayer of thanks to the Stonehenge spirits.

Dad had been asleep for almost an hour when his scream shattered the night. I nearly drove off the highway as terror sliced through me.

"Dad, what is it?" My eyes darted from his face to the road. He jerked straight up, his face a mask of terror.

Toby jumped off his lap, whining nervously.

Dad banged his head against the back of the seat as sobs racked his body. "Can't do it. Can't do it. Can't." He reached for the door handle.

"No!" I screamed and steered the car off to the shoulder of the highway, cars blaring their horns at me. The truck shuddered to a stop on the gravel. Dad looked at me and I didn't know who he was anymore. The lucidity from earlier was gone, replaced by a stranger. A terrified, broken stranger.

My hands trembled as I pulled my cell from my pocket and dialed 911. I couldn't do this by myself anymore.

My rescue mission was over.

CHAPTER THIRTY-SEVEN

The ambulance siren wailed as we flew down the highway. I sat on the bench next to the EMT, holding Dad's limp, sedated hand. The sheriff's car led us, lights and sirens clearing the traffic out of the way, with Toby in the backseat.

The EMT was kind. "Do you want me to call someone to meet us at the hospital?"

"No." My voice wobbled. "I'll do it." The sheriff had wanted to call Mom himself, but I'd insisted that I do it. If a sheriff had called her, she'd have keeled right over. Or started drinking again.

"Please don't say his name over the emergency radio," I'd begged the sheriff. I couldn't handle reporters showing up at the hospital.

"You really need your mother," he'd insisted. "You're a minor, technically. I don't want to call social services. You've been through enough. I can see that."

"She'll come, I swear she will. I'll call her from the ambulance."

My phone shook in my trembling hands as I tried to balance on the bench seat as we flew down the highway. I decided to call Charlie, since he'd be calmer than Mom.

"Charlie." My voice was strangled with suppressed tears. I wanted so badly to break down. But I couldn't, not yet.

"Tell me where you are." His voice was sharp with worry. I knew he heard the sirens.

"Cheyenne. The hospital." I looked at the EMT for help.

"The Regional Medical Center," he said.

I repeated it to Charlie.

"Ty?" Charlie said. "Is he —"

"He's not dead. But he's sick, Charlie."

So very, very sick.

"We're leaving right now."

I told the doctor what had happened, describing Dad's behavior since I'd found him.

"He's malnourished and dehydrated," the doctor told me. "We're getting liquids into him now." He paused and looked at me. "When will your mother be here?"

"Soon," I said. "They're driving up from Denver."

He nodded. "We'll talk more then. Have the nurse page me when your mom arrives."

I nodded and wandered to a small waiting room outside the ICU. It was blissfully quiet. I sank onto a couch and dropped my head in my hands. Breathe. Just breathe.

After what seemed like hours, the sound of running feet made me look up. It was Mom, with Charlie and Lucas close behind her. They burst into the waiting room. Mom grabbed me, crying and exclaiming. Charlie hugged me next, telling me everything would be okay. Finally it was Lucas's turn. His body was like a taut wire, holding me so close I could hardly breathe. He didn't speak, but he didn't let me out of his grip.

The sheriff came into the room and calmed everyone down. He told Mom about my 911 call and the condition my dad was in when he'd found us on the highway. He asked if I felt able to make a formal statement, to tell him what had happened since I'd found my dad at the henge with the hippies.

"Does she have to do that right now?" Charlie asked, looking like a protective archangel.

Lucas's arm tightened around me as we sat on the vinyl couch. I glanced at him and saw his jaw clench. He'd hardly said a word since he'd arrived but he hadn't let me out of his grip.

"She's exhausted," my mom protested. "Can't we do this later?"

The sheriff sighed. "I know the doctor wants to see you right away," he said to my mom. "I can wait a little while."

"Thank you," my mom breathed. She turned her tear-filled eyes to mine.

The doctor arrived, looking slightly taken aback at the room full of people.

"Are you all related to Mr. Covington?" he asked.

My mom shot a glance at Lucas, then looked at the doctor. Her shoulders straightened and her eyes narrowed. "Yes." She paused. "This is his family."

I sagged against Lucas's chest and felt his heart pounding.

The doctor raised an eyebrow. "All right." He glanced at me, then my mother. "Your daughter found your husband, as you know. He was in bad shape. It's a good thing she got to him when she did. His physical condition isn't good." He paused. "But we can fix that. However, his mental condition…" He looked into my mother's eyes. "He's not well, Mrs. Covington. We need to do a psych evaluation." He hesitated. "Nervous breakdown isn't an official medical diagnosis, but it's the easiest way to explain it, until you meet with the psychiatrist and hear it from her. I'm guessing acute stress disorder, possibly dissociation."

My mother nodded. She didn't look shocked. "Do what you need to, doctor."

"He'll need to stay here for a while."

"Then so will I," Mom said, her voice strong and clear.

The sheriff returned and I told him my story. Lucas brought me cinnamon tea from the cafeteria. He sat across from me and watched me with burning intensity while I talked. When I got to the part about the henge builder with the gun, Lucas swore under his breath. Mom gasped. Charlie dropped his head to his hands. Finally I finished. The sheriff snapped his notebook closed. He looked around the room, his gaze resting on me.

"You're a very brave young lady. You probably saved your father's life. If he'd kept wandering, in his condition..."

Mom started crying again. Charlie stood up and walked over to me, resting his hand on my shoulder. "She is her father's daughter," he said. "A force of nature."

I stared at my lap. I didn't feel like a force of nature. I felt like a worn-out rag doll.

The sheriff handed his business card to me. "You can come get your truck and your dog at the station anytime." His mouth twitched. "Though I hear the desk jockeys are getting attached to that mutt."

Mom and Charlie left the room. They stood in the hallway, talking in soft voices, darting glances at me through the window every few seconds.

"Finally," Lucas whispered. "I need to tell you something."

"Me first," I said, taking his face in my hands. "I love you, Lucas Martinez. I should've told you before." I smiled weakly. "If this were one of my favorite movies, this is where I'd make some big flowery speech. Like you did to me." I kissed him softly. "But I'm too tired for speeches."

"That's okay. I'm better at them than you are." He grinned. "Ready for my speech?"

"Make it quick," I said. "I'm very close to fainting from stress, so if you're dumping me, skip right to the end."

He pulled me toward him. "Charlie's right. You are a force of nature. And I couldn't stand to lose you, tornado girl." He ran his hands through my hair but his intense gaze stayed riveted on my face. "I love you, Darcy Covington. But if you ever do anything like this again, I'll chase you down and I won't stop until I find you, and whoever you're trying to rescue."

Tears collected in the corners of my eyes, ready to spill over. "Stupid Lancelot," I whispered. "Always wanting the glory for himself."

His eyes roamed over my face, then drifted down to my neck. His eyes widened in surprise, then he shook his head, smirking. "You totally cheated. You're worse than Pickles. I have to hide all her presents. Guess I have to hide yours now, too."

I tried to look indignant. "Isn't the knight supposed to bring a token of affection when she goes into battle?"

"Still cheating," he said, but before I could argue, he bent his head over mine and kissed me so deeply and urgently I forgot where I was, and why I was there, for a few blissful minutes.

We might have stayed that way forever if Mom hadn't opened the door.

"Who wants something to eat?"

Chapter Thirty-Eight
December 20

"You and Lucas are driving the truck back to Denver. Charlie and I are staying here with your father." Mom's bossy tone reassured me that Dad's condition hadn't sent her back to a dark place. We sat in a diner across the street from the hospital.

"But I want to stay with Dad." I was surprised at the words that came out of my mouth. But I'd found him. I'd gotten him to a hospital. I'd heard his confession. I wanted to see this all the way through. "Besides," I argued, "I don't want to spend Christmas by myself."

Lucas squeezed my hand under the table. "You won't be alone," he murmured.

Mom shook her head. "No, honey, you've been through enough. You can come back to see him again, once he's settled. But for now I want you to go home and rest. I need to stay here for a few days to meet with the doctors and figure out what's next. I'll drive home for Christmas, I promise."

Lucas squeezed my hand again. "Your mom's right."

"You can stay with Liz," Charlie said. "She'd love to have you."

"I might want to go home." I said. "Our new home." I looked at Mom. "I feel safe there."

Mom tilted her head. "Well, you've certainly proven that you can take care of yourself." She sighed and shook her head. "I'll leave it up to you."

I watched Dad from the doorway of the hospital room. Tubes snaked out of his nose and mouth. The click-clicking of the machines hooked up to him were the only noises in the room. I walked toward him slowly, as if the floor were quicksand.

I'd slept like a rock the night before in a motel by the hospital, in a bed next to my mom. When I awoke, I'd hoped it had all been a bad dream.

But as I stood in the hospital room watching my father, part of me was grateful it wasn't a dream, because maybe now he had a fighting chance. My stomach knotted as I looked down at his battered face. Had I really saved him? Or was I too late?

All I could do now was wait, and hope, and pray. I leaned over and kissed his forehead. "I love you, Daddy," I whispered. "Come home. Soon."

Lucas waited for me in the hall. He took my hand and looked into my eyes, but said nothing. He didn't need to.

Charlie and Mom met us in the parking lot by the truck, which Lucas had picked up from the police station. Toby leaned out of the truck window, tail wagging.

Mom and I held each other tightly. "Keep your phone on," she commanded. "I'll call you every day."

I managed a smile. "I promise I won't turn it off again. Maybe now you can learn how to text more than three words at a time."

She laughed and hugged me again. "I just might surprise you."

Charlie stepped forward and smothered me in a hug. "I love you, favorite niece," he whispered in my ear. He released me and looked at Lucas. "Take care of her, Lucas, and the store. I'll be back this weekend."

Lucas nodded. "Of course," he said.

"Darcy can take care of herself," Mom said. She paused. "But I'm grateful to know Lucas is around." She gave him a meaningful look and he returned it, nodding. I knew they were both remembering the night he'd helped her to bed. The night everything had changed between him and me.

Lucas opened the driver's side door of the Grim Reaper, but I put out a hand to stop him.

"I'd like to drive."

He cocked an eyebrow, surprised. "Do you think you should?"

"I got myself here, didn't I? Right now, I'd like to be in control of something."

He dropped the keys into my waiting palm. "As you

wish, Shaker Girl."

I settled myself into the seat. Toby sandwiched himself between us, curling into a ball next to Lucas.

"Ready?" I smiled at him.

He grinned at me, the first real smile I'd seen from him since he'd arrived. "Ready."

We drove out of the parking lot, waving. Mom wiped her eyes. Charlie saluted.

As we idled at a stoplight, Lucas plugged his iPod adapter into the lighter slot and queued up one of my favorite bands.

"Aren't you the Boy Scout? Always prepared."

"I know. It's like I have to do everything. I bet you didn't even think of getting snacks."

He tossed a bag of peanut M&M's on my lap.

"How'd you know they're my favorite?"

His eyes glinted. "I'm very observant."

"Yeah, you are. And full of surprises."

He was quiet for a moment. "Not nearly as many as you." He reached over and ran a finger down my cheek.

Shivering from his touch, I reached out to rub the ninja shakers glued to the dash. "For luck," I told him.

Lucas shook his head. "You don't need luck, Darcy. You never did." His eyes locked on mine and I marveled at the emotion I saw reflecting back at me.

The light changed to green and I took a steadying breath as I revved the engine. "Ready?"

His low voice washed over me like a caress. "Ready for anything, as long as it's with you."

I headed for the highway and rolled down my window to let the cold wind in. My ponytail whipped around my neck, tickling my skin. I shot a grin at Lucas, who gave me his sexiest smirk in return.

The highway unfurled like a ribbon ahead of us. I gunned the engine, feeling the energy vibrate through me, enough to take us all the way to the stars and back again.

Denver Daily News

The Secret Scoop from the Street
by "Crystal Ball"

Reaping Their Harvests

It's been almost a year since Tyler Covington made his last televised appearance on PBS. Since then I've followed his disappearance, rumors of embezzlement, and his hushed return to an inpatient mental hospital. I've been told his daughter was the one who finally found him, at a hippie commune somewhere in the mountains of Montana, but no one will confirm the story.

Here's what I can confirm: J.J. Briggs, acting president of Tri!Umphant! Harvest Industries, was fired by the board of directors in the midst of bankruptcy proceedings. He now faces charges of fraud, embezzlement, misleading stockholders, and a slew of other charges that will keep his attorneys busy for a long time.

Insiders tell me that Briggs knew Covington was troubled and contemplating leaving Harvest, but instead of getting him help, Briggs concocted a crazy plan to "wake him up," starting with the repossession of his daughter's car from her school last fall, seizing the Covington home by forging a signature on the deed, and blaming Covington for real estate investments that crashed when the rest of the market did. Investments that Briggs made, not Covington. But there are rumors about Covington, too, that parts of his inspirational story were fabricated. No one from Harvest will confirm or deny these claims, and you can find just as many Covington supporters as detractors if you scan the internet.

Covington spent his life talking about harvests: planting, reaping, and sowing. It appears that J.J. Briggs is reaping his harvest. I can only hope that Covington reaps his as well, because no matter what other truths come out, he's helped countless people, and been a huge pillar in the local nonprofit community. I hope that someday whatever he plants bears new fruit.

Lucas insists on driving his car to the cabin. He likes to drive fast and the Grim Reaper doesn't do fast. He's wearing sunglasses and a necklace of random beads, specially made by Pickles. I made the twisted copper bracelet that glints in the sun as he downshifts into third gear.

"Pull off here." I point to the exit. His car bounces down the rutted road. "Your precious baby car," I say. "We should've brought the truck."

He snorts in mock disgust.

There's whimpering from the backseat. I turn around. "Hush, Toby. We're almost there." Chocolate eyes lock onto mine. Brown fur shimmers in the sunshine. His tail whacks the seat, sending fur everywhere.

"It's like a dog hair tsunami back there," I say.

Lucas downshifts to second gear. "Like I care."

I turn back around and there it is. Our cabin. Not ours anymore, I correct myself. It belongs to the Sullivan family now, but they agreed to let me come up to do this. I can pretty much talk anybody into anything these days.

We park and Toby half falls, half climbs into the front seat, eager to get out of the car. Lucas removes his sunglasses, watching me with his usual sexy smirk.

"Give it up," he says as I try to rein in my dog. "He's a spaz."

I open the door and Toby leaps out, making a beeline for the forest.

"You ready, Shaker Girl?"

"As much as I can be."

We hike down the trail. Purple crocuses peek out of

patches of spring snow that still linger in the shade. Lucas takes my hand, his grip warm and firm. I remember the first time he almost held my hand, when we'd walked Toby together and he'd told me how his dad had checked out, just like my mom.

Stonehenge is still in shambles from when I destroyed it.

"Show me what to do," Lucas says, squeezing my hand. So I do, and together we rebuild it, using the old photo on my phone as our guide.

When we're finished with the stones, I ask him to dig a small hole in the center of the circle. He does, but I realize we're missing something. Frantically I search for the heart stone, dropping to my knees to dig in the dirt.

"What is it?" Lucas asks.

Toby rushes into the circle, screeching to a stop next to me. I'm about to scold him, when I see the corner of the stone sticking out from under his paw. He's unearthed it for me. I reach out to smooch his head. He slurps my cheek, and then bounds out of the circle, managing to do so without knocking down any stones.

"This." I hand it to Lucas. He takes it, then reaches for me with his other hand and pulls me to my feet.

"Cool."

"My dad and I found it a long time ago. We made wishes on it every time we came up here."

Lucas presses the stone into my hand, his grip warm and reassuring.

"Make your wish," he says.

"Not yet." I hand the stone back to him. I retrieve my messenger bag from outside of the circle, and remove a Ziploc bag that holds all of Dad's postcards. A deep sigh shudders through me. Lucas's arm wraps around my shoulders. My eyes lift to his. Even though I know how much he loves me, sometimes it still takes my breath away when I see it in his face.

I drop to my knees and place the postcards in the hole. Lucas shovels dirt, burying the images forever.

"Now," I say, palm uplifted. He hands me the heart stone.

I place the heart stone on the mound of dirt and close my eyes. A million wishes flood my mind. How can I make just one?

Who says I need to?

So I wish, and wish, and wish.

After a bit, Lucas asks softly, "Are you ready?"

I sink back on my heels and look around at our stones. The Sullivans promised they'd leave it like this as long as they owned the cabin. On the hills surrounding us, many of the old pines are brown from beetle kill, but there's new life, too. Young green flashes of it catch my eye everywhere I look.

I pick up the heart stone and put it in my pocket. I stand, brushing dirt off my pants. I squint into the sun as I smile up at Lucas.

"You're not leaving the heart stone here?" Lucas asks.

I shake my head. "I'm bringing it to my dad."

He smiles down at me, then drapes his arm around my shoulders, pulling me close as we walk together.

"Let me drive your car?" I ask. "I feel like going fast." He grins and tosses me his keys.

Mom texts me as I slide into the driver's seat. *"Okay?"*

"Okay," I send back.

"I visited Dad before work," she texts. *"He sends his love."*

Mom is the director of Sprites, a daycare center less than a mile from our new home. She got a small business loan to open the center. She tried every bank in town, refusing to take no for an answer. Eventually she got a yes.

The truth about Dad and Harvest is out there now, on the web, in the papers, on the business news channels. So is the truth about J.J. Like Dad always said, no matter how deeply a seed is planted, it always finds the light of day. Eventually.

Over the past few months, I've forgiven J.J. because I know he couldn't imagine a different life than the one Harvest provided for him and his family. I know he was terrified Harvest wouldn't survive if Dad told the truth. I also found an old show of Dad's on YouTube, where he talked about forgiveness, and how it opens you up to possibilities you can't even imagine.

And in the end, J.J.'s still the guy who gave me the pink Barbie bike and taught me how to ride without training wheels. That's the guy I want to remember.

"Illness isn't failure," Mom said at the press conference she'd called after she'd returned from Wyoming and gotten Dad settled in a local facility. She'd been so brave facing those TV cameras and clamoring reporters. I'd been so proud of her as I'd stood next to her. When it was my turn to talk I'd taken my inspiration from her, and from Dad, speaking directly to the cameras, my voice clear and strong. "My dad made mistakes," I said. "And he regrets them. But he never meant to hurt anyone. All he ever wanted was to inspire people to do more than they thought they could. To become who they were meant to be."

I'll visit Dad later today and give him the heart stone. We'll sit outside on a bench in the bright Colorado sun. He'll listen while I tell him funny stories from my time at Liz's, about the movies Lucas and I've seen, and the crazy costumes Sal wore in the Woodbridge spring play. I'll tell him I've decided to turn down the scholarship opportunity that Woodbridge offered me. I'm going to do my senior year at Sky Ridge instead. I'll drag Lucas to one last school dance, only I won't puke in his car like the goddess. Since Mark is graduating this year, my only friend left at WA is Sal, and we'll always see each other, no matter what. Friends for life.

Charlie will visit Dad, too, bringing used books from his store and pastries from Liz. From what Charlie tells me, he and Dad have really long talks. Sometimes Dad cries, but he laughs, too. And Charlie says each visit brings them closer.

Dad's treatment time is almost up at the inpatient mental health facility, so he'll be coming home soon. Mrs. Hamilton, his secretary from Harvest, insisted on setting up a desk and tiny office in the basement of our new house. She's convinced the next chapter of Dad's story will be a bestseller, if he's willing to tell it. A lot of other people Dad knows have reached out to Mom, some of them famous, some of them not, but all of them expressing love and support for Dad, and us.

We hear from trolls and haters, too, of course, but we ignore them.

Lucas and I don't say much as we drive down from

the mountains. Toby snores from the backseat, exhausted from chasing rabbits. We listen to one of my favorite songs because the lyrics have propped me up for a long time now, lyrics about bending, not breaking. About the redemptive power of love.

I don't know what's next for my family or me. All I can do is put one foot in front of the other, and sometimes that takes more courage than facing down the fiercest dragon. But I'm not afraid anymore, and I'm not alone.

And in the end, that's all that matters.

ACKNOWLEDGMENTS

It's true that it takes a village, and I love mine:

My writing tribe: the Wild Writers critique group members (past and present) for their collective brilliance, laughter, and snacks! I couldn't have done it without you. Special thanks to Julie Anne Peters, who invited me to join and cracked her metaphorical whip until I "finished the damn book." I'm grateful for new friends from the Heart of Denver and Colorado Romance Writers RWA chapters, YARWA, and the Rocky Mountain Fiction Writers.

Entangled: Heather Howland for pulling this book from the slush pile and believing in the story. Liz Pelletier, my patient and encouraging editor and grand wizard of Entangled: because of you, this book is finally what it was meant to be. Heather Riccio, Debbie Suzuki, and Anita Orr: a million thank-you hugs for championing this book and answering all my questions. Thank you to Julia Knapman for laser-like copy edits.

Nicole Resciniti, agent extraordinaire, for cheering me on with phone calls and emails full of exclamation points, and for being a ninja editor!

My teachers: Kathy Scott for her shoebox of story ideas, Sally McCabe for "One, two, three. Breathe." Nancy Fehrmann for introducing me to Robert Cormier as a "budding author" in high school.

Finally, to my family: my book-loving parents who nurtured me as a writer, my extended "out-law" clan for love and support, my husband who always makes me laugh and whose support never wavers, and my son, who cringes over the kissing scenes, cheers me on anyway, and cooks me awesome dinners.

**Don't miss Vivi Barnes's funny and romantic Paper
or Plastic, available now!
Read on for a sneak peek...**

PAPER OR PLASTIC, by Vivi Barnes

Welcome to SmartMart, where crime pays minimum wage...

Busted. Alexis Dubois just got caught shoplifting a cheap tube of
lipstick at the local SmartMart. She doesn't know what's worse —
disappointing her overbearing beauty-pageant-obsessed mother for
the zillionth time...or her punishment. Because Lex is forced to spend
her summer working at the store, where the only things stranger than
the staff are the customers.

Now Lex is stuck in the bizarro world of big-box retail. Coupon cutters,
jerk customers, and learning exactly what a "Code B" really is (ew). And
for added awkwardness, her new supervisor is the totally cute — and
adorably geeky — Noah Grayson. Trying to balance her out-of-control
mother, her pitching position on the softball team, and her secret crush
on the school geek makes for one crazy summer. But ultimately, could
the worst job in the world be the best thing that ever happened to her?

CHAPTER 1

It was just a cheap tube of lipstick in a shade I would never wear, if I wore lipstick at all.

Which I didn't.

So I couldn't believe I was sitting here, staring at the frosted square of glass in the door, holding my breath every time a shadow moved past.

Court shifted slightly, but her expression was bored. Her mom had already appeared, popping her head in for a few seconds to click her tongue and say, "Courtney Ann," in that slightly disappointed way that made me wish I were going home with her instead of my own mother.

Why did I do it? All I knew was that Mom's pinched expression this morning as she looked from my superstar sister, Rory, to me, the *meh* daughter, had been fixed in my mind. Her words, *Why can't you be more like your sister*, were familiar enough by now. Then she had to add in the fact that I was *throwing away* my future on some ridiculous pipe dream when I could be so much more. And all because I asked to go to Space Coast Fastpitch Softball Camp at the end of summer instead of joining her boring League of Southern Women group. I remember my sole thought as I slipped the lipstick into my pocket: *Take that, Mom*.

Still. The first really wrong thing I did in my entire life, and I got caught.

The annoying ticks of the wall clock reminded me that we had been sitting here for an hour. I wanted to take the stapler off the desk and throw it at the clock as hard as I could.

"What's taking so long?" I asked Court, who was busy with her phone. Probably texting Bryce, her long-time boyfriend and one of my best friends. If it wasn't for Bryce, I don't know if I would've become friends with Court. She liked to live on the edge, way outside my comfort zone. I didn't even *like* shopping — that was her thing.

I wished Syd were here. As my softball teammate and forever best friend, Syd would be a whole lot better at commiserating. She'd know what to say to make me laugh instead of staring at her phone the whole time.

"I don't know," Court finally said. "I guess they're waiting for the cops."

My heart sank to my shoes. Cops? "But it was just a couple of lipsticks."

She shrugged and kept texting. How could she look so calm right now? Was it too much to hope that the store manager would talk to our parents and leave the police out of it?

"What do you think is going to happen to us?" I asked for the third time, trying to keep the shakiness out of my voice.

She sighed and looked up at me. "Seriously, Lex, stop worrying. It's not like they'll arrest us. We're only sixteen. Minors." She stuck out her tongue at the door. "My brother got in trouble for drinking vodka at a party when he was seventeen and got off with just a warning. We'll be okay."

I nodded, but that didn't make me feel better. Drinking vodka didn't exactly match up to outright theft.

The door handle turned, and both Court and I jumped to our feet. *Ha!* I wanted to say. *You're not so cool about this after all.*

The security guard stuck his head in. "Courtney?" He motioned to her. She slipped her phone back into her pocket and moved forward through the door, flipping her black curls and looking back to wink at me. Before the door closed, I could see her mother shaking her head. My throat clenched as I remembered *my* mother would be here any moment, and she'd be doing a whole lot more than just shaking her head. I wished my dad would show up instead, but I knew he was working.

Fifteen minutes later, Court still hadn't reappeared. My stomach churned and my throat was dry. I wondered if it would be okay to ask for water. Most of all, I wondered what happened to Court. Had she been arrested after all? If so, wouldn't they have taken me, too?

It was wrong.

It was wrong.

It was wrong.

If I repeated it enough times like a mantra, maybe I'd get out of this.

I'm an idiot.

I'm an idiot.

I'm an idiot.

Maybe they were using this as a scare tactic. Some kind of "freak the kid out so she'll never do this again" trick.

It was working.

The handle turned, breaking my thoughts, but instead of jumping up, I pressed my back against the wall. The perfumed air reached my nose even before the giant nest of blond hair breached the gap in the door.

Besides the heavy scent of gardenias that floated about her, the first thing anyone would notice about my mother was that she loomed above practically everyone. She could've been mistaken for a women's basketball player, except for the face so heavily made up that it was a wonder the foundation didn't slide off her face. I'd rarely seen her without makeup myself. I doubt my father ever had, either.

The balding, pudgy store manager who followed seemed in awe of her. Or maybe he was just afraid.

"Alexis Jasmine Dubois!"

I cringed. I hated when she said my full name, especially in front of others. It always sounded like a bunch of crappy princess names thrown together. And it was a constant reminder of what she had expected me to be and what I most definitely was not.

She glared at me before turning her sweetest pageant smile on the store manager. "I don't know where she gets these crazy ideas. I'm sure it's all on her father's side. But we really appreciate the opportunity you're giving her, Mr. Hanson."

Opportunity?

Mr. Hanson blinked. "Oh, of course, Mrs. Dubois. I'm only too happy to extend a second chance to Alexis. My own son got in trouble when he was sixteen, so I know how having a record can damage a person's future."

Wait, what?

My mother nodded, still smiling, though it had an edge as she glanced at me. I knew she was going to let me have it later, but I almost didn't care. I wasn't going to get arrested. He was just letting me go. The "Hallelujah" song was reverberating in my head, and I felt like hugging him.

As my mother and Mr. Hanson talked, all I could focus on was the fact that no sheriff was being called in and no handcuffs were being snapped around my wrists. I was happily oblivious to their conversation.

Until a few words yanked me back to reality.

"Just bring her in Monday morning for the paperwork and uniform shirt, and we'll be good to go," Mr. Hanson said, smiling at me.

The happiness I felt inside whooshed out of me as if someone had punched me in the stomach. I stared at him. "Um, what?"

"Mr. Hanson understands that you were acting like a stupid teenager," my mother said. "He has kindly agreed to allow you to work your summer here at SmartMart. In return, you'll get to keep the incident off your record, not to mention a paycheck. That'll be a change."

"But I'm already working this summer. Remember Let's Have a Ball? And I'm supposed to go to softball camp in August, too."

My mother's eyes narrowed slightly. She definitely remembered, and I could see she cared about it as little as if I had said I was going to get a drink of water.

I turned to Mr. Hanson before she could answer. "I'm sorry, Mr. Hanson. I really appreciate the opportunity, but I already have plans this summer."

My mother took my hand in one of hers in what would look like a loving gesture if she weren't digging her fingernails into my skin. I tried to pull away, but she had a grip of steel. "Don't be silly, Alexis. You have plenty of time before your camp, and you don't make money playing ball with little kids." She laughed lightly. She seemed to have missed the point of volunteering. "SmartMart is offering an excellent opportunity here, and I think you need to take it."

"But—"

"Mr. Hanson," my mother said without lifting her eyes from

me. "Would you give me just a moment alone with my daughter?"

No, don't leave me with Crazy! I wanted to shout. But I just watched, helpless in her grip, as the store manager nodded and bowed out, giving me a sympathetic look before shutting the door behind him.

As soon as the latch clicked, my mother's pretense at charm and grace dropped. "I'm going to say this once, Alexis. If you don't accept this man's offer, you'll end up with shoplifting on your record that will follow you around the rest of your life. And think about what everyone will say about my parenting skills."

"This has nothing to do with you—" I started, but she pulled me closer. I got a strong whiff of her perfume and tried not to choke.

"This has everything to do with me, not to mention your sister. Can you imagine if this followed us through the circuit? I'd be criticized for being one of those mothers who can't control her kids, and Aurora's career would be over."

Aurora's career? It was true that my mother loved pageant life more than anything else—her claim to fame was being runner-up in the Miss Florida pageant when she was young. Pictures of her glory days hung in pride on our wall, and we endured story after story about how she should have won, and how the judges just felt sorry for the girl who actually won because of her poor background. She had even tried getting me involved in pageants when I was too young to know better, except I hated every single moment of it and finally refused to do it anymore. So yes, I knew she took the whole pageant thing seriously. But a seven-year-old's *career*? I knew better than to roll my eyes, but in my defense, they kind of moved on their own.

They could've at least waited until my mother's back was turned.

Her lips pressed together in a cold line. "Control yourself," she hissed. "Now, you are going to take this job and be glad about it. And if you don't, you can spend your entire high school career taking the bus instead of that car you want so badly, got it?"

She had me now. I needed that car, and my mother knew it. "Wait a second, that's not fair. I've been saving up—"

"Not even enough to fund the tires," she finished. "You're expecting us to foot the rest. Which we won't do if you don't get serious and take this job. And by the way, your camp is at the end of summer, so *if* we agree that you can go, it shouldn't interfere."

"But Let's Have a Ball camp—"

"You put in what, five or six *unpaid* hours a week there?"

"Eight," I mumbled. It would be more if I had a car to drive myself, but I didn't want to go there.

"Exactly. Plenty of time left for a real job."

"Dad won't—"

"Your father will agree with me. You have your choice. Take it or leave it."

Some choice. I knew I would have to do what she said. The car and my softball camp were the only things she could really hold over my head. "Fine," I whispered.

She turned on a heel and opened the door. "Mr. Hanson?" Her voice sounded musical again.

He entered the room, his face politely inquisitive.

"She'll be delighted to accept the position."

Hanson clapped his pudgy hands together. "Wonderful! Welcome to the team, Alexis."

I reached out to shake his extended hand, trying to smile. I sucked at acting. My eyes dropped to the floor while he and my mother chatted.

SmartMart—Where Everybody Farts. That's what everyone called this place ever since some guy posted a People of SmartMart video on YouTube. It was a contest for whoever could take the funniest video or picture with their cell phone and post it on his blog. I sent in two—one of a woman walking around with a dressed-up dog in a stroller and another of an employee talking animatedly to herself. I didn't win, but the one that did showed a guy bending to pick up something and farting really loudly. The woman's puckered face behind him was priceless.

I felt sick to my stomach as my mother and I left the store. The fact that I wasn't going to jail should've made me feel relieved, but at the moment, all I could do was feel sorry for the situation I'd gotten myself into.

CINDERELLA'S DRESS, by Shonna Slayton

Kate simply wants to create window displays at the department store where she's working, trying to help out with the war effort. But when long-lost relatives from Poland arrive with a steamer trunk they claim holds *the* Cinderella's dresses, life gets complicated. Now, with a father missing in action, her new sweetheart, Johnny, stuck in the middle of battle, and her great aunt losing her wits, Kate has to unravel the mystery before it's too late. After all, the descendants of the wicked stepsisters will stop at nothing to get what they think they deserve.

WHATEVER LIFE THROWS AT YOU, by Julie Cross

When seventeen-year-old track star Annie Lucas's dad starts mentoring nineteen-year-old baseball rookie phenom, Jason Brody, Annie's convinced she knows his type — arrogant, bossy, and most likely not into high school girls. But as Brody and her father grow closer, Annie starts to see through his façade to the lonely boy in over his head. When opening day comes around and her dad — and Brody's — job is on the line, she's reminded why he's off-limits. But Brody needs her, and staying away isn't an option.

LOVE AND OTHER UNKNOWN VARIABLES
BY SHANNON LEE ALEXANDER

Charlie Hanson has a clear vision of his future. A senior at Brighton School of Mathematics and Science, he knows he'll graduate, go to MIT, and inevitably discover the solutions to the universe's greatest unanswerable problems. But for Charlotte Finch, the future has never seemed very kind. Charlie's future blurs the moment he meets Charlotte, but by the time he learns Charlotte is ill, her gravitational pull on him is too great to overcome. Soon he must choose between the familiar formulas he's always relied on or the girl he's falling for.